Journeys

I Found My Heart in San Francisco
Book Ten

Susan X Meagher

JOURNEYS

I FOUND MY HEART IN SAN FRANCISCO: BOOK TEN

© 2010 BY SUSAN X MEAGHER

ISBN (10) 09799254-8-7
ISBN (13) 978-0-9799254-8-1

THIS TRADE PAPERBACK ORIGINAL IS PUBLISHED BY BRISK PRESS, NEW YORK, NY 10023

FIRST PRINTING: OCTOBER 2010

Acknowledgment

Every good thing in my life is due in some part to my
lovely partner, Carrie.

By Susan X Meagher

Novels

Arbor Vitae
All That Matters
Cherry Grove
Girl Meets Girl
The Lies That Bind
The Legacy
Doublecrossed

Serial Novels

I Found My Heart In San Francisco

Awakenings
Beginnings
Coalescence
Disclosures
Entwined
Fidelity
Getaway
Honesty
Intentions
Journeys

Anthologies

Undercover Tales
Outsiders

To purchase these books go to
www.briskpress.com

Chapter One

The huge fuselage of the 767 left the runway, lurching heavily, while the junior senator from the state of California sat in his seat, a contented smile curving his lips. After a few minutes of climbing, the plane reached cruising altitude, and he reclined his seat back, his eyes drifting to the window that his right shoulder was nestled against. His thoughts were scattered, his mind flitting from the unexpectedly wonderful meeting he had just had with his daughter, to the equally surprising talk with his wife the day before.

After a while, Jim began to focus his musings, allowing the very warm feelings he had for both women to come to the surface. But intrusive thoughts kept breaking through. He considered his chronic need to always have a young woman to bed. They'd kept his sexual needs satisfied, and had made him feel younger and more powerful than fidelity ever could have. But at what cost? What did he have to show for all of those years of cheating?

His logical mind got into the game and he carefully considered his current status. On the verge of divorce, he'd seriously eroded his daughter's respect and knew, even without confirmation, that he was viewed as an aging letch at his law firm. Twenty years earlier he and his peers had made lewdly derisive comments about the more indiscreet partners and their serial affairs. And now he was the goat. Even worse, his position as managing partner probably made the associates assume he couldn't get a woman without using his power and title.

The young women he'd seduced had used him as much as he'd

used them. That was his only consolation. He'd never pressured anyone, and he'd made sure that each of them rose in the firm according to their talents outside of the bedroom. At least he'd tried to. It certainly couldn't help to have your peers know you'd slept with a senior partner. There would always be suspicions about your real talents.

But that wasn't what nagged at him. The ache in his gut formed from the thought that none of them had ever truly cared for him. He couldn't trust one word that came out of their mouths. No, the only woman he'd ever been sure of was Catherine. Sighing heavily, he thought of the young woman he had met twenty-two years before, who was far superior to him in nearly every tangible way. Catherine's family had had money, power, prestige, and enough political muscle to have run the city if that had interested anyone in the clan. She didn't want him for his potential…she didn't want him for his money…she didn't need any favors from him. No, she had just loved him—for himself. And he had repaid her genuine trust by being unfaithful time and time again. Each time she caught him there had been a series of promises, each one readily broken as soon as the urge hit and the next opportunity presented itself. And it always seemed as though the opportunity presented itself quickly. Actually, as he rose in the organization and became more visible, it seemed as if the women actually sought him out—rather than the other way around. He had been pleased by the shifting of roles, but when he thought about it, there was only one reason a man got more attractive as he aged, and it had nothing to do with his looks or charm.

His mind wandered to Kayla, and he tried to remember who had made the first overture. It was hard to pinpoint, he realized. Things had happened so quickly that it seemed as though sparks had flown from the start. She had been a first year associate, barely twenty-five, and fresh from graduation at UCLA law school. She was a very attractive woman—lovely long strawberry blonde hair, pale eyes that took on the color of the clothing she wore. A little taller than Jamie, but much slighter, with a body that commanded attention. His attention had been drawn from the first day they'd met, and even then he'd sensed a glimmer in her eye that long years of cheating had alerted him to. There was a receptivity and a frank, open appraisal from her that sent his libido into overdrive.

His position allowed him to suggest assignments for the new associates, and he tagged her as his deputy, a plum job given to the most promising new associate. The job was close to being a glorified clerk, but it was one most associates would have killed for. He was surprised and pleased that their working styles fit together so well, and for a time, he let the sexual tension die down while they concentrated on work alone.

The break had come while on a trip to Brussels. A fellow partner had been unable to make the trip, leaving Jim alone with Kayla for the first time. Everything was very aboveboard until the meetings were concluded, late on a Friday night. Kayla had casually mentioned that she'd never been in the lovely city, and since he was intimately familiar with it he spontaneously asked if she'd like to stay the weekend and let him play tour guide. To his amazement, she looked him right in the eye and suggested that, as an economy measure, they could save the firm several hundred dollars a night if she gave up her room and shared his. His response was unequivocal and enthusiastic, and that weekend started them on a liaison that quickly grew to be an open secret in the firm. He hated the fact that word had leaked out, but he had to admit that it was largely his fault. He'd had a hard time suppressing his desire for the young woman, and he was sure that their peers had noticed his lingering gazes when they were in meetings together.

Even though the affair had begun just about a year ago, things were nearly as hot now as they had been then, quite an oddity for him, since he had rarely pursued an ongoing association with the women he bedded. Kayla was an enthusiastic lover, skilled far beyond her years—how that education had come about was never discussed between them. But Jim knew that her skills at lovemaking were not the hook that kept him connected to her. It was the odd feeling that she was a feminine mirror image of himself at her age. She had the same drive, the same need to impress her superiors by doing anything that needed to be done—no complaints. He smiled as he recalled her enthusiastic suggestion that she be allowed to conduct the preliminary meetings with an important client in Japan over the Thanksgiving holidays last year. She had insisted that she merely wanted him to be able to spend the holiday with his family, but he knew that it was just a chance for her to maneuver herself into position to gain some important experience at a time when most attorneys desperately wanted some time off.

Jim was fairly certain that he didn't love Kayla , and she had never expressed feelings of love for him either. He jerked upright in his seat, feeling a flush come over him. Love between them was unthinkable; loving him would be toxic for her ambitions, and he'd look like an idiot, dragging around a woman not much older than his daughter.

Thinking of his last conversation with Catherine, he reminded himself, that she was the only person he could imagine loving. But when the reality of his repeated betrayal washed over him he was struck with disgust. He'd become a man no one he respected could respect.

A surprising thought struck him, and he fought his self-loathing for a moment, letting the thought roam around in his mind. It was as elusive as a firefly, but he finally caught and held it. There had been something tender in Catherine's voice the day before. He was sure of it. And her recent bouts of anger showed she wasn't through with him. Catherine had always grown distant and unemotional when he'd hurt her. This time was different. Decidedly different. Maybe there was a chance; even a slim one was worth pursuing. But the only way to do that was to give Kayla the heave-ho. He mulled that over for a while, gazing out the window at the achingly clear blue sky. That would be easy enough. Besides, it was better for her to make a name for herself in Washington without the specter of their romance trailing behind her.

The rest of the flight was spent in fierce concentration as Jim made plans to end one relationship, while dreaming of resuscitating another.

❧

As his key slid into the lock of his hotel room, Jim heard a light tread scampering across the thick carpeting. The door was not yet fully open when he found his arms full of his young lover, her voluptuous body barely covered by one of his dress shirts. "Get in here and show me how much you missed me," she demanded, walking backwards as she pulled him along.

The door closed with a quiet whisper, and as the latch clicked, her mouth tilted up and sought his out, his determination of just hours before nowhere to be found. The kiss went on for a long time, the young woman's ardor obviously unquenched during his five-day absence.

He finally managed to pull away and slowly regained his equilibrium. "Wow, that was a surprising welcome," he was actually shocked that she was there. He had given her a key, but to his knowledge she had never used it, always waiting until he was at home to visit. Visit wasn't the proper term, since Kayla had slept with him every night since they had arrived in Washington. But she had her own room in the hotel, and kept most of her things in it. Most mornings would find her struggling into running clothes, then returning to her room to shower and prepare for the day.

"Do you mind?" she asked warily. "I uhm…wanted to welcome you home." A seductive smile crept onto her face as she lifted the tail of the long shirt, revealing just a neatly groomed triangle of dark red hair. "Am I dressed appropriately?"

He blinked a few times, always slightly amazed at Kayla's frank sexual aggression. "Yeah…uhm…that's a great outfit." He wished he could exploit her luscious body one more time, but even his very shaky moral code would not permit it.

Cocking her head slightly, Kayla gazed at him and asked, "Something's wrong, isn't it?"

He nodded, deciding that he had to get this over with. "I had some time to think this weekend, and I think it's best if we stop sleeping together." He carefully watched her face and body language for a reaction.

"Why?" she asked simply, using one of his tricks against him. He had stressed the efficacy of keeping questions as simple as possible to goad an opponent into elaborating more fully than they had planned, and he hated to have his own ploys used on him.

"This can't go on permanently. We both know that. You're wasting your time with me when there's no future for us. You need a young man that can keep up with you."

"Don't I satisfy you any more?" she asked, a frown darkening her eyes to a slate gray.

"Of course you do! This isn't about sex. I think we each need to focus on relationships that can be permanent. This one can't."

Her head cocked slightly, her eyes never leaving his. "You want to get back with your wife, don't you?" Even though her voice rose on the final words, her tone made it sound more like a statement than a question.

Nodding slightly, embarrassed that she saw through him so easily, he said, "I don't know if that's possible, but if it is, I want to try again."

She peered at him closely. "Why does that mean that we can't sleep together? You can have your relationship with her, and have sex with me. I don't want more than this, and, let's be honest, if your wife satisfied you, you wouldn't have started this, or any of the other affairs you've had."

His cheeks burned from the truth of her implications. "We've had problems, of course we have. Every married couple does. But I want to give this a genuine try, and that can't happen if we're sleeping together. I'm very sorry to spring this on you, but I honestly think it's best for both of us in the long run."

She shook her head briskly, her tone confident. "I disagree, but your decision is the final one." She stood up and started to walk towards the bedroom. He stayed right where he was, watching the gentle sway of her hips as she moved. Returning a minute later with her clothing, she started to dress in front of him, taxing his determination to the limits.

She let the shirt drop to the floor, then started to slide a pair of panties over her hips. Feeling the fire start to burn again, he swallowed and revealed the remainder of his decision. "I uhm…I know you won't like this, but I think it would be best if you went back to San Francisco."

Her mouth dropped open, and she stared at him, looking deeply wounded.

"I'm very happy with the work you're doing here, but it would be too hard for us to work together."

It looked as though she was going to say something; instead, she closed her eyes for a moment while continuing to dress. "Okay. It won't look good for me, but I'll do whatever makes you happy. That's all that matters."

"You are such a wonderful woman," he said softly, gazing into her eyes as she pulled her jeans up her sleek legs.

"It's easy to be a wonderful woman when you're with a wonderful man." Kayla walked over to the sofa and straddled his lap, her jeans gaping open. "Can I kiss you goodbye?" Her soft voice floated down to his ears as he drew in a deep breath, imprinting her alluring scent onto his brain.

He didn't have the strength to speak, just nodding his head a few times. She settled onto his lap—her breasts crushed against his chest. Her head tilted down and her lips latched onto his mouth as she kissed him, forcing him to feel all of the passion, all of the lust that enveloped them every time they were intimate. As the kiss continued her hips began to gyrate, skimming across his groin and she felt him begin to respond. "K...Ka...Kayla," he groaned, his hands going to her hips to guide her movements.

"It's okay," she soothed. "I promise I'll let you go. I just need one thing. I want to love you one last time, Jim. Give me this...please. Let me remember how good it was."

He looked up into her eyes, grown bright with desire, her hair swung across her shoulders as she moved against him. His last bit of willpower disintegrated, and he forced himself to stay conscious of the sensations that pummeled his body, reminding himself, *You might as well enjoy this, because if Catherine will take you back this is the last time you'll have sex this hot.*

Chapter Two

It was late, and Jamie felt like she'd been up for three days. Still, she had to get some studying done. Their weekend had been so hectic that she hadn't cracked open a book, and her classes were small enough that she couldn't hide a complete lack of preparation. Ryan was in favor of falling into bed, even though it was just eight, but she had decided that if Jamie could study—she could study. They went to their respective study spots and were quickly engrossed in their work.

The concentrated effort Jamie was putting into her accounting class was paying off, and she felt like she was finally understanding the broad concepts behind the rules she'd been following, rather than just memorizing. She was feeling pretty good by the time she decided she'd be able to go to class and not have to hide from her professor's perceptive eyes. It was nine-thirty, and she had a half hour to get ready for bed and get a full night's rest.

As usual, her cell phone was clipped to her waistband, the habit so ingrained that she barely noticed the small device any longer. The muted chirping caught her by surprise, and she started when she heard it. "Hello."

"Hi, Jamie." Only two words, but she not only knew the voice, she realized that she would probably always recognize it.

"Hi, Jack," she said, her heart skipping a beat. The mere sound of his voice made her anxious—not for any good reason that she could think of—she just uncharacteristically assumed the worst.

"Is it okay for me to call you? I don't want to cause you any trouble."

"Trouble?"

"Yeah...well, I assume that you're still with Ryan, and ah...I also assume she might not like you talking to me."

More than a little perturbed at the assumption, she said, "Ryan doesn't try to control me. I can speak with whomever I wish."

There was a silence that went on a beat longer than was comfortable. "Okay, let me try that again." She could hear him breathe out a sigh before he gave it another stab. "I guess it's easier for me to blame her if you don't want to speak to me."

This astounding show of introspection touched her, and she felt her defenses melt. "I don't understand why you think I wouldn't want to speak to you. I thought we parted on very good terms. Didn't you?"

"Yeah," he said, letting out a heavy breath. "I do. I guess I'm just feeling twitchy today. I have a question to ask you that's really got me spooked."

"What is it?"

"I uhm...I want to ask Natalie to marry me," he said in a rush, the words colliding as they tumbled out.

She paused for just a second, consciously willing down the tiny tendril of jealousy that began to emerge. "That's wonderful. I wish you all the best."

"Thanks," he said quietly, and she smiled as she pictured the shy blush that likely covered his features.

"I appreciate that you called to tell me." She was more puzzled than appreciative, but he didn't need to know that. "I take it that you haven't asked her yet."

"No, I was going to do it at Thanksgiving."

Trying to be tactful, she said, "Any particular reason that you're telling me now? I mean, I appreciate it, but if I was Natalie I don't think it'd sit well with me to know that you told your ex a month before you proposed."

"Well, I wanted you to know before you heard it from anyone, but that's not really why I'm calling."

Ryan entered the room at this point in the conversation, looked at the phone, and cocked her head in question. Jamie hit the mute button and said, "Jack."

Ryan turned and was striding out of the room before the "ack" had been fully enunciated, only to have her fleece shirt grabbed from behind. "Stay," Jamie mouthed, tugging Ryan towards the couch.

She gave Jamie a suspicious look, but shrugged and sat down next to her, placing a warm hand on her thigh. Jamie patted her gently and once again focused her attention onto Jack. "Why are you calling then?"

"I'm having a real battle over what to do for an engagement ring, and I thought of all the people I know, you're the only one that I trust to give me good advice on this."

"Oh," she said, completely shocked that he wanted her to consult with on this question. "Well, thanks for saying so. What did you have in mind?" The image of spending the day shopping with Jack for another woman's ring flashed through her mind, and was quickly dismissed into the 'when hell freezes over' category.

"I want to give her my grandmother's ring."

Her tone was just short of incredulous. "You want to give her the ring you gave me?"

"Bad idea?"

She took a deep breath and tried counting to ten. It was his ring—that's why she'd given it back to him, but the mere thought of him giving it to another woman set her teeth on edge. "Is cost a factor here? 'Cause you don't have to spend a lot to get a nice ring…"

"No!" he said, vehemently. "This is about sentiment. I thought you'd understand that."

"Look," Jamie said, frustrated. "I can't read your mind. Tell me what's up, or I can't be any help at all."

He sighed and said in a voice filled with hurt, "I thought you'd understand what this ring meant to me…and if you did, then Natalie would too."

She let out a breath, feeling a little like he'd punched her. Jack's grandparents had been married over sixty years when his grandfather died and his grandmother had moved in with the family. She and Jack had always been close, but they grew closer still during the last years of her life. She had passed away just a few months before Jack had asked Jamie to marry him, and she recalled that the most emotion she had ever seen from him was when he told her that he hoped they would have as good a marriage as his grandparents had.

"I'm sorry, Jack," she said. "That was very insensitive of me. I do know how much the ring means to you." She paused for a minute, looking at the curious blue eyes that peeked over at her from under long black bangs. She pushed Ryan gently, urging her to scoot down the sofa. As soon as Ryan was against the other arm of the piece, Jamie lay down with her head in her lap. She grasped one of the warm hands and placed it on her head, silently asking for an always-calming head rub. As Ryan's long fingers began trailing through her hair, she sighed and continued. "Even though I'm sure Natalie would be honored by the sentiment, I honestly think that it would always bother her to know that she wasn't the first person you gave the ring to."

His frustration was evident as he said, "But it means so much to me! It'd be like always having a piece of my grandparents with us."

"Jack," she said, her voice even softer than it had been before, "it might also be like having a piece of me with you. I know that you don't want that."

"It wouldn't be like that for me," he insisted. "I'd think of my grandmother when I looked at it."

"You're not the one who will wear it," she reminded him. "I know this means a lot to you, and I'm sure Natalie will wear it if she knows that. I'm just trying to be honest with you, even though it's not what you want to hear."

"Do you think I could ask her if she wanted it or if she wanted me to buy her another one?"

"Not a good idea. If she told you to buy another, she's not good enough for you. I mean that."

"Damn it, Jamie," he said gruffly, "are you sure about this?"

"No, I can't be sure. Want another opinion?"

"Sure, I guess. Is Mia around?"

"No. Ryan's a woman too. She's right here. Hold on." Hitting the mute button, Jamie swiveled her head until she could meet her lover's eyes. "Would you be insulted if I gave you a family heirloom as an engagement ring—if I'd previously given it to Jack?"

Ryan's twinkling blue eyes smiled down at her. "Is this a clever ploy to ask me to marry you?"

She barked out a surprised laugh and said, "I think I could come up with something a little more romantic than this. No, this is really about Jack. Would it bother you?"

"Yes and no," Ryan said thoughtfully. "I'd like the fact that your family meant a lot to you, and that you were making me a part of that tradition. On the other hand, it would always bug me a little that you gave it to Jack first. It might remind me of him more than I'd like."

"My feelings exactly." Just before she hit the button she turned to Ryan and gave her a speculative look, her face twitching into an even bigger smile. "I really should ask you to formally marry me one of these days. It's about time I made an honest woman out of you."

Turning back to the phone, Jamie said, "Ryan feels like I do. Part of her would be honored to wear it, and the other part would be reminded of the other person."

"All right," he said, sounding defeated. "I still might ask her though."

"Jack," she said, her voice still soft, but more determined, "don't try to manipulate her to get your way. That's not how to start off a marriage. Try to think of her feelings too."

"Okay, okay. I get the message."

"I do have one idea that might work. Why not give her the ring to hold until you have a child to pass it on to? Entrusting her with something that means a lot to you would be a nice gesture."

"Thank you," he said, the relief evident. "I'll buy her a ring that reminds me of her—rather than my grandmother. That's a great idea." He paused for a second then asked, "Is Ryan still there?"

"Yeah. Why?"

"Can I speak with her for a minute?"

"Sure." She handed the phone to Ryan with a puzzled shrug of her shoulders. "He wants to talk to you."

Ryan put the phone to her ear. "Hi, Jack."

"Hi," he said in a friendly tone. "Thanks for the advice. I think you two are right."

"Oh, you're welcome."

She started to hand the phone back but his voice caused her

to put the phone to her ear again. "You're a lucky woman, Ryan. Jamie's one in a million."

She chuckled mildly and corrected him. "She's one in a 38th Mersenne Prime."

"Huh?"

"I'm a math major," she said, knowing that simple explanation explained a wealth of her eccentricities. "That's a recently discovered prime number that has over two million digits."

"Ahh," he said, "it's nice to know that you know how special she is."

"I do indeed," she said, smiling down at her partner, "I'd say that she's the most wonderful woman in the world, but that's far too small a number to convey my full appreciation of her."

He laughed at that and said, "It's probably best not to talk to you about how wonderful Jamie is when I'm about to go ring shopping for another woman. Take care of her for…" He stopped abruptly and started again. "Take care of her forever, Ryan."

"With my last breath," she said, locking eyes with Jamie, her voice filled with confidence. Her blue eyes searched the moss green ones that looked up at her. "I'd say yes," she whispered.

"Pardon?"

"If you asked me to marry you, I'd say yes," she repeated, her intent gaze never leaving Jamie's.

"I marry you every day," Jamie said, her heart aching with emotion. "I pledge my love to you every night when I say my prayers, and I thank God for you every morning when I wake up"

"I'm thanking God for you right now," Ryan whispered. Pulling her partner into a tender embrace she kissed her. "All of my prayers have been answered." They kissed a few more times, each kiss adding to the heat that was building. Jamie could feel Ryan start to shift her weight against her and she knew they'd be naked in moments.

Putting her hand on Ryan's chest, Jamie said, "Let's brush our teeth and get into bed. I want to fall asleep after we make love."

Looking at her with the vacant gaze she often bore when aroused, Ryan said, "We're gonna make love?"

"Like you didn't know that." Jamie kissed her gently, then got up and went into the bathroom.

Ryan sat there for another minute, reflecting on the phone call. She'd been observing Jamie thoroughly while she spoke. There was a guarded wariness to her affect that Jamie never displayed to her. Ryan had a suspicion that the wariness was not something that had developed after they broke up, recalling that she'd noticed a polite distance between the couple the few times she had seen then together. With a start, she realized that she wouldn't have been attracted to Jamie if she behaved like that now. That small affect was enough to change her whole personality, and Ryan sat there musing about how the smallest thing can change the course of one's whole life. She was still thinking when Jamie placed a fresh tasting kiss on her lips, and her thoughts changed from the ephemeral to the wholly physical in a matter of seconds.

Aloysius Pender walked into his office on Monday morning and checked his schedule. "Betsy?" he called out to his secretary when he noticed his 7:00 A.M. appointment.

"Yes, Father?" the woman asked as she popped her head in.

"Martin O'Flaherty called for an appointment?"

"Yes, Father. He left a message on the machine yesterday. Is it all right that I scheduled him?"

"Of course, of course," he said absently. "It just surprised me, that's all."

He walked to the tiny kitchen down the hall and poured himself a cup of coffee, checking his watch as he walked back into the office. Like clockwork the front door opened at seven on the dot, and he heard his old friend extend a greeting to Betsy. Soon Martin's large frame filled the door, and he waited to be signaled in.

"Will you come in here, already?" Father Pender said with a warm smile. "In all these years I've never known you to be the formal sort, Marty. Why the bother?"

Martin closed the door and put his hands on the back of a chair. Pausing for a moment, he pulled the chair out and sat down, his weight making the old wooden chair creak. Fidgeting for a moment, he realized he wasn't going to get comfortable, so he cleared his throat and spoke. "I've given it a couple of months, but it's not any better, Father," the formal, almost brusque affect wholly unlike himself. "I'd like to ask Father Villarreal or perhaps someone not associated with St. Philip's to perform the ceremony for Maeve and me."

The priest leaned back in his chair, both taken aback and stung by this announcement. "After all we've been through? You're unable to forgive me for one mistake?"

Martin's dark head shook, his eyes devoid of warmth. "You didn't harm me, Father, you harmed my baby. That's not something I can forgive."

"Will you stop with the Father!" He stood up and paced behind his desk, his face growing red with anger. "For goodness sake, Marty, we've been friends for a quarter century! You haven't called me Father Pender since Brendan was in diapers."

"I respect you because of your position...not you yourself. I don't think you'd like the names I now call you in my mind."

He was so frustrated by his intractable friend that he felt like shaking him. "I thought we'd settled this. Siobhán is perfectly cordial to me, Marty. I know she wants you to get over this. She said as much when she was here with you."

"She's a better person than I am."

"She's a fine woman," the priest said, his voice growing soft as he recalled, "She's the image of her mother."

Martin's voice softened and his posture even grew relaxed. "Even though they look nothing alike, she is that."

"I'm glad she's found someone to share her life with. I've been worried about her these last years, Marty. I heard a lot of rumors about her behavior. The things I heard didn't seem like something your daughter would have been caught up in."

"What *exactly* do you mean by that?"

Knowing he'd only made matters worse, the priest tried to backpedal, but he wasn't effective. "I only meant that I knew you'd want Siobhán to find one person to love."

"That's not what you meant and you know it," Martin spat. "I'll tell you something, Aloysius Pender...it's the ridiculous stance of this church and the interference of a certain blabber-mouthed priest that made the child think she had to find her pleasure in brief encounters with women she hardly knew! She felt like an outcast! She was so filled with self-loathing that she was afraid to talk to me, and that child had never held anything back from me. How many more young people have to suffer the rejection of the *Holy* Church before you come to your senses?"

Stunned by the volume, the vitriol and the sarcasm Martin had used, the priest was almost unable to think of a reply. He had to spend a moment trying to think of some way to make his old friend see his position, and his lack of power over these matter. "You know that the Church's official teachings don't always square with my private beliefs, but there's only so much a parish priest can do!"

"What are your private beliefs on the subject, Father Pender?" he asked, eyes narrowed and intense.

"I think that we should, and I feel that we do, offer a warm welcome to homosexuals. There's nothing inherently sinful in being gay."

"And…?"

"And, if the homosexual person chooses to live a celibate life, they should be welcomed into every level of ministry."

"*If* they choose a celibate life," Martin said, the rancor dripping from his words. "And if they don't?"

"Well, I don't think it's my job to police the members of this parish. I would never withhold the sacraments from someone like Siobhán, even though I know she's openly breaking the Church's clear rules on this topic."

"Well aren't you just the most open-minded person?"

"That's not fair, Martin. I don't think that Siobhán's sins are any worse than a heterosexual person who has sex outside of marriage. Someone like Conor, for instance."

Martin grabbed the edge of the desk and shook it, making a Celtic cross totter and settle again. "Who's next to fall under your inquisition? Duffy? He's been neutered, I'll have you know!"

"Martin, I meant nothing by that. I'm only pointing out that most people in our parish are in a state of sin about something. I'd imagine ninety percent of our parish members use birth control of some sort. Their disobedience is no better and no worse than Siobhán's."

"So Conor's a bigger sinner than his sister, since he obviously has sex, and he's never produced a child," Martin groused, disgust evident.

"Technically, yes. But that's not the point. The point is that we're all sinners. Our mission isn't to point out the sin—it's to offer a path to forgiveness."

Martin's face was dark with anger, the veins on his temples standing out starkly. He spit his words out, each one enunciated sharply. "My child is one of the purest souls to ever walk through the doors of that church."

"She's a fine girl. That's what—"

Louder still, Martin continued. "She's a model of love and compassion and forgiveness. The fact that her biology leads her to love a woman in no way affects that!"

"Of course it doesn't. Look, Martin, we're getting off track here. You came to talk about your wedding, and now we're on a discussion about Church teachings. I think you're confusing your anger with the Church about these topics with your anger with me."

"I'm not confused in the least. You hurt my child. You...not the Church."

"I know I made a mistake in telling Siobhán's principal about her sexuality without talking to you first. But that's been eight years. Siobhán was a high school girl."

"That's no matter," Martin snapped, his chin stuck out in a way Father Pender had seen many times, each time showing his intractable nature.

"I've apologized for what I did. Siobhán has forgiven me. Can't we move on from there?"

"No, I'm afraid we can't," Martin said. His eyes were suddenly sad, and he looked pained. "I appreciate all that you've done for me and my family through the years, but I can't have you ask for God's blessing on my marriage if you can't agree that my Siobhán and her Jamie have the exact same rights to sexual pleasure that Maeve and I do."

"I don't believe that, Martin. I wish I could—believe me, my life would be easier if I could—but I don't. Marriage is reserved for a man and a woman. There's no way around the teachings."

"I appreciate your time, Father Pender," Martin said as he stood. "I'll speak to Father Villarreal about the ceremony." With that, he was gone, leaving the priest shaking with a mix of anger and sorrow at losing one of his oldest and dearest friends.

"Hello, Catherine," the clear, lightly accented voice said in greeting. "It's Maeve Driscoll."

"Would that be the future Maeve O'Flaherty?" Catherine asked, enjoying the teasing that was part and parcel of the O'Flaherty experience.

"One and the same. I have good news on that very front. Everything is settled, I believe, and the wedding is set for November the thirteenth."

"Excellent! That gives us plenty of time to make the few arrangements that we need."

"What needs to be done? I've secured the church and talked to one of my friends who's a printer about having some simple invitations done up."

"We don't have much to do. I can handle all of the details for the reception. What type of food would you like to have?"

"Well," she said, "the lads don't care for anything too fancy—they're a meat and potatoes crowd."

"That's not a problem. Marta and I will work up a sample menu and see if you and Martin agree."

"Now, you remember that we're paying for the food, Catherine."

"I do indeed. I'm a woman of my word. Now your dress is set, but will you have attendants?"

Absolute silence greeted that question. Finally, Maeve said, "I can't believe this, but that has slipped my mind completely."

"You've had a very hectic few weeks. You don't need to decide right now."

"No, I think it's obvious. So obvious I didn't give it a moment's thought," she said, laughing at herself. "I'd like my boys to give me away, and if she's willing, I'd love to have Ryan stand up for me."

"Oh, I can't imagine she wouldn't be willing, but given what Jamie's told me about her wardrobe I doubt she'll have a dress."

"She has a skirt," Maeve mused. "I gave it to her for Christmas a few years ago. She wore it once, or so she told me. Ah well, I'm not going to worry about that. I love her like my own, no matter what she wears."

Catherine was making notes, and she added one in bold print. *Have Jamie find a suitable outfit for Ryan.* "Well, it looks like there's just one detail remaining. What about a honeymoon trip?"

"Oh, I don't think we'll be able to do that. We have so many expenses…"

"Would you like to get away for a few days?"

"Well, yes, I suppose every couple wants to start their lives together away from the concerns of daily life. But we're not teenagers, Catherine. We should just get on with it."

"I have a suggestion. It set Jamie and Ryan off on the right foot, and Tommy and Annie seemed to enjoy their time there also."

"Oh, Catherine, not your house in Pebble Beach. We couldn't!"

Falling back on her now-familiar refrain, Catherine asked, "And why is that?"

"It's just too generous!"

"Offering my completely empty house to you for a few days is too generous? Just how is that, Maeve? The pool is heated every day, the lights come on at dusk, the temperature is set at sixty-nine degrees twenty-four hours a day. Your visit honestly would not cost me one cent, and if that is being too generous, you're going to have to explain how, because I don't understand."

"Oh, I would love to accept, but I'm afraid Martin will think we're taking advantage."

"Maeve, I suggest you accept the Pebble Beach offer. If I have to go to work on Martin, I'm aiming higher. For him, it's my apartment in Milan."

There was a longish silence, then Maeve's warm chuckle traveled along the line. "I would love to see my Marty in Milan," she giggled. "He thinks the Italians are quite mad, you know."

"That's my final offer. You go to Pebble Beach for a few days, or it's two weeks in Milan…with first-class airline tickets thrown in."

"My, but you drive a hard bargain." Maeve laughed heartily. "I'll get to work on my fiancé tonight. I think my powers of persuasion are up to the task, and if they're not, I'll ask Jamie for a crash course in Italian, because I know yours are."

To Maeve's stunned surprise, Martin was completely amenable to accepting the honeymoon gift from Catherine. He seemed distracted during the discussion, and after they had agreed she asked, "What's on your mind, Marty?"

"Oh," he said, his lips pursed and his brow furrowed. "I'm just thinking about my discussion with Father Villarreal this morning. I don't know if it's because he's a younger man, or because of his background, but that fellow knows how to talk to people."

"Tell me more about your talk. You didn't have much time this morning."

They were sitting next to one another in Maeve's small, neat living room. Martin had his arm around Maeve's shoulders, and his fingers were rapidly drumming on her arm. "I'm not a stupid man, you know."

Maeve flinched and turned to look at Martin's profile. "Who implied that you were?"

"No one," he said, absently. "I'm just trying to show that I know Father Pender doesn't have his own little fiefdom here. I fully understand that every priest takes a vow to uphold the teachings of the church in Rome. But there are ways to enforce the rules and ways to insult and demean, and that young man understands the difference."

"Did you talk about Siobhán and Jamie?"

"I did." His fingers stopped moving and Maeve could feel his tense body relax. "He said something that impressed me. He said that he feels we're in a difficult period right now. Society is changing much more quickly than the Church can, or should change."

"Should?"

"Yes." Martin nodded decisively. "I agree with him on this. He said that we're going through a revolution, but the Church can only change through evolution. And we all know how long it takes for things to change evolutionarily."

Maeve nodded and said, "I suppose that makes sense, but I'm a little surprised you agree. Having Jamie and Ryan wait for the Church to evolve will be a long time coming."

"I know that. But I'd be surprised if it happened in their

lifetimes."

Maeve burrowed in closer and Martin squeezed her tightly. "It's so unfair." She leaned her head on his shoulder. "They should have what we have."

"I know," he said, his voice very quiet. "But it won't happen for many years. So all I can hope for is a local priest to express his support for my daughter and her relationship."

"I take it that Father Villarreal does that?"

"He does," Martin nodded. "He said that what matters is that Siobhán has found someone to experience a deep, committed, holy connection with. The fact that the Church isn't able to recognize the sanctity of it doesn't mean that God doesn't."

"You seem very satisfied with this."

"I am. I feel better about the Church than I have in months. I'd really like him to perform our ceremony. Is that all right with you?"

"Without question. I hate to wound Father Pender, but I agree with you on this. It just wouldn't be right to have him bless us while feeling that our relationship was valid and the girls' was invalid."

"I'm no theologian, but any God who would disapprove of Siobhán and Jamie's union is a God I have no interest in meeting. If I'm sent to hell with all of the gay people it'll be fine with me."

"If Michael's not in heaven, I'm not going either. So I'll be right beside you."

Martin hugged her again and placed a kiss on her cheek. "If you're with me, hell would be heavenly."

Chapter Three

When Ryan opened the door on Tuesday night, she was surprised and pleased to find her aunt sitting on the sofa chatting with Jamie while they drank a cup of tea. "Now this is the kind of surprise I'd like to see every day," Ryan said, smiling broadly. She crossed the room to kiss her aunt. "Why did you decide to make my day so special?"

Turning to Jamie, Maeve rolled her eyes as she asked, "Does she speak to you like this, sweetheart?"

"Constantly," Jamie agreed as Ryan came over to kiss her too. "I don't know why everyone doesn't want a lover who has kissed the Blarney Stone a few times."

"Everyone does," Ryan decided, sitting down next to her partner. "So what's up?"

"I came to ask you to do me a great favor, and I wanted to ask you in person."

Ryan's face took on a concerned look, even though her aunt gave no signs of distress. "Whatever it is, my answer is yes."

"It might involve getting dressed up," Maeve cautioned.

"I'd wear an evening gown with a tiara if you asked me to, Aunt Maeve. Now give me the bad news. Where am I going, and how dressed up do I have to be?"

"Well," Maeve smiled, "tradition requires the maid of honor wear a gown of some sort, but I frankly wouldn't mind if you wore your volleyball uniform. All that matters is that you're at my side when I marry your father." She got her entire statement out, but the last few words were a little shaky. Her own watery eyes were soon matched by those of her niece, who went over and sat right next to her, wrapping her in a fond hug.

"Of course I'll do it. Of course." She held her tight. She noticed that Jamie was a little teary, even though Maeve had obviously let the cat out of the bag before Ryan had returned. "I'll happily don a dress. I'll even wear heels, and you know how I feel about them."

"Oh, sweetheart, I hate to have you go against your principles." She sat up and straightened her blouse, which Ryan's strong hug had wrinkled. "Besides, with heels you'd be so much taller than me, we wouldn't fit in the same photos."

"I have an idea," Jamie piped up. "Ryan, you don't have anything dressy to wear to the symphony or out to dinner."

"Yes, I do. I have that outfit you bought for me in Pebble Beach."

"Honey, that's an unlined silk tank top and pants. You can't wear that in San Francisco in November! It might be fifty degrees out."

"I could wear a coat over it. It's always warm inside, anyway."

Jamie mentally ran through Ryan's inventory and decided that a casual summer-weight outfit with a motorcycle jacket topping it was really not the type of thing she was thinking of for the wedding. Not wanting to insult her partner, she said, "Yes, you could, but that's too casual. I'd love to buy you a nice dark suit...a pantsuit. You could wear flats with that and look absolutely perfect."

"I just don't think I'd wear it very often," Ryan sulked mildly.

"We'll get you something understated and very simple. You'd be able to wear it for years and years."

"If I say okay, will you not try to get me to buy any more nice clothes for a few years? I'll have two nice outfits then, a winter and a summer."

Jamie wanted to remind her that she wasn't in the military, but decided that Ryan wouldn't appreciate that. "It's a deal. We'll get you something elegant and dark, and I won't bug you to buy anything new until our kids get married."

"Now you're talking!" Ryan beamed, looking relieved to have won a major concession in the ongoing skirmish.

The ringing phone had chirped five times when Mia pulled herself away from the torrid embrace that Jordan had her wrapped in. "Be right back," she murmured, as she tried to focus enough to find the phone. "Hello?"

"Hi, this is Brendan O'Flaherty. Is Ryan home?"

"Hi, Brendan, it's Mia. I thought they were home, but they didn't pick up. Let me go check." She straightened her shirt and slipped off the bra that Jordan had just unhooked by snagging the loose fabric through the sleeves of her shirt. Her smirk was firmly fixed on the long, lean, blonde who relaxed on the bed, trying to look innocent. "I thought you had to study," she whispered, shaking a finger at her lover.

"I was studying you."

Mia shook her head at the playful woman and went into the hall. "Ryan?" she called out. There was no reply, and she walked down the hall and poked her head in the open door to her roommates' room. "Ryan?"

Ryan was lying on the love seat, her head on a cushion, her very long legs dangling from the knee over the opposite arm. "Are you thinking?" she asked as she approached, familiar with her roommate's odd habits.

When Ryan didn't reply she touched her shoulder, still getting no response. A mild shake didn't work either, which puzzled her, since Ryan was notorious for her ability to wake from the smallest noise. It took a rather rough shake, which Mia hated to do, to finally pull Ryan from her sleep. "Hey," Mia said, squatting down so she was at eye level, "your brother Brendan is on the phone. Do you want to talk to him?"

Ryan was blinking so slowly that Mia wasn't sure if she knew what she was saying. She smacked her dry lips together a few times and nodded, mumbling something that Mia couldn't make out. Tossing her legs from the furniture she got to her feet, grasping Mia's offered hand for stability. "Tell him I'll be there in a sec," she said as she walked into the bath.

Mia picked up the phone next to the bed and relayed the message, then went into her room to hang up. She spotted Jamie coming up the stairs and crooked a finger, inviting her into her room. "What's up with Ryan?" she asked after hanging up the extension phone.

"I don't know. What is up with her?" Jamie took a seat on the bed, sharing the surface with Jordan, who had taken a book out and was idly looking at it.

"She was nearly unconscious when I went to tell her that her brother was on the phone. I've never seen her sleep that soundly."

Jamie blew out a breath that made her lips flutter. "She's still trying to get her strength back from having the flu. I actually called my doctor, just to ask how long it might take for her to be normal again, and she said it might take a month or more—and that's if Ryan was really babying herself. With the way she runs herself down, it'll probably be twice that long."

"She seems fine at practice," Jordan piped up. "And her play in games has been phenomenal."

"Yeah, I agree," Jamie said. "It's like she uses all of her energy to play her sport, and then collapses at the end of the day. I'm sure she's fine, but she could use a lot more sleep."

"Doesn't help that we have our Oregon trip this week," Jordan supplied. "That one's always a bitch because of the travel situation. Lots of time on a bus."

"Are you going, James?" Mia asked.

"Hmm…I thought about it, and I know that Ryan likes it when I go with her, but I honestly think she goes to bed earlier when I'm not there."

"I can vouch for that," Jordan agreed. "She normally doesn't even join us for the team meal. She goes right to bed as soon as the game's over."

Jamie nodded, "Well, there's that, too. I make her eat better when I'm with her. Plus, Saturday is her birthday, and I'd really like to be with her at midnight." She looked at her friends and shrugged her shoulders. "Silly, huh?"

"No, sweet," Mia insisted, sharing a smile with Jordan.

"But if I was with her I'm sure she'd sleep less—especially since we'd probably want to see her birthday in with a celebration." Her eyebrows waggled a little, making Jordan, who had never seen her version of the expression, giggle. "I just wish I could be sure she'd eat right. Then I wouldn't worry about her."

"Make you a deal," Jordan suggested. "If you don't want to come, I'll go back to the room with her and make sure she eats something before she goes to bed."

"Would you really do that?"

"Sure. I care about her, and I know that she tends to ignore her body's signals."

"It's a deal," Jamie said. "I'll go to the store right now and buy some granola, or some other dry cereal, and some fresh fruit. That's her favorite bedtime snack."

"I'll force feed her if I have to," Jordan assured her as Jamie left the room.

"You're such a nice person," Mia said, brushing the fine blonde hair back from Jordan's face. "Generosity turns me on," she whispered, climbing astride her lover's hips.

"I'll brush her teeth when she finishes her cereal," Jordan teased, smiling gently as Mia pushed her to the bed and gave her a well-deserved reward for her consideration.

⁂

"Hi, Bren," Ryan said after splashing some cold water on her face and giving her teeth a quick brush.

"Am I bothering you?"

"No, I just fell asleep studying. You saved me from getting a horrible crick in my neck."

"You sure? I can call back another time. This isn't vital."

"I'm sure. What's up?"

"I wanted to talk to you about Maggie."

Her voice was softer and showed a little tension. "Is everything all right?"

"Oh, yeah. Everything's great. That's part of the reason that I think I need to make some decisions. It's only going to get harder from this point on."

"I was tracking you until the everything's great part. Then you lost me."

He sighed and said, "I'm frazzled, to tell you the truth. I feel like we're really getting close, closer than we were in law school. If this continues, I'm going to ask her to marry me."

"That's great, Bren! I think she'd be a great partner for you."

"Yeah, I'm sure she'll fit into the family." He paused for a second and added, "That's not that easy for some people to do, ya know."

"I know. Tracy Stewart would be your sister-in-law if she'd loved all of you guys." She shivered a little at the thought that she could have missed out on the opportunity to love Jamie, and forced herself to concentrate on Brendan again.

His next statement shocked her right back into the conversation. "Do you think Da would have married Mama if he knew she would die young?"

"Brendan! Does Maggie have...cancer?"

"No! Thank God, no. She's not even sure that she has the gene, but Huntington's disease runs in her family. Her father has it now—he's in very bad shape."

"Oh, Brendan, that's so sad."

"You know about Huntington's?"

"Yeah. I learned about it in one of my genetics classes. It's a horrible disease," she understood his concern. "Has Maggie been tested?"

"No. That's part of the problem. I'd like her to get tested—I think it would help her make decisions about having kids—and if she doesn't have the gene, I think it would really free her up."

"But she doesn't want to?"

"No. Several of her siblings have been tested, and only her oldest brother has it. She says it's thrown him into a depression that she's afraid he'll never come out of. He broke up with his girlfriend because of it—now he says he'll never marry because he doesn't want to be a burden."

Ryan sighed, letting out a deep breath. "I don't know, Bren. I might feel like Maggie does. When there's no cure...no real treatment... do you really want to know?"

"When there's a fifty-fifty chance that she doesn't carry the gene; it's worth the risk to me."

"That's to you, Bren. Obviously not to her." She was quiet for a few moments, letting it all since in. "How old was her father when he developed symptoms?"

"Not very old. He's been affected most of Maggie's life. He became bedridden just last year." Brendan considered the timing and said, "I think that's one of the reasons she decided to come out here, to tell you the truth. It just kills her to watch him deteriorate.

They had to put him in a nursing facility because he's unable to swallow any more. He has to be watched constantly, and her mom just couldn't do it any more."

"Wow," Ryan said quietly. "Doesn't her family need her for support?"

"Her mom's the one who urged her to go. Maggie was really close with her dad, and when he lost his ability to recognize her she had a very, very tough time of it. In a way, it's hard for her to be away, but in another way, it's easier to not have to be surrounded by it. I think it was the right decision for her—even though she still has her doubts."

"How many other sibs does she have?"

"Oh, she has a full baseball team," he chuckled. "She's the fifth of nine. Her oldest brother and the two youngest aren't married. The rest are—and they all live in the Chicago area. Her mom has a lot of support."

"Wow," Ryan said again, feeling slightly overwhelmed by the information. "This must have ruined them financially."

"Yeah. Her dad was a cop, so he has good medical benefits, and he was able to hang in until he qualified for his pension, but they aren't very well off. Maggie pays for all of her dad's care when insurance doesn't and it takes a huge chunk out of her paycheck. He's in the best facility available—I think she does that as her penance for not being there."

"So that brings us back to your original question. Would Da have married Mama if he knew?"

"Yeah. What do you think?"

"I can't answer for him, Bren, but I'd be with Jamie if I knew we didn't even have a year together. If you can walk away from Maggie because of this—you should." She knew that her words were harsh, but she meant every one of them.

The silence carried on a little longer than she was comfortable with, and she was afraid she had deeply offended him, but he finally said, "I can't, Ryan. I won't. I love her—no matter what's in store for us—I love her."

She sniffed away the tears that were forming and said, "I had a feeling you'd say that. I love you, too."

"Thanks, Ryan. I guess we'll just have to work out the details as time goes on."

"Hey, Bren?" Ryan recalled a detail from an earlier conversation that she wanted to follow up on. "Did this have anything to do with her previous boyfriend breaking up with her?"

"Yep. It was the whole problem. He wanted to be with her, but he didn't want to have kids together and he refused to even consider adopting. I think he was just scared."

"I bet you're scared, too, Bren, but you won't let that stop you."

She could hear him smiling through the phone as he said, "No, you're right. I won't let that stop me."

At nine-thirty on Thursday night, two tired volleyball players relaxed on their respective beds. The dark haired one was methodically shoveling spoonfuls of cereal into her mouth, with the other continually trying to add a little something to the bowl. "Let me put some more raisins in that," Jordan suggested.

"Did Jamie offer to pay you by the calorie?" Ryan smirked, knowing her partner was behind this conspiracy.

"No, although that's not a bad idea."

Ryan flicked an almond at her, laughing when her quick-reflexed friend caught it in her mouth. "Well, that's all I can get down," she said, setting the bowl on the table.

"How about another banana? You need the potassium."

"Okay," Ryan sighed. "Toss me one." Jordan did so and Ryan started turning her bed down as she ate. "I can't wait to sleep." As soon as she swallowed the last bite, she brushed her teeth and hopped in.

She tossed and turned a bit, trying to get comfortable. "It's hard to find a good spot without Jamie here," she mumbled, punching her pillow in frustration.

Jordan got up and went into the bath, emerging with a bottle of moisture lotion. "Let me rub your back for a while."

"Did Jamie put you up to this too?" Ryan asked as she tugged off her T-shirt and lay face down on the bed.

"Yeah, it was mentioned. She said that the best way to relax you was...I believe the term she used was a skin massage, rather than muscle massage."

"Yep. That's the ticket," Ryan agreed. "She just moves my skin around with her fingertips. Lots of lotion please."

"Have you always had a retinue of people tending to your every need, Boomer?" Jordan asked fondly as she squirted a cool trail of lotion down the center of Ryan's back.

"I hate to admit it, but I really have. Being the youngest, and the only girl, and having a bunch of aunts who all only had sons really helped, I think. They all wanted to pamper a sweet little girl."

"Well, I guess you'd do in a pinch, huh?"

Jordan was quiet for a while as she played with the smooth skin under her fingers and Ryan asked, "You didn't have that, did you?"

"No. My brother got all the pampering. I was supposed to take care of both him and my mother. It was a little Cinderella-like, but it wasn't a step-family…I was related to the jerks."

"What about your dad?" Ryan asked, her voice growing soft as she felt herself start to relax under Jordan's gentle stroking.

"He wasn't home much when I was little. He was just getting his career going, and work took precedence. But when he was there, I was the favorite. As long as I was doing well at school and accomplishing something in one of my sports, he was very supportive."

Ryan turned her head around to be able to look into Jordan's eyes. "Did you never feel loved just for being who you are?"

Jordan head shook slowly, Jordan's fine hair skimming over her shoulders. "No. Never."

Lying back down, Ryan reached behind herself and patted Jordan's leg. "I love you for who you are. I think you're just perfect."

Jordan leaned over and kissed Ryan on the cheek. "I love you too, Boomer." She ruffled the dark hair affectionately and added, "You're the best friend I've ever had." She handed Ryan her T-shirt and ordered, "Now cover up so you don't catch cold, you tender little thing. And don't you dare try to get out of bed before eight, Jamie's orders."

"Will do," Ryan agreed, shrugging into her shirt and collapsing heavily onto the mattress. "You be careful if you go out. And if you want to sleep with me you can, okay?"

"Mmm…that wouldn't be a good idea," Jordan chuckled. "My

hands wind up in some pretty interesting places when I sleep these days. Besides, I haven't had a nightmare since our first road trip."

"That's good to hear," Ryan murmured sleepily. "See you tomorrow. Thanks for caring about me."

A smile bigger and brighter and more filled with emotion than it would have been if the light had been on covered Jordan's face. "Night, Boomer."

The next morning, Ryan lay in bed, hands laced together behind her head, trying to make herself remain right right where she was. Jordan got up and stumbled into the bathroom, and when she came back she shot her roommate a look. "It's after eight, Boom, you can get up now if you want."

"Nah," Ryan yawned. "I'm trying to get used to sleeping late. It's the only way I'm ever going to feel better."

"Might help if you closed your eyes." Jordan curled up in her still-warm bed, humming a soft, happy tune.

Ryan didn't reply, recognizing that Jordan's comment was rhetorical. She rolled over onto her side and tried to sleep, but was largely unsuccessful. A few minutes later she heard Jordan flopping around. "You up?"

"Yeah. I can't go back to sleep. You're starting to rub off on me."

"Jamie can always put me to sleep," Ryan said, her voice wistful and soft.

"Hey, I rubbed your back and helped you nod off last night."

"Yeah, but she can put me to sleep when I'm fully rested. That takes talent."

Jordan rolled over to face Ryan and caught the impish look on her face. "I have a feeling I know what her technique is. I think you're gonna have to wait until you get home for that treatment."

"Mmm...nobody could compare. She's the only one for me."

"Is that really true?"

Sitting up and staring at Jordan, Ryan said, "Are you kidding? Haven't you been paying attention?"

"Oh, I know you're totally into her. But is Jamie the best sex partner you've ever had?"

Ryan gave the question its due consideration, as she always did. "Hmm…let me answer that two ways," she said thoughtfully. "Yes, we have the most fulfilling sex life that I could even imagine. No comparison. But I've been with people who were a lot more experienced and pushed me a little more than Jamie ever does."

"Pushed you? Like how?"

"Let's see, how do I explain this?" Ryan mused. "It's hard to put to words, since it's such a physical concept, but I'll try." She rolled onto her side and supported her head with one braced hand. "I've been with women who played me like an instrument. Women who had so much experience and loved sex so much that they dedicated themselves to it." She laughed gently as she said, "I'm generally pretty quiet in bed, but I've had women drive me so crazy that the neighbors were pounding on the walls to get us to shut up."

"It's not like that with Jamie?"

Ryan smiled as she admitted, "Well, sometimes it is, but that's the exception, rather than the rule."

"So, it doesn't bother you to not always have wild sex?"

"No, not at all. Those women made me feel something so they'd feel something, too. But it never really worked that way. I felt plenty physically, but very little emotionally. It's like we had to fuck each other's brains out to feel connected." She paused and considered how it was with her partner. "It's never like that with Jamie. I feel so much from the slightest touch, from the softest kiss. If she pushed me sexually the way these women did, it'd probably kill me. I honestly don't want that kind of thing with her very often."

"Hmm…I don't know if I really understand the difference. It seems like you'd want the woman who was the absolute best in bed if you were going to be with her for the rest of your life."

"I'm not expressing myself well," Ryan decided. "Jamie is the best in bed—by far. Making love is more than just the physical sensations. Jamie's like a volleyball player that can do it all—set, kill, pass, serve—and do it all very, very well. Now if you compared her to the world's best passer, she might come out a little short. Likewise the best server. But if you wanted one particular player to be on your team, you'd choose her every time, because she's the best overall. Does that make any sense?"

"Yeah, I guess so. I just wonder about these things because of

Mia."

"What about her?"

"I'm trying to figure out what's going on with us, you know, how I feel about her. I don't have anything to compare it to, and that confuses me." Jordan had rolled onto her back again, making it difficult for Ryan to see her face clearly.

"I can't tell where you're going here. What has you confused?"

"It's hard for me to pin down. I just wonder what it all means." She sat up and tossed her legs over the side of the bed, looking intently at Ryan. "I don't really know where we're going, ya know?"

"Well, you've only been seeing each other a few weeks. That's not odd to feel a little unsettled."

"Yeah, I guess you're right. I'm just not used to not knowing where I'm going. It feels weird."

"I know the feeling." Ryan chuckled. "When I first realized I was falling for Jamie, I was more confused than I'd been at any time in my life."

Jordan hopped to her feet and loomed over Ryan, her eyes wide. "That's not what I'm talking about. I'm not falling in love. I just…I just…I was talking about sex!"

Ryan blinked up at her, completely puzzled. "Oh. Sorry. It didn't feel like you were talking about sex."

"I am. I'm only talking about sex."

Still clearly confused, Ryan said, "What about it?"

"You know Mia's the only woman I've ever been with. I want to know…" Jordan sat down on her bed, looking as though she didn't know how to form the words she was seeking. "How do I judge the sex we've been having? Is it really good, or just good because I've never had it?"

Now Ryan sat up, and gazed up at her friend speculatively. "You want to know how to tell if the sex you're having is good?" The tilt of her head and the tone of her voice combined to show she doubted that the question was sincere.

"Yeah. How do you know if it's really good?"

Ryan scratched her head. "Isn't that like asking how you know if you've enjoyed a meal?"

"No, no." Jordan crossed her legs in a yoga pose. She started using her hands to emphasize her words, something Ryan had never seen her do. "What if I've only had fast-food my whole life, and I go to a fabulous restaurant and have all sorts of dishes I've never had. I might want my more experienced dining companion to tell me if the escargot we just had was really good or not. I'm trying to expand my palate here."

"Okay, I guess I see your point. Tell me this. How do you feel when you make l…have sex with Mia?"

Jordan laughed gently and smiled at her friend. "It's pretty awesome, and I mean that in every way. Sometimes I lie there and I'm actually in awe of the feelings."

Ryan smiled back and assured her, "I've been in awe a few times myself. What else?"

"Well, it's hard to explain, but she makes me feel really important, you know? Like she'd rather be with me than anyone else on earth. She makes me feel really attractive, too, and that hasn't happened to me very often."

Ryan was amazed at that comment, but Jordan was staring at some distant point and didn't take in her startled expression. "She makes me feel aware of my body in ways I never have been before, if that makes sense. It's funny, but sometimes I feel like she's actually worshipping me." Her eyes moved to Ryan's, and she cocked her head slightly as she asked, "Do you know what I mean? She lavishes so much attention on my body that I feel like a goddess sometimes."

Ryan nodded, having felt that way a time or two, also, but only with Jamie.

"Like the other night…she spent a good fifteen minutes just kissing my hands." She looked down at her hands, which were lying palms up upon her knees. "They didn't even feel like my hands when she was doing that. I looked at them like they were really special too—rather than just tools for beating the hell out of a volleyball." Ryan laughed at her joke, and Jordan looked at her intently. "Does that sound like good sex?"

"Does your heart start to beat wildly when she looks at you in a certain way—and you know she wants to touch you?"

"God yes!" Jordan cried, falling onto her back, her legs still crossed—knees pointing towards the ceiling.

"Do you find yourself thinking of her when you really should be doing something else?"

"How about match point last night? It was really hot in the gym and I lifted my arm to wipe my forehead. I smelled my own perspiration and it reminded me of some of the scents we throw off when we have sex, and I almost forgot what I was doing out there!"

"Uh-huh," Ryan said, recalling seeing Jamie's face in a few glass beakers in chemistry lab. "Is being with her the highlight of your day?"

"Yep. Being with her is better than beating Stanford."

"When something happens, does it have more meaning once you share it with her?"

Jordan thought for a second and said, "Yeah...it does. I felt great about beating Oregon last night, but it wasn't until I called her that it really sank in. It's like I could feel that she was proud of me for playing well, and then it meant more to me."

Ryan nodded, having felt the same way while on her own phone call. "I feel qualified to render my expert opinion now," she said solemnly.

"Yeah?"

"You are most definitely having great sex. I'd stake my reputation on it."

Jordan nodded, smiling broadly. "That's what I thought. Thanks for listening. You really are great to talk to."

As Jordan hopped to her feet to head for the shower, Ryan smirked at her departing form. *Ooh, Baby. Are you ever in deep!*

"Hey, Mia, it's Ryan. Is the love of my life at home?"

"Yep. Now that we've covered that, let me talk to my sweetie, okay?"

"Wait your turn," Ryan growled playfully. "I want to say goodnight and hit the sack. Then you and Jordan can stay up and giggle all night."

"Oh, all right," she pouted. "Here's Jamie." The phone was handed off amidst a muted rustle.

Jamie's sleepy sounding voice said, "Hi, sweetheart. We were almost out."

"We?" Ryan asked, eyebrows shooting up. "Are you sleeping together?"

"Uh-huh," she said, a half-captured yawn escaping. "We were sitting in my room, listening to the game on the Internet, and generally moaning about how we hated to have you two gone, and we decided to at least have a little companionship."

Mia squawked in the background. "Hey, thanks!"

"You know I love you," Jamie soothed to her friend. "I'm just not in love with you. Big difference, as I've discovered."

"Well I should hope so," Ryan interjected. "Are you two trustworthy? I don't want a pair of 'Dear Jane' letters waiting for us when we get home."

"We've slept together many times before now." She giggled, recalling, "Of course, neither of us knew about the other's Sapphic tendencies at the time."

"You know Jordan says she doesn't want to sleep with me any longer because her hands don't behave. Maybe you'd better take some precautions with Mia." Ryan thought for a moment and added, "I've got some handcuffs in my bag of tricks."

"Hey, Mia, Ryan wants me to put handcuffs on you. Do you mind?"

After a pause Jamie got back on the line and said, "She says she'll agree to a little bondage, but that she has to be the top. She claims that she and submission are incompatible."

"I don't even have a rejoinder for that," Ryan chuckled. She lowered her voice slightly and Jordan took the hint and went into the bath to get ready for bed. "I'm glad you have each other. Just don't warm your hands like you do with me."

"Hey, it's not my fault that I could melt chocolate on your breasts. You're my space heater."

"You know," Ryan said reflectively, "the thought of seeing you with another person now is horrendous for me. But I have this image of the two of you when you were still in high school. It's kinda hot to think of you fooling around a little bit when you were on a sleep-over."

"It never happened," Jamie insisted, her voice dropping as she added, "but I'll be happy to make up a little erotic story about that for your birthday."

"Ooh, tempting. But I don't think you have to go to that much trouble to turn me on. Just hearing your voice does it—quite well as a matter of fact."

"Works for me too. You just hold that thought until tomorrow. I'll make steam come out of your ears."

"I'm going to sleep right now, so I can start dreaming of you. I love you, Jamie."

"I love you too, Ryan. Now put Jordan on so Mia stops pinching me."

Chapter Four

As expected, Jamie was patiently waiting for Ryan when the plane landed just after noon on Saturday. The unexpected twist was the colorful bunch of helium balloons that she held in her hand. "Happy birthday, honey!" she called out when Ryan had barely passed through the doors of the jetway.

Ryan grinned broadly, good-naturedly accepting the delighted congratulations of her teammates, none but Jordan knowing that this was her natal day. As Jamie hugged her, Ryan was patted on the back repeatedly, with a few of the other women ruffling her hair as they passed. Jordan hung back, waiting to greet Jamie. When Ryan was released, Jordan hugged her and kissed her cheek. "Mission accomplished," she said. "She was fed every hour on the hour, and she got ten hours of sleep both nights. Actually, she slept on my shoulder all morning too, so she's in good shape."

"Excellent job. Coming to our house by any chance?"

"Hmm." She acted as though she hadn't given the idea any real thought. "I guess I could swing by at some point."

"Let's go. Mia's waiting in the car. We were running late and didn't have time to park."

"Mia, huh? I guess it would be nice to see old Mia. How is she anyway?"

"Seems fine since you were on the phone with her half of the night," Jamie commented dryly.

"Yeah, well, I'm just checking. It's good to be careful."

"You're busted, Jordan. Don't make it any worse for yourself." Ryan slung her arm around her friend and they walked through the terminal together, drawing dozens of looks from people who were amazed by the sight of the very tall twosome.

❦

Ryan was in a hurry to get home, so they stopped by the Berkeley house just long enough to disgorge passengers. Jamie ran into the house and emerged with two extremely large rectangular baking dishes, both covered with foil. "Since you guys are coming over to party in Castro with us tonight, why don't you come for dinner too?"

"That'd be great," Mia said. "Jordan?"

"Yeah. I'd love to. We just have to spend the afternoon figuring out costumes."

"Ours are all set," Ryan said, grinning, "although I think my partner is having second thoughts."

"Well, it sounded like a good idea when I saw it, but now it seems kinda juvenile," Jamie admitted. "It might be fun to do something a little sexier. I mean, this is my first Halloween as an official lesbian."

"Oh, I could fix you right up if you want to look sexy," Ryan promised, "but I think the costume you bought is really cute."

"We'll see," Jamie said, patting her cheek. "Now let's get home. See you guys around six?"

"Cool," the pair replied in tandem.

❦

"So, what's in the pans you so neatly secured in the trunk?" Ryan asked as they pulled out of the drive.

"Birthday girls shouldn't ask too many questions." Jamie was giving her an adorable smile, and Ryan had to pull over to the curb and give her a kiss—even though they'd traveled less than fifty feet.

"I really missed you," she murmured as she nuzzled her face into Jamie's neck. "More so this time than usual."

"Do you wish I'd come with you? I hope you know I stayed away just so you could rest better."

"No worries. I appreciate that you tried to do what was best for me. I really did rest up pretty well—even though the travel for this trip was tiring. We spent far too much time on the bus for my tastes."

"That's what happens when you play the PAC-10 schedule. When the town is too small for an airport, you've gotta do it the hard way."

Ryan started the car up again and commented, "I think I missed you because Jordan and I talked a lot about how she feels about Mia. It made me think of you even more than I normally do—and then I started to miss you more and more."

"What does Jordan have to say about Mia?"

"Oh, nothing much," Ryan said, obviously evading the question. "She seems to like her a lot."

With a wry chuckle Jamie said, "Well, I can certainly understand how such a scintillating conversation could make you pine away for me. You two need to calm down a little—your hearts can only take so much."

The tips of Ryan's ears reddened, embarrassed at being caught dissembling. "She tells me some really private things. I have to respect that."

"I understand. I don't like it, but I understand."

Trying to change the subject, Ryan said, "Hey, Jordan hasn't had a nightmare since she's been seeing Mia. Cool, huh?"

"That's very cool. I really think they're good for each other, don't you?"

"I do. Hearing about Mia from Jordan's perspective gives me a whole new frame of reference on her," Ryan mused. "It sounds like Jordan would be lucky to land her."

"True. She just has to allow herself to be vulnerable enough to be caught."

❧

Every member of the O'Flaherty family was at home when they arrived, and the group made over Ryan effusively the moment they entered the house. Jamie stood back a little remembering what she'd thought when Ryan first told her that her family didn't exchange gifts on birthdays. *I actually felt a little sorry for her,* she smirked internally. *Boy, was that wrong! Having a group like this show you how much they love you is worth so much more than any gift.*

"Have you had lunch yet?" Martin asked as he went into the kitchen.

"Not really, Da. I just ate some fruit that Jamie sent with me."

"I'll make something for you both. Name your pleasure, Siobhán. All of your wishes will come true on your birthday."

"Hmm…" She pondered her options for a few minutes, finally deciding, "How about a club sandwich. Can you manage that?"

"I can as soon as one of your brothers goes to the market for some turkey."

"I'll go," Rory said, heading for the door. "Anything else?"

"Root beer?" Ryan asked.

"Done," the youngest brother said as he grabbed Duffy's leash taking the excited pup with him.

"Is this a family tradition?" Jamie asked, grabbing a kitchen stool as Martin started to cook some bacon.

"Yes, each child got to do whatever they wanted on their birthdays. Siobhán always asked for the same thing," he said smiling at his daughter.

"What was that?"

"She always asked me to arrange to have the day off, and she would take the day off school if her birthday fell on a weekday. She never cared what we actually did—she just wanted to spend the day together." He was giving his daughter such a fond look that she blushed again, looking very adolescent.

"That is so sweet," Jamie said, getting off her stool to give her partner a lingering hug.

"I loved being with the whole family, of course, but I rarely had Da all to myself. I looked forward to my birthday for months," Ryan recalled. "Kids at school would always ask me what I got— they didn't understand why I was so excited to tell them about going to the zoo or something simple like that."

"Silly kids," Jamie murmured, still holding her partner in her arms.

"Having a nice day so far?" Jamie asked when they were back in their room.

"Unh-huh." Ryan smiled, jumping onto her bed and folding her hands behind her head—all in one smooth move. "Very nice day so far. Of course, just being with you improves every day."

"I need to go upstairs and tend to a little something. Can you entertain yourself for a little while?"

"Sure. I think I remember how to do that. Hurry back."

As soon as Jamie left the room, Ryan set about trying to find alternative costumes for them to wear that night. Jamie was only gone about fifteen minutes, but in that time a delightful transformation had taken place in their room. Gone was the lanky, twenty-four-year-old jock, dressed in her volleyball warm-ups. Instead, a stunningly sexy schoolgirl sat on the bed, blinking up at Jamie with all of the innocence she could muster. "Hi there," she whispered, her lusciously sexy voice at odds with the faux innocent smile.

"Oh my God!" Jamie had to grab for the desk chair to prevent herself from falling to the ground at the sight. "Where…where did you get that…outfit?"

"It's my uniform from high school," she said, still blinking up at Jamie innocently. "Do you like it?"

"Ryan O'Flaherty, you most certainly did not leave this house in that uniform!"

"I most certainly did," Ryan insisted. "Every day, as a matter of fact." She stood and smoothed the pleats of her skirt, doing a twirl just to show off. "Of course, it fits a little differently than it did then."

"Come over here, you sexy thing," Jamie commanded, a lascivious grin on her face. "I'd walk over to you, but my knees are still weak."

For the first time that Jamie could remember, Ryan actually flounced over to her, swinging her hips in a scintillatingly sexy fashion. "Yes?"

Smacking her dry lips together, Jamie started at the top of the dark head, taking her in, first up were the adorable twin ponytails that bounced along as she walked. Ryan had applied blush to her cheeks, enhancing her schoolgirl image, but the innocent image took a beating when Jamie's eyes slid lower and landed upon the voluptuous breasts straining to free themselves from the several sizes too tight short-sleeved white blouse. The lacy white bra that peeked out from the straining buttons didn't help with the innocence illusion, but she was the last one in the complaint line.

The blouse was so small that it was only half tucked in, revealing smooth tanned skin where it failed to meet its goal. The skirt, which Jamie still had a hard time believing her partner had worn, was a bright red and navy blue plaid, one-inch knife pleats surrounding her entire body. The skirt was short, to say the least, and Jamie was fascinated by the discrepancy of lengths, the rear appearing at least two inches shorter than the front. It didn't take a brain surgeon to figure out the cause of the problem, Ryan's very toned butt took up more than its allotted portion of the fabric. Ryan twirled again, this time revealing just a hint of white lace panty.

"Honey," Jamie gasped, "it's your birthday, not mine."

"True," she murmured pushing her partner onto a chair and straddling her lap. "You wanna party with me?" She had a large piece of bubble gum in her mouth, and as she asked the question she blew a huge bubble that took every bit of Jamie's self-control not to pop.

Jamie's head was bobbing like a puppet's, and Ryan giggled at her enthusiasm. She climbed off and walked a few feet, then looked down at the carpet. "Oops. Dropped something." The method she used to retrieve the imaginary object was not approved by the American College of Orthopedic Surgeons. Her feet were close together, and Jamie took a moment to appreciate the navy blue knee socks and cordovan penny loafers. With nary a flex to her knee, she bent from the waist, folding her long body in half to reach the rug, the short skirt climbing…climbing…climbing… until it revealed a scandalously erotic white lace thong.

Her teasing had pushed Jamie to the brink, and before she could straighten up she was tackled from behind, laughing wildly as Jamie threw her to the bed. They wrestled roughly for a few minutes, this kind of play completely foreign to Jamie, but something she found she enjoyed immensely. Ryan was so much stronger and so much bigger that it was clear she wasn't putting her all into the game, making the contest more equal.

Rolling onto her back, Jamie started to undress, her hands flying to her shirt to unbutton hurriedly. "No, let me," Ryan urged, gently pushing the hands away, "I absolutely love to undress you."

With a deep, contented sigh, Jamie tried to relax, placing her hands alongside her head. "I love it too. Although it drives me absolutely crazy." She gave her lover a smile, knowing that Ryan would take at least six times longer to complete the task than she would have.

"Patience is a virtue," Ryan reminded her gently, bending to nibble on her neck and ears. "We learned all about virtue in school, you know."

"I just bet you did," Jamie gasped as Ryan took a playful nip on her neck. "What else did you learn in school?"

"Mmm." Ryan's whole face was burrowing into Jamie's neck, as she took a series of deep breaths trying to fill herself with her lover's scent. "My best subject is anatomy," she whispered. "Will you help me do my homework? I have to identify all of the parts of the body…with my tongue."

"What was the name of your school again? Sacred Heart Academy for Wayward Girls?"

"That's the one," Ryan agreed. "I'm trying to win the Most Wayward Girl award for the year. Wanna help me practice?"

"If you'll get those little fingers busy and get my clothes off of me I'll do anything you want. We're awfully overdressed."

"You have a lot of buttons here," Ryan whispered as she bent her head over Jamie's chest and surveyed the mint green oxford-cloth shirt. "I'd better get started." To Jamie's combined dismay and pleasure, Ryan bent further still and started to work at the first button with her mouth, her tongue expertly pushing the button through the hole. She was making adorable noises as she worked—soft sounds that were not quite moans escaped her lips. Jamie laced her fingers through the ponytails and held on, content to feel the powerful body poised over her and observe the lovely features as Ryan concentrated upon her task.

By the time Ryan had reached the belt, Jamie was pulling her head down forcefully, moaning softly as Ryan's hands roamed all over her body. Tugging at the shirt with her teeth, Ryan resembled a frisky puppy with a chew toy, her sexy grin revealing itself amid the bunched up green fabric. When she had the shirt open she prudently decided to use her hands to unbuckle the belt, then went right back to her tongue and teeth to pop open the five metal buttons from Jamie's new jeans. Ryan had to cheat and use her hands to make the fabric taut, but Jamie was loath to complain. Her partner got so much pleasure out of undressing her that she always felt her own arousal increase as she watched.

When all of Jamie's clothing was spread open to Ryan's gaze she started to lick and suck all of the bare skin she could reach. It was so much easier to just remove all the clothing, but so much more arousing to feel like every kiss was the result of a hard-won gain. She kissed lower and lower on Jamie's belly, finally reaching her low-cut panties. Grasping the waistband with her teeth she gave the smooth material a few firm tugs, her bright blue eyes dancing impishly.

"I've never had anyone give me a wedgie while making love," Jamie teased, fondly brushing her hand through Ryan's bangs.

"See all of the new and exciting adventures I can give you?" Ryan grinned, lightly resting her chin on her partner's pubic bone.

"I do." Jamie rolled over and shed her blouse in the process. "Sorry to infringe on your turf, but some of my more assertive parts are signaling me that they're ready for some action."

"Anatomy class quiz time, huh? Would that be the labia majora? Or maybe the minora?" Ryan twisted on the bed so that her face was peeking into the open fly of Jamie's jeans. "That pesky clitoris isn't whining again, is she?"

"Yes, yes and yes." Jamie thrust her hips into Ryan's face a few times. "They're all very needy."

"Mmm, I can see that," Ryan murmured, staring at her partner's cleavage and painting a path of warm, wet kisses up her chest. "But the party just started. We've got all afternoon. I hate to rush."

"A little rushing can be a good thing." Jamie slid her hands up her chest to unhook her bra. She shook her shoulders slightly, letting the soft mounds bounce lightly. "Why don't you rush over here and kiss me," she growled, her hands hefting her breasts tauntingly, leaving nary a doubt that she wasn't referring to her lips.

"Ooh, rushing can be nice." Ryan climbed up her partner like a hungry panther, dropping her head onto a pert breast. They both let out faint gasps, each slightly stunned by the magnitude of the sensation. They'd tasted and touched each other dozens of times during their months together, but Ryan found that each time felt brand new when it was proceeded by a long bout of teasing foreplay. Something about the delayed gratification made her nearly crazy to touch Jamie, and seeing the longing and pent up desire on her partner's face increased her need dramatically.

"Oh God, this feels fabulous," Jamie moaned, her hands stroking Ryan's face. Ryan groaned in response, her exclamations limited to an occasional slurping sound as she devoured the sweet flesh with boundless enthusiasm.

Jamie's head lolled from side to side, the sensations building so quickly she felt like she couldn't keep up. The insistent throbbing between her legs was growing by the second, and she knew that she was already on the edge. Her hands slid to her hips, her thumbs into the waistband of her panties and she tossed her legs into the air, shimmying jeans and underwear down to her ankles.

Ryan's head whipped up in surprise as Jamie lowered her legs, trapping her in the tangle of denim. "You're mine now," she growled, settling her feet onto Ryan's back.

"I'm yours always." With a gentle smile that conveyed her love, Ryan dipped her head and started to explore.

After just a few moments, Jamie grasped her shoulders and squeezed. "Wait, baby. Wait…" Ryan lifted her head and made eye contact. "Wow," Jamie said, smiling. "I was almost gone and you've barely started."

"I've got all day. Besides, I love the neighborhood." She turned her head and rested her cheek low on Jamie's belly. "I'll just hang out 'til you're ready."

"You are so silly." She sighed deeply and fluffed her partner's bangs. "I love playing with you in bed. It's so nice to relax and do whatever feels good at the moment."

"Mmm-hmm." Ryan kissed Jamie's smooth belly. "This feels good right now."

"Can I have a little more? I don't think I can take much, but I love this high I'm on."

Ryan smiled up at her. "I meant what I said. This is pure pleasure for me. The best birthday present I could have." She shifted down until she was comfortable and resumed her gentle nuzzling, quickly getting back into the rhythm of their lovemaking.

They moved against each other, Jamie's hips twitching gently. "Whoa!" she cried abruptly, grasping Ryan's shoulders again. "Whew. Just in time. Just in time," she gasped as she fell back against the bed. Ryan busied herself kissing and nibbling on the tender thighs so conveniently located. They lay there in perfect silence, with Jamie relishing the feelings flowing through her as Ryan continued to love her. "Okay," she finally said once she felt she had control, "let's give it one more try. This time we'll go all the way."

"As long as I don't miss dinner, you can't take too long."

Once more, Ryan snuggled close and delicately traced every part of her lover, her warm, wet tongue gliding over smooth skin made smoother still by her growing excitement. "Oh, Ryan, I love you," Jamie cried out, her hands gaining purchase on the white blouse where they flexed convulsively. She gasped repeatedly, her climax building and building while brilliant colors flashed in her eyes when she squeezed them tightly shut.

As the spasms died Jamie reached out for her partner, needing the full contact of her body. It took a little maneuvering, but Ryan freed herself from her restraints and climbed up the bed to wrap her still-trembling lover in her arms. "Happy birthday to me," she mumbled softly, drawing a weary chuckle from her depleted partner.

❧

"Hi, Mr. O'Flaherty…I mean Martin," Mia said as the head of the family opened the front door.

"Hello there, girls. Good to see you both. I haven't heard a word from Siobhán or Jamie since lunch. Would you like me to roust them?"

"Nah. We can go on down." Mia was scampering down the stairs even as she spoke. She knocked lightly, waiting politely until she heard a mumbled, "Yeah?"

When she opened the door a much more awake voice cried,

"Whoa! Give us a second!"

Mia poked her head all the way in and said, "It's just us. No worries."

"Jesus!" Ryan flopped onto her back. "I thought my father was gonna get a lot more information about our frequent naps than he wanted."

"Ooh, somebody got lucky on her birthday." Mia looked around the room, seeing all of the usual signs. Clothes were strewn everywhere, the blanket and sheet had been pulled from their moorings and now covered the women in a most irregular fashion. Mia picked up the tiny plaid skirt and held it up for Jordan to view. "Somebody got very lucky on her birthday," Mia corrected. "Way to go, Jamie."

"Nope," Jamie smiled, her tousled hair and pink cheeks giving her a very youthful appearance. "I'm the one who got the present. Ryan wore that little number for me." She was chuckling as she said this, and Ryan gave her a tickle for revealing her secrets.

"My, my, Boomer, this is a side of you I wouldn't have guessed. Do you have any other naughty outfits lying around here?" Jordan started inspecting the closets, allowing Ryan to wing her with one of her loafers.

"I was getting my Halloween costume ready. Not my fault that my partner succumbed to my charms once I had it on."

"Oh, like that wasn't your intent," Jamie giggled.

"Hey, you're the one who didn't want to wear the outfits we agreed on."

"I couldn't come up with anything," Mia said. "Can I wear your cast offs, James?"

"Why don't you wear Ryan's school uniform?" Jamie suggested. "She sure as hell isn't going out in public in it."

"Jealous streak?" Jordan asked.

"No, I'm being kind. There'll probably be twenty women there who've slept with her, and I don't want to hear them cry when they find out they'll never lay a hand on her again."

They rushed to get a shower while Jordan and Mia looked

through Ryan's closet, trying to come up with acceptable outfits. Still undecided at dinnertime, they all went upstairs to get the meal started. Maeve had just arrived, bringing a large platter of Ryan's favorite cookies as a treat. Jamie was in charge for a change, and Martin sat on a stool and watched her work in his kitchen for the first time. "I might just get used to this," he said, smiling at his betrothed.

"I have a feeling we're going to have to come to an agreement of some sorts on the kitchen, Mr. O'Flaherty," Maeve said. "I don't think I can bear to give up control of my kitchen completely."

"We'll figure it out. No problem is insurmountable."

Conor came in and said hello to everyone, pausing awkwardly when he got to Mia. He'd seen her since their brief affair, but they'd not been in such close quarters before. "How've you been, Conor?" she asked.

"Good. Nothing much going on. I think I'll go and clean up before dinner. I've been playing basketball all afternoon." He exited quickly and Ryan shared a discreet shrug with Mia.

For reasons that eluded her, Ryan was surprised when she sniffed the scent of lasagna baking away in the oven. Pulling Jamie into the dining room for a moment alone, she rested her forearms on her partner's shoulders, loosely linking her hands behind her neck. "I don't know why, but it didn't dawn on me that you'd make lasagna for me. Thank you, baby. I really appreciate it."

"That's our new birthday tradition. Hours and hours of lovemaking, then I'll fill your tummy with your favorite food."

"Could you have a better idea?" Ryan mused, not seriously thinking it was possible to outdo this one.

Ryan put herself in charge of fixing Jordan up with a costume, and Jamie agreed to help Mia get into the schoolgirl outfit. Mia and Jamie went upstairs, and Ryan and Jordan stayed downstairs where the wardrobe was. "Do you have any ideas?" Ryan asked.

"Yeah. I'd like to look as different from normal as I can. I wanna mix it up for a change."

Ryan regarded her friend for a moment. Jordan generally either looked like a high-end print model, which she was, or an athlete. She usually dressed a little more stylishly than her peers, and looked quite feminine, not having even a touch of androgyny in her makeup. "I can make you look like a pretty authentic construction worker or a tough leather woman," Ryan decided. "Any interest?"

Jordan swallowed. "Well, I guess I could, but if Mia's gonna wear that school uniform I won't look like I belong with her. I'd kinda like to have the same theme."

"Hmm," Ryan said, thinking about the challenge for a moment. "I think I can hook you up."

A little while later, Jordan emerged from the room, heading upstairs for a vote. Martin caught sight of her first, and he laughed heartily. "Maeve, look! Our little Siobhán is back!"

Maeve turned and they both laughed at the shyly grinning woman. Jordan wore a pair of Conor's carpenter's jeans, his size thirty-six-inch waist dwarfing her twenty-eight-incher. The waistband was rolled over several times to make them stay up on her slim form, but they still sagged dramatically. Conor's barn jacket likewise hung on her body—the sleeves rolled up so she could use her hands. One of Ryan's baseball caps sat on her head—backwards, as was the style of the owner. Under her arm she carried Ryan's skateboard, and Ryan's Bad-Badtz-Maru backpack was astride her shoulders. In total, she looked unbelievably goofy and so unlike herself it was shockingly funny.

"Do I pass?" she asked.

"Are you trying to look like a little hoodlum skateboarder?" Martin asked.

"That's the general idea."

"You pass with flying colors," Maeve smiled, sending Jordan in search of additional votes.

With a light knock, Jordan poked her head into Martin's room. "I'm ready, how about you?"

"Come on in," Jamie said. Jordan did and broke into a grin so broad it was comical.

"I didn't realize I had a thing for Catholic school girls until just this minute."

"That's exactly what I said, not six hours ago," Jamie echoed, "Who knew?"

Mia did look adorable, and Ryan was giving her such a frankly appraising look that Jamie came up and backhanded her in the gut. "Off limits."

Ryan actually blushed, much to Mia's pleasure. She said, a bit defensively, "I was just reminiscing. Thinking of how much more fun high school could have been if there had been girls like Mia running around."

"I would have given you a run for your money," Mia agreed.

"I called dibs on this one," Jordan insisted, snaking her long arms around her lover.

"You look absolutely adorable, Jordan," Mia said. "You look just like the kind of ruffian I would have been attracted to in eighth grade."

"How about now?"

Mia didn't answer verbally. She merely nodded her head and pulled Jordan close for a very friendly kiss.

"Well, our work here is done," Ryan said. "Now it's our turn, Spot."

"Spot?" Jordan asked, wondering what she had missed.

"You'll see," Jamie promised, taking Ryan's hand as they walked downstairs to dress.

It didn't take either of them long to prepare. Martin had bent the regulations of the San Francisco Fire Department by borrowing the gear of one of the members of his battalion who was on vacation. The young man was close to Ryan's size, and he gave his permission easily, knowing that Martin's daughter would treat his uniform with respect. It was a cool night, making Ryan glad that her costume would provide some much needed warmth. She wore a San Francisco Fire Department T-shirt, navy blue with a red Maltese Cross emblazoned across the front, large crossed axes bisecting the cross. A bright yellow slicker, with strips of reflective tape on the hem and the placket, matching pants with red suspenders to hold them up, and her own boots finished off her costume perfectly. In Jamie's opinion, her cutest accessory was her father's helmet, which fit her surprisingly well once he had made a small adjustment.

San Francisco firefighters still wore the old-style black leather helmets, with the long duckbill in the back to keep water from running down their necks, and Ryan looked like she was born to wear it. Jamie was so impressed with her look, she found herself wavering on her reticence to have Ryan join the department. "Wow…there would be a massive increase in pyromaniacs if you joined up," Jamie teased.

"And people would join up in droves if all of the mascots were as cute as you," Ryan insisted, tweaking Jamie's black nose. Jamie had ordered an adult sized full-body dalmatian outfit for herself, reasoning that if Ryan was a firefighter, she was going to be her faithful mascot. The white fleece suit with the big black spots really did look adorable on her, and her extra touch of using make-up to produce a black nose and whiskers just added to the look.

Jamie turned and wagged her tail at Ryan, earning herself a kiss. "You've got a little black on your cheek, love," she said.

"It'll look like soot," Ryan assured her, taking her hand to go back upstairs.

Jamie didn't have to take too much teasing, everyone agreeing that she and Ryan looked adorable together, and the group finally set off. Conor took pity on them and offered to give them a ride over the hill in his truck, to which they all gladly agreed. As they approached Castro, Conor shot Mia and look and asked, "Have you ever been over here for Halloween?"

"No. I don't think I've been over here for anything. Is it fun?"

"Well, you won't find many eligible men," he said, chuckling.

"That's not why we're here." She noticed that Jordan had tensed up beside her. "We're just going to party with our friends."

"Oh, you'll have fun," Conor assured her. "Even though you won't meet any eligible guys, I'd bet a few women wouldn't mind picking you up."

"Also not interested," she said, giving Jordan a surreptitious pat on the leg.

❧

They had a marvelous time together, just as Conor had predicted. Both Mia and Ryan attracted more than their share of looks, neither Jamie nor Jordan being up to their own usual babe-magnet status. Most of the evening was spent looking at the costumes that the other revelers wore, with the leather look being the choice of a full twenty-five percent of the crowd.

Through most of the night, Mia held Jordan's hand or grasped her upper arm when the crowd got too thick. Jamie noticed this and was pleased with her friend's comfort with the situation. She was about to mention this to Ryan when a voice from behind called out, "Mia? Is that you?"

Mia dropped Jordan's hand like it was a hot rock, turning to find her old friend from high school, Melissa, and her lover. "Yep, it's me," she said, her tone overly happy. "How are you?"

"I'm great," she said, wrapping Mia in a hug. "Mia, this is my lover, Andi. Andi, this is Mia Christopher. You remember Jamie Evans and her partner Ryan O'Flaherty, don't you?"

"Yeah. How are you both?" Andi asked, extending a hand for both women to shake.

"We're good," Jamie said, her eyes shifting to a very uncomfortable looking Jordan.

"So Mia, what are you doing here?" Melissa asked, glancing furtively at Jordan, who had yet to be introduced.

"Oh. Well, I've never been to Castro, and Halloween seemed like a good time to start," she said, not elaborating any further. "Jamie and Ryan are our tour guides."

Jordan was staring at the ground by this time, so Jamie jumped in. "Melissa, this is Jordan Ericsson, one of Ryan's teammates from the volleyball team."

"Hi, Jordan," Melissa said, echoed by Andi. "Have you been to Castro before? Or are you a novice, too?"

"I'm a novice. Just passing through."

"Well, it was great to see you all again," Melissa said, her eyes fixed on Mia. "You should call me sometime."

Jamie piped up and said, "You can call us too, Melissa. We're listed under my name."

"That's a deal," she said, giving Mia one final gaze as she and her lover departed.

Without a word, Jamie tugged on Ryan's sleeve, trying to give their friends some room. As soon as they were alone Jordan asked, "Old friend?"

"Yeah. She's the girl I slept with in high school. I told you about her."

"Yeah, yeah. I forgot her name. Kinda didn't think I'd ever have the pleasure."

"San Francisco is kind of a small town. Especially when you don't want it to be."

Jordan bent down and looked Mia in the eye. "Did it bother you to see her?"

"Yeah, it did a little. Thanks for asking," she said softly.

"Hey, I care about you," Jordan reminded her, tucking an arm around her waist. To her surprise Mia patted her hand and removed it, instead holding her hand for just a minute before dropping it.

They caught up with Jamie and Ryan but the mood had been ruined, and within a short while both Jordan and Mia were ready to go. It was late, after midnight, so they all agreed to walk back together.

Ryan and Jamie did their best to hold up their end of the conversation, but it didn't help much. The walk seemed longer than usual, probably because of the awkward silences. Just before they reached the house Ryan offered, "You guys are welcome to stay over if you're too tired to drive home."

"No, thanks," Mia said immediately. "We're fine."

They changed back into their clothes and took off just a few minutes later, promising to return the next day for Ryan's party. As Jamie watched them drive away, she said, "It's tough being in a relationship when you're trying to stay in the closet, isn't it?"

"I wouldn't recommend it. To anyone."

🐎

"I guess Jamie's prediction was wrong," Jordan said, trying for a light tone of voice.

"What about?" Mia asked absently, as she concentrated on getting them out of the often confusing streets of Noe Valley.

"She thought Ryan would run into a bunch of old lovers, and I don't think she did."

"Yeah. Must have been a slow night," Mia chuckled. "Apparently it happens frequently."

"Uhm…does it happen…frequently…to you?" Jordan was staring intently out of the passenger window, and when Mia shot a glance at her she could see some lines of stress around her mouth and eyes.

Mia sighed. They were still on 24th, and she pulled up to an empty meter and put the car in park. "What do you really want to know?" she asked quietly. "You know that I'll tell you anything, don't you?" She placed her hand on her friend's thigh, but Jordan didn't respond to her touch.

"Did you sleep with Conor?" Jordan asked, still not looking at her.

Mia blinked, not having expected the conversation to head in that direction. "Yes, I did. I went out with him twice, and I slept with him once."

Jordan head swiveled in her direction and tilted in question. "You didn't like him enough to go out more than twice, but you still slept with him?"

There was just a hint of censure in her tone, and Mia found her hackles rising. It was the first time she'd felt her temper starting to flare with Jordan, and she didn't have any idea how to put a damper on it. Sounding more angry than she was, she spit out, "I won't ever justify my sexual behavior to you or anyone else." She crossed her arms over her chest. "It's *truly* none of your business."

Jordan slumped down in her seat, her long body not having much room to move, but taking every inch she could manage. "I apologize. You're right. It's none of my business. I was just curious."

Mia wanted to say that it was Jordan's business to know about her, but she didn't think Jordan was receptive. "Can we talk about this later? I'm really beat."

"No need. That's all I wanted to know."

Sighing heavily, Mia put the car into drive and proceeded to the East Bay, finally turning her CD player on just to cut the silence in the car. She pulled up in front of the house, but to her surprise, Jordan gave her a light kiss on the cheek and announced that she was going home. "Jordan," she said, her frustration showing, "why didn't you say so? I don't want you walking home. It's after one."

Jordan shrugged while looking at the sidewalk. "I'm used to it. I'm faster than any of the criminals, anyway."

That didn't reassure Mia in the least, and she grasped the sleeve of Jordan's jacket and pulled her close. "I'm sorry if I hurt you tonight.

Please don't shut me out."

Jordan's head shook slowly. "I'm sorry I upset you. I've just gotta go now." After an awkward, one-armed hug she took off, running down the street with her easy, loose-limbed stride.

Chapter Five

When Ryan came into the dining room the next morning, there was a basketful of mail for her. "You didn't get your mail yesterday. It seems like many of your fans remembered you," Martin teased.

"Looks like one of my fans even sent a present." She picked up and hefted a square box. Her smile quickly faded as she looked at the postmark. "Do you have any buddies on the bomb squad, Da?"

He got up and looked over her shoulder, nodding somberly when he saw the address. "He does seem to be making an effort, sweetheart. He even sent it Federal Express so it got here on your birthday."

"Yeah. I know. I just don't trust him, and I hate to let my guard down."

"Reminds me of the old blessing. May those who love us—love us. And those that don't love us—may God turn their hearts. And if he doesn't turn their hearts, may he turn their ankles, so we'll know them by their limping." Laughing softly he met his daughter's eyes and said, "I think you're wise to keep an eye out for his limp, darlin'." He walked into the kitchen to begin breakfast for the young women, leaving Ryan alone to open her present.

She was mildly pleased that Jim hadn't used the franking privileges of his office to send the package for free. After inspecting the package from every angle, she set it aside and opened all of the other mail. She was working on the last card, one from Ally, when Jamie came into the dining room. "Ooh, somebody's a popular little birthday girl."

"Yep. It's nice to have my friends remember me." She tossed Jamie the package from Jim and said, "I have a feeling that you were instrumental in this one."

Jamie kissed her on the top of the head. "I merely mentioned that your birthday was coming up. He asked for our address and said he wanted to send something. That was my only contribution. He didn't even ask for ideas of what to buy, so God knows what's in there."

Ryan took the package back and shook it a few more times, finally admitting, "I don't have a clue. I'm usually pretty good at guessing, but I don't have enough to go on this time."

She looked mildly depressed and Jamie reminded her, "You could open it."

"But I like to guess. That's half the fun."

"Want me to open it, and then you can ask for clues?"

"Nah. That's cheating. I'll just open it myself." Her mood brightened appreciably when she opened the present. She hadn't even known that devices like this existed, but Jim had bought her a very tiny portable DVD player. "This is so cool!" she said, bringing Martin from the kitchen.

"What is that little thing?"

Jamie explained the purpose while Ryan opened the card.

Dear Ryan,

I know you are forced to travel a lot, and I thought this might help you pass the time—when you're not thinking, of course. You can use the gift certificate to purchase some of your favorite movies. I hope you enjoy the gift, and have a wonderful birthday.

Best wishes, Jim.

Ryan looked at her partner and said, "This was really thoughtful. He tried to find something that fit me—rather than just throwing some money at me. I really appreciate this—even though I'm sure it was ridiculously expensive. He's really trying, isn't he?"

"I think so, honey. I really think so."

When they returned home from Mass, Ryan decided that she wanted to call Jim to thank him for the gift, even though she always sent written thank you notes. She tried his apartment first, but there was no answer, so Jamie suggested she try his private line at his office. He answered immediately, and Ryan identified herself.

"Well, hello, Ryan. How did the birthday go?"

"Very well, thank you. I wanted to thank you for the fabulous gift, Jim. It was too generous, but I really do love it."

"Don't forget to buy some movies for yourself."

"Oh, I don't have to. I can use that gift certificate to rent for a whole year." Her glee at having figured out a way to make the gift last was obvious.

"You're something else," he said, his voice containing a note of fondness that she had never heard from him before.

"That's what they've been telling me for twenty-four years now. While I have you on the phone, I do have a favor to ask."

"What's that?"

"I'd like your permission to get the address and phone number for Tory Knight from the private detective that you had investigate me."

"Pardon?"

"The married woman that I had the affair with," she reminded him. "I want to contact her to apologize for any part I played in destroying her marriage. I don't know how to get in contact with her, and I assume that the detective wouldn't reveal that information without your permission. So I'm asking for your permission."

"Does Jamie know you want to do this?"

"She does now," Ryan said, since her lover was astride her lap. "Do you mind, honey?"

Jamie took the phone from her and said, "Hi, Daddy. I didn't know Ryan wanted to contact that woman, but I'm glad that she wants to."

"Okay, I'll have the investigator call Ryan with the information." He paused for a moment and said, "She's a tough one to figure out."

"No she's not. She's the easiest person to figure out that I've ever known. She always tries to be kind—no matter the consequences. Just remember that, and she's a breeze."

The party was scheduled to begin at two, and the first of the relatives wandered over at twelve-thirty. Shortly thereafter, Jordan called. "Hey," she said, "how do I get to your house on public transpo?"

"Why do you need to? Isn't Mia coming?"

"I'm sure she is. We didn't sleep together last night, and I haven't heard from her yet, so it's looking like she's going without me."

"Did you guys have a fight?"

"I guess. I'm not really sure, though. We didn't yell at each other or anything, but I asked her a question that seemed to piss her off and we stopped talking."

"I'm happy to give you directions, but I'm equally happy to come get you. It's kind of a hassle to get here from Berkeley. You've gotta take BART and switch to MUNI and then take a bus if you don't want to go up some hellacious hills. It could take you over an hour."

Jordan sighed and said, "I don't want you to go that far out of your way." She paused and said, "Hang on a sec, will ya?"

"Sure."

Jordan came back a minute later and said, "Mia just got here. We'll be over in a bit. Thanks."

"Hope it goes well, pal. My motto is to apologize—even if you don't know why you're doing it."

Catherine had learned her lesson, and she arrived just after one, no longer content to be the last to join the party. This time she brought a guest, and Jamie ran to the door to greet her grandfather with a warm hug before he was halfway through the door. Catherine carried a lavish bouquet of flowers, with Casablanca lilies, anthuriums, ginger, and birds of paradise artfully arranged in a basket. A bottle of wine peeked out of the basket, and Ryan pulled it out to find that it was a rich, dark Pommard, bottled in the year of her birth. "This is beautiful, Catherine," she smiled. "Just perfect. And these are some of my favorite flowers."

"They suit you. Charles and I were just discussing that on the way over. Most of these come from the wilder, tropical climates, and those types of flowers remind me of you."

"I truly do appreciate your thoughtfulness," Ryan said, giving her a generous hug and a kiss on each cheek, as was Catherine's habit. "And I'm really glad that you could join us too, Charlie."

"The pleasure is all mine, Ryan."

"Daddy sent Ryan a present, Mom," Jamie informed her. "He seemed to put some thought into it, too."

"Oh, he's actually quite good at that. With all of his international business experience, he's had to learn how to buy gifts."

Ryan brought her DVD player over to show Catherine and Charlie, and they marveled over the technology for a few minutes. Caitlin became aware that her best friend had entered unnoticed, and she made up for that by making her way across the crowded room, her path supported by quick grabs to assorted pant legs as she walked.

Ryan noticed that Catherine wore neither earrings nor a necklace, and she had to offer a teasing comment as Catherine stooped to pick up her delighted little friend. "You seem to be accessorizing a little less these days. Any particular reason?"

"Oh, just the fact that I've nearly been strangled by this strong little grip. It took me long enough, but it dawned on me as I was walking up the stairs. I've got my jewelry in my pocket," she said, smiling as she patted her slacks.

Jordan and Mia arrived right on time, and after they spent a few minutes greeting everyone they signaled Ryan that they wanted to see her in her room. Ryan grabbed Jamie and they all went down together. Mia said, "Jamie said that your family doesn't do gifts, but we both wanted to get you something, so we thought we'd give them to you down here. Is that cool?"

"Of course it is," Ryan said delightedly. "I'm certainly not antagonistic to gifts. We just stopped doing it because there were so many of us. It wasn't for moral reasons or anything. We just didn't have enough money."

"Cool," Mia said. She handed Ryan a neatly wrapped package and said, "I don't think you have one of these, and I love mine, so I thought you might like one, too."

"Thanks," Ryan said, ripping the package open enthusiastically. "Ooh, a portable MP3 player! Thanks, I really have wanted one of these." She kissed her roommate and gave her a hug, then released her and spent a moment looking at her new toy carefully. Mia explained how it worked and offered to put some of Ryan's music on it when they got home.

The box Jordan handed her was quite a bit bigger, but Ryan ripped through it in record time. Inside was a hard-shell backpack in a bright blue. "I love the backpack you normally carry," Jordan said. "But I hate to see you put your laptop in it when we travel. This should keep your little baby safe."

"This is great!" Ryan exclaimed. She fussed with the straps with Jordan's help, and got it adjusted properly, really liking the way it conformed to her back. "I love this, Jordan. It's really perfect." Smiling at her friends she admitted, "I got such great gifts this year."

"What did Jamie get you?" Jordan asked.

Jamie rolled her eyes and said, "We've been playing the 'guess the gift' game since we got home last night. She refuses to open it until she can guess."

"Has she gotten close?" Mia asked.

"Not in the least. We're still on the 'is it bigger than a bread box' part of the game. At this rate she won't open it until her twenty-fifth birthday."

"I told you that I like to guess as much as I like the present," Ryan reminded her. "When I was little, we each got two presents for Christmas. I found that if I spent a long time guessing what they were, it seemed to last longer."

"Oh, you're all about making things last long," Jamie teased, recalling their extended love play from the day before.

They were barbecuing, as usual, and Ryan volunteered to watch one of the grills, taking Jordan with her. "So, how did things go on the way over?"

Jordan gave her friend a swat to the seat. "Thanks for the advice. I apologized, and she just looked at me and said, 'For what? Exactly.'"

"Oh-oh. There's always the risk of that. Sorry I didn't give you the whole scenario."

"Oh, that's okay. I pulled it out pretty well. I told her that I was sorry we were so distant from each other, and that I was sorry if I hurt her."

Ryan smiled and draped an arm around her friend's shoulders. "Excellent recovery! Great save."

Jordan nodded and said, "Things seem a little better, but it's still tense. I don't even know why I'm mad, and I really don't know why she's mad."

"How did it start?"

"Like I told you—I asked her a question."

"Yeah, well, there are questions and there are questions."

"Okay, it was a bad question. I asked her if she'd slept with your brother."

"Oh-oh…"

"Yeah," Jordan nodded. "That wasn't so bad, but when I said that I was surprised she slept with him after just two dates…"

"Yipes! You didn't!"

"Oh, yes I did. I know that was a stupid thing to say, but it really surprised me, and I let that show. That just doesn't seem like Mia."

It sounded just like Mia to Ryan, but she thought it wise not to say so. "I know this is easier said than done, but it's never a good idea to comment on someone else's sexual past. It buys you nothing."

"I'm learning that," she smiled wryly. "I'll put that in the 'things that would have been helpful to know yesterday' category."

"Why did you bring it up? Does it bother you that she had a thing with Conor?"

"No, not really. I know she's been with a good number of people, and that's fine. I think I was just pissed off in general, and I was picking on her."

"Why were you pissed off?"

"It was that Melissa woman," she admitted. "I knew all about her, but it pissed me off that Mia acted like she didn't even know me. She didn't bother to introduce me," she grumbled, looking very wounded.

"I can imagine that hurt. But that's how you set this up, isn't it? I thought you wanted to be totally discreet, and if I recall, you were more insistent on that than Mia was."

"I know, I know," she groused, kicking at the grass with the toe of her shoe. "I just felt like crap when it happened. I felt like she was ashamed of me."

"I can understand that. But isn't it possible that Mia was respecting your boundaries? It's kinda tough to be angry with her for following through on your agreement."

Jordan tucked her hands into her armpits and rocked to and fro for a few seconds. "This is exactly what I was afraid of. I told you I'm not the kind of person who likes to be inauthentic. I don't want to hide how I feel about Mia. It feels awful to do that."

Ryan waited a beat, considering the intense sadness on her friend's face, then gently asked, "How do you feel about her?"

The light blue eyes drifted up and Ryan could clearly see the hesitation reflected in their depths. "I like her. A lot." She looked back down at the ground and added, "I don't want her to tell the world we sleep together, but I also don't want her to act like I don't exist. She would have introduced me if we were just friends. Why should I get less respect than someone she takes a class with?"

"That seems fair," Ryan agreed. "Why don't you tell her that your feelings were hurt? You've both got to practice with this, and the only way you'll both get better is with some feedback. She probably thinks you're mad that she slept with Conor, when that doesn't seem like what's bothering you at all."

"Okay, I will. That's one of the things I like best about her, to tell you the truth. We talk about everything—really honestly. We have to do that now, too."

Ryan nodded somberly. "Now more than ever."

When Jamie saw Ryan leading Jordan off, she did the same with Mia, taking her back down to Ryan's bedroom. "You guys don't seem like yourselves today. Is everything all right?"

"No," Mia sighed, as she flopped down on the bed. "Everything's kinda sucky as a matter of fact."

"What's up? Do you feel like talking about it?"

"I'm not sure, James," Mia reflected. "We had a little fight last night, and Jordan went home. I was awake most of the night—just trying to figure out what was wrong. I guess seeing Melissa kinda threw me."

"How so?" Jamie asked. "You don't still have a thing for her…"

"No, nothing like that. It just made me feel funny, James, like an outsider, I guess."

"Huh? You lost me."

Mia rolled over onto her side and faced her friend. "I'm finally taking a look at myself, and I'm…confused. I mean, I don't feel like I'm a lesbian That's just not me. But I'm clearly not straight. I couldn't feel like I do about Jordan if I was. Seeing Melissa last night made me think about how it was with her." She turned and lay on her back, then crossed her legs. It took her another minute, but she finally said, "I really cared for her, but I wouldn't let myself. I held back."

"Yeah, I can see that. So what do you feel like?"

"That's where I'm stumped," she admitted. "If I tell people I sleep with Jordan, they assume I'm a lesbian, but I'm not. If I tell them that I slept with Conor, they assume I'm straight, but I'm not. It was easier before when I just felt like an open-minded kinda girl, but that's not really true, either. I'm not just experimenting with Jordan. And it's not just sex," she added somberly, not surprising Jamie in the least.

Jamie sat down next to her and Mia immediately turned onto her side. Jamie ran a hand up and down her back, asking in a soothing tone, "Does she know how you feel?"

"I don't know how she couldn't," she scoffed. "Sometimes it's almost a religious experience when we make love—that doesn't happen with casual sex partners."

"I'd think not," Jamie agreed. "Are you going to tell her that you love her?"

"Don't go off the deep end," Mia warned. "I didn't say that. I said I care for her. That's different."

"Oh, right. That's different." It would have been nearly impossible to ignore the teasing tone, but Mia seemed to.

"I don't know what I'm going to do. She's like a wounded animal some times, James. It's obvious that there are times when she wants to run and hide, but she generally hangs in there and works things out with me. I don't want to scare her by being too needy, you know?"

"Caring for someone doesn't make you needy. I think it's just the opposite. It makes you stronger."

Mia shook her head and said, "I don't know. Maybe that's true, but I don't think we're at a point to have those discussions yet. Things are going along fine, and I don't see any reason to screw it up. I think I'll just apologize for being in a bad mood last night and try to get close to her again. It was only one night, but I missed her," she admitted, a wistful look on her face. "I've really grown used to having her sleep next to me—it was odd to be alone."

"I know the feeling," Jamie sympathized, dreading the next away game, which was coming up in just a few days.

⁂

"Is it bigger than the dining room table?" Ryan asked, sneaking up behind her partner and whispering the question in her ear.

"No, Ryan, it's not bigger than the dining room table."

"Is it bigger than Jordan?" Ryan followed up, chuckling a little.

"It's not comparable to a human. Try again."

"But it was comparable to the dining room table, eh?"

"Only in some ways," Jamie decided. "You're still way off."

"I'll get there, just you wait," she warned, narrowing her deep blue eyes dangerously.

⁂

By the time all of the guests had been fed, all of the cake had been eaten, and Caitlin was asleep in Jamie's arms, Ryan had ascertained that her gift was not clothing, not books, not related to a sport, and was bigger than Martin's easy chair, but smaller than the refrigerator, when laid on its side. It wasn't much, but Ryan was still brimming with confidence that she would figure it out.

Rory came up and asked, "Any chance I can move your present out of my room tonight? I almost killed myself when I got up in the middle of the night."

Ryan whirled and faced her partner. "It's in Rory's room? Why would you choose Rory's room, hmm? Maybe Rory helped you with it!" She said this like she had just deciphered the Rosetta Stone, and Jamie just laughed and rolled her eyes.

"Okay, let's say he did. How does that help?"

"Oh, for the love of Mike," Rory said. "Is she still trying to guess what it is?"

"I'm getting close," Ryan insisted, waving her brother off.

"No, she's not," Jamie smiled, shaking her head.

"Well, it's gonna be out in the hall when I go to bed, so you'll know one way or the other." He walked off, chuckling to himself.

"Big question," Ryan said seriously. "Did Rory help you decide what to buy?"

"Yes."

"You didn't ask Conor, or Brendan, or Da?"

"Nope. Just Rory," she smiled, knowing that Ryan was getting close.

Ryan nodded slyly, a wide smile settling on her face. "I've got it! And if I'm right, you'd better give Caitlin to your mom, 'cause she's gonna wake up screaming from the noise."

When Rory saw his sister taking the stairs two at a time, he followed her up, coming up alongside Jamie, who was lagging behind. "Did she guess?"

"I think so, but she might still be a little surprised."

Indeed, Ryan was surprised. She stood in the doorway, looking at the impressive set-up, a puzzled expression on her face. "Electronic drums?" she asked. "Electronic?"

"Trust me, Sis," Rory said. "These babies have come a long way." He took a pair of sticks off his dresser and handed them to her. Leading her over to the stool he urged her down, then handed her a pair of headphones. He flicked a few switches on the module that was located right at eye level and said, "Give 'em a rip."

She looked a doubtful, but started to play, a thoughtful look on her face that quickly turned into a smile. The smile grew as she experienced each element of the set, until she was beaming an iridescent smile at her partner. Removing the headphones so she could hear, she said, "These are absolutely phenomenal! I love them!" Turning to Rory she said, "I had no idea electronic could come this close to acoustic."

"Yeah, they've done a great job with these. Most good drummers have acoustic and electronic now, just because these are so much more versatile. I think you'll really love 'em."

"I love them already," she smiled, "but you really shouldn't have been so generous. These must have cost a ton."

"Yes, they were expensive," Jamie admitted, "but these fall in the 'as much for me as for you' category."

Ryan knew just what that meant, but Rory did not. "Do you play the drums, Jamie?"

Ryan gave her lover an impish smile and replied for her. "Nope. She plays the drummer."

On their way home, Mia looked over at Jordan and asked, "My place or yours?"

"Mine," Jordan said, surprising and displeasing Mia. She started to look at her, but Jordan touched her leg lightly. "You've never even seen my apartment. I think it's time."

"Does the tour include the bedroom?" she asked with a suddenly sunny smile.

"That's where the tour starts. I missed you last night." She shot Mia an adorably shy smile, making Mia's heart clench with emotion.

"I missed you, too, sweetheart." The term of endearment escaped before she could pull it back in.

Another shy grin accompanied Jordan's soft response, "No one has ever called me sweetheart before."

"Their loss." Mia smiled, reaching over to grab her lover's hand and press it against her breast.

Catherine and Charlie were among the last to leave, after having helped clean up and put everything away. After a fond goodbye from Jamie and Ryan, they got into Catherine's car for the trip to Nob Hill. "I didn't want to bring this up during the party, but I am interested in how things are going for you, Catherine. How have you been?"

She smiled at her father-in-law and said, "I don't think I could get through this time without Jamie and Ryan, but with their support I'm actually faring pretty well. I'm not sure what will happen between Jim and me, but I feel more confident that I can handle whatever comes."

"Do you want to end the marriage?" he asked gently.

"No. No, I don't. We have a lot of problems, but I would prefer to work them through together and try to save our relationship." She gave Charles a look and said, "My therapist said something not long ago that I've been thinking about a lot. She said that you choose your mate for both healthy and unhealthy reasons, and that leaving them when things get tough doesn't necessarily insure that you won't have the same issue pop up again with the next partner you choose. If I'm going to have to really investigate the issues that led me to Jim, and that kept me with him through his betrayals, I'd like to have him there while I do it." She spared a look at her father-in-law and asked, "Does that make any sense?"

"Yes, I think it does. I know that you make a good point about repeating your mistakes. That's something we humans seem programmed to do."

"I suppose what I mean is that I love Jim deeply, and I don't want to lose him. Yes, he has flaws, but so do I. Even though he has betrayed my trust on many occasions, in other areas I trust him completely. I trust him to work on our problems with me—if he'll agree."

"What do you think the likelihood of that is?" he asked, not seeing much evidence of his son's willingness to do so.

"It's hard to tell. He calls me every few days—usually without much reason. He seems lonely in a way I've never seen. It's hard to put a finger on, but I occasionally see glimpses of the young man I fell in love with, and that gives me hope."

"I can understand that," Charles agreed. "I certainly hope he comes through for you, Catherine. You're the best thing that ever happened to him—if he can only wake up and see it."

A few minutes after their last guest departed, Jamie climbed into bed. She curled up next to Ryan's side and placed her hand on her belly. She was so tired that she drifted off in seconds. A subtle rocking woke her just minutes after she'd fallen asleep. Perplexed, she sat up and looked at Ryan who was clearly wide awake. "What are you doing?"

"Oops. Sorry. I didn't think you'd feel that."

"What are you doing?" she asked again.

Ryan cleared her throat and admitted the truth. "Playing my drums."

"Lord, you are an adorable woman," Jamie sighed as she snuggled next to her again. "How are you playing your drums? You don't have your sticks in here do you?"

"No. I'm playing my thighs. I understand why you did it, but having my new toy upstairs is pretty cruel. They're so close I can taste 'em, but I can't reach 'em."

"Even though they don't make much noise, I'm not about to hear that slapping sound all night long. And that's just what you'd be doing, so don't even try to convince me otherwise."

"Point taken. I really, really like 'em," she whispered. "I never had my own set."

Jamie sat up on her elbow and peered at Ryan in the dim light. "Never? I thought you played in school."

"I did. The school owned a set and I stayed there to practice. I always dreamed of someday having my own kit," she said wistfully. "I should have realized that you'd be the one to make my dream come true."

"Rory helped. He was certain you'd love them."

"He knows me well. You know I never would have bought them for myself," she said softly. "They just seem like such a luxury."

"My goal is to one day have you not think of luxury as a dirty word."

"My goal is to have you holding my hand on my 100th birthday, wishing our guests would leave so that we can make love."

"Our guests are gone now." She put her lips on Ryan's neck and nibbled delicately. "As long as we're up you can put those twitchy hands to use."

"I'd rather play you than a drum any day," Ryan agreed, folding her partner into her warm, welcoming embrace.

Chapter Six

When Ryan came home from practice on Monday, she picked up the mail on the way into the kitchen. "Hi," she said, greeting Jamie absently as she examined the package addressed to her.

"Hey, how about showing me as much interest as you show a box?"

"Sorry." Ryan scampered over to kiss every exposed inch of her lover's neck. "Better?" she whispered catching a tender earlobe in her teeth. A sexy hip grind was her only answer, but it was fairly definitive.

"What do you think this is?" Ryan asked as she went back to her package.

"What does it say?"

"It's from J. Giovacchini in Palo Alto." She shook the box experimentally.

"I hate to belabor the obvious, but you could just open it."

"Where's the fun in that?" She sat down at the kitchen table and hefted the box in her hand for a moment. "It's not very heavy, but something moves when I shake it."

"Maybe you broke it," Jamie supplied helpfully.

Ryan shot her a chiding look. "Not that kind of movement. There's no sound, but there's definite movement. Like it's muffled."

"Well, it is in a box."

"Nope. More muffled than that. It's in another container within the box." She shook it gently and then more forcefully. "Do you know what this is?"

"Uhm, no."

"But you do know something."

"Well, I should hope so. I'm due to graduate soon from a prestigious university."

"You're evading the question," Ryan said as she tossed the box from hand to hand. "Since it's from Palo Alto and since you obviously know something, it must be from your mother."

"Do you want confirmation or are you in this alone?"

"Confirmation, please."

"Okay. You're dead on correct so far."

"Great. Now since it's from your mother and since my birthday was Saturday, I can only assume that it's a present."

"Also correct."

"And I assume that this Giovacchini person was the person who sold this to her."

"Bullseye."

"Hmm, do you know this person?"

"Mmm, too broad."

"Okay." Ryan rephrased. "Do you know who this person is?"

"Yes."

"Have you met them?"

"No, but I was going to meet them."

"But you didn't."

"Correct."

"Hmm, is that important?"

"Not really. It's a clue, but you'd have to really think to get it, and even if you did it wouldn't let you know what was in the box."

"But I love clues," she said with a gleeful look in her eyes.

"Okay, here's another. Someone else was going with me to meet this person."

"Hmm, can't be your mother because she must know them. Who would...I know, Jack!"

"Very good!" Jamie proclaimed as she took the saucepan from the stove. "Dinner's ready. Do you want to eat or guess?"

"Both."

The little box didn't leave Ryan's grasp through the entire meal. It was either in her hand or resting on her leg or being used as a weight when balanced on her fork. During the meal she guessed that it was a jeweler, so the surprise was really over but she was still reticent to open it.

After she cleared the dishes Jamie came over to sit in her lap. "Why don't you want to know what's in it?"

"Oh, I do. But when I'm done, the surprise is all gone. Before I know what's in it, it can be anything in my imagination; but once I know, the fun is kinda gone."

"But what if you really like the reality?"

"Good point," she said as she tore the wrapping without a moment's hesitation. Inside the paper was a slightly rectangular dove gray velvet covered jewelry box. It was at least nine inches long and six inches wide. Ryan stared at it for a long while before she said, "I hope it's not earrings!"

"Open it, silly," Jamie demanded, finally tiring of the game.

Ryan creaked the box open to stare wide-eyed at the most gorgeous necklace that she had ever seen. The silver-colored piece was very substantial and clearly looked like it had been hand crafted. Each oval link was slightly hammered to cause the light to reflect off the delicate hammer marks and make the piece sparkle. The links were quite large, each one almost an inch long; and they were about three-quarters of an inch wide. When Ryan delicately lifted the piece she murmured, "It's so heavy!"

Jamie slid her hand under the necklace and held it in her palm. "Good thing you have such a strong neck."

Now Ryan took the piece and examined it with precision. After she had spent a good three minutes in silent contemplation Jamie finally asked, "Do you like it?"

Ryan looked at her like she was stark raving mad. "How could I not? It's the most beautiful necklace I've ever seen."

Jamie had to agree that the piece was not only magnificent, she thought that it reminded her exactly of Ryan. It was strong and sturdy and substantial, but with so many delicate little facets that it was impossible to decipher it completely at one glance. The piece was starkly modern, but could also have been found in a Sumerian temple, so simple was the design.

Jamie took it from her and unclasped the hook. She started to put it on her, but decided that one equipment change was needed. "Take off your shirt."

"I would ask why, but I guess I don't really care." Ryan yanked off her T-shirt and waited patiently until Jamie decided the bra had to go, to."

Without hesitation she shed her sports bra and waited for her partner to place the necklace on her. Jamie clasped the piece around her neck, smirking as Ryan let out a yelp when the cold, heavy, metal touched her skin. "You look like the queen of some tribe of Amazons," she murmured as she took in the sight. "I want to take you upstairs and worship you all night long."

"Honey, I have to call your mother to thank her," Ryan protested. "I haven't even read the card."

"Later."

Ryan was wearing only her necklace and her jeans as Jamie led her through the parlor. The front door opened as Mia and Jordan came in from dinner.

Mia grabbed her mail and started to leaf through it as the pair passed her. "Nice necklace," she said idly. "It goes great with that outfit."

It was nearly ten o'clock when Jamie had finished admiring the necklace from every angle. She was moments from sleep when Ryan shot up and said, "I have to call your mom to thank her."

"She won't mind if you wait until tomorrow," Jamie said, her voice sleepy and slow. "She'll be glad to know how much we both enjoyed it."

"No can do," Ryan said as she crawled out of the tangled mess of sheets. "I'll be back. Go to sleep," she urged as she placed a gentle kiss on Jamie's cheek.

Slipping into a T-shirt and her discarded boxers, she headed back downstairs to find Mia sitting in the living room with Jordan sprawled across the small sofa, her head in Mia's lap. "Let me see that necklace, princess," Mia demanded as soon as she spotted Ryan.

Ryan decided that their recent bout of lovemaking precluded her from being too close to the ever observant Mia, so she reached behind her neck to unclasp the piece. Handing it to her she said,

"Nice, huh?"

"I'll say." She hefted it in her hand. "This must have cost a fortune."

"I'm sure it did. Silver isn't cheap."

"This isn't silver, silly. It's platinum."

"Are you sure?" Ryan asked, sitting down heavily on the arm of the sofa.

"Yeah, of course I'm sure. Platinum and silver don't really look alike at all. Silver is much shinier and more reflective."

Ryan rubbed her face with both hands, and when she spoke she sounded completely fatigued. "It's gonna take me a long while to get used to being in this family."

"Well no matter what it cost, it looks gorgeous on you. It fits your style and your personality. You'd look goofy with some delicate little chain."

"That's what I like best about it," Ryan admitted. "Catherine obviously put a lot of thought into this to get something just for me. That's the cool part."

"I'll take the pound of platinum, you can have the sentiment."

Ryan had to tickle Mia mercilessly to get the necklace back, but she finally had it, and the card, in her hot little hands. In the kitchen, she sat down to read the handwritten card before she called Catherine.

Dear Ryan,

Please forgive me for breaking the O'Flaherty rules, but I simply had to buy you something to commemorate your birth.

I know this was an unintended consequence, but your love for my daughter has allowed me to experience a re-birth this year. I fear that I would not have come out of my emotional torpor if it had not been for you, and I want you to know that I am forever grateful for that gift.

Being with you both and being allowed to be an honorary member of your family has permitted me to see what a real family can be. I am going to spend the rest of my life trying to live up to the example that you and your family so beautifully model.

Knowing you has been a wonderful experience for me, Ryan, and I hope you will think of my regard for you when you wear this necklace.

With love and affection,
Catherine

Ryan brushed the tears from her eyes as she read the note at least six more times. *She is so precious. So much like Jamie. Like a beautiful pearl just waiting for someone to help open her shell. I hope to God that Jim can wake up and see what he has right in front of him.*

🐎

Ryan strolled in the front door after practice on Tuesday night. Jamie was idly sitting in a chair in the living room, an usual occurrence. "You look thoughtful or troubled," Ryan said. What's going on?"

"I just spoke with Jennie."

Ryan sat on the arm of a chair and placed a hand on Jamie's thigh. "Is everything all right?"

Jamie shook her head and tried to put a name to the discomfort she was feeling. "She says they're sending her to live with her father."

"Oh shit." Ryan slumped against her partner. "That's so not going to work."

"I got that impression too. But I can't put my finger on why I feel that way. Jennie sounded pretty upbeat."

Ryan sighed heavily. "She adores her father, and I'm sure she thinks that things can work out. But he hasn't gone out of his way to see her in over a year, and no loving father abandons his child for that long."

"What are we going to do? She seems happy at the group home. Why won't they just let her stay there?"

"They have their reasons. And in Jennie's case there's no obvious answer on a permanent placement. I guess I see that they want to give the birth parents a chance, but I'll be amazed if this works."

"She sounded funny," Jamie said. "I'm not sure what it was—but she was giving off a vibe that just didn't match her words."

"When is she leaving?"

"Tomorrow night. Apparently her father is being deployed at sea for six months starting Monday and they want to give them a few days together to bond."

"Did you make dinner?" Ryan asked.

"Oh! I was so preoccupied I forgot to start it."

"Skip it. Let's call Jen and see if she can go out with us. I want to give her a pep talk before she leaves." Ryan stood and started to remove her jacket as she walked up the stairs, mumbling to herself, "They wonder why she doesn't do well in school. She's eight weeks into the term and she's changed schools twice. Can't anyone buy a clue?" As she rounded the stairs to go into the bedroom, Jamie heard her final comment. "I still don't have my damned drums set up!"

They all had a quick dinner together since Jennie had an early curfew. On the way home Ryan said, "I know what you mean about her mood. She seems off somehow."

"Yeah. That's the only term I can think of. It's like she's acting like she thinks she should."

"Well, at least she didn't seem upset. I guess we'll just have to see how it goes. Miracles can happen." She gave Jamie an unenthusiastic smile that showed how small a chance she gave to this particular miracle.

Since it was still early, Ryan decided to get in a little work on their stock portfolios, even though she would have preferred to set up her drums. But Jamie had to make a weekly report on her progress for her investments class, and since Ryan kept the books, her preliminary work was required.

Jamie had caught up a little, showing good progress, but Ryan was still confident that she'd prevail. Jamie came up behind her and observed her for a minute, saying, "You took a beating on that big block of General Motors, didn't you?"

"Yep, sure did. I have confidence, though. I'm not going to change my position until they have two disappointing quarters in a row. I think this is just a momentary blip."

"Ooh…I did well."

"You sure did. You're starting to catch up, sparky."

"Where are we?"

"I'm at $967,000, and you're at $725,000. I think we're both doing great."

"I'd say so," Jamie laughed.

"Thank God this is a game. If this was real money I'd be in front of the computer all day."

"Just what you need. Another fixation."

"One is quite enough," Ryan agreed. "And you're it."

"Hmm…that's interesting," Jamie commented, trying to see as much as she could before Ryan scrolled past her own holdings.

"What's that?"

"I'm surprised to see you loading up on 3Com. Do you know something?"

Ryan turned and gave her a dazzling smile, blue eyes twinkling with delight. "I know plenty, but I don't share." With that, she turned back to the screen, stifling a giggle.

"Come on," Jamie moaned dramatically. "Give me a little break! I'm doing this for a grade."

The dark head turned slowly as the contemplative eyes traveled up and down Jamie's body. "What's it worth to you?"

For a few moments, Jamie considered how she could entice her reluctant partner to share her thoughts. A smirk settled onto her face, and she leaned over and whispered into Ryan's ear.

Shaking her head, Ryan turned in her seat, gazing at Jamie with fond regard. "I don't know why I find this so adorable, but I love the fact that you can't say things like that aloud. You sure don't seem to have a problem doing it."

Jamie shrugged her shoulders and wrinkled up her nose, unable to explain her quirks.

"Okay. Even though I'm sure I could convince you to commit that act without giving you a stock tip, I'll spill it." She turned back to her computer and went to another screen. "Okay, here's 3Com's history over the past eighteen months. See what the price did here in September?"

Jamie nodded, assessing the graph.

"That was when they announced that they were spinning off Palm. I think that's gonna be a massive IPO, and I want to own it. I also think that 3Com will get a boost after the IPO, if it does as well as I think it will."

"How much are you putting into it?" Jamie asked, trying to assess Ryan's confidence.

"Well, I'd never do this with real money, but I'm going to unload a bunch of under-performers." Her brow furrowed as her eyes slid down her holdings. "I'll probably stick a hundred thousand into it. I really have a hot feeling about this one."

"Hmm, maybe I'll do it too, if you're that hot for it."

"Well, ya could. But the IPO isn't going to happen until February or March. That's too late to do you any good for your class." She was grinning like the Cheshire Cat and Jamie slapped at her while making an outraged squawk.

"You suckered me into offering sex acts for information that you knew I couldn't use?"

"So it would seem," she happily agreed. "You really ought to ask the right questions before you start compromising your virtue, sweetheart."

"I'm gonna kick your ass!"

"No," Ryan said thoughtfully, her brow furrowed, "that wasn't part of the deal. Right part of the anatomy, though."

∗

They were already in bed when the phone rang, and Jamie crawled across her partner to answer. She was in a very vulnerable position, and Ryan had to stick her hands under her own butt to fend off the nearly irresistible impulse to grab some of the attractively displayed merchandize.

"Hi, Mom," Jamie said, shooting warning daggers at her partner. "No, you're not interrupting us." She listened for a few minutes, nodding occasionally, a very thoughtful look on her face. "How long would be you gone?" Another pause. "No, I don't think you're crazy...not at all. Besides, how often will you get an opportunity like this?" She smiled at Ryan, as she crawled back across her body and settled herself into her usual position. "If you're asking my advice, I'd say that you should go." She nodded again and said, "Sure. I'm always up for a shopping trip. Friday mid-day would be best for me. Will you come to Ryan's game on Friday night?" After yet another short wait she said, "Yes, I know it's a silly question, but you never know. Something could tear you away. Okay, Mom, I'll tell her." She cast a look at Ryan who was gesturing at her. "Ryan's blowing you a kiss, Mom. Okay, I will. I love you."

"You will never, ever guess where she's going next week," Jamie said when she hung up.

"Do I really get to guess?"

Jamie looked at her watch and said, "Nope. Too late. She's going to Washington to attend a state dinner at the White House. With my father!"

"Darn it!" Ryan cried, hitting the mattress in frustration.

"What's wrong? Don't you think that's a good idea?"

"Oh, sure, I think it's a good idea. I just know I could have guessed that eventually."

After they finished dinner on Wednesday night Ryan went upstairs to study, while Jamie staked out the library, as usual. She realized she needed something from her room and went up to get it, finding Ryan lying on their bed, talking on the phone. "I know we have to have a consistent time," she said, "but I can't commit to any one day right now." Her massive day-planner was open in front of her and she thumbed through the pages idly. "I have games on Tuesday, Thursday, Friday, Saturday and Sunday. Hmm...I guess I could do it on Monday night, but I've got a few conflicts between now and the test." Her shoulders shrugged and she said, "No, I agree that one day a week hardly makes it worthwhile." She met Jamie's eyes and said, "I don't like it, but I guess we have to. Let's do Monday, Wednesday and Thursday. Yeah, six-thirty until eight. That should give us enough time to make a dent." She chuckled mildly and said, "Well, at least we'll know that people who join the group are serious about it—or idiots." She started to pencil in the times in her day-planner, nodding the whole time. "Yeah. We may as well start tomorrow. See you then Vijay—and thanks for this. I really appreciate it."

She hung up and cast a glance up at her partner, who was perched on the arm of the love seat. "Wanna yell at me now, or after I explain what I agreed to?"

"Oh, I think I'll be rational for a change. Just to mess with your mind," she chuckled. "Care to explain what you're committing to?"

"Studying for the Putnam," Ryan said, her expression far from happy. "If it's gonna be worthwhile I've got to commit a significant amount of time to it. The only time I can be consistent is early in the morning. Vijay Khan, my student advisor for my independent study, is willing to get up at the crack of dawn to help me, so we're going to try to get some of the other alternates to join us. The more minds the merrier with this stuff."

Jamie sat down on the love seat and looked at her partner for a moment. Ryan started to feel a little uncomfortable under her penetrating gaze and finally said, "What?"

Shaking her head, Jamie said, "Sorry. Sometimes I really wish we could speak the same language on this stuff."

"Me too."

"I know this is probably a silly question, but why do you have to study? Isn't this stuff obvious for you?"

Ryan sat up and gazed back at her partner for a few minutes, trying to think of a way to explain her mental processes. "I've been thinking about this a lot," she admitted. "And the analogy isn't perfect, but it's the best I can do."

"Come sit by me," Jamie said.

Ryan did so, sitting in the quirky manner that she often did when she was thinking of math concepts. The posture reminded Jamie a little of Caitlin's favorite position, and it dawned on her that Ryan probably started to develop her amazing abilities at about Cait's current age, and she briefly wondered if that's when the habit began. Ryan placed both of her feet on the cushion of the love seat, her heels almost touching her butt, and locked her arms around her shins. She was half-sitting/half-squatting, with her chin resting on her knees—bright blue eyes peering out to stare at a point in space. "The best analogy I can think of is comparing math to houses.

Let's say that each of the disciplines is an individual house. Now some of them I built with my own two hands—I know every brick and beam, and I installed the electrical system, the heating system, the plumbing—everything. I know that house so well, that when I walk in there, I don't think about the individual systems, I simply live there. I don't say, 'Oh, I want the lights on, let me go to the switch and send a signal down the line to the fuse box that will tap into the main line to the power for the house'. I just flip the switch without a thought."

Jamie nodded, observing the tranquil, even tone of voice that Ryan used. She could actually see a kind of peace settle over her when she spoke like this, and she offered up a little prayer of thanks that Ryan had this guiding force in her life to center and calm her.

"When I'm thinking of my specialties, that's just how it is for me." She broke her stare and gazed at Jamie. "I don't think in words or symbols or concepts. I just…live."

"That's so far beyond my ken," Jamie said. "I think in words."

"No, you don't," Ryan giggled. She leaned over and caught her partner by surprise, pressing her lips to hers in a slow, lazy kiss. Her tongue tickled her lips open and languidly explored the warm recesses of Jamie's mouth for a long while. When she pulled away, a smug grin covered her face and she asked, "What words were you thinking of just then?"

"More?" she murmured, reaching for Ryan to merge again.

"Uh-uh-uh," the dark beauty said. "I was making a point."

"It felt like you were starting to make love."

"That too," Ryan smirked. "But I think I made my point. There are some things that your brain doesn't process as language. It's more elemental than that. My math specialties are like that for me."

"Okay. I guess I see your point. But what about the other areas?"

"That's why I have to study. I don't have to study like someone would who didn't have a very good foundation in math. It's like I have to look at the blueprints for the new house. Since I'm a builder, I understand all of the concepts already. I just have to take some things on faith—rather than building the house with my own hands."

"So what will you have to study?"

"I know the fundamentals of math very well. But they have a lot of questions in group theory, set theory, graph theory, lattice theory, and number theory. Those clearly aren't my specialties, so I need to spend a lot of time looking at blueprints."

"I think I have some idea of what you're talking about." Jamie smiled broadly. "I understand this explanation a lot better than when you've tried before."

"I want you to understand this. I'll keep trying to explain it to you."

"I appreciate that you do this. As I've told you, I find you completely fascinating."

"The feeling is mutual. Now I'd better get to sleep or my head will be hitting the desk tomorrow morning, and I'm sure Vijay would like a little more interaction from me than that."

Chapter Seven

Ryan decided she'd be more alert for her early morning meetings if she got up at the same time every day. So she started getting up at six on the dot. Her early mornings combined with volleyball games on Thursday, Friday and Saturday had her dragging and grouchy on Sunday morning. She slapped the alarm so hard that the "snooze" function was disabled and she didn't budge until eight.

When she finally got out of bed and came downstairs she looked like she was spoiling for a fight.

Having been through this travail a few times now, Jamie tactfully asked, "I need a few things at the drug store. How are you doing on tampons?"

"I should be doing fine, since I haven't used any in more than a month," Ryan grumbled, her face mostly obscured by a huge coffee mug.

"Are you overdue?"

"Yeah. Third time in a row. This never happened to me before, either. I chalked it up to living with you—I thought our cycles might be trying to synch up, but it can't be that now."

Jamie had been standing at the sink, and she walked over to the table to put her arm around her partner. "Are you worried about how you're feeling?"

Ryan leaned her head into Jamie's hip and said, "No, I'm not worried, but I should feel better by now, and I don't. It's been a long time, and I should have bounced back."

"I know it seems like that, but Dr. Aiken said this was fairly normal for a severe case of the flu. I don't think you have anything to worry about."

"I said I wasn't worried," Ryan replied frostily as she got up and rinsed her coffee cup out.

Jamie rolled her eyes as her partner left the room. *I'm not worried about your energy level, but I am worried about your mood.*

⁂

Ryan's mood had improved by the time they reached the O'Flaherty house for Sunday dinner, but she was still a little out of sorts. Jamie was bound and determined to get her grouchy lover down for a long nap, and for a change, Ryan didn't protest. As a matter of fact, she suggested it, deciding to head downstairs as soon as they arrived. Jamie opted to stay upstairs and get some studying done, and she sent her partner on her way, shooting a slightly worried glance after her.

Ryan descended the stairs quietly, as usual, and her light tread didn't alert Martin to her arrival. To her frank surprise, her father was standing in front of her bookcase, carefully looking over the titles as his index finger trailed along the spines. "Looking for something?" she asked, a bit miffed to have her privacy invaded.

A deep flush climbed up Martin's cheeks, a rare occurrence for the dark skinned man. "Oh! You're home!"

"Yep." She walked over to the bed and climbed on top of the mattress after kicking off her shoes. "I'm home. Were you looking for something?"

"I ahh…I was just wondering about a few things…and I didn't have the kinds of books that I thought they might be in…and you weren't home…" He looked at her with his embarrassment growing by leaps and bounds. "I'm sorry for looking through your things, Siobhán. I've no right…" he finished weakly.

"Hey, what gives?" she asked, throwing her legs off the bed as she sat up. "What's bothering you, Da?"

"Nothing…nothing is wrong. I'm just embarrassed." His head had dropped, and his blush actually grew in intensity.

"Da, it's okay. I don't mind if you look at my books. I know you don't snoop around in my stuff as a matter of course. Tell me what you're looking for and I'll help you find it. I've got my computer to look things up, too. Now, what is it?"

He looked as embarrassed as ever and started to back out of the room, saying, "This was a bad idea, sweetheart. Don't trouble yourself."

"Da, wait! Come on, now, you can tell me," she urged. "God knows you know more embarrassing things about me than I care to remember."

Her warm smile and reassuring tone gave him the courage to stay, and he finally revealed his quest. "I was ahh…trying to catch up on new trends or techniques," he admitted awkwardly. "It's been a long, long time since I've been in this position, and I figured that I've missed out on a lot."

He still had not stated the subject that he was interested in, but Ryan had talked to enough people about sex to recognize the warning signs. "Come sit by me," she said, patting the mattress. He did so, still vaguely gazing at the floor. "There's nothing to be ashamed of. It has been a long time, and it makes perfect sense that you'd feel a little uncomfortable."

He looked up at her, his blue eyes showing his vulnerability. "It does?"

"Yes, of course it does. Everybody's a little uncomfortable when they're with a new partner. It's completely natural."

His mouth curled up a tiny bit as he said, "You must have been chronically uncomfortable before you met young Jamie."

She slapped his leg, adding a bump with her shoulder. "Hey, that was a low blow," she laughed. "But you make a good point. I wasn't uncomfortable with those women—they didn't mean enough to me to care enough to be nervous. But I was trembling so badly the first time Jamie kissed me that I looked like I had a nerve disorder."

He chuckled at her recollections and said, "That doesn't make me feel much better, sweetheart."

"Tell me what you're worried about—specifically," she said, gazing into his eyes.

"Well, I suppose I worry that it's been so long that I've missed something important," he said. "Your mother and I didn't have a clue, Siobhán, we just did what came naturally."

"I am surprised to hear myself ask this question, but did you and Mama have a good sex life?"

He couldn't help the smile that settled on his face. "Yes, love, I'd have to say that we did."

"Then why won't the same be true with Aunt Maeve? It's not about technique and performance. You should know that more than anyone. Aren't you the fella who told me how special sex was when you shared it with someone you love?"

"Yes, I'm the one," he agreed. "It was a lot easier when I was speaking theoretically. It's the reality that has me puzzled."

Ryan stood and went to her bookshelf. She pulled down one of her lesbian sex manuals, a book she hadn't looked at since she was eighteen. "Just to help you feel a little more comfortable, take a look at the first few chapters of this one." She took the paper bookmark out of the book and placed it carefully. "Don't bother reading past the bookmark…that's lesbian stuff and a lot more than you need to know. The early chapters cover all of the technical stuff and talk about different ways that some women like to be touched." She looked through the book again and pointed out one chapter. "Chapter seven talks about sexual communication. That's an important one. I guarantee you'll have a great time together if you can talk about things." She smiled at him and asked, "Did you and Mama talk about how you felt about sex?"

"Goodness no! Your mother was very shy about talking about those sorts of things. She greatly enjoyed our time together, but she was completely unable to talk about it. She was the typical Irish girl, Siobhán, with a little more guilt than was good for her."

"I'm sure Granny had a bit to do with that."

"Of that I'm certain. I just hope Maeve threw all of that nonsense out long ago."

"I do too, Da, but if she didn't, send her my way." She was smiling broadly, and he wrapped her in a gentle hug.

"I should have talked to you weeks ago," he admitted. "I've lost a lot of sleep over this."

"I hope you lose a lot more sleep, Da, but I hope it's in pursuit of pleasure."

"Darlin' this is one part of you that doesn't resemble your mother in the least."

Ryan slept most of the afternoon away, and when Jamie went down to check on her she was still groggy. "Hold me," her small voice asked when Jamie quietly approached the bed.

Jamie kicked off her shoes and climbed in behind her partner, snuggling close to her warm body. "I wasn't sure if you were awake yet."

"I'm not sure I am," Ryan grumbled, her voice still sleep-clouded. "I hate long naps."

"You must have needed it, or you wouldn't have slept so long. You have to let your body heal."

"I'm sick of healing. I'm sick of sleeping so much. I'm sick of being grouchy," she added, in a very grouchy voice. "I don't feel like myself."

"I can tell, sweetheart. I think it's time to go see the doctor."

Ryan's body tensed appreciably when this suggestion registered. "I don't have time," she said tersely. "I'll go during winter break if I don't feel better by then."

"That's nearly a month from now. Why wait that long? If there's something wrong with you they might be able to fix it by then…"

Ryan flipped over onto her back, dislodging Jamie's arms. "You said earlier today that you were sure nothing was wrong," she growled. "Which is it? Is there something wrong with me, or not?" She scooted off the bed and stomped into the bath, closing the door loudly.

Jamie gave her a few minutes alone, knowing that it would do no good to try to force her to interact. There was a very fine line between smothering her partner and making Ryan feel abandoned, and she still wasn't very good at staying on the right side of the line. When she thought enough time had passed, Jamie went to the door and knocked softly, "Honey, can I talk to you?"

There was a long silence, finally punctuated with Ryan's tight voice. "I need some time alone. Please."

Hated to leave her partner sulking in the bathroom she offered, "I'll go upstairs for a while. You can have your room back."

Taking no response as acquiescence she went upstairs. Martin and Maeve were in the kitchen, trying to figure out how to share the space without stepping on each other's toes. "Hi," Jamie said lethargically as she grabbed a stool.

"Where's herself?" Martin asked. "I thought she'd be foraging for food by now."

"Bad mood. Very bad mood as a matter of fact. I'm worried about her. I mean, I'm sure she's just fatigued, and this getting up early three days a week to study isn't helping, but she isn't herself."

"I think you'd better take her to the doctor," Martin decided. "Do you want me to call?"

"Does she have a gynecologist?"

"No, and she should," Maeve chimed in. "She goes to Dr. Terry—and has since she was in diapers. He's a good doctor, but even he thinks she should have a gynecologist."

"Do you think there's anything seriously wrong with her?" Martin's voice was wary, and his eyes reflected his concern.

"No, I really don't. I think she's just fatigued and has never fully recovered from the flu. I guess I'll take her to my gynecologist. Ryan likes her and she's very thorough."

"Good luck," Martin warned. "Getting her to the doctor is like wrestling a tiger. I've never seen a child so antagonistic to a simple check up."

"I think I can handle her," Jamie decided, not being absolutely sure that she could.

Dinner was nearly ready, and Jamie decided that she needed to fetch her partner since she obviously wasn't going to come up of her own accord. Ryan was sitting sideways on the love seat, knees drawn up almost to her chin, long arms tightly wrapped around her shins. She was crying softly and Jamie felt a stab of regret that she had left her. "Ryan, honey, don't cry," Jamie urged as she knelt on the floor next to the sofa and tucked her arms around her shoulders. "Don't worry, everything is fine," she soothed, pleased when Ryan began to relax against her.

"I'm worried that I'm really sick," she sniffed.

"No, no, no you're not. You might be a little anemic or run down, but you're not seriously ill. You're generally fine, it's just your stamina that's off." She pulled back so that she could see Ryan's eyes. "I know it feels like you're always tired, but you seem fine most mornings. Just like your usual self. I think it's the travel that really takes it out of you."

"Don't forget the bad food. If I never see another pizza from a student union it will be too soon." She lifted her head and fixed Jamie with a look, searching her eyes as she asked, "Do you swear that you think I'm okay?"

"Yes. I'm certain there is nothing seriously wrong with you. But I think there is something minor and completely fixable that's affecting your mood. I think we need to get you checked out."

"Okay," Ryan agreed. She wiped her eyes and swung her feet onto the floor. "As soon as winter break starts I'll go to the doctor—if I'm not feeling better by then."

Sheesh! Maybe I can't handle her.

"Well, hello," Ryan said as she walked into the house after her Monday morning class. "I didn't expect to see you at home today. It's a very nice surprise." She crossed over to Jamie who was seated on the love seat, and placed a gentle kiss on her soft lips.

"I'm kind of caught up, so I thought I'd hang around today. How about you? Is there much on your agenda?"

"I could obviously keep busy, but I don't have anything I have to do until practice." She sat down next to her partner. "You sound like you have something brewing. What's up?"

"Oh," she said casually as she slowly trailed her fingers up and down Ryan's leg, "I thought I might talk you into playing hooky from studying today. I just feel like we didn't have much of a weekend."

Ryan looked a little abashed as she conceded, "You mean that you didn't have much of a weekend because I was such a jerk."

"Nope," she disagreed. "Not what I said—not what I meant. You had games on Friday and Saturday, and you didn't feel well yesterday. Speaking of not feeling well, did you get your period today?"

"Nope."

"How overdue are you?"

"Just a few days. No biggie," Ryan said dismissively.

Jamie let that slide, even though she didn't agree. "So, are you interested in my offer?"

"Yeah, I could take the day off. Do you just want to go back to bed, or do you want to interact with humans?" Ryan asked with a rakish smile. As Jamie regarded her, she reminded herself that Ryan really was fine—early in the day, before she had drained all of her resources.

"Let's go out. I'll be in charge of our day, okay?"

"Sure. You don't often come up with bad ideas. You're in charge of our day. I just need to be back by four for practice. How should I dress?"

"You look perfectly fine," Jamie said, glancing at the "Cal Volleyball" T-shirt and black jeans. She extended her hand and pulled Ryan to her feet, saying, "Let's rock."

※

"Palo Alto?" Ryan asked as Jamie steered the Porsche down the sedate, tree lined streets of the city.

"Yep." She pulled the car up to a meter and put in enough quarters for two hours. "That should do it," she said, popping the money in. They walked down the street and turned the corner, but Ryan stopped dead in her tracks when she spotted the quaint little building that they were headed to.

"What's wrong?" Ryan demanded with a note of panic as she grasped Jamie's hand.

"Nothing, nothing at all. I decided yesterday that I was going to take you to the gynecologist and I thought there was a good chance that you wouldn't agree if I asked you, so I decided to trick you into it." She smiled, looking particularly proud of herself.

Ryan's hands were placed firmly upon her hips as she said with a slightly stunned look on her face, "And you're proud of that accomplishment?"

"Kinda," she said as she grasped Ryan's hand to lead her down the street.

Ryan pulled to a halt again and shook Jamie's hand away. "How do I convince you that I don't like you to make my decisions for me?"

"Sweetheart, you were sitting in your room yesterday crying because you feel so bad. I'm not going to stand by and do nothing. I'm not going to let you wait until winter break to go to the doctor. I have to take better care of you than that. You're just too important to me." She was looking at Ryan with such a sweet, loving look on her face that Ryan didn't have the heart to stay angry with her, but she wasn't ready to completely forgive her so she merely rolled her eyes, shoved her hands in her pockets and strode down the street to the door of the medical office.

Jamie trotted up behind her and immediately went up to the front desk. "Hi," she said in her usual friendly manner. "Ryan O'Flaherty is here for her ten o'clock."

"I need her to fill out some forms since she's a new patient," the receptionist told her as she handed over a clipboard with a few pieces of paper attached.

Ryan spent a few minutes filling out the myriad of forms and after she was finished, the nurse came out to call her in. Jamie hopped up with her and they were shown into the doctor's office. "Dr. Aiken will be with you in a moment," the nurse said as she closed the door.

"I don't have to strip in here do I?" Ryan asked as she looked around.

"No, no. She talks to you for a while, and then they'll show you to a room for an exam."

"Hmm, I'm not used to a lot of talking," Ryan said suspiciously.

"It's okay. She's a real doctor. See, she even went to U.C.S.F.," she indicated as she pointed to the framed diploma on the wall.

"I know, I know," Ryan grumbled, pacing back and forth across the floor nervously.

The door swung open and Dr. Aiken came into the room. She extended her hand and said, "Hi, I'm Alison Aiken," as Ryan stood and shook her hand.

"Hi. Ryan O'Flaherty. We've met twice before," she said tilting her head towards her lover.

"Jamie?" Alison said as she sat down. "Am I seeing you today?"

"No. I brought Ryan in for a check up. Ryan was here a few weeks ago with her young friend. She also came with me when I had that pregnancy scare last year," she added, smiling at her partner. "She's the good luck charm for women who don't want to be pregnant."

"Right," Alison said slowly as she looked at Ryan's paperwork. "So how are things for you, Jamie?" she asked absently as she continued to look at the forms.

"Everything is great, and I feel marvelous since I stopped taking the pill this summer. I have a new, foolproof birth control method," she said as she picked up Ryan's hand and gave it a squeeze. "My new partner has permanently resolved my birth control issues."

"Well, well, well," the doctor said, quirking a smile. "That's a bit of a change."

"Yeah, it caught me by surprise too, but I couldn't be happier."

"Well, congratulations, Jamie. I hope things work out well for you…I mean for both of you," she amended as she turned her gaze to Ryan.

"Things have been blissful," Jamie said. "But I'm concerned about my partner here. Can you reassure both of us today?"

"I'll do my best," Alison said as she looked down at her notes. "So, Ryan, tell me about how you feel."

"I guess I feel like I have a really bad case of PMS," she said thoughtfully. "But it seems like it's lasted since September."

"Since you got the flu?" Alison asked.

"You read my chart?" Ryan asked in amazement.

"Well, yes," she said with a laugh. "Why have you fill it out if I don't read it?"

"I thought it was just a way to make people not notice that the magazines are months old."

"No, I read every word. Now tell me about the flu."

"I got sick right at the beginning of September. I had a pretty high fever for a couple of days, and it took me two full weeks to get most of my strength back. But to be honest, I've never recovered more than about seventy-five percent of my former energy level."

"Hmm, that has been quite a while. Did you take it easy for a while and get extra rest?"

"Umm, well, yeah, I'd say so…"

"No, she most certainly did not," Jamie interrupted. "She's on the volleyball team at Cal, and she works out like a maniac! She exercises anywhere from three to four hours a day, and it's very high intensity stuff. And she's lucky if she gets seven hours of sleep a night, even though I know she needs at least nine."

"It's hard to bounce back when you don't get the rest you need. How has your weight been? Any fluctuations?"

"Some," Ryan prevaricated.

Jamie rolled her eyes and said, "She should be around one-ninety. You can weigh her today and get the real story. She won't get on the scale at home because she thinks I'll yell at her."

"Why do you think you've lost weight?" Alison asked.

"I dropped about twelve pounds with the flu, and I was playing better at the lighter weight so I didn't try to gain it back."

"Honey," Jamie jumped in again, "you were low before the flu. You didn't gain the weight back from the AIDS Ride either."

Alison smiled at the interplay between the young women. "You say you feel like you have PMS. Tell me about your usual experience with your cycle."

"Usually I get a little grouchy on the day I get my period. And sometimes I'm a little sensitive for a few days before. I've been incredibly lucky in that regard. My cycle is very regular—usually twenty-eight days right on the button. If I take ibuprofen, my cramps go away immediately, so I'd say everything is generally perfectly normal."

"But how do you feel now?" Alison persisted.

"Now I feel like I could go off at any time. My mood is very unpredictable, and I've been snapping at Jamie for no reason; and that's just not like me. I've been cold too, and that normally only happens when I'm getting my period. I've been much more easily fatigued too."

"When's your period due?"

"I should have gotten it last Wednesday, but I didn't."

"Is anything else worrying you or causing you stress?"

"No, things are great other than this…"

"Alison, she's had the most stressful summer and fall on record. I'm sure you don't have time to go into everything that's happened, but trust me on this. She's had an incredible amount of stress—plus being ill—all of her athletics, plus the stress of falling in love."

"Okay, I think I'm getting the picture. Anything else you'd like me to know? Any questions or concerns you have about your health?" She looked at her notes again and said, "Why don't you tell me about your mother, Ryan."

"She was diagnosed with breast cancer when she was only thirty. She died in four years even though she had good medical care. So I'd like to have a mammogram as early as you think I can."

"Do you worry about getting cancer?" she asked gently.

Ryan was pensive for a moment, but she finally nodded slightly. "More so since I've been with Jamie. I want to be with her for a very long time, but there's a part of me that's afraid I'll die young like my mother."

Jamie knew that this was a part of Ryan that was very difficult to reassure. So she just reached over and lightly grasped her hand and gave her a small smile when she turned her head to make eye contact.

"I think a long, healthy life is a very attainable goal. Have any other women in your mother's family been affected by breast cancer?"

"No. My Granny is still alive, and my mother's sisters are both healthy. Come to think of it, no one in my mother's entire extended family has been affected by cancer." She looked up at Alison and said, "That's good news, isn't it?"

"Indeed it is. Now, anything else you want to discuss?" Alison asked. "Any other health issues?"

"No, that's it," Ryan said.

"Okay, I'll have the nurse show you to a room and we can do an exam. If you want Jamie to stay in the room it's perfectly all right with me, but if you want privacy that's okay too."

"Since she does most of my talking for me, I guess I'd better keep her around," Ryan said with a fond smile at her smirking partner.

Almost as soon as she was undressed the nurse was back to do a few preliminaries. After the woman took her blood pressure and got a urine sample, she led Ryan out to a common area to weigh her. To her own shock, Ryan was down to 165 pounds. The nurse started to lead Ryan to a chair to take a blood sample but Jamie interrupted to suggest, "You might want to do that on a table."

The nurse gave her a quizzical look but Jamie informed her, "Even though she only weighs 165, she's still tough to pick up."

The woman finally understood the situation and led Ryan back to the examining room. She placed her flat on her back and as she got the materials ready, Jamie tried to distract her by talking in her normal rapid fire way; but as soon as the needle went in, Ryan's eyes rolled back in her head and she was out cold.

Luckily she came around in just a second or two, but the nurse stayed in the room to monitor her for a few minutes. When Alison came back in she asked, "Do you always pass out from needles?"

"Yep. Every time. I live in fear of getting diabetes."

Alison did all of the standard parts of a routine exam, but when she got to Ryan's breasts she asked, "Do you do monthly self exam?"

"Yes. Every month on the first day after my period."

"That's good to hear." After she performed a pelvic exam on Ryan, she stripped off her glove and said, "Everything seems perfectly fine, but I'm concerned about your weight. That's a tremendous amount of weight for an athlete to lose. And I'm going to guess that you didn't have much fat to lose to start with."

"She was rock hard at one-ninety," Jamie informed her.

"I'll run all of the standard blood tests, but I don't expect to find anything. I think you've been burning muscle which could contribute to fatigue and irritability and sensitivity to cold. Weight loss can easily upset your menstrual cycle also. Have you ever heard of the Female Athlete Triad?"

"Uhh, yeah, but I thought that affected women who had eating disorders."

"Losing twenty-five pounds when you don't want to is a disorder. It doesn't really matter why you're underweight. Your body needs fuel, and if it doesn't get it from your daily intake, it starts stealing from places you don't want it to."

"Like what places?" Jamie asked, her alarm growing.

"Like muscle and even bone," Alison said. "Ryan's delayed period could be the precursor to cessation of her period. When you stop menstruating, your body can start leaching calcium from your bones. As a preventive measure, I'm going to prescribe that you start taking a calcium supplement, along with Vitamin D. Up until age twenty-five, calcium loss can be replaced with supplements.

After that, all we can do is halt the loss. Your bones won't accept the replacement."

"She'll take the supplements—religiously," Jamie insisted, glaring at her partner.

"I don't doubt that," Alison smiled. "Will you be able to relax once the volleyball season is over?"

"Not really. I'm going to play basketball too."

"When does that season start?"

"Well, the season starts this weekend," she said with a sheepish smile. "I'd like to join them as soon as possible."

"See what I'm up against, Alison?" Jamie sighed.

"You've got to concentrate on getting some weight back on, or you'll never make it through another season. Didn't I refer you to a nutritionist Jamie?"

"Yeah. She helped me a lot. I'll call and get Ryan in as soon as possible."

"Until you get in, you may want to drink some of those meal supplements that they sell for senior citizens. They're not just empty calories, and they're not terribly high fat. And I know it's difficult when you're in school, but if you could get nine hours of sleep a night it would help tremendously."

"Okay, I'll do that," Ryan said. "Now what about a mammogram?"

"You're going to have to make that decision. I'd advise against it because of your age and your history. Having just one relative with pre-menopausal breast cancer doesn't increase your risk much. And false positives are so common in young women with firm tissue that it can cause a lot more stress than it relieves. But if you spend much time worrying about cancer and you think a mammogram will relieve those fears, you can certainly go ahead."

"But you wouldn't do it if you were me?"

"No, I'd wait until I was at least thirty-five."

"Just thinking about waiting that long makes my stomach clench," she admitted softly.

"Tell you what," Alison said. "I know a wonderful radiologist in the city. I'd be happy to call Dr. Steinberg and tell her why you want to have one done. She can give you her expert opinion on whether it's right for you. Would that reassure you?"

"Yeah, it might. I guess I just worry because I imagine that my mother could have been saved if she'd been screened earlier. I don't think I can wait past the age she was when she died before I have my first screening test."

"Is mammogram the most accurate test?" Jamie asked.

"For older women it's very good, but again, it is not a great test for younger women. Given Ryan's age, she'd probably get the most accurate result with an MRI, but that's a significant expense that your insurance will definitely not pay for."

"Money's not an issue," Jamie said clearly. "Any expense is worth it if it will ease Ryan's mind."

"Let me give you the radiologist's card. I'll call her and tell her the whole story and see what she thinks since she's the expert. Good enough?"

"Great," Ryan said. "It's been a pleasure," she added as she extended her hand.

Alison shook both of their hands and said, "Your blood results will be back by Wednesday. The nurse will tell you how to get them. It was very good to meet you again, Ryan. And good luck with both of your sports."

As soon as she left Jamie wrapped her arms around her partner and asked, "Did today reassure you at all?"

"Yes," Ryan said softly. "It reassured me that you love me and that you care for me and that I'm the luckiest woman in the world."

"It's all true," she agreed. "One minor correction. *We're* the luckiest women in the world."

Chapter Eight

After a very nutritious lunch, Ryan sat down in front of her computer and didn't move until quarter to three. Jamie was studying in the library, and she looked up in surprise when her lover came jogging down the stairs in her warm ups. "Gotta go, babe," she said casually as she laced up her inline skates.

"Why so early?"

"I've gotta make a stop before volleyball practice." She kissed Jamie and dashed to the door. "I'll be home by seven or eight."

Seven or eight? She leaving early and coming home late? That doesn't make any sense. She sat there for a moment, trying to think of any reason for Ryan to spend extra time after practice. Unable to come up with any guesses, she assumed Ryan was hiding something. Probably something bad for her. She hopped up and grabbed her bike from the front porch, slapping her helmet on as she unlocked it and took it down the stairs. She knew that Ryan could beat her to campus, but she also knew that she was headed for one of the athletic facilities, given her outfit, and she already had a pretty good suspicion of her destination. Jamie arrived at the Recreation and Sports Facility and locked her bike up before flashing her student ID for admission. The gym was usually sectioned off for volleyball practice, but today it was wide open and she noticed that the normal resilient surface wasn't in place. She was afraid she'd guessed wrong when Ryan came out onto the court with Coach Hayes and Lynette Dix of the basketball team.

Jamie didn't want to be seen, so she lurked just outside of the court area. The voices carried well, given the silence of the gym, but she nearly broke that silence when she heard the coach ask, "Are you sure you're up to double practices, Ryan? I can't afford to go easy on you if you're going to be any help to us."

"I'm in tip top shape. I actually just had a check up today, and the doctor cleared me to play both sports."

Jamie was clenching her fists so firmly that her knuckles turned white. *She did not clear you to play both sports you idiot!! She told you to sleep for nine hours a night and gain weight so you don't collapse!*

"As I told you when we spoke on the phone last week," Coach Hayes said, "I won't let you suit-up unless you've practiced for two full weeks. Now just because you suit-up certainly doesn't mean that you'll play…but you'll have a chance if you work hard enough."

"Working hard is never a problem for me, Coach," Ryan said, her earnest face focused on the older woman.

"I'm sure that I won't be comfortable with your familiarity with our offense after only two weeks, so don't get your hopes up that you'll play much. Lynette is willing to work one-on-one with you for an hour a day to get you familiar with our system. Is three o'clock good for you?"

"Yeah. Then I can go to volleyball practice from four to six and run over to Haas for the last hour of your practice."

"Okay, I'll let you be the judge, but you look awfully thin. Were you this skinny when you tried out for us?"

"Uh…no, not really," she admitted. "I like to play volleyball really light, but I'm already working on increasing my weight for basketball."

"There are some big girls in this league, and you're going to get tossed around a lot at your current weight. I'd bulk up as much as you can. I don't anticipate using you as a center, but you're too thin to even be an effective forward right now."

"Not a problem. I've already made an appointment with a nutritionist to make sure I gain it properly."

"Okay, I'll let Lynette be the judge of your progress. If you do well over the next two weeks, we'll add you to the roster for the Colorado game."

"How about Nevada?" Ryan asked hopefully.

Scowling dubiously, the coach said, "That's next Sunday."

"I know, but I've been studying the playbook, and I think I can help. The offense is very much like I played at U.S.F., so I don't think it'll be that hard for me to learn."

"We'll see," the coach said, her doubt obvious. "Does Coach Placer know you want to play next weekend?"

"Uhm, no. But we'll know by next Saturday if we get an NCAA bid. If we don't, it doesn't matter what we do in our last game."

"But if you *do* get a bid?"

"Then I'll focus on volleyball," she said decisively. "But the odds that we'll get a bid are poor."

"Okay. We'll see how you do. I'll let you two get to work, and I'll see you at Haas a little after six. Oh, and Ryan?"

"Yes?"

"To me, a good practice is when the hem of your shirt is wet. Get ready to work."

To Jamie's relief, the first hour of practice consisted of slow motion walk-throughs of the offense. Ryan was not even damp when she grabbed her gym bag and waited for the maintenance staff to put the resilient surface the volleyball team used in place.

Jamie finally smiled as she saw her lanky lover take out a can of a meal supplement and gulp it down as she sat on the floor and waited for her teammates. *Good girl!* She had to laugh at the face that Ryan was making, so when she pulled out another can and gulped it down, she gave her an even bigger smile and thought, *Even better girl! You're not in nearly as much trouble as you were an hour ago.*

"Hi, honey," Jamie called out brightly as Ryan came in the front door at around seven-fifteen.

"Hey." She started to trot up the stairs. "Gotta take a quick shower."

Jamie waited until she could hear the shower going before running up the stairs and checking out Ryan's discarded clothes. The wet mess on the floor of the bedroom was testament to Coach

Hayes' maxim.

Dinner was just being set on the table when Ryan came back down in a pair of the cotton pajamas that Jamie had bought for her. Mia joined them for dinner and as Ryan dug in, Jamie casually asked, "Why were you so late tonight?"

"Oh, uhm, no special reason," she said as she shifted in her chair.

"And did you start early too?"

"Yeah, I started a little early."

"Is Coach Placer going to keep you this late all week?"

"I might be this late all week, yeah…I might be."

"It seems odd to me that you'd need extra practice this late in the season."

Ryan just nodded briefly, but offered no comment. "Mia, didn't Jordan call you a long while ago?" Jamie asked.

"Yeah, she called around six-thirty. She's gonna come over later and help me study."

"Why didn't Jordan have to stay late, honey?" she asked sweetly as she batted her big green eyes at Ryan. "Are you just a special case?"

Ryan carefully placed her fork down and took a deep breath. "Did you follow me or can you smell the leather on my hands?"

"I followed you, of course! And you can thank your lucky stars that I didn't go down onto that court and thoroughly embarrass you in front of your coach!"

"What going on?" Mia demanded.

"Rockhead here has decided to play basketball and volleyball simultaneously. Of course, this is in addition to the three early morning study sessions for the Putnam competition. We just went to the doctor this morning because she's feeling so bad, so she thought it was the perfect day to begin practicing four hours a day instead of two!" Steam was nearly rising from the top of Jamie's head.

"But the doctor said I could," Ryan whined.

"She most certainly did not! You told her you were going to start basketball as soon as volleyball ended, and she said that if you didn't start sleeping more and gain some weight that you would never make it through another sport. That's not exactly a ringing endorsement."

"Well she didn't say I couldn't," Ryan reminded her as she stuck her lower lip out in a pout.

Jamie dropped her head to the table and lightly hit it repeatedly. "I don't know what I'm going to do with you."

Ryan turned to Mia and gave her a childlike grin as she admitted, "I'd bet I've heard that refrain at least a thousand times."

The next morning when Ryan got back from working out at the gym, there was a note taped to the refrigerator. "Open Me!" it read. Grinning, she opened the door and found two complete meals and a snack all ready for her consumption. A large container of oatmeal was labeled, "Add two bananas and blueberries and eat by ten" A container of hearty potato soup was marked, "Eat by two", and a pint container of plain non-fat yogurt bore the legend, "Add strawberries and blueberries and take to gym to eat between practices." The blender was in the refrigerator, and it had been filled with orange juice, a sliced banana and strawberries. Its label read, "Add non-fat frozen yogurt and drink whenever you wish as long as it's before three" There was a little heart or a series of x's circled with o's on each note. *I would have had a girlfriend years ago if I'd known it would be this nice,* Ryan thought fondly, kissing the container of oatmeal as a substitute for her partner.

The downside of having a concerned partner made itself known when Ryan showed up at three o'clock for her workout with Lynette. The older woman gave her a look and said, "Jamie called me today. You really should have told us about your weight loss. Losing twenty-five pounds to illness is a lot different than playing light."

"I know," she said, both chagrined and miffed with Jamie for interfering. "I just didn't think you'd let me play if you knew I kept losing weight."

"That's a good guess, and if I told Coach Hayes, that's just what would happen. But I know how much you want to play, and I'm willing to keep this our little secret. Two things I need from you, though."

"Name it."

"One—no weight lifting until you've gained a little weight. You're working plenty hard at practices—you don't need any more strain on your body."

"Okay. That's a good idea."

"Two—no more running. It's not doing you any good at this point, and it's sapping calories. Do we have a deal?"

"Yes, Coach, we do."

"One more thing," Lynette said. "Don't be angry with Jamie for calling me. She's worried about you, and I think she has good reason."

"Yeah, she does," Ryan agreed. "I get too focused and forget to take care of myself sometimes."

"You're going to have to do a better job of that, or this schedule will eat you alive. It's a lot more demanding than the volleyball schedule. The games are often longer, and Coach Hayes is a hell of a lot harder to play for than Coach Placer." She gave her a worried look and said, "I just hope that you don't regret your decision to play."

"I won't," she assured her. "I love to play, and this is the highest caliber of competition I'm ever going to have. It's worth it to me, Coach."

"I hope so. I sincerely hope so."

Chapter Nine

Catherine walked into the luggage retrieval area of National Airport in Washington, D.C. and immediately noticed the uniformed driver holding aloft a sign that read "C. Evans." She signaled the man and he helped her retrieve her luggage, escorting her to the limo just minutes later. The flight had been uneventful, but she had not been able to sleep, her mind far too active to allow her to relax. She'd flown most of the night, and dawn was just breaking over the Washington skyline when the car reached the hotel. The bellman took her bags, and before she was halfway across the lobby Jim appeared, looking fully awake and ready for the day. He was dressed in a dark blue suit, crisp white shirt and a gold and navy print tie that she had given him after a trip to Italy. She smiled broadly and allowed him to give her a warm hug. "God, it's good to see you," he whispered, squeezing her tightly.

"How did you know I was here?"

"I asked the doorman to alert me as soon as a limo carrying a gorgeous blonde woman pulled up." He was giving her one of his most rakish smiles, and she could only respond with a small shake of her head.

As he led her to the elevator she said, "You look good, Jim. You actually look more well rested than I've seen you in years."

"Don't tell anyone," he whispered conspiratorially, "but this job is a day at the beach compared to practicing law."

"Your secret's safe with me," she chuckled, charmed by his boyish exuberance. When they arrived at his apartment, he gave her a brief tour and directed the bellman to put her bags in the spare bedroom.

"I'm sure you want to spend most of the day sleeping, but I'd love to give you the grand tour of the Capitol if you're up for it. I think you'd enjoy it."

"All right. Either today or tomorrow. My flight back isn't until five."

"That's great. I can arrange for a special lunch in the Senate dining room. I'm sure you're too tired to do that today."

"Yes, I think I'll need most of the day to make myself presentable for tonight. I don't bounce back like I used to."

"That's where you're wrong, Catherine," he assured her, looking deeply into her eyes. "You'd be the most beautiful woman there if you went just as you are. You look absolutely lovely," he added, his green eyes boring into her.

She blinked at him, on the verge of tossing off a self-deprecating comment, but the sincerity in his expression stopped her. He was acting exactly as he had when she was in college and he was wooing her. This realization caught her completely by surprise, but it was somehow charming.

"I have a breakfast meeting this morning, so I have to get going," he said, as he crossed to the closet to retrieve his overcoat. "If you need anything, anything at all, call my secretary. She can reach me at a minute's notice. Also, the concierge of the hotel is wonderful, and room service has a great salad that I know you'd like." He was smiling broadly at her the entire time he talked, and his tone showed more excitement than she had heard in years.

"I'm sure I won't have any problems. I honestly think I'll sleep most of the day—I was unable to on the plane."

"Oh, I almost forgot." He walked across the room and handed her a slip of paper from a pad resting near the phone. "I arranged for a massage for you later this afternoon. I thought that would help you feel refreshed for tonight. I know what a tough time you have sleeping on airplanes."

His expression was that of a schoolboy waiting to hear if he had passed an important test, and she smiled broadly in return. "Thank you, Jim. This is very thoughtful of you."

"All of the details are listed right here. You can walk to the spa. It's almost across the street."

"Thank you again," she said, and was surprised again by the enthusiastic hug he gave her.

"I'm just glad you're here, Catherine," he said softly. "I'm very, very happy to see you."

⁂

Once she was unpacked and dressed in her pajamas Catherine tried to get to sleep, but her mind was still racing. She decided to call Jamie to get some sort of order to her thoughts. Jamie answered on the third ring. "Hello?"

"Hi, it's mother."

"Hi, Mom," Jamie whispered. "Hold on a sec. I've got to go outside." She was quiet for a moment, then said in a normal tone of voice, "Okay, I can talk now."

"Am I disturbing you?"

"No, not at all. You just saved me from actually falling asleep in the middle of class. Wow, who knew accounting could be so boring."

Catherine laughed and said, "It doesn't seem like that's a subject that matches your personality, but it's a good thing to know."

"Yeah. I keep telling myself that. Maybe I'll convince myself eventually. So, are you there?"

"Yes. I'm going to try to go to sleep for a while, but my mind won't let me relax."

"How come? Did something happen?"

"Did you see that movie where aliens come to earth and infiltrate the country by starting with the President, and then working their way through the Congress?"

"Uhm, no. Was that the movie on the plane?"

"Hardly. Anyway, I think it's happened, and they've obviously gotten to your father."

Jamie chuckled. "He's seemed like he's been under someone's mind control this year. Do you have any further evidence?"

"He must have found the fountain of youth at the same time. He's acting like he did when we were dating. No, actually he's nicer than he was then. He honestly acts like he's trying to impress me, and he hasn't done that in a very, very long time."

"Maybe he really is sincere in his desire to try again. Do you think you can trust him?" She tried not to betray her doubts.

"No, I see no reason to trust him yet. He's got a very long way to go before I do that again. But he is trying, and that's very good to see."

"I'm glad to hear that, Mom. If he's got a brain in his head he'll put all of his energies into trying to win you back."

🐴

"The limo should be here soon, Catherine. Are you about ready?"

The door to the second bedroom opened, and Jim took a step backwards, his mouth gaping open as he took in the vision of his wife. Catherine always looked lovely when she was attending a formal dinner, but she was ravishing tonight, and the look on Jim's face left no doubts that her extra effort had paid off.

Jamie had convinced her to buy a dress she would not normally have been drawn to—a burnished gold silk, strapless gown with a form-fitting bodice and full train. The bust line of the dress emphasized her slight cleavage to very good effect, with the smoky topaz solitaire pendant she wore helping to set it off. Catherine didn't have a distinctive tan, but she had been swimming recently and the sun had managed to penetrate the protective sun block that she wore. The kiss of the sun showed faintly across her shoulders, making her look healthy and robust and very attractive.

"I'm stunned," Jim murmured, walking slowly around his wife, looking at her from every angle. "I've never seen you look lovelier." He took her hand and walked down the hallway with her, his eyes never leaving her. "I don't think I've ever seen you in that color before," he mused. "I don't even know what it's called, but they should name it after you."

She couldn't remove the smile that settled on her face, even though she knew his compliments were ridiculously outlandish. "You look very nice yourself, Jim. I like this tuxedo better than any you've ever had."

"Thank you." His smile was somewhat sheepish. "That's because I finally listened to you and had one made in Italy. I don't know why I ever argue with you about fashion. You clearly know what's best."

"I'm actually excited about tonight," she said as they walked to the door. "Believe me, I can't remember the last time I was looking forward to a formal dinner."

"No, I've had my fill also, but this one should be special... particularly because you're here," he added as he placed his hand against the small of her back and guided her out the door.

Catherine wasn't sure if she had forgotten, or if Jim had failed to tell her that this dinner was in honor of the president of Italy. Various members of the Italian consulate were in attendance, scattered among the tables, and Catherine was seated next to one such dignitary. Jim watched her out of the corner of his eye as she managed to charm the Ferragamos right off the fellow, chatting easily with him and his wife about all things Italian. She was the only other person at the table who spoke Italian, and even though the man spoke perfectly good English, it was clear that he and his wife preferred conversing in their native tongue, so Catherine became the translator for the table.

After dinner they adjourned to the red room for dancing. "Are you having fun?" he asked, as he led her around the polished floor, his breath warm and moist as it passed over her ear.

"Very much so." She tilted her head to gaze into his eyes. "Are you?"

"Yes, but I'd like it even better if all of these other people would leave us alone."

"It looks like someone's about to cut in," she whispered, and his face flashed a frown of displeasure. "Oh, I'll be right back," she chided softly. "You can't say no to the leader of the free world."

When Jim was reunited with his wife, he sulked for a few minutes about the temerity of the President. "Two songs! Why did he have to dance with you for two songs! He's got his own wife," he grumbled.

"Uh-huh," Catherine said, thinking that Jim and the President had some of the same habits where women were concerned. "You could have asked Hilary to dance."

"I don't think he'd have noticed," he groused, clearly angry that he couldn't trump the man. He blinked down at Catherine and said, "He's as stupid as I am. He clearly doesn't see what a wonderful woman he's married to. After all she's been through I can't imagine it's not over for them." He paused for a second, taking in a deep breath. "I hope it's not over for us."

She patted his back and leaned against his chest, not speaking for a few minutes as they moved gracefully around the dance floor. "It's not over yet. I don't know what's in store for us, but it's not over yet."

When they were back at their table, Jim sipped a cognac and mused, "I wish I hadn't had to leave my cell phone at the guard station. I'd love to call Jamie from the White House."

Catherine gave him a puzzled glance and raised an eyebrow at one of the hovering attendants. "The Senator needs to make a long distance phone call. Can you help him?"

"Yes, Senator, right this way, sir," the tuxedoed man said.

Jim smiled as he rose and extended his hand to his wife. "Mrs. Evans will be joining me for the call," he said, and they were escorted to an elegant sitting room, far down the hall from the dinner.

After securing a line the man handed Jim the phone and said, "Do you need the operators to connect you sir, or do you know the number?"

"I know it," Catherine said, and proceeded to dial.

Jim smiled at the man and said, "See why I need her?"

On the way back to the apartment, Jim sat closer to Catherine than she was used to, and after a few blocks his arm was resting lightly around her shoulders. "Remember the first formal dance we ever attended?"

She looked at him as if he was mad and said, "Of course. How could I forget? I have a permanent reminder of that night, and we just spoke to her on the phone."

He smiled and said, "I meant a little earlier in the evening."

"Oh, before I got so drunk that I had unprotected sex with you in the car." She had never spent a day regretting the gift of their daughter, but if she could turn back time she would have been in her right mind at the time of her conception.

He looked a little taken aback by her tone, and he blinked at her slowly before he asked, "Do you regret it, Cat?"

She patted his leg and assured him, "Of course not. I didn't like the timing, and I wish I hadn't been so drunk, but I don't regret sleeping with you, I don't regret marrying you, and I certainly don't regret having Jamie. It doesn't do much good to complain about the details—especially when the outcome is so wonderful."

"She is wonderful, isn't she?" he asked rhetorically, sliding his arm lower and drawing Catherine close. "She's the best parts of both of us. How did that happen?"

"I don't have a clue, but I'm very grateful for it." She snuggled more comfortably against his body, feeling a certain comfortable familiarity that she realized she hadn't experienced for a long, long time.

"She seemed very happy to hear from us."

"I think she was. How often do your parents call from the White House?" She was quiet for a moment, and then said, "I think she'd be very happy if we got back together."

"I know I would," Jim whispered, pulling her still closer, his arms wrapped tightly around Catherine's body.

"I'm willing to try, but we have to go slowly. I need a lot of proof before I can trust you again."

"I've stopped seeing Kayla. As soon as I returned here after the unfortunate incident with Jamie and Ryan—I broke it off that night."

"Why?"

"Because I know it's wrong," he said softly. "It's childish and immature. I'm like a four-year-old. I see a new toy and I immediately lose interest in the one that I was perfectly happy with. I've turned into the man I used to make fun of. I don't want to be known as the old letch who can't be trusted around a pretty girl. It's not how I was raised, Cat."

"No, it certainly isn't. You had a very good role model that you chose not to follow."

"It's not too late," he insisted. "I can change this time. I know I can."

"I'm willing to try," she reiterated. "You're going to have to be patient, though. I won't rush into anything."

"I will be." His promise was whispered directly into her ear, and she felt a shiver roll down her body. "I'll do my very best."

"Care for a nightcap?" Jim asked, holding up a bottle of cognac.

"No, I don't think so. Feel free to have one, if you wish. I'll stay up and keep you company." She'd had wine with dinner, but she wanted to have her faculties about her, having a feeling that Jim would try to re-ignite their sexual relationship immediately.

Her guess was proven correct just a few minutes later. He sat down next to her on the couch and leaned dangerously close. "I've been thinking about what you said in the car earlier," he mused as he let his fingers trail down her neck, pausing to lightly touch her necklace.

"What's that?" she asked lazily, unconsciously tilting her head to give him better access.

"I think it's a shame that our first time together was such a frantic, clandestine coupling. Wouldn't you like to have another chance to do it right?" He leaned even closer and began to place tender, moist kisses from the tip of her bare shoulder all the way to her sensitive ears.

"You can't re-write history. We made our choices."

"Perhaps," he said softly as he nibbled lightly on her ear lobe, "but I think we could start off the second act of our relationship by re-living that night. We're sober, we're in a nice, comfortable place, I have a nice, comfortable bed, your sorority housemother isn't waiting up for you, and we don't have to worry about you getting pregnant."

"We didn't worry about that the first time."

"We did from then on," he protested, as though that made a difference.

"Yes, we did." She laughed softly. "I guess we have the benefit of knowing exactly when our child was conceived. Most people don't know that."

"May the fifteenth," he recalled. "I've always been partial to that day." He tilted his head as his body shifted closer, his lips meeting hers in a tender kiss. "We could christen our new beginning on November the tenth."

She placed her hands on his chest and pushed him away just an inch or two. "I'm partial to that May anniversary. I want to try again, but I won't let you break my heart again. I have to know that you'll be faithful to me, and that's going to take a lot of convincing. It's just too soon tonight."

"I understand," he said softly, laying his head against her shoulder. "I really do understand, Catherine. I haven't given you any reason to trust me."

"No, you haven't, but I still love you. I very much want this to work out. Can we date for a while?"

"Sure." He smiled, and she felt his mouth move against the skin of her shoulder. "Do you remember what we did on our first date?"

"Yes, as a matter of fact, I do. We went out for hamburgers, and then you walked me back to the sorority house and we made out like we were on fire—sitting on a stone bench in the yard."

"You had my heart racing that night. I thought you were very experienced."

She laughed softly and said, "No, just desperate to grow up. I had been so closely supervised at home I went off the deep end a bit at college."

"You didn't go far enough to please me," he chuckled, "but you could kiss like no one I'd ever been with. That kept me coming back for more."

"I was so amazed that this mature law student wanted to go out with me, that I'm sure I was a little more forward than I would have normally been. I didn't want you to think I was a child."

"Oh, you were no child. You kissed like a woman."

She shifted under him and moved her head until she was gazing into his eyes. Her lids fluttered closed as she leaned forward and kissed him, letting the embrace go on for quite a while. As she moved away she sighed and asked softly, "Do I still kiss like a woman?"

His slow, sly smile assured her that she did, and she leaned in for another. They cuddled and kissed for a long time, not going any further, even though she knew he badly wanted to. There was a part of her that was testing him—seeing if he would honor his promise not to push her. He behaved admirably, letting her lead the dance—responding immediately, but never pushing her. She pulled away at one point when her breathing began to grow ragged. Taking his hand in hers, she placed it over her breast and whispered, "You have my heart racing tonight. I'm going to go to bed while I still have some control."

"Control is highly overrated," he protested mildly, letting just one finger slip beneath the bodice of her dress. With a sultry smile, she leaned over and gave him one last kiss, this one the hottest of the evening.

His eyes were glazed as she pulled away and patted him gently on the cheek. "Goodnight, Jim. I had a fantastic evening."

"G'night," he murmured, wanting to walk her to her door, but knowing his knees wouldn't hold him up. As he watched his wife glide down the hall he marveled, *We haven't kissed like that in years. Maybe dating isn't such a bad idea.*

After a leisurely lunch in the Senate dining room, Jim walked Catherine all around the Capitol, smiling inwardly at the vast number of people who already knew him by name. They were standing next to one another, overlooking the rotunda when she reached down and grasped his hand. "Hard to imagine that the earnest young man I feel in love with would one day be a United States Senator. I'm proud of you, Jim. Your hard work and sacrifice has paid off."

He shook his head slowly, gazing into her deep brown eyes, "I'd trade it all to have your love and Jamie's respect once again. I mean that, Cat. I swear I do."

She reached up and brushed a tear from his cheek, then stood on her tiptoes and kissed the spot. "We'll work together to get there. I'll support you in any way that I can."

"That's so much more than I deserve," he whispered then hugged her close to his chest, his feelings for her welling up until he thought his heart would break.

Chapter Ten

"I think the star of the game deserves a nice long back-rub, don't you, Boomer?"

"Not a bad idea, Jordan," Ryan smiled, starting to tug off her T-shirt.

"Uh…Boom?" Jordan said as she extended the bottle of moisture lotion. "I'd think even a casual observer would give the MVP nod to me, don't you?" She batted her eyes at Ryan in her trademark style.

"I can't argue with your logic. You did rock tonight."

"Kinda sucks not to have our women here, doesn't it?"

"Our women?" Ryan chuckled. "I don't tend to refer to Jamie as my woman. Don't think she'd appreciate it."

"I'd never say that to Mia's face." A satisfied smile settle onto her features as she admitted, "I do think of her like that though. As mine, I mean." Twisting her head around so she could see Ryan she said, "That's silly, isn't it."

"What could be silly about that? It's hard not to feel like that about someone that you're growing close to."

"I just wish I knew how she felt about me," Jordan mused, resting her chin on her linked hands. "I still don't know if this is just a fling for her, or not."

"You know, I've only known Mia a little over a year, but she doesn't seem like the type to spend this much time with you if she was just playing around. I think she likes you a lot. She might even be falling in love with you." Jordan's body flinched.

Ryan didn't think she had ever heard a more hope filled voice as

Jordan asked, "Do you really think that could be true?"

"Don't say it with that disbelieving tone of voice. You're an extremely lovable person."

"Maybe," Jordan muttered. "But I don't think that's how she feels. I mean, look at how she behaved on Halloween. Mia's so open about things, and she doesn't care what people think about her. If she was in love with me, she'd tell me and everybody else in her life." She let out a defeated sigh. "No, I think she likes me—a lot—but I think she's planning on just being friends when we're done with the affair."

"When are you going to be done?"

"I don't know," Jordan mused, her voice quiet and laced with sadness. "I guess whenever she says we are."

⁂

Reticent to go to sleep with Jordan seeming so down, Ryan was just not able to keep her eyes open a moment longer. Her lethargy was really irritating her, even though she was now confident that she wasn't seriously ill. She fell into a fitful sleep, her mind racing while her body collapsed.

She wasn't sure how long she'd been asleep when a muffled sob woke her. "Jordan?" she mumbled, her eyes too heavy to open. "Jor?"

A very quiet, very shaky voice said, "Go back to sleep. It's okay."

She heard the bed creak when Jordan got up and a moment later the fan in the bath begin to run. But even over the background noise she could hear muffled sobs. Tossing the covers back Ryan padded over to the bath and knocked lightly. "Jordan? Come out and tell me what's wrong."

"It's all right. Don't worry about it. I'm just having a rough night."

"When you have a rough night I have a rough night. Now come out here and tell me why we're upset."

Something about that statement struck Jordan as funny and Ryan heard a short bark of laughter. "You're a kick in the head, O'Flaherty," she said opening the door.

Ryan tucked an arm around her waist and led her back to bed, then went back into the bath and wet a cloth with cool water. Jordan's eyes were swollen and red and she gratefully accepted the soothing cloth. "Thanks."

"No problem. Now tell me what's got you so upset."

"I had another one," she said quietly, dabbing at her eyes.

"A nightmare?"

"Yeah. First one in a long time."

"I know you've told me that you don't want to talk about them, but it really might help. Is there a recurring theme?"

"Yes, Ryan," she said tiredly. "It's always the same damn dream, and I've been having the fucker since I was seven." She looked at Ryan and shook her head. "Are you sure you want to hear it?"

"I'm sure."

"Fine." She lay down on her back and stared at the darkened ceiling. "I'm a little kid and I come home from school one day. I walk into the house and my dad's gone. Only no one else knows he's gone because no one else knows he exists. I'm the only person who knew him. None of his stuff is there, and my mother's stuff is arranged in the closet like nothing had been moved or taken away. I'm afraid to ask where he is, because I know it'll make her mad." She sucked in a breath and finished. "I go into my room and everything looks normal—just like I'd left it that morning. All of a sudden the whole house starts to shake and the house rips apart. There's this gaping chasm right in the middle of my room and the shaking is so bad that I start to slide across the floor. I'm grabbing onto anything I can get my hands on—the bed, the rug, my desk chair—but it all slides into the hole. I scream bloody murder and slide in too—knowing that I'll be dead in just a second—and then I wake up."

"Wow," Ryan muttered. "That would scare the piss out of me."

"It's done that a time or two. I'm just so sick of it."

"Do you have any idea of what it means?"

Jordan sighed heavily. "I'd damn well better after more than ten years of therapy." She rolled over onto her side and gazed at Ryan's darkened form. "It's nearly factual. I came home from school one day and my mother told me that my father was gone. There was no real explanation, and the look in her eyes told me I'd better not ask for one. I went into my room and sat down on the floor and started to bawl. I cried for hours, but she never came in to check on me.

I must have fallen asleep right where I lay, because I was still on the floor when the Whittier earthquake hit early the next morning. It wasn't even that bad of an earthquake, just a 5.8, but we lived in an old house and we were very close to the fault line. Everything in my room started to dance around on the floor and I got pinned against the wall by my bed. I still don't know how long I was there, but I screamed myself unconscious. After that, all I remember is getting yelled at by my mother for scaring her and Gunnar when I didn't run outside with them."

Ryan didn't have a thing to offer in response to Jordan's story. She just got up, sat next to her on the bed and enveloped her in a warm, comforting embrace. She rocked her for a long time, intent on giving the poor, fractured woman as much sympathy and concern as she was able. Jordan finally spoke. "Thanks. A few of those hugs would have knocked a couple of years off my therapy tab."

"Does Mia hold you like this?" Ryan asked softly.

"Yeah." Jordan let out a deep sigh and revealed, "She hasn't had to do it much. I've been pretty secure since we've been together."

"We were talking about a few things that might have shaken your moorings right before we went to sleep."

"My therapist calls that my 'loss nightmare'. I have it whenever I feel that something important is going to be taken from me."

"There's no reason to think that Mia's gonna give up on your relationship. You're really just speculating."

"It's what I do," she mumbled.

"Well, you can just as easily go the other way. Roll over."

"What?"

"Roll over on your tummy."

Jordan did so and waited until Ryan shifted to sit next to her. "I'm gonna rub your back and I want you to focus your mind on how it feels to hold her and be held by her. I want you to think of every little comfort that she gives you and how it makes you feel when she does. Think about kissing her and holding her when you sleep. I forbid you to have one glum or negative thought. Do you hear me?"

"I hear you."

"Good. The next sound I want out of you is a snore."

"I do not snore!"

"No, you don't," Ryan chuckled. "Guess that means you're done talking for the evening, huh?"

Ryan got to work and after a surprisingly short time Jordan was sound asleep, her breathing deep and relaxed. Ryan bent over to give her a kiss on the head and was pleased to see a warm, gentle smile on her face.

"This would have to be the day that our flight gets canceled," Ryan grumbled as the volleyball team sat in the Phoenix airport waiting to learn if they could be accommodated on the next flight. The student manager, Coach Placer and both assistant coaches were engaged in a long-running discussion with airline personnel, but from the expressions on their faces, it didn't look good.

"I guess I'd better call Jamie and tell her not to bother coming to the airport. I hate to have her waiting around for us."

"Doesn't she ever have class?" Jordan asked. "How is she available on a Friday morning?"

"Yes, she has class—and she attends all of them, as a matter of fact. She just scheduled Friday as a very light day since she had a lot of Friday golf meets during the early part of the fall."

Ryan was dialing as she spoke and reached Jamie on the way to the airport. "You might as well go home," Ryan advised. "I'll go back to Berkeley with the team."

"No, I'm almost there. I'll go hangout somewhere and study. Call me when you know what flight you'll be on, okay?"

"If you're sure."

"It's easier this way. And since we're going to the city, this will save time. Talk to you later. Be safe, sweetie."

"Do my best. I'll call later."

The coaching staff somehow managed to convince the airline to squeeze another twenty people on the plane and they were able to board the next flight, making them only ninety minutes late. When Ryan called Jamie, Jamie told her to come to the international lounge, since she had frequent flyer status.

🐎

"You guys going to Berkeley?" Jordan asked as they exited the plane.

"No. We've got to get home and help get set up for the wedding. What time do you guys think you'll come down?"

"The reception starts at two?"

"Yep."

"Then I guess we'll be there at two," she smiled. "Jamie's mom gives great parties—I don't want to miss anything."

"Bring some casual clothes," Ryan advised. "I have a feeling this party is going to run late—and wild."

🐎

Ryan grumbled to herself as she made her way through the miles of concourse to reach the international portion of the airport. She didn't have a lot to carry, just her gym bag and her backpack, but she didn't appreciate having to traipse all over the airport just to snag a ride home. It was perfectly fine with her that Jamie was concerned for her own comfort, but she wished she had been able to get comfortable somewhere in Ryan's section of the airport. *She can probably stretch out and drink an espresso with her paisans in the international terminal. Don't be such a baby!*

It took her twenty minutes to make the long trek and she had to go through security again…opening her backpack and booting up her laptop just to make the ordeal take longer. She'd wrestling with her mood for the last ten minutes, and she thought that she had a pretty authentic smile pasted on by the time she got to the lounge. Of course, she wasn't able to enter, since she wasn't a member. The uniformed man at the door actually sniffed when he saw her, attired in her volleyball warm-ups with a backwards Cal baseball cap on, but he agreed to test her theory that she actually knew a member of his little club. Moments later, Jamie came out and wrapped her in a big hug, immediately dispelling Ryan's bad mood. Her mood lightened even more when she saw the look of outrage on the doorman's face, and she gave him a wink as she grasped Jamie's hand to leave.

"Come inside for a minute. I just ordered a cappuccino, and my stuff's in here."

Forcing herself not to roll her eyes, Ryan did so, breezing past the doorman, who continued to glare at her. "Can we get going soon?"

"Yes, love. I just have to get something very important that I left here. Then we can go."

"Why would you leave something that was important?" Ryan groused, as they made their way through the sumptuously appointed lounge.

"Because we wanted to surprise you," she announced as they rounded a corner and came upon a small, auburn-haired woman, sitting at a table sipping a cappuccino.

"Aunt Moira!" Ryan gasped, collapsing heavily into a chair when her knees betrayed her.

"The one and only," the older woman smiled, tossing her arms around Ryan and enveloping her in a hug.

"How in the world…?" Ryan looked from her aunt to her partner and back again, clearly confused, as well as totally delighted.

"This young woman of yours certainly knows how to get things done." Moira smiled brightly at Jamie. "I still don't know how she convinced me to leave my family and sneak off to America. But here I am."

"She has that effect on people." Ryan smiled at her partner fondly, still shaking her head in surprise. "Was your mother involved in this little caper, Jamie?"

"I told you that she had three vouchers for international travel. Maeve used one, your father used the second…it seemed silly to let the third go to waste." She was blinking up at Ryan innocently, not quite able to pull that ruse off any more.

"I did well for myself, didn't I, Aunt Moira?" Ryan was beaming with pride, her blue eyes sparkling with affection as she gazed at her partner.

"If she's half as special as Maeve and your father say, I'd have to wholeheartedly agree with that claim." Moira stood and smoothed her dress into place as she said, "Let's get this show on the road, girls. We've got a wedding to prepare for!"

Moira's arrival threw the house into a tizzy, and wedding plans were largely ignored for the better part of the afternoon. All of the other aunts had to come over to greet their visitor, and she and Maeve finally went back to Maeve's house so Moira could take a much needed nap.

The children had planned a rehearsal dinner at a small, neighborhood restaurant, so everyone agreed to meet back at the house before the seven o'clock rehearsal. Ryan's suit was ready for pickup, and she and Jamie left to run that errand as soon as Moira left. "I can't get over how thoughtful it was for you to bring my aunt over for the wedding," Ryan said as they drove along.

"I knew how much it would mean to Maeve," Jamie said simply. "If I can do a little something to make her happy, why wouldn't I?"

"You've really come to love my family, haven't you?"

Jamie paused for a minute and said, "I don't think of them as your family anymore, I think of them as mine. Even though I've never met Moira, I feel a bond with her because of you. She's very special to me, because she's so special to you."

Ryan reached over and clamped her hand on Jamie's thigh, the emotion of the moment causing her to squeeze a little harder than was prudent. "Thank you, sweetheart." Her voice was shaky as she said, "Moira is truly a wonderful person. She's been there for me when I really needed her, and she's protected me just like my own mother would have."

Jamie recalled that Ryan had gone to stay with her aunt after the debacle with Sara, and she assumed that's what she was speaking of now. "She sure seems comfortable with us as a couple, and I can't imagine she has a lot of experience being around gay people."

"Yeah, she's generally very accepting, but she's known about me since I was seventeen, so it's not surprising for her."

"Still, knowing something and seeing something can be very different things," Jamie reminded her partner.

"Yeah, I guess I forget that sometimes. It would never dawn on me that Moira would be anything but totally accepting of me and the woman I love. That's just who she is."

"That must be a wonderful gift," Jamie said softly. "To know that your family will support and embrace you—no matter what."

"It is. I have that from almost everyone in my family. I really have been blessed." They were close to the tailor's, and Ryan shook her head at the dearth of parking spaces. "We're gonna have a hike."

"There is a pay lot close to the place," Jamie said, knowing that she was wasting her breath.

Ryan shot her a look and offered, "I'm happy to drop you off, but it'll be a cold day in hell before I pay ten bucks to park for an hour. Ain't gonna happen."

"I'll hike with you. It wasn't a serious suggestion any way. I know you better than that by now."

"I should hope so," Ryan chuckled. "Pinching pennies is one of my core traits, and I can't imagine that changing."

It was just four when they returned home, and Martin was out running a few of his own errands, accompanied by Rory. Conor was working at a house in Atherton, and he was going to have to rush just to make it to the rehearsal, so Ryan and Jamie had the house to themselves for a change. "We've got three hours. How about a nice, long nap?"

"Only if you'll agree to put me to sleep the fun way," Ryan teased, her blue eyes dancing merrily.

"It has been a while, hasn't it, Tiger?" They hadn't been intimate in over a week—Ryan's fatigue, coupled with her bad mood to seemed to conspire against them.

"Yeah, it has." Ryan placed her arms on Jamie's shoulders and clasped her hands together behind her neck. "But I'm feeling much more normal now that I finally got my period. I think the old Ryan's back."

"Ooh, I like the old Ryan," Jamie teased. "Of course, any old Ryan's fine with me. I'm crazy about all of her incarnations."

"Yeah, but you mated with the old one—I'll try to keep her front and center."

"Sounds like a deal. Do you need a snack? We won't get to eat until eight-thirty or so, you know."

"Ya know, I could stand a snack. I think I'll make myself a big bowl of ice cream." As she walked into the kitchen Jamie could hear her mumbling to herself, "What flavor goes best with, and on, Jamie?"

Ooh, she is back, thought Jamie with delight.

🐎

Ryan was still sensitive to cold, and the large dent she'd put into her enormous bowl of ice cream had her shivering by the time Jamie emerged from the bath. The comforter was pulled up almost to her ears, and when Jamie saw her she couldn't help but tease her. "Hey, Tiger, where are those hands? Come on, let me see 'em. I don't want you to start without me."

A dark look flashed across Ryan's face, and for just a minute Jamie thought that her guess had been wrong, and that the new and unimproved Ryan had returned. But just as quickly as it appeared, it vanished; and Ryan composed her face and seemed to force a smile. "I won't start without you," she said, a little too brightly. "You're the guest of honor."

"Hey," Jamie said softly as she slid into bed, "why did my teasing bother you?"

Ryan shook her head and tried to slough off her reaction. "No biggie. It just reminded me of something."

Jamie cuddled up close and started to draw neat little designs on Ryan's skin. "You don't have to tell me when things bother you. I just want to make sure you know that I'm always interested in what you have to say. So, if you want to keep it to yourself—that's one thing, but if you don't tell me 'cause you think I'm not interested—you're dead wrong."

Ryan gave her a squeeze and said, "I guess I should talk about this a little, 'cause it's obviously on my mind." She sighed heavily and said, "I guess it's what we talked about earlier about my Aunt Moira," she admitted. "I'm totally glad that you brought her here, but Moira's entwined with my Granny in my mind, and little memories have been bombarding me all day. As a matter of fact, that's been true ever since Da and Aunt Maeve went over to Ireland. I just had a flashback to a really hard time when you made the comment about my hands."

"But, honey, I didn't mean anything—"

"Shh, I know you didn't mean anything by it, love," Ryan insisted. "Don't give it another thought. It's just a bad memory. Nothing to do with you."

"Wanna tell me about it?" Jamie asked softly, her hand still gliding over Ryan's skin.

"It's…it's kinda embarrassing." Jamie could hear her swallow, and feel the tension in her body.

"Sweetheart, you never have to be embarrassed to tell me anything. I would never judge you…don't you know that?"

Ryan bit her lip. "I don't want to make this into a bigger deal than it was, and I don't want you to think less of my Granny because of it. It sounds pretty harsh when I put it into words."

"Baby, I won't think less of her. I tend to make up my own mind about people. Don't let that influence you. If you want to tell me about it—please do."

"Okay." Ryan sighed and closed her eyes, obviously trying to remember the event. "I'm not sure how old I was…oh, wait…yes I am. I was in third grade. I was staying with Granny for the whole summer, and it was the first time I went alone."

Jamie still struggled with the fact that Martin had let his precious daughter fly to Ireland alone at such a young age, but she knew he must have had his reasons. "Granny and I always…and I do mean always…had our disagreements," Ryan revealed. "I wasn't an obnoxious kid, and I was polite and respectful of my elders. But I was, as you would expect, pretty hard headed, and Granny didn't like that. I got swatted pretty hard when I did something that she didn't like, and I received more than my share of spankings, but she had a real thing about lying. It was…a real hot button for her."

Jamie's eyes had narrowed, and she knew her heart rate was picking up at the mere thought of someone hitting the vulnerable child that her precious lover had been. She tried her best to control her reactions, though, because she knew Ryan wouldn't be open about her feelings if she reacted badly.

"We had this ongoing fight about taking an afternoon nap. I was in third grade, and I hadn't had an enforced nap since I was four. But that didn't matter to Granny. She made me lie down on the sofa in the living room every afternoon. There were two rules. You had to close your eyes, and you had to keep your hands outside of the blanket."

"Because...?" Ryan just raised an eyebrow, and the implication dawned on her. "So you wouldn't touch yourself?" Jamie asked slowly, amazed that someone would supervise a young girl's personal habits so closely.

"I assume so," Ryan said. "She didn't explain herself, and I didn't ask, 'cause I knew I wouldn't get an answer. She didn't really like to offer reasons for her rules."

"That must have been hard for you. With your quick little mind, it must have driven you nuts to be forced to do things that made no sense."

"Yeah, it did, but I wanted to be in Ireland, and staying with her was the price of admission. Anyway, one day it was kinda cold, and I pulled the blanket up to my chin...you know...like I always do."

"Yes, I know," Jamie said, finding the habit one of Ryan's most adorable traits. Coming into the bedroom to see nothing but that shock of jet-black hair and those vibrant blue eyes poking out of the blanket always put a smile on her face.

"I had forgotten the rule until I heard Granny come into the room. I whipped my arms out, but she saw me. She marched right over to me and demanded to know if I'd been 'interfering' with myself. Now, I had no earthly idea what she was talking about, but I assumed she was asking if I had broken the rule about my hands. Since I had my eyes closed I wasn't sure if she'd seen me or not. So I told the truth. I'd been interfering with myself." She smiled wryly. "I figured that was just another Irish word I didn't know."

"So you told what you thought was the truth. Even though it wasn't."

"I had to. Even though I knew I'd get in trouble for breaking the rule lying wasn't an option—I knew that was a capital crime in Granny's world."

"My God, she sounds like a tyrant." Jamie said, unable to control her reaction any longer.

Ryan shook her head and insisted, "No, no she wasn't. She's an older woman from a very different time. She's just a product of her environment. If you don't know the influence that the Church had with that generation, you really can't understand this."

"I'm sorry, honey." She closed her eyes briefly while she struggled with her emotions. "I don't want to criticize her. Please, go on."

"You're not gonna like the end of the story," Ryan warned, but she continued anyway. "She grabbed me by the arm and hauled me to my feet and gave me a lecture about how touching myself was sinful and would send me to hell. God, she scared the shit out of me, and I still didn't know what she was talking about!" Her voice rose with righteous indignation, still fresh after so many years.

"You poor little thing." Jamie was about to cry, but she wanted Ryan to finish so she bit her tongue to keep from interrupting again.

"She demanded to know how long I'd been doing it, and whether my father knew. Knowing her, she probably thought he told me to do it. There was no love lost there. It finally dawned on me that she was accusing me of doing something that I didn't do, even though I wasn't sure what it was. I tried to explain that I'd just been trying to stay warm, but I'm sure my excuse didn't sound very convincing at that point."

"I take it that she didn't believe you," Jamie said quietly.

"No." Ryan shivered at the memory, and related, "She went to her room and came back with this leather strap."

Jamie's whole body tensed, and she willed herself not to comment.

"She gave me one chance to tell the truth, but I had been," she said softly. "I wasn't going to lie, no matter what. I didn't care if she beat me to death." Ryan's voice was hard and bore the marks of years of bitterness over the false accusation. "She made me hold out my hands, and she gave me a dozen lashes on each one. It hurt... God, did it hurt...but what hurt worse was that she didn't believe me."

Unable to hold herself back any longer, Jamie wrapped her partner in her arms and began to cry softly. "That's so wrong. So very wrong. That's child abuse!"

"Yeah, it would be here," she admitted. "I could hardly hold a fork the next day my hands were so swollen. I was eating lunch at my Aunt Moira's, and she saw that I was having trouble feeding myself. I still remember the look on her face when she saw my hands. She didn't even ask me what happened. She stormed out of the house and didn't come back for the longest time. I wouldn't tell Aisling what was going on, but I think she knew…she had been at the wrong end of Granny's temper a time or two, also. I was so worried that I couldn't eat, but when Moira came back she was carrying my little suitcase. She squatted down in front of me and said that she and Granny had decided that I'd be happier staying at her house from then on."

"I like Moira better and better," Jamie said, sniffing her tears away.

"Yeah, she's a great mom," Ryan said, in her mind all three Ryan sisters had co-mothered her. "She held me on her lap that night, even though I was nearly as big as she was by that time. She told me that it was perfectly all right to touch my body any way that I wanted. That it was my body and no one had the right to tell me what to do with it."

"Good for her," Jamie whispered fiercely.

"Yeah. I told her the whole story, mainly because I was so confused. She tried to explain what she thought Granny's point of view was. But Moira clearly told me that she thought Granny was wrong. There was nothing wrong with any part of my body. And the best thing." She took a breath, trying to keep from crying. "She told me that she knew my mother would feel the same way."

"You still must have been horribly mixed up about the whole thing."

"Yeah, I was. But the important part is that I understood that my aunt would look out for me. That she wouldn't let anyone, even her own mother, hurt me. That was worth getting a beating for."

"I wish you could have learned that lesson in a gentler way," Jamie sighed, still reeling from the thought of a grandmother beating a small child for such a ridiculous thing. "I can't think of what I'd do if someone beat our children."

Shivering at the mental image, Ryan said, "That will never happen. I'll never trust our children to someone I don't trust."

"Were you angry with your father for letting you stay with her?" Jamie asked, a note of hesitation in her voice.

"No. He didn't know. I'm sure my mother never told him that they were beaten when they were kids. It's really humiliating, baby. It's not the kind of thing you like to talk about."

"Do you think your father ever knew?" Jamie silently wondered why the woman was still alive if Martin had known she'd struck his daughter.

"Yeah. He knew. We never talked about it, though. When I got off the plane that fall, he squeezed me until I thought my ribs would break. Then he looked at my hands. I swear he studied them for three minutes, obviously making sure there were no permanent marks on them. It was never an issue of where I would stay from then on, though. I've not slept in my grandparents' house since."

"I hope your granny lives to a very ripe old age," Jamie said, her voice filled with emotion, "but our children will never be with her alone. She's lost that privilege."

Ryan nodded, agreeing completely. She thought it wise to not tell Jamie about the other times she had been beaten for even more inconsequential reasons. Like when she was whipped with a switch for not being home by dinner, or the time she had been spanked right in the front yard for trampling her Granny's flowers. As humiliating as those incidents had been, they hadn't stuck with her long—since she thought that each was somewhat deserved. It was the injustice of the accusation that she had never been able to forgive…and she pledged once again to always try to listen to her own children, no matter how compelling the evidence against them.

They made love for a long time that afternoon—even though they didn't technically have sex. The story had cooled Ryan's ardor, and Jamie was much more interested in expressing her love for her partner than in slaking her desire.

Jamie took out a bottle of moisture lotion and rubbed and stroked nearly every inch of Ryan's body, whispering loving sentiments the whole time. When she was finished, Ryan returned the favor, both of them feeling refreshed and well loved when their alarm went off. "Well, we didn't get that nap and we didn't get to put each other to sleep the fun way, but I'm very pleased with how we spent our afternoon," Jamie said when they got up to shower. "Knowing everything about you, good and bad, is always a positive thing for our relationship. Thanks for sharing this with me, even though I know it was hard for you."

"You make things easy. Ya know," she said speculatively as she regarded her partner fondly, "your listening style reminds me very much of my Aunt Moira. I wonder if that's one of the reasons I was instantly attracted to you."

"I'd like to be like your aunt," Jamie decided. "Actually, I'd like to be like any of your relatives. Even Duffy is worth emulating."

Chapter Eleven

The restaurant was only about seven blocks from the church, and the entire group walked down 24th Street together. The crowd was smaller than usual, with just the happy couple, their children, Moira and Catherine in attendance. Jamie was pushing Caitlin's stroller, and her mother was walking alongside, her hand loosely wrapped around her daughter's arm. Just in front of them, Ryan was holding her Aunt Moira's hand, the two women chatting companionably during the entire trip. Ryan stood a good foot taller than the diminutive woman, and they did not share a single common feature. Hair color, texture, and wave—all strikingly dissimilar. Moira's eyes were a pale green, nothing like the startling cornflower blue that Ryan had been blessed with. Moira's bone structure was slight and delicate, two words that had never been uttered about Ryan. Still, there was something about the pair that would make even a stranger assume they were mother and daughter. Ryan had speculated that part of the reason she felt so close to her aunt was because the woman bore such a striking resemblance to her mother, but Jamie thought it went deeper than that. She had a sense that this woman embodied some of Fionnuala's personality—in a way that Maeve did not. Moira seemed to have a fire to her that the placid Maeve did not possess, and Jamie guessed that Ryan's mother might have shared that trait—especially since Ryan surely had more than her share of spark in her own determined personae.

Whatever the reasons, it was clear that Ryan was very fond of the woman beside her, and that fact alone was enough for Jamie to make a little room in her heart to welcome in yet another member of her family of choice.

※

"Are you sure you don't want to go to the Dubliner with your father and all of the guys?" Jamie asked, once they were snug in bed.

"No," Ryan said thoughtfully. "I want to be well rested for tomorrow. It's gonna be a long day. Plus, I don't want to have a hangover."

"I've never seen your father drink more than one beer," Jamie laughed. "Surely he won't have a hangover tomorrow."

"No, he won't. But all of the cousins will be there, and at some point one of them would challenge me to some sort of drinking game and I'd give in, and...well, you know the rest."

"Honey, you don't even like to drink much. Why would you do that?"

Ryan shrugged and said, "It's part of being a member of the clan. Group dynamics, I guess you'd call it. I don't always use my brain when I'm around the cousins."

"Then I'm glad you didn't go. I want you bright eyed and bushy tailed tomorrow. You're going to look so pretty in your new clothes. I'd hate to see bloodshot eyes and a greenish pallor to that pretty face."

"It'll be fun to be the only one in the crowd who feels just ducky." Ryan smiled at her partner fondly. "Nine hours of cuddling by my best girl, and I'll be on top of the world."

"You're on, love. I'll race you to sleep." For a change, Ryan won, hands down.

※

"Morning, cuddle bear," Jamie murmured into her pillow early on Saturday morning. Ryan was wrapped around her so tightly that she was quite sure they had finally reached the limits of human connectedness.

"Hi," a wide-awake voice replied. "I'm gonna go for a run. You can stay in bed if you want." Ryan started to disentangle, but her partner reached behind her and placed a restraining hand on her hip.

"Want me to go with you?"

"No. I need a little time to myself today." There was a long moment of silence, and then Ryan added, "I need to talk to my mom for a while."

Jamie sighed and rolled onto her back, regarding her partner with gentle care. "I know today is going to be hard for you. Do you want to talk about it at all?"

Ryan's dark head shook. "No. I'm fine. I just want to feel Mama's presence this morning. I do that best when I run."

"I'll wait for you to have breakfast."

"Good deal. I'll try not to stay out too long."

"You stay as long as you need to, honey. We're not in any rush."

Ryan started to roll out of bed, but she impulsively drew her partner into another hug and placed several kisses on her exposed neck. "Thanks for understanding," she whispered, then rolled away and hit the floor all in one smooth move.

Ryan managed to stay close to home, satisfying herself with running up and down the hills of her immediate neighborhood. She had covered about five miles, and had just passed her Aunt Maeve's house when a familiar voice said, "How about slowing down a bit, and giving your aunt a chance to catch up."

Turning to greet Moira with a grin, Ryan ran back to the house and waited for her to come down the stairs, pausing to wipe her sweaty face with the hem of her T-shirt. "This is quite the coincidence, eh?" Moira asked.

"Not really." Ryan chuckled. "This is the fourth time I've been by this morning. I was hoping you'd come out for your usual walk."

With an exasperated look Maeve asked, "Why didn't you knock? You know we've been up for a while. My poor sister is so nervous, I don't think she slept a wink."

"I don't know," Ryan said, gazing at the street with an adolescent expression on her face.

"Doesn't matter," Moira assured her, taking her hand. "I've got you now."

"It's kinda wet," Ryan said, looking pointedly at her hand.

"Oh, please! Like a little sweat would bother me? I've changed a few dozen of your diapers, Siobhán," she said with a big smile. "Sweat is a definite improvement." They walked along the quiet street, their footfalls the only sound. "How are you feeling about today, sweetheart? I haven't had the opportunity to talk to you about the whole thing."

"I'm okay," Ryan said, pausing just a second to reflect on her mood. They merged their strides into a brisk pace, Moira quite used to an invigorating walk every morning. "Is it okay if I tell you what's on my mind? I've got a lot of things floating around upstairs that I can't get comfortable with."

"Of course," Moira said, squeezing her hand. "Tell me whatever you want to share."

Ryan nodded and took a breath, her thoughts organized after her run. "The biggest part of me wants both Da and Aunt Maeve to be loved, and to have them find that with each other is absolutely fantastic. But that's the twenty-three...no...twenty-four-year-old that feels that way. There's a younger part that doesn't want anybody...not even my beloved aunt...to take my mother's place. And even though I know Aunt Maeve doesn't want to do that... it's a bit unavoidable."

"I can see that," Moira said. "It's understandable that would be hard to get used to."

"I think it'll be a little easier because they'll be living in Maeve's house," Ryan said thoughtfully. "On the other hand, I don't want Da to move out. That's really going to be hard for me. I know that sounds silly, since he's only going to be two blocks away, and I just live here on weekends...but it really bothers me."

Seemingly switching topics completely, Moira asked, "I assume you know about Aisling's boyfriend?"

"Uhm, yeah. She's told me all about him," Ryan agreed, wondering why they were discussing her cousin at this point.

"I just bet she has," Moira laughed. "And don't you give me that look, I know you two tell each other everything."

"Well, she is my best friend," Ryan reminded her. "Besides, Jamie, that is."

"Well, he's a perfectly lovely young man. John Houlihan. She's brought him to the house several times when she comes home from school." Moira turned to her niece and gave her a deceptively innocent look. "I'd like to crush his head with a brick!"

"What!" Ryan cried, stunned at this uncharacteristically violent wish.

"He looks at her with those big doe eyes of his. He honestly looks like he'd like to have her for tea! Every time he touches her, I want to go over and slap him silly. 'Get your hands off my baby!' I want to cry, but of course, I don't. I behave myself very well, thank you. I offer the man a good meal and polite conversation, but I'm secretly plotting his demise," she added, a fiendishly satisfied look on her face.

Ryan had been chuckling through this whole revelation, and by the time her aunt was finished, she was laughing out loud. "I can just see you bumping off Aisling's first serious boyfriend, Aunt Moira. That's priceless!"

"Her father's worse than I am," Moira assured her. "The first time we met him, he leaned over to me as they came up the walk and said, 'I think I saw him on the telly. I think he's an escapee from the county gaol'."

Ryan was laughing heartily by this time and her aunt insisted. "I'm not pulling your leg. Eamon calls him 'Beady Eyes' or 'Pasty Face'."

"Since I've never known you to tell a story without a point, you might as well get to it."

"It's a simple point," Moira assured her. "We all have roles for the people we love. Your father and your aunt are both changing their role, and it's going to take some time for you to get used to it. Just like Eamon and I have to. Aisling isn't our baby any longer. She's a twenty-four-year-old woman who has probably been thoroughly kissed a time or two." She gave Ryan a gentle elbow to the ribs and said, "Agree with me, darlin'."

"Yes, Aunt Moira. Aisling has been kissed a time or two. I don't think she enjoyed it, though," she lied outrageously.

"Good girl! Now, we've all got some adjusting to do, but we can do it, because we all love each other. This is truly the best thing that could have happened. And just for the record, I am one hundred percent certain that your mother would give her wholehearted approval. I actually think she'd be disappointed in your father for going so long without love in his life." She turned to Ryan and said, "I know she'd want him to share his love, and what better person to share it with than her beloved sister. This is truly a time for celebration. Let's do our best to put our mixed feelings aside and show them how happy we are for them."

"I will," Ryan said as she brushed a tear away. "I will."

They walked for a while longer, and by the time they passed by the O'Flaherty house they had discussed every little detail about the wedding. When Moira told Ryan all of the elements of Maeve's costume, Ryan had an idea and dashed into the house to fetch something, calling out, "Be back soon," when Jamie stuck her head out of the bathroom, fresh from her shower.

After changing into a dry T-shirt, Ryan escorted Moira back to Maeve's house. Her aunt was a nervous wreck, just as Moira had described. "Oh, Ryan! If I had any idea this little wedding would take this much out of me, I swear I'd just live in sin."

"Over my dead body," Ryan decreed, laughing softly at her aunt's obvious distress. "My poor father would never recover from the mere suggestion. No, Aunt Maeve, you're in too deep now. Just try to relax, and in a few hours it will all be over."

"That's what they told me when I gave birth to Kevin," she scoffed. "Thirty hours later I was begging for a pistol."

"This will definitely be over in a few hours," Ryan assured her. "Besides, you've done this before. Wasn't it scarier the first time around?"

Maeve shared a look with her sister. "Oh, the innocence of youth," she smiled. "No dear, it was not scarier the first time. When you're young, you don't have enough sense to know how hard it is to be married. You just assume that everything will turn out fine."

"Well, call me innocent, but I know that everything will turn out just fine. I've been living with your groom for twenty-four years now, and I can assure you that he's one of the easiest people in the world to get along with. He's neat, clean, doesn't drink to excess, clearly doesn't chase other women, and he can cook. How many men have that many good traits?"

Maeve gave her niece a hug and said, "You're right, of course. I'm just being silly. I think I'll feel better when I can start doing something. It's too early to get dressed."

"How about a nice long bubble bath?" Ryan suggested. "Put on some good music, light some candles, and relax in the tub. Jamie has convinced me of the relaxing properties of a good soak, and if I can do it, so can you."

"Ooh, that does sound nice, but I don't have many candles."

"You will when my father moves in. We've got enough to provide light for the whole neighborhood during a power outage. I'll have Jamie bring some over."

"Oh, don't go to so much bother," Maeve insisted.

"No bother. I think we women should stick together today, anyway. I think I'll have Jamie bring over our clothes, and we can get dressed here. Can you feed us?"

"Of course. I'll start breakfast, love. That will give me something to do."

"All part of my plan," Ryan muttered to herself as she went to call her partner.

🐎

After Jamie arranged an idyllic setting for her, Maeve soaked for a solid hour, and her mood was much improved when she emerged from the tub. "I honestly do feel calmer." Jamie had insisted on providing a spa-like experience, and she set about removing the mud masque she had applied before the bath. She was about to help Maeve with her makeup when Catherine arrived, carrying Maeve's wedding suit and a selection of jewelry that would provide the proper accent. Being long-skilled in the artful application of make-up she took over from her daughter.

While Ryan showered, Jamie got all of their things organized, and when Ryan emerged she offered to do her hair. Ryan's hair had grown out since her summer cut, and was now much closer to her original length. Jamie decided that she needed a little something special today, so she parted it off center and created two long braids, which she twisted and secured at the back of her head with bobby pins. "I don't think I have any hair clips here," she muttered. "I'll have to run home and get something."

Overhearing the comment, Catherine looked over and said, "I brought a little something for Ryan's hair, dear. Look in the kitchen."

Jamie found a sprig of tiny sterling silver tea roses woven around a simple silver hair clip, and shook her head at the thoroughness of her mother's planning.

Ryan looked lovely with the delicate display of roses in her hair, and she even consented to allowing Jamie to apply a bit of makeup to her normally cosmetic-free face. Then the tall woman sat on the bed and watched Jamie and Maeve's transformations. Jamie was finished first, and Ryan wished she could nibble all of the soft pink lipstick off her luscious lips, but she didn't think Jamie's careful application should be ruined this early in the day. There would be plenty of time at the reception for that.

Catherine did an excellent job making Maeve look absolutely lovely for her big day. The makeup she applied was understated and tasteful, just perfect for a morning wedding. They decided that Maeve should not put her suit on until she was ready to walk out the door, but Catherine wanted to decide on jewelry. Everyone gathered around and looked at the selection she'd brought. Moira and Jamie were in favor of a sterling silver necklace with a matching bracelet, but Maeve decided that she wanted to wear her one piece of nice jewelry. "I have a pearl necklace that was my grandmother's," she said. She pulled it out of its case and everyone agreed that it was just perfect...a single strand of cultured pearls that would hang down just to the second button of her jacket.

"I thought pearls would be nice," Catherine agreed and pointed out a lovely pair of pearl earrings in a setting of tiny diamonds.

"I have something you might fancy, Aunt Maeve," Ryan said, pulling out a small box lined with tissue paper.

"Oh, Ryan," Maeve said, looking like she was on the verge of tears. In the blink of an eye, all of the other women left the room, allowing Maeve and Ryan a moment alone. "Are you sure, sweetheart?"

"Of course I'm sure," she said as she bent over to fasten the tear-shaped pearls onto her aunt's ears. "You got the necklace, Mama got the earrings. I think the set should be reunited on your wedding day."

Maeve wrapped her niece in a tender hug, holding on for a long time. "It's nice to have something of Fi's with me," she whispered. "Besides her Marty, that is," she added with a small laugh. She looked up at Ryan with a hint of doubt in her green eyes and asked, "Are we doing the right thing?"

"Yes," Ryan said, her voice strong, and full of conviction. "You are most definitely doing the right thing. You're going to make my father a very happy man, Aunt Maeve, and I know he'll make you happy, too. This is absolutely as it should be." Ryan placed a tender kiss on her aunt's cheek and said, "You know, I'm a little afraid of being too greedy today. I'm going to walk Da down the aisle and be your attendant. Don't you think maybe we should share the wealth?"

The older woman blinked up at her and asked, "What do you mean?"

"I think Aunt Moira should stand up for you. "I think it would mean a lot to her."

Maeve gave her niece yet another hug, and whispered, "I think you're right, love. I think it would mean a lot…to both of us. Thank you, Ryan. Thank you for being so thoughtful."

"Just trying to be fair."

The older woman sniffed a little, smiling when Ryan handed her a tissue. "Sweetheart, do you still want to refer to me as your aunt?"

Ryan smiled back and said, "I found myself referring to you and Da as my parents the other day," she admitted. "It sounded right… strange, but right."

Maeve gave her another fierce hug, on the verge of losing the war with her composure. "I'd be proud to call you my daughter," she sniffed, "and I'm honored that you feel comfortable calling your father and I your parents. But what about just me? You could drop the 'aunt' and call me Maeve," she suggested.

Ryan nodded, smiling the whole time. "I'll give it a try," she agreed. "It will take a while, and I might not do it in private, but it would be nice not to have to explain why I call my father's wife 'Aunt Maeve'."

"I'm sure we're not the oddest blended family in the area. This is San Francisco, you know."

"Indeed it is, and you're going to be the loveliest bride in the whole city. Now let's get you dressed and prove it!"

Maeve was just slipping into her jacket when Annie and Caitlin showed up, and befitting her years of experience with toddlers, Maeve took the jacket right off and went out to greet the pair in her robe. After receiving a sloppy kiss, she went back into her room and got dressed, this time with Moira's assistance.

The pair came out a short time later, and everyone made over Maeve's striking appearance. Moira said, "My lovely sister has just asked me to stand up for her. Isn't that grand?"

"That's wonderful," Jamie agreed, having had a feeling her partner was going to bow out.

"I just wish I had something to wear that fit in better," she said. "I only brought a dark dress."

Catherine went to her large suit bag and looked into its depths. "Aren't you close to my size?" she asked speculatively.

"Yes, I suppose so," Moira replied.

"Well, I couldn't make up my mind this morning," Catherine related, "so I brought a few things. Why don't you see if one of these outfits pleases you, Moira?"

All of them blinked as Catherine pulled out three absolutely gorgeous suits…each completely complementary to Maeve's outfit. "How…how…?"

"Don't ask, Aunt Moira," Ryan warned. "Catherine works in mysterious ways."

While Catherine and Maeve fussed over Moira, Jamie took Ryan into the bedroom to finish getting dressed. "Some sweet girl offered up her spot to her aunt, didn't she?" she asked wrapping her arms around Ryan's waist.

"Uh-huh," Ryan murmured. "And I think some sweet woman

brought some extra outfits knowing that my aunt might not have a very extensive wardrobe."

"That's a definite possibility," Jamie agreed, smiling as she thought of her mother's planning for the day. "She's pretty sly, isn't she?"

"She's adorable," Ryan insisted. "Just like her daughter." The dark head tilted as Ryan said, "If this had been left up to us, poor Aunt Maeve would be wearing her one nice dress, I'd be in jeans and a T-shirt, and we'd be having the usual barbecue in the back yard afterward."

"There's nothing wrong with that, if that's what you want. But I don't think that's what Maeve really wanted."

"No, it's not. I think the little touches the Evans women have provided will give her years and years of fond memories."

"I haven't done anything. This is my mom's work."

"Uh-huh. Who went out and bought Da that beautiful new shirt and tie? Who talked me into buying this lovely suit? You've had your sweet little hands in this affair, too. And I appreciate it very much."

"It's been fun," Jamie said. "And seeing how excited your aunt is makes me really glad that I could help."

"She is excited, isn't she? It's great to see her this way. Her first marriage was really rough. She deserves some sunshine in her life."

"I agree completely, Tiger. Now let's get dressed and let the fun begin."

The pair emerged to a series of "oohs" and "ahhs". Everyone except Caitlin expressed their pleasure over the young women's attire, but they didn't hold her abstention against her. Fashion was just not Caitlin's thing, even though she looked divine herself. To everyone except Annie's surprise, Catherine'd had a dress made for the child in fabric that perfectly matched Maeve's dress. The sterling silver color looked fantastic on the toddler, with her pale skin and white-blonde hair, which had recently been trimmed for the occasion, courtesy of Conor's latest trip to Giancarlo.

Moira was beautifully attired in a pale mint green suit, and Annie had decided to jump on the Evans' fashion bandwagon as well. She wasn't quite as small as the other women, but so long as she didn't breathe very deeply or eat much, the third suit, a blue silk, looked marvelous on her.

Jamie and Ryan were the only ones who did not exactly mirror the cool colors theme, although Ryan wore a sterling silver top under her elegant black suit. The top was a heavy satin with spaghetti straps that left her broad shoulders bare. The loose fabric flowed attractively when she removed her jacket, which Jamie was sure she would do at the first opportunity. Her blue diamonds were nestled against her earlobes, and the maiden appearance of her platinum necklace was a definite success.

Ryan's suit showed off her long, slim body perfectly. When Jamie told the tailor that Ryan was twenty-five pounds underweight he agreed to leave room to let the pants and jacket out, but to tailor the clothing to her current size, and he had done a beautiful job.

When Ryan first put on the jacket, Jamie had to stifle a laugh as she stood in front of the mirror for a few minutes, flexing her arms in every direction, obviously amazed to have a jacket fit properly.

For her part, Jamie chose a completely different look, deciding on a peach suit in a soft, rich Ultra-suede. The jacket was long, coming to mid-thigh, and the skirt was a little shorter than she normally wore, extending just a few inches below the hem of the jacket. Ryan thought she looked absolutely scrumptious, and her wandering hands had been teasingly slapped quite a few times while they were trying to get dressed.

"Well, I suppose we're off, eh?" Maeve asked looking around.

"Do we have enough cars?" Catherine asked. "I found a parking space just a block down. I can take three people."

"Oh, we'll walk," Maeve decided. "It's only a few blocks." Everyone agreed that walking was just as easy as trying to fit into the available cars, but as they exited the door they all stopped abruptly at the sight of a huge white limousine double-parked in front of the house, taking up most of the narrow street.

All eyes turned to Catherine, but she protested, "Don't look at me! This wasn't my doing—although it's a fabulous idea."

Now all heads turned to Jamie, but she shook her head too. "Not me."

Ryan piped up and warned, "Don't even ask!"

The driver got out of the car and asked, "Maeve Driscoll?" horribly butchering her first name.

"That would be me," she agreed, approaching the car cautiously. "May I ask who arranged for this?"

The driver pulled some paperwork from his pocket and looked at it quickly. "Martin O'Flaherty ma'am."

Maeve nearly fainted at the thought of her notoriously frugal fiancé throwing money away so frivolously, but she was thoroughly pleased with the gesture. "He never ceases to surprise me," she said as she allowed the driver to help her in.

"That's what being married to an O'Flaherty is all about," Jamie laughed as she made eye contact with her grinning partner. There was room for all, but Ryan didn't want to bother with the trial of securing Caitlin's car seat, so she volunteered to take the baby in her stroller, since she was the only one wearing flats. Receiving only token complaint, she and Cait set off, with Ryan reminding herself that she had to act like an adult today, and not challenge herself to try to beat the limo to the church.

Even though she didn't try to, they nearly beat the big car, mostly because the car was too big to turn around, and had to go down to 24th Street to do so. They all gathered in a small room in the nave of the church, just out of view of the guests who were still arriving.

Ryan peeked into the church to see her three uncles serving as ushers. "Ooh...Uncle Malachy has a new suit," she whispered.

"Get back in here and behave," Jamie said, tugging on her suit jacket.

Kevin and Tommy poked their heads in, and Ryan gasped as she realized, "Hey, I'm not supposed to be here! I've gotta go find Da." Jamie kissed her goodbye, and Ryan paused just long enough to give her aunt a tender hug before she took off.

Ryan dashed around the side of the church and found her father and brothers huddled around the entrance, fussing with each other's ties. When Martin spied his daughter his face broke into an enormous smile as he said, "Well, if it isn't the second prettiest girl in the whole county."

"Smart, Da, very smart," she smiled, kissing him on the cheek.

"Aunt Maeve should always be the first."

He looked down the walk and asked, "Where's Jamie?"

"Oh, she's going to hang out until they're ready, then go in with Catherine."

Martin gave her a look that seemed to question her sanity. "Why isn't she with us, Siobhán? I thought my whole family was going to escort me."

Ryan blinked at him and said, "She didn't walk with us during rehearsal, Da. Why didn't you say something then?"

"She was running around with her mother and the florist. I assumed she could figure out her part without extensive practice. It is just walking down an aisle, ya know."

"I…I had not idea you'd include her, Da." Ryan's expression was thoroughly befuddled.

"Oh, for the love of Mike. I'll go get her myself."

"No, Da, you aren't supposed to see Aunt Maeve. I'll go get her." Ryan took off before he could say another word and got to Jamie just as her uncle Malachy was set to escort her to her seat. "Jamie!" she whispered loudly from the door of the church. The blonde head swiveled and cocked in question. Ryan made a frantic gesture, and Jamie released Malachy's arm and dashed over to Ryan.

"What's wrong?"

"I screwed up. Da assumed you knew you were supposed to walk down the aisle with us. I don't know why, but that didn't even dawn on me."

"Oh, that's so sweet!" She gave Ryan a hug, but pulled back. "Are you okay with that? It's fine with me if you want it to just be you and your brothers."

"Did you get into the Communion wine?" she asked with falsely solicitous concern. "Don't be ridiculous! Of course I want you there. Let's go."

When they approached the men, Martin looked at his daughter and gave her the bad news, "I'm afraid you've dropped down to the third spot on the prettiest girl contest, Siobhán. Jamie has you beat by a mile."

"Thanks for including me, Martin," Jamie said as she hugged him. "It means a lot to me."

"I'm so sorry I didn't make myself clear, love. It never dawned on me that you wouldn't know you were part of the group."

"I do now," she smiled. "The music has started. I think that's our cue."

They walked around to the entrance of the church and lined up in birth order. Brendan led the way, with Conor and Rory behind him. Ryan and Jamie each took one of Martin's arms and escorted him up the aisle to the whispered greetings and bright smiles of the assembled guests. When they reached the front pew, each of the children kissed Martin and slid into their seats. Martin's brother Francis emerged from the side door and stood beside him, clapping a firm hand onto his shoulder for support.

When they were all in place, the music changed, alerting all to the procession about to begin. Annie led the way carrying Caitlin, who was determinedly trying to remove the small satin pillow that had been secured to her wrist, two simple gold wedding bands sewn onto it.

Moira was next, looking absolutely elegant in her flattering suit and the sterling silver jewelry that she had easily been convinced to wear.

Last in the procession was Maeve, flanked by her two sons, both looking handsome in their dark suits and silver ties. When they reached the front of the church, both of them kissed Maeve, and then Tommy placed her right hand in Martin's and the beaming couple stood next to each other in front of Father Villarreal.

The priest made a few brief opening remarks, and then began the Mass. The Catholic tradition required a full Mass as part of the wedding ceremony, but it didn't seem as though many people were able to concentrate on it. All eyes were on the pair who stood next to each other, unable to stop the furtive smiles and little handclasps that they continued to share, their attention focused solely on each other.

Father Villarreal had the grace to keep his homily short, spending just a few minutes reflecting on the path that had brought the couple together. As soon as his remarks were finished, he questioned Martin and Maeve on their decision, asking if they were prepared for this lifetime commitment. When they had answered the questions, Moira and Francis stood next to their siblings as witnesses while the couple took their vows. They spoke the traditional vows, neither being the sort of person who thought they could do a better job than had already been done in the scriptures.

Martin's hand was shaking visibly as he partially slipped the band sequentially onto Maeve's second, third and fifth fingers, as he pledged his love in the name of the Father, the Son and the Holy Spirit. Letting his eyes lock onto her mist-green orbs he whispered, "Amen," as he slid it onto her ring finger, where it nestled comfortably. Maeve recreated the tradition, then Father Villarreal blessed the couple and said a final prayer, officially marking them as husband and wife.

To the surprise of the non-Catholics in the crowd, now the heart of the Mass began, clearly an anti-climatic event. The church was still buzzing with excitement, the couple was brimming with joy, and their families couldn't wait to shower them with affection; but that all had to wait while the most solemn part of the Mass was celebrated.

Catherine privately mused that anyone with an iota of theatre or opera knowledge would know not to put the focus of the piece so near the beginning of the performance, but she never pretended to understand Catholic traditions, so she kept her opinions to herself.

The rest of the Mass proceeded apace, and after the recitation of the Lord's Prayer, Father Villarreal gave a blessing to the couple and invited the congregation to offer one another the sign of peace. That was the opening the families had been awaiting, and they all poured out of the front pews to hug and kiss the bride and groom. This normally short element of the Mass took a good ten minutes, but once again, they all had to return to their seats for Communion. Catherine was quite surprised when Jamie got up with the rest of the O'Flaherty's to participate in the ceremony, and when her daughter returned to the pew she leaned over and asked, "Have you joined the Catholic church?"

"No." Jamie smiled, looking a little impish. "But I believe in a lot more of the elements of the faith than Ryan does, so I think I'm entitled."

When the Mass finally drew to a close, the newly married couple exited the church followed by the attendants, then the immediate families. They decided to stand on the front steps and have a quick receiving line, since some of their guests would not make it down to Hillsborough for the reception. All of the children, both attendants, and Martin and Maeve lined the stairs, with the line getting slowed repeatedly as Ryan doggedly introduced every stranger to her partner.

Ryan and Jamie were standing near the entrance to the church, so they were the first ones to spot Bryant. He gave them both a sheepish look and said, "Sorry I didn't get here in time to say hello before the service. I just barely made it."

"It's great to have you here, no matter when you come," Ryan said, wrapping him into a hug.

Maeve spotted his tall figure and reached across Jamie to draw him close. "You get right into this line, young man," she said. "You're a part of my family."

"Oh, Maeve, you don't want to do that," he said, trying to beg off.

"Nonsense," she insisted. "It's like having Michael here with us. Please stay."

He looked into those warm green eyes and felt all of his excuses fade away. "Where do you want me?" he asked.

"Right here," she indicated, drawing him next to her. Martin greeted him warmly, then Kevin and Tommy added their hellos and they settled down to meet the rest of the slightly perplexed guests.

After a quick stop at the rectory to sign all of the appropriate documents, the couple entered their limousine for the trip down to Hillsborough. Maeve wanted some of the children to ride with them, but Martin gave her a look that quickly made her rescind the offer. As the door closed, he raised the window between the driver and the passenger compartment, pleased to see that the glass was heavily smoked so they had complete privacy.

"Do you really think I'm going to spend the next hour in this car with a bunch of kids babbling away, Mrs. O'Flaherty? I don't part with my money easily, ya know, and I want my full value for renting this boat." Maeve just beamed at him, too overjoyed to even bring herself to tease him. He leaned over to the refrigerator, extracted a split of champagne, and opened it with more skill than Maeve knew he had. He was giving her a sly grin the entire time, and it was only as he clinked his glass with hers that his face grew serious. "I've had more happiness in my life than any man deserves, Maeve, and you've been with me through most of the best days of my life. First as a sister-in-law, then as a second mother to my children, but always, always as the best friend that a man could ever wish for. Our relationship will be very different in some ways after today, but the essence of what we have remains exactly as it's always been," he pledged. "I've always considered that you were one of the greatest blessings of my life, and our marriage will only serve to enhance that feeling." He leaned forward and placed a gentle kiss upon her lips, moving just a few inches away as he said, "I love you, Maeve. I always have, and I always will."

They drank from their glasses and she snuggled up against his broad chest. "I don't know what I've done to deserve a man like you, Martin, but I'm forever grateful that you've chosen me."

"Now, that's where you're wrong," Martin decided. "You're the one who chose me. I've been under your spell for years, Mrs. O'Flaherty, and I'm quite sure that enchantment is unending."

After loading up the Boxster with a change of clothes, Jamie and Ryan took off for Hillsborough, wanting to arrive before the rest of the guests. Jamie was driving, and as they got onto the freeway Ryan mused reflectively, "You know, it was kinda fun to be one of the girls today. I don't think I've ever done that."

"What do you mean? You do girl things with me all of the time."

"Ahh, not really." She chuckled. "Although I clearly enjoy the fruits of your womanhood, we don't really do girl stuff. I mean things like doing each other's hair and putting on makeup. I honestly don't think I've ever been in a room with a group of women while we all got dressed for an event. It was kinda cool," she decided. "I think I'm on an estrogen high."

"I'm glad you enjoyed it. I sometimes forget how male-centered your upbringing was. Didn't you ever have slumber parties with your friends in elementary school? That's when you start doing all of that girlie stuff."

"No, I didn't do that. I stayed at Sara's a lot, but we never did that kind of stuff. We were more into playing on the Internet or watching TV. They had cable," she informed her partner, her eyebrows twitching.

"What did they have…porn?"

"No. Just regular cable. But we didn't have it, so it seemed really exotic to me."

"You still don't have cable, do you?"

"Huh-uh. My cousins all have it, so we used to go to one of their houses to watch a game that wasn't on broadcast channels. Da didn't want us to watch TV much, and he figured we wouldn't be tempted if there wasn't much to choose from. Course, he might have just been being cheap," she added.

"He sure surprised the heck out of your aunt," Jamie laughed. "Springing for a limo was quite out of character."

"Yeah. I think he's really gotten into the whole thing, to tell you the truth. He really looked happy today, didn't he?"

"Oh, yeah." Jamie smiled broadly at her partner and said, "I've never seen him smile so much. His cheeks are gonna be sore."

"He deserves it," Ryan decided. "He's been alone far too long."

Chapter Twelve

Maeve let her hand drift down to capture Martin's left hand, looking carefully at his new ring. "Are you sure that you want to wear this, Marty? It's really all right if you—"

"Hush," he whispered, touching her lips with his index finger. "Of course I'm sure." They had discussed the issue of rings on two occasions, with Martin assuring her that he wanted to replace the ring he had worn for over thirty years with one that she would give him. But she had noticed that he still wore the band at dinner the previous evening, and she knew that he was struggling.

Unbeknownst to Maeve, Martin had risen early that morning and traveled down to old St. Patrick's Church, where he and Fi had been married. He'd sat in the sparsely filled church as the six-thirty Mass let out, awash in the memories of his first wedding. He knew that the vow he took that day was no longer in effect—that since death had parted him and his beloved wife, he was free to move on. But he had never taken off the ring that she had given him that day, and it was harder than he could have imagined to even contemplate doing so.

Tears had rolled down his cheeks as he reached for the ring and tried to tug it off, suddenly alarmed that he might have to stop by the firehouse and have one of his co-workers cut it off. But determined pressure finally did the trick, and the band had come free, resting in the shaking palm of his right hand. He'd cried so hard that the band ad been all but obscured, but he'd managed to lift it to his lips and kiss it, just as he had done on the day that Fionnuala had given it to him.

He'd stayed in the church for nearly an hour, memories of the life they'd shared settling over him like a warm blanket. It had been nearly eight o'clock when he was finally composed enough to leave the church, but he'd managed to return home before he was missed. The last thing he'd done before he left the house for St. Phil's was to tuck the ring into the inside pocket of his jacket, unable to part with it.

Maeve watched the panoply of emotions cross her new husband's face and knew that the issue was still not settled for him, no matter his protestations. "I know this isn't the common thing to do, Marty," she said softly. "But I think it's fitting in our case."

"What's that, sweetheart?" he asked, cocking his head in question.

"I'd like it if you wore the ring that Fi gave you on your other hand," she said, lifting the unadorned right hand and brushing her lips across the knuckles. "One of the things I most love about you is how much you still love her. Having you wear that ring would just remind me of what a loyal, devoted man you are."

His composure failed him for the second time that day, as he buried his face into his wife's neck, shaking as tears once again streaked down his cheeks. "Are you sure?" he rasped.

"Yes," Maeve whispered, rubbing her hand in soothing circles on his back. "I'm very sure."

With a trembling sigh, he sat up and reached into his inner pocket, pulling out the ring that Maeve had been certain was on his person. His watery smile nearly broke her heart, and Maeve's hand covered his as he struggled a bit, but managed to get the ring over his knuckle. "Thank you," he said, gazing into her eyes with all of the love he felt for her. "Thank you for understanding."

"She'll always be a part of both of us, Marty. Let's not try to shut her out of our memories."

"I won't," he whispered, his smile growing brighter. "I promise that I won't."

After surveying the grand buffet that Marta and her assistants had created, Jamie went inside to express her appreciation to the cook. "Marta, how did you do all of this? Mother told me what your budget was."

"I had a challenge," she admitted. "And you know I love that."

"Come on, tell me your secret."

"It's not a secret. I go to the Costco to buy things for my church. Since your mother told me about the party, every time I see they have a special on something I buy it, and then figure out how to make it part of the menu. The freezer was bursting."

"Thanks so much for working so hard, Marta. It means a lot to all of us."

The older woman hugged her fondly. "I love to do things like this. It makes me feel like I finally earn my salary."

The guests began arriving relatively close to the announced time, instead of hours early. Catherine assumed this was in deference to the party being at her house. At one-forty-five she sought Martin out and said, "I think your family is taking it easy on me. I said two o'clock, but I assumed they'd come directly after the service."

"Oh, give them a chance. Soon they'll be imposing on you routinely."

It was quite nice to have just the immediate family together for a while, allowing everyone to spend a few minutes congratulating the happy couple before the crush of guests arrived. Catherine had arranged for a valet service so the neighborhood wouldn't be filled with cars, and as the first guests arrived Jamie asked Martin if the limo was going to wait for them to take them back home. He looked at her with a puzzled smile and said, "They charge by the hour, love," as if that made the question moot.

The guests began to pour into the back yard, and as more and more arrived Maeve went up to Catherine and asked, "Where should we put our gifts?"

"Gifts?"

Maeve blinked at her and rephrased. "People have brought gifts for us. Where should we put them?"

"They brought gifts here?" she asked, astounded that someone would actually bring a gift to the reception.

"Well, yes, of course, they did. Don't your people give gifts for a wedding?"

"Yes…of course they do," she nodded. "They send them to the bride's home well before the ceremony."

Maeve blinked again and said, "Oh! Well, we don't do that. We bring them along and then we open them after the meal."

"You open them?" Catherine gaped.

Maeve tilted her head and said, "They're gifts, dear, of course we open them."

Her eyes still wide, Catherine excused herself, saying, "I'll have Helena set up a table or two, all right?"

"Brilliant!" Maeve agreed, puzzled over the odd habits of the Evans family.

Jordan and Mia arrived right on time, both women tastefully attired in dresses. Mia's was a clingy black strapless with a short multi-color nubby silk jacket in shades of blues and greens. Jordan's was a cool blue sheath that nearly matched her eyes. Her long, lean frame looked even longer than usual in the striking dress, serving to accentuate the difference in the couple's heights. Mia obviously didn't mind the discrepancy, since she hadn't even chosen to wear heels, telling Jamie, "I wore flats so we could dance. We are gonna dance, aren't we?"

"Count on it. Rory's band is getting set up right now."

"Cool." Mia scanned the grounds and smiled. "Your mom really outdid herself. The place looks amazing."

"Well, my mom had the ideas," Jamie reminded her. "The staff did the work. Go tell Marta and Helena that you appreciate them, will you?"

"Sure. Does she have any of those homemade biscotti lying around?"

"Probably. Especially since my mom knows that Caitlin loves them."

"She's not the only one," Mia said, setting off in search of the cook.

The O'Flaherty children had sprung for a professional photographer, and he was busily recording the event, rushing to obtain a majority of the pictures "before everyone's shoes and ties come off" according to the groom's predictions. Once the formal photos were completed, Annie took Caitlin inside and removed her silk dress, knowing that it was only a matter of time before it was ruined. She came back out in a pair of pink overalls and a pink, yellow, baby blue, and mint green plaid shirt, a recent gift from Jamie. Someone was assigned full time to watch the toddler, due to her propensity to head for water. The pool was a powerful lure, however, and only her beloved biscotti could tear her attention away from it. Mia took over watching the baby for a while, and the pair sat in a chair together, both contentedly chewing on their treats.

As soon as everyone had arrived they began to serve lunch. Catherine had set up for a buffet, deciding that the group was too large for a formal meal. Round tables had been arranged on the lawn, each seating eight. Martin and Maeve ate quickly, then moved from table to table, chatting with each group of guests for a while.

Bryant fit right in with the Driscoll brothers, and he joined them, Annie and Caitlin at a table. Within a short while, Caitlin was deeply in love with the tall, dark, stranger, and they were inextricable bonded for the rest of the afternoon.

Mia and Jordan, Jamie and Ryan, Brendan and Maggie, Conor and Rory sat together, the group teasing and joking as usual. Maggie was sitting next to Jordan and they were engaged in an intense discussion, neither of them looking up when Brendan stood to return to the buffet. "I'm getting some more of that fabulous soup. Refills anyone?"

Mia nodded, then Brendan gave Jordan a questioning look but Mia told him, "She can't eat it, Brendan, she's allergic to peanuts." Conor gave her a funny look at that comment, but she didn't notice his puzzled glance.

They all ate more than was prudent, and after the meal everyone was slumped a bit in their chairs. Mia's hand was on the back of

Jordan's chair, and she unconsciously began to stroke the soft, bare skin that was so delightfully exposed to her touch. Jordan gave her a warning look, but Mia either didn't understand or didn't care if their relationship was revealed. The band set up, and as soon as they started to play, Mia looked at Ryan and asked, "Do we have to wait for the bride and groom to start the first dance?"

"No way. My father would kick Rory's butt if he put him on the spot like that. Go right ahead, girls."

Mia stood and stuck her hand out. "Okay, let's go!" Jordan took her extended hand and followed her to the stone pool surround, where the surface was most conducive to dancing. Jamie and Ryan followed, and soon many of the guests had joined them.

The young women danced as though their bodies were quite used to being in close proximity, and when Brendan spotted the dark scowl on Conor's face he discreetly asked, "Hey, what's bothering you?"

Conor twitched his head in the direction of the dancers and asked rhetorically, "Who says they don't recruit." With that he pushed his chair back and left the party, headed in the direction of the gardens.

After dancing to a few songs, the young women returned to the table. "Where's Conor?" Ryan asked.

Brendan shrugged and said, "He looked like he wanted a little space." He gave Ryan a meaningful look, and she shrugged in response, not really understanding Brendan's comment.

Jordan, however, did, and she leaned over and whispered something in Mia's ear. Mia flinched and nodded a couple of times, finally standing up and asking Brendan, "Which way did he go?"

As Mia got up, Maggie leaned over and smiled at Jordan, continuing their conversation. "So, how long have you and Mia been dating?"

Jordan's eyes widened, and she looked at Ryan for help. "How long have we been 'dating'?" she asked, her face paling a little.

Ryan smiled at Maggie and patted Jordan's back. "They've only been dating a short time. She's still getting used to it."

Maggie smiled in return, looking a little puzzled, but hiding it well. "You make a very cute couple."

"Thanks," Jordan said, brightening a little.

"I didn't know Mia was a lesbian," Brendan commented, just trying to stay involved in the conversation.

Three voices joined to say, "She's not!" Jamie, Ryan and Jordan shared a glance and then broke into a laugh, rendering Maggie and Brendan thoroughly confused.

⁂

"Hi," Mia said as she found Conor sitting on a garden bench, his feet stuck straight out in front of him. He looked to be sulking, and she felt a flash of irritation at his mood.

"Hi," he replied, not meeting her eyes. "What's up?"

"That's what I wanted to ask you," she said, sitting down next to him. "Are you as pissed off as you look?"

He folded his arms across his chest and asked the question that had been racing through his mind since he'd realized what was going on between the two women. "Did you stop seeing me because of her?"

"No," Mia said clearly. She paused and looked at Conor for a moment then added, "Not that it's any of your business, but no, I didn't."

He finally made eye contact, and she was shocked to see the pain he obviously felt reflected in his deep blue eyes. "Are you serious about her?"

Mia took in a breath and decided to tell the truth—to both herself and Conor. "Yes, I am," she said softly.

"So you used that 'I don't wanna be tied down thing' just as an excuse to get rid of me, huh?" He actually looked like he was going to cry, and Mia felt a little sick to her stomach. She knew that Conor had been more serious about her than she'd been about him, but she assumed he'd shrug it off and forget about her in a short time.

"Conor," she said, her voice gentle and soft, "I didn't lie to you. I'm not ready to settle down and get married any time soon. I don't want to have children until I'm at least thirty. I was completely honest with you about that—really."

"Then how can you be serious about her so soon? What do you even mean when you say you're serious about someone?"

"That's a good question. I wish I knew." She got up and paced, the stone crunching under her feet. "I think I'm more serious about Jordan than she is about me."

"Sucks, doesn't it?" he asked, staring at the ground once again.

"Yeah, it does," she agreed, placing her hand on his shoulder. He looked up at her, his eyes still carrying pain. "I'm sorry that I hurt you, but I want you to know that I meant exactly what I said. If I was a few years older, I would have fallen for you—hard. You're exactly what I'd love in a man...in a husband."

"But I'm not what you want in a woman," he said, stating the obvious. "Did you know you were a lesbian when you slept with me? Is that what the problem was?"

She rolled her eyes, surprised at the way he framed his question. "I'm not a lesbian, Conor, but if I was, it wouldn't be a 'problem'."

"I didn't mean it like that..." he started to say, but when she fixed him with a raised eyebrow he admitted, "I guess I did mean it that way. I guess I'd prefer to think you were a lesbian than that you just like her better than you like me."

"I guess I can understand that," Mia said, as she patted his shoulder. "But it's not like that. It's not that I like her better than you. Things just kinda clicked with Jordan. We're the same age, we're both afraid of commitment, we're both a little hazy on our sexual orientations...I don't know...it just felt less serious with her. It felt more like we were just playing around, you know?"

He nodded.

"This was nothing I'd planned, and I swear I would never have gone out with her if I'd thought she wanted to get serious."

"So my mistake was being honest?" he asked, his voice still reflecting his hurt.

"That's never a mistake, and I think you know that. Would it have been better to go out for a few months, or a year, and then find out I didn't want to get married for another eight years? Gimme a break!"

"What if she wanted to be with you forever? Would you marry her?"

It was really bugging Mia that Conor refused to say Jordan's name, but she wouldn't give him the satisfaction of knowing that it irked her. "I can't answer that. It's not gonna happen, and it doesn't do any good to speculate. I do know that even if we got together and stayed together, I still wouldn't have kids for another eight or nine years. I refuse to give up my youth until I've really lived it, and I think that was the biggest problem between you and me."

He nodded somberly. "You're right. I'm a lot closer to wanting to settle down than you are. It just caught me by surprise. I didn't expect to feel like I did about you. You just felt right to me, ya know? I've never really felt like that before…especially so soon."

"We just had bad timing. You were born a little early…I was born a little late. It just can't be helped."

He sat there in silence for a few moments, and she could tell he was considering his thoughts carefully. Finally, he took in a breath and said, "If you were ready to settle down, would you have taken a chance on me? Be honest with me," he said, showing his vulnerability so clearly that it shocked her.

Mia answered instantly. "Yes. If I wasn't with Jordan, and I was ready to settle down, I would chase you down and never let go. I'd be like a little pit bull grabbing onto your pant leg."

"Okay," he sighed, finally giving her a small smile. "That makes me feel better. When I saw you with her I just felt like you'd lied to me."

Mia extended a hand, and Conor took it as he got to his feet. "I know this is hard for you, but if you don't start calling Jordan by her name I'm going to belt you one."

"You're my kinda girl," he said fondly, slipping his arm around her shoulders. "Jordan," he enunciated carefully, "is one lucky woman."

"I'm not sure she knows that, but thanks for the vote of confidence."

By the time Mia and Conor returned, most of the younger generation had changed into casual clothes and the gift opening had begun. Mia spotted Catherine standing in the back of the crowd, and she sidled up next to her. "What in the world is going on?"

Assuming Mia had been schooled in traditional WASP gifting, Catherine couldn't resist teasing her. "They're opening their gifts, of course. Is yours up there?"

Mia blinked at her and said, "Uhm, I sent a gift to the house… last week."

Catherine laughed and said, "I'm just playing with you. I was a bit surprised by this myself." They watched for a few more minutes and Catherine said, "You know, this does look like a lot of fun. Rather like a birthday party."

"Yeah. Plus, doing it in public shames people into giving you really nice stuff."

Conor decided to go to the bar for drinks for the table, and he nodded in Ryan's direction and asked, "Help me carry?"

"Sure."

As they were alone he said, "It would have been nice of you to tell me that Mia was seeing someone else."

She blinked at him and said, "Why would I do that? How does it even concern you?"

"I looked like a fool today, and you could have prevented it."

She bit back the sarcastic reply that was itching to leave her mouth and said, "Look, I'm sorry you feel like you looked foolish, but I'm not in the business of giving updates on my friends and their dating lives. I respect your confidences, so I have to respect hers, too."

"Well, you could have at least told me Jordan was a dyke. That would have given me a clue."

The bar was set up near the entrance to the garden, and Ryan grasped Conor none-too-gently by the upper arm and pushed him down one of the paths. "Look," she said, her eyes flashing with anger, "I know your feelings are hurt, but don't you dare use that term with that tone of voice. That is unacceptable!" she said fiercely as she gave his arm a good shake before she released him.

"I'm sorry," he muttered, the tips of his ears turning pink from embarrassment. "I didn't mean that like it sounded. I'm just…

I'm…"

"You're hurt," she snapped. "You really liked Mia. It didn't work out. Someone else is with her now, and she seems happy. It makes sense that you're hurt, but that's no reason to blame Jordan." She gave him a rough push. "She didn't take Mia from you. Mia wasn't yours."

Conor looked at her, obviously stung by her harsh tone. His expression morphed quickly from embarrassment to a touching vulnerability. "I'm sorry. I really am. This kinda thing…" He held his hands up, showing his confusion. "Has never happened to me before."

She wracked her mind, and realized that he was speaking the truth. Conor had never been dumped by anyone he cared about. He was actually more phobic than she had been about getting close—with the exception of his one long-term girlfriend, Melissa, whom he dated for two years. She intentionally gentled her voice and said, "Conor, I know this is hard for you, but you need to look at reality. You went out with Mia twice. I know you felt there was a lot of chemistry there, but you don't know her that well, and she doesn't know you very well, either. She wasn't rejecting you—heck, she didn't know you well enough to reject you."

He gave her a startled look and she assured him, "You know what I mean. I think you see Mia more as an archetype than as a person. You just don't know her well enough to be this bothered by her choice to be with Jordan."

"I don't know what an archetype is, but I see Mia as a person. Maybe this has never happened to you, but I just clicked with her. I don't want to give up on her."

"Fine." She tossed her hands in the air, as though ridding herself of the problem. "You can sit around and waste you time waiting for her to break up with Jordan, but I wouldn't advise it. They're really getting close, but even if they weren't, Mia decided not to be with you even before she met Jordan. That's not an insignificant fact, Bro."

"Maybe," he said. "I guess we'll just have to wait and see."

He started to walk back towards the party, but she placed her hand on his chest to stop him. "Don't let this get to your ego. Mia isn't a prize—she's a person."

Shaking his head he said, "That's where you're wrong, Sis. She's both."

·ঌ

As the afternoon went on, more and more neighbors, fellow firefighters and people from the parish took their leave. By the time dusk fell, about thirty people remained, most of them family members. A few of the cousins had brought dates, and eventually most of the clan wound up on the dance floor. The crowd was no longer paired off in couples; now all of the women danced with all of the men, without regard to sexual orientation. Ryan noticed that Conor made it a point to dance with Jordan a time or two, and she was pleased to see that he was sulking less.

The band was playing mostly Irish music, most of their selections very sprightly, and easy to dance to in an exuberant manner. They threw in an occasional ballad, some of them popular songs, just to appeal to everyone. As one ballad began, Ryan spotted her mother-in-law standing near the pool, checking on some detail, taking her role of hostess very seriously. Ryan walked up and adopted a formal air and asked, "Would you care to dance?"

Catherine blinked at her in surprise, but then her mouth twitched into a grin and she placed her hand in Ryan's and allowed herself to be led to the dance area.

"Have you ever danced with a woman before, Catherine?" Ryan's eyes were shining merrily.

"Let's see now…have I ever danced with a woman?" She acted as though the question merited great thought, finally saying, "I think not, Ryan, not unless you count junior high."

"I don't," Ryan said, and drew her close by placing a hand in the small of her back. "This doesn't make you uncomfortable, does it?"

"No, of course not." She looked up at Ryan and smiled. "You know, given how most men feel about dancing, I should always dance with women. The only problem would be who would lead." Grinning, she added, "I bet you never have that problem, do you."

"No, I tend to lead. Byproduct of my size, I suppose."

"I think your personality might be a small contributing factor," Catherine said dryly. "You're no shrinking violet." She let out a light chuckle, adding, "Besides, you dance beautifully."

"Thanks. I don't tell many people this, I wanted to be a dancer for the Niners when I was a little girl."

"That's a switch," Catherine laughed. "I could see you dreaming of being a defensive back, but I can't see you as a dancer."

"Yeah, I think that was my only sex-typed goal. Of course, Jamie thinks I wanted to be a dancer just to be around a lot of good-looking girls." She paused a beat and said, "She might be right."

Catherine slid her arm around Ryan and gave her a squeeze. "I'm having such a good time today."

"I hope you know how much we all appreciate this. It's made all the difference in making this day memorable for Da and my aunt."

"The pleasure is definitely all mine."

Just then Jamie swept by, leading Maeve around the dance floor. "Will you give me lessons in how to lead, honey? This is harder than it looks!"

"It's not a bed of roses being a top. Lotta hard work involved, babe."

Ryan looked around at their fellow dancers and saw that most of her aunts were now dancing with each other, a common event in her family since none of her uncles would set foot on the dance floor. Her aunts Peggy and Eileen were always in demand, since they were both very good at leading, always finding their dance cards full at the Hibernian's socials. When Rory noticed that all of his aunts were now on the dance floor, he continued to play songs that were conducive to dancing. Soon, Jordan and Mia got into the act, with each of them taking a turn with Catherine, Maeve and Moira. Ryan danced with each of her aunts, finally ending up with Moira.

"What's your tall friend's name again, love?"

"That's Jordan," Ryan said.

"Yes, Jordan. She's a very good dancer. She'd never have a chance to sit at one of our parish dinner dances."

"I'll tell her that," Ryan smirked. "She likes to be the best at everything…that'll make her day."

"You have nice friends," Moira said thoughtfully. "They seem very fond of you."

"Yeah, they are."

"I have a favor to ask of you," Moira said.

"Anything, Aunt Moira. All you have to do is ask."

"Cait has a little Internet computer now. She saved all year and finally got enough money to buy it and pay for a connection. Will you start corresponding with her?"

"Sure," Ryan said immediately. She noticed the slight look of concern on her aunt's face and asked. "Is Cait giving you trouble?"

"No, no, not at all. She's just…I see a lot of similarities between Cait and you, Ryan, and I think she could use someone to talk to. Someone who might understand and help her through this time in her life."

"I take it that you don't mean she's gifted in math," Ryan guessed, "and I know she's not extraordinarily tall. That leaves one main theme. Do you think she's gay?"

The worried look became more pronounced as Moira said, "I don't know. I haven't even spoken to Eamon about this. I just see how she is with her good friend, Maddie, and it reminds me of you. I know it's common for girls her age to have a good friend…but there's something more, and I'm a little afraid to ask her."

"That's probably wise," Ryan decided. "Asking her directly might upset her…especially if she doesn't know yet."

The song finished and Moira stayed right where she was, her arms loosely draped around her much taller niece. As the music started again she looked up at Ryan and asked, "How do you mean? How would you not know that you were in love with someone?"

"It's different when you're gay. It's hard to explain, but most young lesbians aren't aware that what they're feeling for another girl is love, or sexual attraction. It's tough growing up as a member of such a small minority group—we're really quite invisible. And we're the only minority group that doesn't share our status with our parents—for the most part, at least."

"Yes, I suppose that's very true."

"It takes most girls a little while to get comfortable that what they're feeling is normal—for them, but isn't what most of their friends are experiencing. I swear that I didn't know I was gay until I was seventeen—even though I'd always been attracted to women. I just assumed that's how everyone felt."

Moira nodded and said, "I've never thought of it like that. I just assumed it was something that you always knew—but you had to wait for the right time to share it with others."

"Maybe it is for some girls—especially ones who have positive role models—but it wasn't for me…and we live in the most lesbian neighborhood in the city. It just didn't click."

"Well, I can assure you that we don't live in the most lesbian neighborhood in Ireland. If Cait is a lesbian, she's not getting much in the way of positive role models. That's why I'd like your help. I'd really like you to make it safe for her if this is how she's feeling."

"How do you feel about it?" Ryan asked gently.

"Well, I've thought about this a lot, and while it's not what I'd choose for her, I'm fine with it. I just worry that she'll head off to Dublin as soon as she finishes school so she can be around other girls like her."

"That's a definite possibility. Killala would be a lonely place to be gay."

"Yes, and I want her to be happy, so I suppose I have to prepare myself for that eventuality."

"Well, don't assume that she's packing her bags, Aunt Moira. Maybe she and her friend are just very close."

"Maybe," the older woman said hesitantly, "but I don't think so."

⁂

It was fully dark by six. The band was taking a break, and Martin came by to say that he and Maeve were thinking about leaving, since they had a long drive to Pebble Beach.

"How will you get there?" Ryan asked, knowing that he had released the limo.

"Kevin drove Maeve's car down. Our things are already packed in it."

"Great. Well, all you have to do is dance with your bride once, and we'll let you go."

"Oh, Siobhán, you won't make your poor father embarrass himself that way, will you?"

"Of course I will," she laughed. "Aunt Maeve would be disappointed if you didn't dance with her, Da. I know you don't want to disappoint her."

"That threat will lose its effectiveness one day," he threatened, as his eyes narrowed. "But it's still working just fine now. I'll go find her." He was just a few feet away when he stopped and said, "Let's get everyone together and do a reel. I can't believe we haven't done one yet."

She knew this was just a ploy to have the spotlight diffused, but Ryan knew her father well enough to know that it was nearly painful for him to have too much attention focused on him. "That's fine idea, Da. Jamie doesn't know any reels, and it's high time she learned."

While Martin arranged for all of the remaining guests to join them, Ryan gathered up the few neophytes and demonstrated the rudiments of the simplest dance she knew. She had Jamie, Catherine, Mia, Jordan, Bryant and a few of the cousin's dates mimicking her steps in short order, and by the time Martin had instructed the band, all were ready.

Following Martin's instructions to a T, the band started off rather slowly, letting everyone get used to the pace. The lilting melody carried the inexperienced dancers along, and soon nearly everyone was up to speed. Speed soon became the operative word, as the band increased the tempo slowly, but inexorably. Soon, the entire group was nearly flying around the dance floor, the energetic, joyous beat causing everyone to laugh helplessly as they passed each other in the chaotic whirl. With a loud crescendo, the piece finally ended, most of the participants forced to bend from the waist to catch their breath. "Good Lord!" Martin gasped, "they're trying to kill us!"

"That was a blast!" Mia piped up, the energetic dance barely raising her heart beat. "Let's do another."

All of the O'Flaherty brothers decided to sit the next one out, but everyone else stayed, even though there were a few very flushed faces. The band slowed down a bit out for humanitarian reasons, and eventually Martin joined the group again, gamely participating in the fun. Ryan was even a little winded when they finally stopped, but since she was holding Caitlin upon her shoulders, she had a valid excuse.

"That was grand!" Maeve exclaimed. "Now we need a nice, slow piece so I can dance with my Marty." She gave him a look that he was unable to resist, and he found himself approaching her with his hand extended, waiting to begin.

Knowing this was difficult for him, Ryan made an offer. "We'll accompany you, Da. Come on fellas," she said to her brothers. "Let's give them a nice send off."

Rory suggested a traditional Irish tune that he knew their father liked. Instead of the drums, Ryan decided to play the bodhrán. The instrument resembled a tambourine, consisting of goatskin stretched over a round wooden frame. But the sound wasn't similar since the bodhrán was more of a timekeeper than melodic or percussive. Brendan took the acoustic guitar, Rory handled keyboards and Conor played the fiddle, not his first choice, but the band did not usually carry a mandolin.

They hadn't played together in over a year, but their previous years of practice allowed them to get comfortable quickly. As the boys tuned up, Ryan was struck by the memories of when she was a child—sitting in the living room, playing simple tunes with her brothers. She had started off playing the Irish whistle, mainly because her small hands weren't able to play any of the more complex instruments. Even though she'd taken up other instruments over the years, she still felt a special place in her heart for her whistle. She didn't think Rory had one with him, however, so the bodhrán was a good substitute.

As agreed, Martin led his bride onto the dance floor, pleased that everyone didn't abandon the space when he and Maeve entered. Jamie could see that he was uncomfortable, so she enlisted Mia and Jordan to join her as they asked Martin's brothers to join in. Even though the men never danced with their wives, none of them were foolish enough to pass up a chance to dance with pretty, young women, and by the time Martin had taken just a few steps, all of his brothers had joined him. Regrettably, if Martin and Maeve had any hope of being able to have a quiet, unnoticed dance, that chance flew away when the brothers were lured onto the floor. Now all of the aunts and all of the cousins paid rapt attention, but thankfully, the attention was split between the four of them, lessening Martin's discomfort. In fact, of the four brothers, he was the most graceful, but that wasn't saying much. As much as Maeve appreciated his attempt, by the time the song ended she was privately resigned to dancing with her sisters-in-law at the next dinner-dance they attended.

The applause at the end of the song was as much for the dancers as the band, even though the siblings had performed admirably. Maeve came over to thank them for playing and asked, "Have you no whistle, Ryan? Your father would love to hear you play a tune."

"I have one," Rory volunteered, and Ryan immediately switched instruments. They decided to play an ancient tune, one that had been heard in the west of Ireland for centuries. Ryan hooked the heels of her low boots onto the lowest rung of a stool and concentrated for a minute, looking over the sheet music that Rory provided. The boys agreed to accompany her and, after calling out the time, she began to play.

It was fully dark, and the band was nearly outside of the perimeter lighting that illuminated the yard and pool. Ghostly shadows were cast over them as they started the sad, haunting tune. All their faces were indistinct, and as the music wafted over the crowd in the darkened evening, thoughts of previous generations of their ancestors joining together for music and camaraderie settled in the hearts of the family members, the music evoking emotions that none of them could name, but all felt strongly.

Martin was transfixed by the tune as he stood behind his bride, his long arms wrapped around her in a tender embrace. Maeve's head was resting against his shoulder and she let the music transport her back to her youth, the tune, one she had heard hundreds of times, and one that her father often whistled.

When the song was finished, the family insisted on another, and the siblings continued to play until it was too dark to see the music any longer. Some of the cousins moved the large gas heaters close to their set-up, giving them just enough light to read their music, but Ryan checked her watch and decided that it was time for the happy couple to leave.

It took quite a while for the assembled guests to say goodbye, and they were only about halfway through the crowd when someone remembered that Maeve hadn't thrown her bouquet. There was a paucity of single women, and it was only by force that the small group was convinced to gather in front of the band. Maeve tossed the bouquet, giving it a good ride and having it hit Mia right in the chest. She acted as though it was a live grenade, throwing it right back into the air, where it dropped into Ryan's defensive grip. She waved the flowers good-naturedly at her partner, calling out, "Oh, Jamie…I'm next."

"You'd better change that to we're next, Tiger," she called back, to the laughs of the assembled family members.

The band members abandoned their instruments to bid farewell to their father and Maeve, with each of the children giving both of them generous hugs. Determined not to cry, Ryan practically bled from the pressure she put on her lower lip. She managed remarkably well, then almost lost it when her aunt let a few tears slip down her cheeks. "You'd better go, or we'll be out here crying all night," Ryan whispered, still trying to stay composed.

Maeve nodded, and grasped Martin's hand, dabbing at her eyes with a tissue as she tugged him towards the house. Martin gave his daughter one final look, all of his conflicting emotions swirling in the depths of his blue eyes. She dug her fingernails into her palms to present a happy face to her father, but as soon as he turned for the house she whirled and made a hasty retreat to the garden. Jamie was right on her heels, and when they were out of sight, Jamie wrapped her in a hug and held on tight as Ryan unleashed some of the emotion she'd been holding in all day. She cried soundlessly for a long time, allowing herself to feel the mixture of joy, loss, pleasure and pain that had buffeted her ever since the ceremony.

Jamie shed a few tears herself, knowing how hard this was for Ryan, and how much she felt the loss of her mother during this celebration. "Are you all right, love?" she asked softly.

"Yeah, I'm fine," Ryan murmured. "Thanks for being with me. I just needed to let some of that out. It's been building up all day, but I was determined not to spend the day crying."

"You did very well," Jamie soothed. "I know it wasn't easy for you, but you were very composed today."

"It wasn't that hard, 'cause I really am incredibly happy for them. It's just that when they left it all hit me."

"I know. I was sad, too."

"I'd better go check on the boys," Ryan decided, taking her role as the emotional center of the family seriously. "Today was as hard for Brendan as it was for me."

As they walked through the garden, Jamie spotted Brendan sitting on a bench with Maggie, his dark head resting against her chest as she calmly ran her fingers through his hair. Ryan saw them and squeezed Jamie's hand, "I think I've been replaced. Brendan finally has a shoulder he can cry on. Two down…two to go," she gave Jamie a watery smile.

※

Catherine had to ask the boys to turn off the amplifiers at eleven, knowing that she would be receiving a visit from the Hillsborough police if she didn't. They played on even after they were unplugged since the crowd was now small. All of the uncles and aunts had gone, along with Bryant, who wanted to visit some friends before returning to Los Angeles. Now it was the cousins, their dates, the O'Flaherty children and Mia and Jordan.

Ryan went on a mission, spending a few minutes talking with each of her cousins, deciding who was in shape to drive and who wasn't. Luckily, the ones who were sober were the designated drivers, and she didn't have to wrestle the keys out of anyone's hands. She thought Conor was a little over the limit, but he agreed to let Rory drive, so all was safe on the family front.

Mia and Jordan were another matter, both women having imbibed too much, probably trying to cool themselves down after dancing for hours. "You two are staying over," Ryan said, not even giving them the opportunity to complain. "Give me your keys so I don't have to worry about you again." Mia docilely handed them over.

"I love a woman that takes charge," she purred as she placed the keys in Ryan's outstretched palm.

"Do I take it that you're ready for your room?"

Mia's hand slid up the center of Jordan's chest and she touched her chin with her fingers, turning her head slightly. "Ready for bed, sweetheart?"

Jordan's head nodded up and down slowly, her expression giving the clear impression that she'd follow Mia anywhere she wanted to lead.

"I'll go ask Helena to show you to your rooms. I'll ask for two, just for propriety."

"Doesn't matter," Mia said breezily.

"Doesn't matter tonight," Ryan called over her shoulder. "It might tomorrow."

⌖

Ryan encountered Catherine coming out of the house, and she gave her the update on everyone's sobriety and transportation plans.

"Oh, Ryan, thank you for doing that! I was worried when I saw some of your cousins looking a little wobbly during that last dance."

"They're good about having a designated driver. They all take turns, so they each only have to behave every fourth or fifth party."

"Well, it looks like we're about ready to wrap it up," she looked around at the dwindling crowd.

"I think we'll stay over, Catherine. We can help get everything organized for the rental service in the morning."

"That's not necessary, but I'm always happy to have you. It will be nice to have company for breakfast."

"We'll need a good one. We have to move Da out and Kevin in tomorrow."

"I think that's one family gathering that I'm going to miss," Catherine teased, her good sense overtaking her loyalty.

⌖

After seeing that the band's gear was properly put away and saying goodbye to the boys, Jamie and Ryan headed off to bed. They had to pass by Jordan and Mia's room, and they shared a meaningful look as they did so. "Think they were making that much noise when your mom came up?" Ryan asked ruefully.

"Maybe she thought Jordan was performing a really rigorous aerobic conditioning program," Jamie mused. "Athletes are a strange bunch, you know."

"Oh, I know," Ryan agreed as she stood next to her partner and wrapped her in a hug. "Did you have fun today?"

"Oh, yeah," Jamie smiled. "I particularly liked two things. I loved it when you played your whistle. I got shivers up and down my spine when you played that first song. It sounded like something the Celts would have played on some primitive instruments. It was really moving."

"Thanks. I really should practice more, but it went surprisingly well. What else did you like?"

"I loved it when you caught the bouquet," she smiled. "The look on your face was just priceless."

"Think it'll come true?" Ryan asked, as she focused her attention on methodically undressing her partner. Her blue eyes were intent on her task, but they rotated up to meet Jamie's and locked on for a long minute.

Jamie nodded, a smile affixed to her face. "I certainly hope so. I think we'll be able to have a ceremony this year. We just have to make some decisions about when to have it, and how we want to conduct it."

"Do you think your father will come?" Ryan asked, slipping her partner's shirt off and kissing her neck.

"I think he's at the point where he'd be well behaved. I'd like him to have a little more time, but he's close. He's made a lot of progress."

"Yeah, he has, but the hole he dug for himself still has him well below ground."

"This is also true," Jamie agreed, shivering as Ryan blew a stream of cool air over her bared breasts, the nipples popping up in response.

"Your turn, Tiger," Jamie purred, performing the same service for her partner. Soon they were both in their jeans, their warm breasts rubbing against each other as they shifted their shoulders slightly. "Mmm…feels marvelous," Jamie moaned, suddenly realizing how their recent reduction in sensual couplings had affected her. "Need more."

"Oh, greedy tonight, are we?" Ryan murmured as she bent over to grasp her partner by the waist and lift her until her legs wrapped around Ryan. "I absolutely love holding you like this," Ryan soothed, her strong, warm hands playing over Jamie's smooth skin.

Jamie leaned back as far as she could, holding on with both hands clasped around Ryan's powerful neck. She sighed heavily and said, "This is bliss. I can feel all of the muscles in your back—they twitch when you move. I can hold you tight and feel your breasts against mine, and make your nipples hard rubbing against them. God, Ryan, your skin is so soft...and the way it glides over your hard muscles makes me throb."

"Throbbing is good," Ryan sighed, tossing her head back and letting the sensual pleasure of moving so intimately with her partner wash over her. She twirled a little bit, one heel firmly planted to provide stability. "Oh, you make me dizzy." She sat on the edge of the bed and slowly dropped back onto the mattress.

Jamie slid from the prone body landing on her knees. Staying on her knees she reached up and started to unbutton Ryan's jeans. Ryan co-operated, lifting her hips when instructed. She laced her hands behind her head and let her partner undress her.

When Jamie had the jeans off, she scooted closer to the bed and asked, "Remember when I bought you these shorts?" Her hand started to sketch abstract patterns at various spots on the white cotton, sending shivers up Ryan's spine at the unpredictable contact.

"I have a vague memory," Ryan teased, chalking that experience right up there with her most erotic. That tender, shy, but determined exploration of her body by her, then, completely inexperienced partner had nearly driven her mad, and she had thought of the touch often during their months together. "Wanna do it again?" she asked, hopefully.

"Huh-uh." Jamie shook her head and looked up at Ryan from between her legs, letting her face twitch into a sexy grin. "I wanna do it the way I wanted to that night. My imagination was way ahead of my body at that point."

"All righty then," Ryan decided, having not heard a better idea in weeks. "Shall I stand...if I can?"

"Nope. I like this angle." The saucy look she was giving Ryan was revving Ryan's engines enough that foreplay was really unnecessary, but Ryan knew a great offer when she heard one. During their months together, one of Ryan's most pleasurable experiences had been sharing her partner's burgeoning interest in sexual play, and she was bound and determined to always respond favorably to Jamie's overtures. Besides, Jamie had quickly figured out Ryan's triggers, and Jamie had yet to have an idea that wasn't a complete success.

Jamie's hands began to wander all over Ryan's thighs, and her gaze slowly became softer. She looked like her imagination had taken over. "I remember you standing in front of me in your new boxers," her voice was soft and smooth as silk. "You had on a polo shirt, and I kept running my hands all over your legs. I was amazed at how muscular and strong they looked in your shorts…just like carved marble," she purred.

Ryan's hips started to twitch as Jamie spoke of that night, nearly six months previously. Jamie's hands were never idle, continuing to tease Ryan's sensitive skin through the knit fabric.

"You shirt kept getting in the way, so you just yanked it off. " She licked her lips and looked across Ryan's body, making eye contact with her lover. "That was the first time I'd seen you in a bra and panties. I nearly fainted," she recalled, shaking her head, the scene had been so arousing. Ryan's warm chuckle reached her ears and she tickled her a little for her insolence. "You laugh now, but that was a whole new level of desire for me. I wanted to rip that sports bra off of you and fill my mouth with one of those luscious breasts."

"That would have been fun," Ryan mused.

"No, I wasn't ready for that yet," Jamie could remember the pull. "I had to get my mind off of them though, so I concentrated on your adorable butt. Remember that?" She urged Ryan over on her tummy, and even though it was difficult with her legs dangling off the bed at that angle, she executed the move.

Jamie started to knead her cheeks, feeling the fabric slide over the firm flesh. She bent forward on her knees, the better to apply strong pressure to the muscle. "You started to moan when I was rubbing your ass, and I could feel my heart start to race. I'm surprised you didn't hear it. It was pounding!"

"So was mine," Ryan said, gasping a little as Jamie hit a sensitive spot on the inside of her cheek.

"Do you know why I focused so much on your ass?" Jamie asked, her fingers now lightly stroking the curved mounds.

"No. Why?"

"Because I wasn't ready to do this," she ran both of her thumbs down the cleft of Ryan's cheeks, just barely grazing her mound.

"Yow!" Ryan's legs jerked together, but her partner was still between them, holding them apart.

"Ooh...did I startle you, love?"

"Yes you did, but it would have startled me even more then. I should be used to your tricks by now," she chuckled.

"Turn over again, honey," Jamie urged gently, helping her partner onto her back. "As I was saying," she continued, bending her head until it was less than an inch from the apex of Ryan's thighs. "I was afraid to touch your breasts then, and I was certainly afraid to touch you here." Her eyes lingered on the tempting sight right in front of her, and she added, "I'm not afraid any more." Her head traveled the rest of the short distance, and she opened her mouth to cover as much of Ryan's mound as she could. She blew a long stream of warm air onto the flesh, delighting when Ryan's hips began to twitch harder, trying to direct her mouth downward just a few inches.

"Jesus, Jamie, you're killing me," she groaned, her fists grabbing onto the bedspread.

"I wanted to do this to you that night," Jamie insisted. "I wanted to drop my head right between your legs and consume you." She nuzzled her face into the spot she had denied herself earlier and rubbed every bit of hypersensitive skin. Ryan's legs spread wide— so wide that it looked painful, but she needed the touch so badly she was ready to do the splits if need be.

Jamie began to nibble on Ryan through the fabric, her white, even teeth tugging gently on one sensitive spot after another. Ryan's hips were quivering so badly that Jamie had to hold onto her, she grasped her hips firmly, unintentionally increasing Ryan's desire. "Oh, God. Come on, Jamie, touch me."

Ryan eyes were locked on her partner, unwilling to look away with snapping teeth so close to her favorite spots. Tilting her head Jamie met her eyes, giving her a devastatingly sexy look as she opened her mouth and bit down and grabbed the fabric covering Ryan's thigh. She started to tug, twitching her head repeatedly, making some progress removing the shorts the hard way. She moved her mouth to hover above Ryan's mound for just a second, meeting the startled blue eyed gaze as her teeth clamped down on the soft fabric. She began to pull, managing to draw the shorts off her partner smoothly, with the aid of Ryan's raised hips.

Ryan let out a sigh of relief, now that Jamie's sharp teeth were no longer a threat. Her sighs quickly switched from relief to pure pleasure when her partner maneuvered her feet onto her shoulders and started to please her with her warm mouth, loving every inch of her overheated flesh with a fervent focus that curled Ryan's toes. "My God, you're good at that," she gasped, her arousal spiraling out of control so fast that she could barely keep up. Giving up all pretense of control, Ryan just grasped Jamie head and pulled it closer, offering herself up to her lover's voracious appetite. Her entire body shook and jerked, her legs splaying wide open as she lost her fine muscle control.

Since her partner always liked to be cuddled tight after she was loved, Jamie climbed onto the bed and wrapped her in a snug embrace, thoroughly enjoying the feel of her steamy breasts that rested against her own. "You've ruined me," Ryan muttered, her voice nearly indecipherable through her fatigue.

"Oh, I haven't ruined you, I'm just breaking you in," Jamie teased.

"Nope. You've ruined me. I used to be able to lie back and spend a good long time letting someone please me. Now, I barely have time to lay my head down before I explode. Where is the famous O'Flaherty control? No one would recognize the woman you've made me," she moaned, in her mock-serious tone.

"That's my plan. I want to render you unrecognizable to all of my predecessors. How am I doing, babe?"

"So far so good," Ryan decided, bestowing her partner with a warm smile. "I think it's a very sound plan, and you're just the woman who can pull it off."

Much later, the young women lay tangled in the disordered sheets, their naked bodies pressed tightly against one another, Jamie's heart was slowly reverting to its normal rhythm. Ryan was methodically kissing her partner, her tender, yet insistent kisses giving a good indication that Ryan's ardor had been slaked but not sated.

Jamie kept opening her eyes just to enjoy the passionate look on Ryan's face. Her eyes were shut tight, a little furrow of concentration on her brow. Her tongue slid into Jamie's mouth repeatedly, and with each gentle foray a low, sensual moan accompanied the invasion. Jamie's hand slid down Ryan's overheated body and slipped between her legs, questing fingers asking a silent question. "No" Ryan murmured, lifting her head just enough to be able to speak. "I'm completely satisfied. I just need to kiss you." Her mouth quirked into a sexy half-grin as she said, "I can't get enough of you tonight."

"This feels so nice," Jamie sighed lazily, her body completely relaxed. She tightened her grip and returned Ryan's kisses with as much emotion as she could generate. Stopping for breath she whispered, "It makes me feel so intimate to kiss like this after we make love. Now it's not foreplay…there's no goal to work towards. It's just love."

"It's just love." Ryan smiled serenely as she lowered her head and continued to love her partner deep into the night.

Chapter Thirteen

Late the next night, Ryan lay on her stomach, her body splayed out diagonally across their bed. Jamie was astride her thighs, working diligently to relieve a sore muscle that Ryan had tweaked during their day of moving. "I don't know why you had to try to help move Kevin's dresser," Jamie chided her. "Brendan and Rory were right there. Why didn't you ask them to do it?"

"I don't like to act like a girl," she muttered into the hollow space created by her crossed arms.

"Oh, honey," Jamie sighed. "You're twenty-four years old, and you've proven yourself time and again to the boys. Can't you try to let it go…just a bit?"

"No," she said honestly. "I like to show I can do what they do."

"Why? You don't think women are less than men. Why can't you accept that we're different, rather than inferior. There's lots of things we can do that they can't."

"Yeah, but they don't want to do the things we can do. If there was a way to take a pill to start menstruating—believe me, guys would not be lining up to get it."

"Maybe not, but this competition you have with the boys seems to be pretty one-sided. I don't see that they're invested in it."

"No," Ryan agreed, "I guess they're not when I look at it honestly. I'm not sure it's a girl thing, though, to be honest. I actually think it's more about being the youngest."

"Maybe," Jamie said, not really agreeing with her partner. "But I think it's more about wanting to be included when you were growing up. I can't imagine they would have wanted you around as much as they did if you were focused on dolls and tea parties."

"You're probably right. I guess I knew I had to develop the same interests to get their attention. They always thought it was cool that I knew about cars and sports and stuff." She paused reflectively as she said, "I used to wonder if some of that contributed to my being gay."

Jamie rolled off and lay down next to her, reclining on her side so she could see Ryan's face. "You say you used to wonder...what changed?"

"Oh, I learned more about being gay, and discovered that most scientists don't think environment is the primary trigger. It's probably a combination of environment and genetics. Or it might be hormonal—maybe something that happens in utero. I don't really care much anymore, but I used to try to figure out why I was different."

"It must have been hard for you to have so many unanswered questions...and no place to go for answers."

"Yeah, that first year was tough. That's why it's so rewarding to work with Jennie, you know? It's really nice to provide positive role modeling for a kid who has a tough time at home."

"Speaking of tough times at home," Jamie said, "I've been thinking a lot about what you told me about your grandmother the other day."

"Yeah?" Ryan asked a little warily. It was important to her that Jamie not judge her grandmother harshly for disciplining her, even though she knew the older woman's actions had been over the line by today's standards.

"Yeah. I was wondering how you felt when you first discovered that your body could give you pleasure. I know how bright you were, and I can't help but think you put two and two together and realized that's what your grandmother was worried about."

Ryan nodded, relieved that Jamie wasn't focusing on her grandmother per se. "Yeah," she said softly. "I can still remember the first time I touched myself sexually."

"You can?" Jamie asked, stunned.

"Yeah." She rolled onto her back and laced her hands behind her head, a wistful look in her eyes. "I was in fifth grade, and we had a new girl in our class. She was an American, but her father worked for an international company, and she had spent the previous four or five years in Indonesia. We got to be friends, mostly because she was in band with me. She played tuba, but she didn't have one at home, and since I didn't have a drum set we would stay after school and practice. We were good kids, so they let us be in the music room alone. We talked more than we practiced, and I had quite a little crush on her."

"Did you know it was a crush?" Jamie asked softly, as her hand drifted down to rub Ryan's belly.

"No, not at all. I just liked her—a LOT!" she laughed.

"What was her name?"

"Cari Scott," Ryan recalled. "We didn't touch each other or anything, but I thought she was the most fascinating, experienced, worldly woman I had ever met." She chuckled mildly at her perceptions. "One night I was lying in bed, thinking about her, and for some reason I put my hand down between my legs and started to touch myself. I don't even think it was conscious. It's like my hand knew where to go without my brain even telling it to."

"It probably did," Jamie smiled. "I think our bodies know how to help us out if we listen to them."

"Yeah, maybe," Ryan agreed. "Anyway, I slowly became aware that I was touching myself in a way I had never been conscious of doing before—and it felt fantastic! The sensations built and built, and I kept going—no way I was getting off that ride if I didn't have to."

"God, I would have loved to have known you then," Jamie sighed. "I bet you were absolutely adorable."

"Ehh…maybe. You'll have to ask someone who can give you an unbiased opinion. Anyway, I kept going until it was almost painful, and right before I got there I thought about what it would feel like to kiss Cari…and bam! I had my first climax." She smiled over at Jamie and said, "The euphoria lasted about three seconds until I realized that this was what Granny was talking about. I wasn't supposed to touch myself to feel good! This was exactly what she said that I would go to hell for!"

"What did you do?"

"I wigged out about it for a couple of days. But one night soon afterwards, those urges started to build up again, and I couldn't stop myself," she recalled, shaking her head. "I felt really bad, and I went on this campaign to prevent myself from even having the urge. I'd try not to go to bed until I was really, really tired, sometimes staying up until all hours of the night. I even asked Da to read to me until I fell asleep—but the first time he was at work and I was all alone…bam! I did it again."

"So my little twelve-year-old Tiger had a strong drive even then, huh?"

"Yeah," Ryan said, thoughtfully. "In retrospect, the fact that I knew it was wrong probably made it much more attractive." She grinned over at Jamie and said, "You know how hot I think it is to do things that are just a little wrong."

"Yes, I do, love. It's one of your most endearing traits. But it sounds like you were tormented about this. How did you get past it?"

"Poor old Brendan came to the rescue again," Ryan smiled. "God, it must have been hard for an eighteen-year-old to have to talk to his little sister about masturbation, but he did it." She looked at Jamie and said, "He's the best brother in the world."

"I couldn't agree more. I'm eternally grateful to him for helping you through some very hard times."

"Yeah. This one was a pisser," she recalled. "I wasn't sleeping well, and I had dreams almost every night of being in hell and having my whole family up in heaven. He finally asked me what was going on—since I was so grouchy from lack of sleep. I was so desperate that I swallowed my fears and told him the whole story."

"The whole story?"

"Well, my version of the situation," she grinned. "I told him that Granny had told me that I'd go to hell if I put my hands under the covers when I took a nap…just trying to see if he had gotten the same story, you know?"

"Yeah," Jamie laughed. "What did he say?"

"Apparently he hadn't gotten the lecture, 'cause it took him a while. I finally told him that I tickled myself before I went to sleep, and asked him if it was wrong to do that."

"You tickled yourself?" Jamie said, thinking the expression was so charmingly Ryan.

"Yeah…that's what it felt like to me," she agreed. "I don't recall the conversation all that clearly, but he finally got what I meant, and he did a great job of reassuring me. He just said that Granny had some funny ways of thinking, and that we didn't always have to do what she said. He left me with the impression that there were differences between Ireland and America, and that we did things the American way." She was chuckling now, recalling her brother's tact in handling the situation. "He did tell me that I should always check with him before I disregarded Granny's instructions, but he helped me see that things weren't always black and white...and that was a very big help."

"He is quite a guy," Jamie agreed, her already high esteem of Brendan growing as they spoke.

"Yeah, he is. Always has been."

"So, did your guilt go away after that?"

"Mmm...mostly, but not entirely. I still feel like it was a little wrong to masturbate...even though it didn't stop me from doing it," she admitted.

"You know, you've never done that in front of me," Jamie said thoughtfully. "Are you embarrassed to?"

"A little," she said, blushing slightly as she admitted this holdover bit of guilt from her childhood. "Plus, I prefer to have sex with you, so it seems silly to touch myself if you're there."

"Unless my hands are all busy," Jamie reminded her.

"Yeah. Then I don't mind lending a hand."

"Well, if the occasion ever arises, I want you to feel comfortable doing it in front of me. I don't want you to have any leftover guilt about that."

"I'll try," Ryan said. "Hey, I don't know your history. How did you discover the joys of masturbation?"

"Mia made fun of me for never having done it when we were in high school." She laughed. "I went to the store and bought a book that told you how to touch yourself. Strangely enough, the book helped and I kinda liked it."

"That's my girl," Ryan smiled. "Always the good student."

"Are you bummed about having your aunt leave today?" Jamie asked when they woke the next morning.

"Yeah. I normally spend a lot more time with her on her visits. I feel like we've barely spoken this time."

"Well, she was only here for a few days, babe. She just didn't feel comfortable leaving Brenna for long."

"I understand," Ryan said. "I just don't like it."

Moira was packed and waiting when they arrived to take her to the airport. "I've been on the phone with my sister for over an hour," she related when Ryan was loading her suitcase into the Lexus. "She's having a marvelous time, by the way."

"I should hope so," Ryan grinned. "Lord knows that Jamie and I enjoyed our time down there."

Moira patted her back and said, "I've gotten the impression that you and Jamie enjoy most of your time together."

"Oh, we do," Ryan beamed.

She was getting into the car when she said this, and Jamie couldn't help but ask, "We do what, honey?"

"I was just telling my aunt how much we enjoy having sex," Ryan said, adding a rakish grin and a wink.

With a flush coloring the tips of her ears Jamie blinked slowly. "Wh…what…"

"Relax," Ryan smiled, giving her thigh a squeeze. "I was merely referring to how much we like spending time together."

Jamie's head fell back against her shoulders and she moaned, "I never know with you. It wouldn't be out of the question for you to reveal all sorts of mortifying details."

Moira was chuckling from the back seat and she commented, "I'd wager that my Aisling is at my door the moment I arrive asking about you, Ryan. I must say that I'll have an awful lot to tell her."

Jamie turned around in her seat and gave Moira an inquisitive look. "What will you tell her? Has Ryan changed much since you last saw her?"

"Goodness yes!" She gave Jamie a long look and said, "The last time we saw Ryan was just after her she was attacked. She was a different girl then. Some of the fire had been taken from her." She reached up and squeezed Ryan's shoulder, giving her a fond look.

"She wasn't our Ryan that time."

Ryan nodded. "I didn't feel like myself for a long time, Aunt Moira. You know," she said reflectively, "I was really flat all that summer. The first thing that I can remember being excited about was this cute little blonde from my psych class. I didn't think I had a chance with her, but something about her made me start to recapture some of my optimism again." She turned her head just enough to fix Jamie with a love-filled gaze, and the older woman in the back seat made a mental note to relate to her daughter that the old Ryan was back and better than ever.

That afternoon, Ryan was sitting on the floor of the gym, stretching a little before volleyball practice began. The gym was totally silent since she was the only one on the floor, and the silence allowed her to hear the very muted tune coming from her cell phone. By the time she got to her gym bag and retrieved the device the call had already gone to voice mail. She didn't even bother to dial into the system, just hit speed dial number one and waited for her partner to respond. "Hi," Ryan said. "I assume that was you?"

"Yeah. I'm not bothering you, am I?"

"Not possible. What's up?"

"I'm not sure. But there was a very ominous sounding message from someone named Sheila Hawthorne on the machine. She said she's from the Department of Children and Family Services. Do you know her?"

"That's Jen's social worker. Do you have her number?"

"Yeah. Call me back as soon as you talk to her, okay?"

"Will do."

Ryan spent the next fifteen minutes trying to track the woman down, finally reaching her only to receive a load of very bad news. She was on the verge of being physically ill when she called Jamie back. "I'm going to see if I can skip practice," she began without preamble.

"What's wrong?"

"Jen ran away. Her step-mother isn't sure if she left last night or this morning, but she didn't show up at school."

"Oh, Ryan."

Jamie's voice reflected her fear and her tone just magnified the knot in Ryan's stomach. She growled in frustration. "I don't know what to do, but I feel like I have to do something!"

"Honey, there's nothing that you can do right now. Stay at practice and get some of your frustration out that way. When you get home we'll figure out what to do next. I'll make some calls while you're gone, okay?"

"Are you sure I can't help right now?"

"No. I'm going to call the private detective that my father uses. He's an expert at finding people who don't want to be found. By the time you get home I should have some leads."

Ryan's voice dropped into a near-whisper and Jamie could hear a lot of activity in the background. "I'm scared to death, Jamie."

"I am too, but try to stay positive. We'll find her and bring her home safe and sound."

"Where's home?" The question was both simple and profoundly complex, and Jamie knew that it was a question that would have to be answered soon.

🐎

Ryan and Jordan ran into the house together, both severely out of breath. "What have you found out?" Ryan gasped.

"A lot," Jamie said. She twitched her head in Mia's direction. "Mia's on the phone right now with Jennie's homeroom teacher. She's agreed to violate school policy and give her the phone numbers of some of the kids that she's seen Jen talk to."

"What else?"

"I've talked to the private detective, her old social worker and the new one from San Diego, Sandy and several of the girls that Jen knew at the Safe Haven, and her stepmother. None of them had any idea that she would bolt, and none of them have any idea where she might go."

"I know where she'll go," Ryan said quietly. "She'll come here."

"That's almost six hundred miles! How could she possibly get here?"

"Does she have any money?" Jordan asked.

"No. Her stepmother says she only gave her five dollars a week for spending money." Jamie's expression showed what she thought of this largesse, but she didn't comment further.

"She'll hitch," Ryan said. "She's done it before."

"How do you know?" Jamie asked.

"She was in two foster care placements before they placed her at Safe Haven the first time. One was local, but the other was way the fuck up in Placer County. She ditched both of them and hitchhiked her way back here."

This news didn't help Jamie's churning stomach. "A fourteen-year-old girl hitchhiking up the state. What a nightmare."

"Can we at least call the highway patrol to be on the lookout?" Ryan asked.

"The social worker did that. I don't think there's anything we can do but wait," Jamie advised.

"Wait and worry," Ryan corrected, her body slowly collapsing onto the love seat.

⁂

To Jamie's surprise, Ryan actually fell asleep before she did. But her slumber was neither deep nor restful. Ryan woke at least once an hour, and finally got up at three to make herself some hot cocoa with a shot of Bailey's. She was in the kitchen, idly stirring the cocoa when she heard a creak that sounded like it was coming from the living room. Sticking her head into the room, she decided that she must have imagined it and went back into the kitchen. The sound startled her once again, and she realized that the wind must be rocking the chairs on the front porch.

She finished making her drink and was about to go back upstairs when she heard it again, it seemed best to bring the chairs in if the wind was that strong. She switched on the porch light and opened the door to the sight of Jennie, huddled on a chair in an embryonic shape, her backpack nestled against her chest for warmth. She looked utterly exhausted, and nearly frozen—her small body covered only by a threadbare sweater and a pair of ripped jeans. Her head fell forward and she moaned softly in her sleep at the disturbance.

Ryan fell to her knees and wrapped her arms around Jennie so tightly that she could feel every bone. She started to cry, twelve hours of mad anxiety unleashed in a torrent of emotion.

Jennie woke and started to cry too, nearly as hard as Ryan. Her body was shivering so badly that Ryan collected herself enough to pick her up and carry her into the living room, managing to kick the door shut with her foot. They sank into the love seat as one, Jennie clutching Ryan as if she was her lifeline. Neither woman could stop crying but Jennie slowly started to warm and her body stopped shivering from the cold. She finally managed to ask, "Why are you crying?"

"Why am I crying?" Ryan looked at her incredulously. "I've been so worried about you! I love you, Jennie! Don't you know that?"

"Y…Yeah, I guess I do," she mumbled. "You don't have to worry about me. I can take care of myself."

Ryan grasped her by the shoulders and held her at arm's length, glaring at her with tears still running down her cheeks. "No you can not! You're still a girl, Jennie, and you need adults to help you and guide you. If you'd met the wrong person out there you could have been raped or killed. It's a miracle that you got this far in one piece!"

"I did meet the wrong person," she admitted, her tears starting again.

"What happened?" Ryan was frantic with alarm when she saw the look on the girl's face.

"It was last night," Jennie said. "A guy picked me up in San Diego and he made me smoke grass with him."

Ryan didn't comment, she just held her tight and let her talk. Her eyes closed in pain as she listened to the story unfold.

"I didn't want to do it 'cause I promised you I wouldn't," she sobbed. "I haven't smoked since that last time." She looked at Ryan to make sure she believed her and was met with eyes brimming with love and warm regard. Jennie pressed her face against Ryan's chest and allowed herself to feel the concern and compassion that radiated from her entire body.

After soaking up as much love as she could accept, Jennie continued. "I kept telling him that I didn't want any grass, but he put his hand on my neck and started squeezing." She pulled away from Ryan's embrace and tugged her sweater down to show livid purple fingerprints on her pale skin. "I thought he was gonna kill me." Her voice was soft and low and Ryan could hear the same flat affect that she had often heard from teenagers who had been violated. Her stomach was churning so badly that she feared she'd be sick right on the floor, but she stayed with Jennie, offering as much comfort as she could.

"I don't know what was in this stuff but I got so high so fast," she mumbled. "It was sickening. I kept feeling like I was gonna throw up, but I never did."

"Was the car moving the whole time?" Ryan asked.

"Yeah. We were on the 5, I think, but we were going the wrong way. He was going to take me to Mexico," she related. "He was drinking beer and smoking the whole time. I don't know how he did it. I could barely see I was so stoned."

"What happened then?" Ryan's voice was thin when she asked.

Her face colored in shame and her head dropped against Ryan's shoulder. "He started touching me," she sniffed. "I begged and cried but he grabbed my throat again and said he'd kill me if I fought him. So I just sat there and let him." She sounded so thoroughly disgusted with herself that Ryan just had to interrupt.

"You did the right thing, Jen. You did exactly the right thing. You're here now and you're alive, and that's all that matters. No matter what you had to do—it's not your fault."

"But I let him," she sobbed.

"No." Ryan moved her body so they were eye to eye. "You survived. That's all that matters. He was a cruel, violent adult who was drunk and high. Anything you had to do to live through that is okay."

"Okay," she said quietly, nodding her head slightly. "You wanna hear the rest?"

"Anything you want to tell me is fine, Jen. Anything at all."

"We started to get closer to the border and they had these barricade things up that you had to go through. His hand was…in my pants," she said with a voice full of self-loathing, "but I jerked myself away from him when he slowed down to go through. I opened the door and jumped out and rolled down the embankment."

"Oh, God," Ryan moaned, pressing the child to her body in an automatic reflex. "Are you hurt?"

"A little," she admitted. "I started running through all this really sticky sharp stuff that was growing down there. I don't know how long I ran, 'cause I was so high. I finally got so exhausted that I found a big drainage pipe and just stayed there until I came down. It took a really long time and it was light by the time I felt like I could walk again."

Ryan pulled back a little and noticed that Jen's clothes were not threadbare, they were ripped and torn from the scrub she had run through. She grasped one of her legs and pulled the pant leg up, grimacing when she saw hundreds of deep scratches and cuts lancing her fair skin. "Do you want me to take you to the emergency room? You're awfully banged up."

"No, no," she said her agitation beginning to come back. "It's just some scratches. Really, Ryan."

"Did anything else bad happen to you? Did anyone else touch you or hurt you?"

"No. I just hitched the rest of the way. A truck driver picked me up and took me all the way to L.A., but I couldn't get another ride for a couple of hours. A really nice lady picked me up in Glendale and she took me to Valencia. Then another trucker brought me to San Fracisco. I still had my Muni pass, so I took a bunch of buses and finally got here."

"Why didn't you ring the bell, Jennie? Do you really think I'd want you outside freezing?"

"I didn't want you to get mad," she mumbled.

"Oh, Jen, we've got a lot of work to do here. I've got to somehow convince you that I really do love you and only want what's best for you—even when it's inconvenient for me."

"I know that sometimes," she admitted. "I just get scared."

"I know," Ryan soothed. "We just have to work at making you not so scared." She patted her and said, "Let's go upstairs. I'll make you a nice warm bath with some baking soda in it. That should help with your cuts."

"But we'll wake Jamie up," she said with no small amount of alarm.

"She loves you too, Jen. And she'll only care that you're safe—not that it's four a.m.."

By seven Jennie was clean, warm, fed and all of her more serious scrapes had been cleaned and dressed. Ryan tucked her into the bed in the spare room and went back into her own bedroom. She looked longingly at her own bed, but banished the tempting thought and sat down at the desk to start making phone calls. When she related all of the details to the social worker, they agreed that Jennie had to go to the police to make a statement, but they also agreed that time was not of the essence, since more than twenty-four hours had passed, and Jennie could not recall many details of her attacker's description or his car.

"When she wakes up will you bring her down to my office, Ryan? I'll have her placed in one of the emergency shelters until we decide what to do with her."

"Can't she stay here until you figure out a solution? We have a spare room and I'd take her to school every morning."

The woman sighed and said, "I don't think I can do that. We'd need Mrs. Willis' permission for an arrangement like that, and I'm sure she wouldn't give it."

"What about Safe Haven? For God's sake, it's the only place she's agreed to stay at!"

"I know that, but it's far more expensive than a foster home and we're uncomfortable putting that many children into a single home."

"What if I paid for her? I'd be more than happy to pay the entire bill."

Sheila nearly laughed. "Do you have any idea how much money that is?"

"It doesn't matter. I'm…quite well off. It wouldn't be a problem."
Well, that was the winning entry in the "things I swore I'd never say" competition.

"Well," she hedged. "It's not unheard of to have a family pay for a private placement. I suppose it's possible to have a non-related individual do that. I'd have to have Mrs. Willis' permission, though."

"Do you want to call her, or do you want me to?" Ryan asked, ready and willing to resort to any means necessary to get Jennie back into the home.

"I'll do it," Sheila sighed. "I'll call you later." Ryan started to hang up but she heard her say, "Wait!"

"Yeah?"

"I forgot to say thank you. It's not very often that I run into someone willing to go this far out of their way for someone they're not even related to."

Ryan smiled and said, "We are related. She's my sister."

Chapter Fourteen

When Jamie came home from school Ryan was just going down the front walk to head over to volleyball practice. "Two questions," she said after giving her a quick kiss. "One, where's Jennie? And two, why do you look happy?"

"Same answer to both," Ryan said, giving her a very tired smile. "I just got back from taking her to Safe Haven. She's going to stay there."

"Stay there...like permanently?"

"Well, no. The social worker took pity on me when I started to cry," she admitted.

"What?"

"I offered to pay for Jennie to stay at Safe Haven." She gave Jamie a half-anxious look and said, "That's okay, isn't it?"

Shaking her head, Jamie said, "I'm not even going to dignify that ridiculous question with an answer."

Ryan have her an adorable grin and said, "Sorry. Anyway, Mrs. Willis won't hear of it. She wants Jennie in a foster home. So now we're going to go through the whole fiasco of having a hearing to determine a permanent placement for her. It's a fucking mess."

"So why are you happy?" Jamie was sure she'd missed something vital in the explanation.

"Well, until they have the hearing Jennie can stay at Safe Haven. I'm gonna work on Mrs. Willis between now and then." She gave her partner an evil look and said, "I can be very persuasive."

"That's an understatement," Jamie chuckled.

"Oh, I called those therapists that Anna recommended. Jen's got an appointment tomorrow with a woman who specializes in helping troubled kids. She claims she doesn't need any help, but I want her to have someone to talk to about that asshole that molested her. It's gonna prey on her mind if she doesn't have someplace to vent her feelings about it."

Jamie threw her arms around her partner's neck and gave her a very enthusiastic hug. "You are such a good person."

"Me? What did I do?"

Jamie released her and stepped back to look at her closely. "You really don't know, do you?"

"No," she said blankly. "Anyone would have done the same thing."

Jamie impulsively tossed her arms around her waist and squeezed her tight. "God, this would be a wonderful world if that were true."

When Jamie got out of bed on Wednesday she began the refrain she had finally stopped when sleep had overtaken her the night before. "Are you sure this is something you want to do?"

"Yes, dear," Ryan replied patiently. "I want you to attend your father's speech. I'd like to go too, but I really can't get out of practice. I've already checked with Jennie's housemother, and she says it's perfectly fine if she eats with us. I don't know why you're stressing about this."

"I don't know," she said, a little embarrassed to be caught in her nervousness. "I guess I'm just anxious about seeing my parents together. I feel like there's always a chance that something will go wrong and they'll be feuding again. This is also the first time Daddy's eaten with us, you know. What are you going to make?"

"Something appropriate to the day," Ryan replied mysteriously.

Jamie snuck another peek out the window and said, "I don't know what goes well with forty-three degrees and driving rain but I trust you to make the correct decision."

Ryan joined her at the window and gave her a hug as they watched the rain pelt down in sheets. "'Tis a bit of a sickener," she agreed. "When I was a kid in Ireland my grandmother would look at weather like this and say, "Sure and there's a break in the clouds just over the hills. You go out and play Siobhán, but wear your slicker."

"God, she was that much of an optimist?"

"Not at all," Ryan laughed. "She would have sent me out in a hurricane just to keep me from being underfoot."

When the Evanses came in through the back door a little after seven the rain had tapered down to a steady drizzle, but the wind was absolutely bone chilling as it whipped off the Bay. "I'm freezing!" Jamie cried as she ran up to receive Ryan's warm embrace.

She was wearing a cream colored turtleneck with a dark green wool sweater and a pair of tan corduroy slacks, but her light jacket obviously had no insulating properties. "Where are you winter clothes?" Ryan demanded. "No hat? No gloves?"

"It was raining so hard when I left that I thought the biggest issue was staying dry. This is the only rain jacket I have."

Ryan shook her head in mock anger and tightened her embrace. "How did you ever survive having this scamp in the house for eighteen years?" she asked Jim and Catherine, who were taking off their perfectly adequate rain gear.

Ryan went to hang their things up in the mudroom, and when she returned Catherine gave her a hug and a kiss as usual but Jim just extended his hand. Jamie was peeking in the oven but Ryan lightly slapped her hand and said, "Uh-uh-uh, no peeks."

"Ooh, but it smells so good," Jamie said trying to get past her partner to take another look.

But Ryan didn't move an inch as she tweaked Jamie's nose and said, "Set the table and I'll not only let you look at it, I'll let you eat it. I'll go let our other guests know that you're here," Ryan offered as she left the room.

"Guests?" Jim asked. "Someone other than Jennie?"

Before Jamie could reply Ryan returned with Rory and Jennie in tow. Both Jim and Catherine looked pleased to see Jennie again and when it became clear that Rory bore him no ill will Jim relaxed and took on his normal personae.

"Jim was giving a speech at Cal today on a bill he's proposing to fund research grants in the pure sciences," Ryan said. "I really wish I could have come. I'm very much in support of your plan."

"Thank you, Ryan. I should have assumed that. It's always nice to hear that one of my constituents is supportive."

Catherine accepted a glass of the Pinot Noir that Ryan was pouring and asked, "I wasn't aware that you liked to cook Ryan."

"I do actually," she said. "I'm not terribly creative but I'm pretty adept at executing old family favorites. Tonight's dish is a Casey heirloom," she added in her adorable brogue.

"Casey?" Catherine asked.

"My mother's mother is a Casey. She got this recipe from her grandmother on her father's side. So technically I suppose it's a Ni Mhuiri recipe, but it came down through the Caseys."

"I'm going to hazard a wild guess that that's a Gaelic name," Catherine said with a smile.

"Yep, one more unpronounceable name. I can only thank my mother for naming me after her father's family. Almost everyone can pronounce Ryan." She opened the oven and took out a large enameled Dutch oven and transferred it to the table. Trotting back over to the lower over she removed a tray of fluffy biscuits and put them into a basket with a warming stone hidden beneath the gingham napkin that covered them.

As Jim passed by on his way to his seat he gave Ryan a smile and said, "Thank you for cooking for us. We both appreciate it."

Ryan's natural ebullience took over and she placed her hand on his arm and gave it a squeeze. "My pleasure," she smiled.

When Ryan sat down she looked around the table and asked, "Anyone mind if I lead grace?" When no one voiced a complaint she extended her hands and gripped Jamie's and Jennie's. Looking at Rory she began, "It's fitting that we're sharing a dish that came down from our mother's family. Today would have been her fifty second birthday, and I know nothing would make her happier than to have at least some of us gather and think of her. She's never far from my thoughts and I thank God every day for having given her to us. We didn't have her for long but we had every bit of her for every day that she was with us." She could feel herself starting to tear up, but she fought for and gained control. "I suppose all we can hope for out of life is that we love and are loved well while we live and that we're remembered fondly when we're gone. She was all of that and so much more." She lifted her glass and toasted all of the guests and got up halfway to lean across Jamie and kiss Rory. "And one thing she enjoyed more than anything was to have people enjoy the food she prepared, so let's eat heartily in her honor."

As Ryan removed the lid to the heavy pot every eye went to the dish to try to figure out what the delectable aroma was. "Nothing warms a cold body like a bowl of Irish stew," she said as she began to ladle the stew into the earthenware bowls.

Everyone made over the dish enthusiastically, with Jim passing along some very sincere sounding compliments. As they ate he asked Jennie, "How have things been since you moved back into the home in Oakland?"

"Pretty good. I like some of the girls I'm living with and the housemother has always been nice to me."

"How about school?" he persisted.

"It's okay," she said noncommittally, shrinking a little bit in her seat.

"What exactly are you taking?"

"Well," she blushed. "I can't go back to my old class 'cause I've missed too much. They put me in this thing called 'Accelerated Learning'."

"What does that mean?" Jim asked, his eyes narrowing.

"Umm, I think it's supposed to help new kids and kids who've had to miss a lot of school catch up."

Ryan fixed her laser-like blue eyes on Jennie and asked, "What is it really?"

Her blush deepened as she admitted, "It's where they stick the pregnant girls and the kids who've been kicked out of regular classes."

"Why have the others been kicked out of regular classes?" Catherine asked, her alarm sounding in her voice.

"Um, some of them were kicked out for drugs or fighting. One scary guy got suspended for a whole year for having a gun on campus. And some of them are kinda slow," she said delicately.

"Are these all freshmen?"

"No, I'm the only freshman. The scary guy's nineteen. He should have graduated last year, and he doesn't want to be there, but he has to show up as part of his probation."

Catherine's eyes had grown wide, but she tried to sound like this was all normal. "Tell us about what you study. Do you have classes for math and English?"

"Um…this was my first day, so I'm not really sure…"

Ryan again fixed her with her gaze and said, "What did the other kids tell you that you'll do. I'm certain that they gave you all the dirt."

"Well, they said we don't have to do anything. We don't even get books."

"Jennie," Jamie said, visibly alarmed, "What do you do all day in school if you don't have books or regular classes?"

"The other kids said they just try to keep us quiet." She said this last statement so quietly that it was nearly impossible to hear her. Her head was dropped down and she stared at her plate in shame.

Ryan felt her stomach begin to turn again, and she realized that Jennie's problems were even more complex than she had guessed.

"Were you in regular classes at your previous school?"

"Yeah, but my mom lives in a different part of Oakland. When I stay at the house I have to go to school near there."

"That doesn't make any sense!" Jim cried, his frustration getting the better of him. "Why can't you stay at your old school?"

"I don't have any way to get there. It's in a pretty bad neighborhood and I'm afraid to ride my bike that far. It's really hard to get there on the bus, 'cause I'd have to change twice, and wait on a really dangerous corner. I can walk to the school by the home."

"Jennie," he asked carefully as he put his spoon down. "Did you like your old school?"

"It's okay. But they didn't have any classes in art or music and that's what I do best in."

He nodded briefly and went back to his dinner without another comment on the topic.

❧

Thankfully the dinner conversation moved on to brighter topics, with Jim showing genuine interest in Rory and his career. They spoke about the wedding, and the one phone call the family had received from the newlyweds, telling them that things were fine and they'd see them all on Thursday.

The entire Dutch oven was empty by the time dinner wound down, and Catherine leaned over and speared the last bite of carrot from Jim's plate, giving him an impish grin as she did so.

He regarded her fondly for a moment, as he leaned back in his chair. "You know, Catherine, I don't think I've ever seen you clean your plate in the twenty-two years I've know you. Your healthy appetite is quite a surprise."

"I've been working out," she said proudly. "I ride my bike nearly every day and I use our gym three days a week. It's wonderful to be able to eat real food."

"Well, you look marvelous." He smiled at his daughter and said, "Doesn't she look marvelous, Jamie?"

"Indeed she does, Daddy," she agreed, smiling at the faint blush that covered her mother's cheeks.

Jennie had a nine o'clock curfew so Rory offered to give her a lift on his way home. After all of the goodbyes were said Jim went into the parlor to make a few business calls while the women cleaned up.

They were nearly finished when Jim came back into the room. "After the fiasco we had the last time I was here I decided to take care of a little paperwork," he said as he held out an official looking document to Jamie.

She carefully read the single sheet and gazed up at him with a delighted smile on her face. "This," she said as she shook the paper, "is so very thoughtful of you Daddy. Look honey," she said, extending the sheet to Ryan.

Ryan dried her hands and read the document. "Thank you, Jim." At Catherine's raised eyebrow she explained, "Jim had the title to the Porsche transferred to both of our names." After looking at it carefully she teased, "You even spelled Siobhán correctly."

"The keystone of legal work is detail, Ryan. Speaking of legal work, we've got to do something to make sure that Jennie can stay in one place to finish high school. The way they're treating her is criminal"

"I agree," Ryan said. "At this rate she'll drop out at sixteen—and that will just consign her to menial work her whole life. What do you think we can do?"

"I think we have to go to her mother and force her to allow Jennie to remain at the group home until she's out of high school," he said decisively, his normal take-charge attitude in full force.

"Force her?" Ryan asked weakly as she shot Jamie a look.

"No, not force her. Convince her."

"What tactics were you planning on using?" Catherine asked, her voice showing her wariness.

Scowling, her said, "Just verbal persuasion, Catherine."

Ryan looked at him for a long minute as she gathered her thoughts. "I don't normally agree with strong arm tactics but I think Jennie's only chance of survival is to remain out of her mother's house. After what we've learned tonight, we need more of a plan than just keeping her out of the house, though. We need to get her into a decent school, and that's not going to be easy."

"We have to do first things first, Ryan," Jim said. "I'm going to be in town most of tomorrow. I'll have one of my aides call her mother and see if he can make some progress. I'm happy to get involved and go see her if need be."

Jamie went up to her father and gave him a hug, saying, "I'm so pleased that you're willing to help, Daddy. That's very generous of you."

"Not at all. She's a lovely young girl who's at a very critical turning point. If we can step in and help her now it might make the difference in her entire life. We can't just stand by and do nothing."

"No, we can't," Ryan agreed. "This will go much easier with your involvement, Jim. Thanks for caring."

As the couple cuddled in bed that night Ryan mused, "You know, that was the most animated I've ever seen your mother around your father. Normally she's pretty flat—but today she was very much like normal."

"Yeah, I noticed that too. I was also pleased that they each only had one glass of wine. I don't remember the last time one bottle lasted an entire evening at my house."

"You know, she doesn't drink much at all when she's around us. Is she consciously trying to cut back?"

"I don't know," Jamie said thoughtfully. "I don't want to interfere, or make her think I'm supervising her, so I haven't really ever discussed her drinking. I'm just pleased that I haven't seen her drunk in a couple of months. That's progress."

"It is," Ryan agreed. "It was quite the shocker to have your father be so passionate about Jennie's problems. That really impressed me."

"Yeah, he's acting more like he did when I was younger," she mused. "He used to seem like he really cared about people. I think being in the senate has been a good thing for him. He seems a little more open minded."

"Boy, I felt like a dunce for not knowing how bad Jennie's school was. I've asked her about school every time I see her, but I obviously wasn't asking the right questions. It's like you have to know the answer before you can ask the question with a teenager!"

"Don't worry. Our kids will be babies first—we'll be used to their tricks by the time they're Jennie's age."

Jim called Ryan around lunchtime the next day. His aide had discussed the issue with Mrs. Willis, and she'd said she needed to pray on the issue before she could discuss it again.

"That sounds like she's going to that minister of hers to see what he says to do," Ryan said. "She's given her life over to some guy at a church in Oakland. I hope he doesn't make matters worse."

"I can do a little investigation into his tax-exempt status," Jim mused, but Ryan quickly interrupted.

"Let's just see how it goes before we use the big guns, okay?"

"As usual, I have to be reminded of the moderate path. Thanks, Ryan. I'll let you know if I hear back before I leave. And Ryan?"

"Yes?"

"I really appreciate the hospitality you showed me last night. I was honored to be with you when you celebrated your mother's birth. I know she meant a lot to you."

"Thank you," she said, smiling into the phone. "I'm pleased that you recognize that."

"I'm not such a bad guy when you get to know me."

"Of course you're not. You're Jamie's father—nothing all bad could produce something so good."

The next call came from the plane. Jim hadn't had time to call before he boarded, but senators are never out of touch. "I know I shouldn't talk about this when people can hear me," he said, his anger obvious, "but I'm so mad I could punch that woman."

"Yeah. It's probably not a good idea to hear a senator threaten to punch a woman."

He sighed and let out a deep breath. "Could you travel around with me to kick me in the pants a few times a day? I think I could really use an attendant sometimes."

"I take it that you spoke with Mrs. Willis?"

"Yes. What a miserable excuse for a parent! She shouldn't be allowed to have a fish, much less a child."

"What in the hell happened?"

"Well, after my aide spoke to her again I decided to go over there. I thought that having a senator visit her could help make up her mind."

"Yeah…what happened?"

"That slimy, disgusting minister you speak of was there at the time," he said, his voice dripping with disgust. "They were 'praying', but it sounded like a bunch of hogwash to me. He launched into this diatribe about gay people and how they prey on youth. They think that you've lured Jennie into being gay!"

"Well, that's just wonderful. I didn't think this could get worse. So where do we stand?"

"Well, this idiot thinks that Jennie's too far gone to be saved. He told her mother that having her in the house would be inviting the devil in. Can you believe that?"

"No, but it sounds like that's the outcome we wanted."

"On one front, it is," he agreed. "But I have a feeling she's going to cut off contact with the child. I know that would break Jennie's heart," he said, his voice quavering with emotion. "How could a parent do that to their little girl? How can you stop loving your child?"

"I don't know," she said honestly. "I don't think you really can stop, to be honest. I can only assume that she never loved her."

The silence hung between them for a minute, both of them recalling just a short time earlier when Ryan had asked Jim if he had ever loved Jamie. He finally broke the silence, saying, "Well, for better or worse, she claims that she's willing to allow Jennie to stay in the group home until she's of age. She also doesn't care where she goes to high school—as long as she doesn't have to pay for it."

"What a piece of work," Ryan muttered.

"When I was leaving that idiot minister hit me up for a contribution!" Jim said, still irate over the encounter.

"I'm guessing that you didn't give him one."

"No, not hardly. I still would like to have him investigated, but at this point I guess we'd better leave well enough alone."

"This is going to be very, very hard on Jen," Ryan said, already worrying about what she would tell the child.

"I know that, Ryan," he agreed somberly. "It won't be the same, but I know that you and Jamie can provide the kind of support that she could never have received at home."

"True, but nothing can make up for the loss of your mother...no matter what kind of a mother she is."

Chapter Fifteen

O n Thursday night Ryan should have been concentrating on warming up for the University of Washington, but her attention was torn between pre-game preparations and repeated glances into the crowd, hoping to see her father and Maeve in the stands. They were due home today, but no one knew exactly what their plans were. Rory had brought Caitlin, and they were sitting next to Jamie and Mia, but there was no sign of the honeymooners.

Just before player introductions, Ryan caught sight of the pair out of the corner of her eye, and immediately felt her body relax. Both of them were smiling so broadly that they glowed, and she offered them both a hearty wave and a blown kiss. Ryan could hear Caitlin's enthusiastic greeting—a rapid-fire repeat of a hard "g" that she had recently mastered. Her vocabulary had grown, but she was still having trouble getting past the "g", even though they all assumed she would soon have an epiphany and settle on a recognizable word for her grandmother. Standing there, it occurred to her that Caitlin would probably refer to Martin as her grandfather. Somehow that didn't sit right, but she reminded herself that's what her father would be to the child.

Martin sat next to Jamie, giving her a warm hug as the team was introduced. They weren't paying a lot of attention as the announcer began his usual spiel, but they perked up when he called, "Starting at outside hitter, a senior from San Francisco, California, the PAC-10 student athlete for the month of October, Ryan O'Flaaaa-her-ty."

Martin looked at Jamie and she stared back in open-mouthed

shock. They turned their heads in unison to lock eyes with the PAC-10 player of the month. She shrugged her shoulders just a tiny bit and gave them an adorable crooked grin. "She's an enigma," Martin mused.

"Wrapped in a conundrum," Jamie added with a smirk as she blew her secretive lover a kiss.

Catherine arrived very late, traffic not cooperating this evening, but Ryan spotted her as soon as she arrived, and gave her a discrete thumb's up sign.

As soon as the last point was scored, Ryan ran up into the stands to kiss her father and Maeve and welcome them home. Jamie informed her that the group was coming to the house for dessert so the couple could tell them all about their trip.

Ryan hugged her father and stepmother, and ran to get changed, skipping her usual impromptu autograph session. "Boy, she really missed you two," Jamie smiled to Martin. "For her to rush out of here like this is remarkable."

Martin winked at Jamie and said, "Don't tell Siobhán but I don't think we spent a moment missing anyone in the family. Even Caitlin's name wasn't mentioned, and you know she's the focus of most conversations around here."

The small group sat around the living room eating ice cream and cake that Jamie stopped to buy. "So, Da, what did you think of the house?"

"Oh, my! Can you even call a place like that a house, love? Shouldn't there be another name for it, like castle or mansion? I've never seen anything like it in my whole life."

"That was one kitchen that Marty and I could share peacefully," Maeve decided. "We made all of our meals together, and we didn't run into each other once."

"So you didn't go to any of the restaurants Jamie recommended?" Ryan asked. "I didn't think you'd want to cook all week."

"No, we didn't go out for any meals, did we, Marty?"

"No, no, I don't believe we did," he agreed.

"Did you go over to Pebble Beach and walk along the pedestrian paths?" Jamie asked.

Maeve gave Martin a look and said, "No, we didn't get a chance to do that, either."

Martin was blushing a little and Rory went to the heart of the issue. "Did you leave the house, Da?"

He gave his youngest son a slightly perturbed look and said, "No, lad, we did not." He added, "It's a very big house, ya know, and we were only there four days. It took a while to explore the entire place."

Jamie shot her partner a look and they both had to struggle to refrain from laughing, but neither wanted to make the couple uncomfortable, so they behaved themselves. "It is a big house," Jamie agreed. "It could easily take four days to see it all." Turning back to Martin she said, "Did you spend any time in the gym? I know you like to work out."

He pulled on the collar of his shirt and said, "No, no, we didn't get over there, Jamie. Maybe next time."

"How about the pool, Aunt Maeve?" Ryan asked, having a feeling what the answer would be.

"No, we're not much for swimming, dear. We…didn't venture very far."

"How was the weather, Da? Or did you not make it to a window?" Ryan asked innocently, ineffectively batting her blue eyes at her father.

He shot her a look and reminded her, "Siobhán, I have a series of embarrassing stories, going back to 1975 that I'm sure everyone would love to hear. Before you go teasing your father, perhaps you'd like to step back and consider that."

"Who wants more cake?" she asked brightly, smiling at her now smirking father and his blushing bride.

❧

"Mmm…Saturday," Jamie sighed early in the morning, sounding a little like Homer Simpson.

"Yeah, it's nice to be able to lie in bed and not worry about class or golf practice."

"Or basketball or volleyball games," Jamie added.

There was a brief silence, and then Ryan said, "Well, you're technically correct. I don't have a game today."

"Ryan…" It always meant trouble when that name sounded like it was made up of three syllables.

"Yes?"

"What's up? You played volleyball Thursday and Friday evenings, and you don't have your first basketball game until tomorrow."

"True. But we have practice today. It'll probably be a long one."

"You have to practice on Saturday?" Jamie sounded absolutely horrified at this development.

"Yep. Especially when we have a Sunday game." Ryan had a chagrined look on her face as she said, "I think the schedule's gonna be pretty tough. Coach Hayes seems like she expects a lot more from us than Coach Placer did."

"I don't like it," Jamie grumbled, "but I guess I don't have a choice. Can I come?"

"No, you can't come this afternoon," Ryan said as she started to kiss a wet path from her ear, down past her collar bones, around one perky breast, down to linger at her tempting navel. "But you can definitely come this morning," she growled as she climbed on top of her giggling partner to fulfill her prophesy. "Several times."

When Ryan got home from practice, there was a definite slump to her shoulders.

Jamie looked up from her book and asked, "What's wrong, honey?"

"I went by the volleyball office to check on the NCAA selection results. We didn't make it," she added needlessly.

"Oh, Sweetheart, I'm so sorry." Jamie got up and offered a comforting hug.

"Yeah, it kinda sucks. If we were in any other conference, I'm sure we'd be in, but they took four PAC-10 schools, and it just looks bad to take half the conference." She unzipped her jacket and started to strip for a shower. "I'm disappointed, but Jordan's gonna be devastated. She needs the exposure for USA Volleyball to see how good she is."

"I think it's so sweet that you're more focused on Jordan's disappointment than your own," Jamie said softly.

"I'd really love to play in a NCAA tournament, so I'm disappointed. I know we won't go in basketball, so this was my best chance. But this is Jordan's future. It's a very big deal for her."

"You gonna call her?"

"Yeah. After I take a shower and wash my disappointment down the drain," she said, a half-smile curling up one side of her mouth.

Chapter Sixteen

Just after Mass on Sunday, Ryan ran downstairs to change clothes while Jamie helped Martin make brunch. The O'Flaherty kitchen was bigger than the one at the Driscoll house, and since all of the children now lived together, the newly married couple found themselves automatically drifting into eating their meals with the boys. No one complained, of course, since the boys were more than happy to have a pair of built-in cooks.

A few minutes later Ryan was back in her new "Cal Basketball" warm ups. The unveiling was a little anticlimactic since the new suit was identical to the old except for the legend, since a different sponsor had paid for the basketball team's uniforms.

"Oh, you look so cute," Jamie said fondly, ignoring the fact that only one word had changed.

"I've really gotta go," Ryan said as she looked at her watch. "Is there something I can eat on the run?"

Martin shook his head, but immediately started to make her an energy shake. He added a couple of spoonfuls of protein powder as the nutritionist had recommended, and Ryan gulped it down without complaint. Jamie went to the cabinet and got out some energy bars that she placed in Ryan's generously sized pockets. "Is that enough to keep you going?"

"Yeah, I think so. I had two bowls of oatmeal before Mass, so this should do it."

"Did you take your vitamins?" Jamie asked.

"Yep. Every one—even the big one that makes me gag," she said proudly.

"Okay, you're released," Jamie decided. Martin smiled at his daughter as she kissed her partner goodbye.

"I could have used you around the house when the lass was young, Jamie. You certainly have a way of handling her."

Ryan replied by raising one eyebrow to dangerous heights, causing her father to blush fiercely. "I didn't think that one through," he mumbled.

The mostly completed Haas Pavilion was the site of the game, and Jamie was excited to see the new building. The men's team had, of course, received the honor of opening the gym, but there was still a little excitement for the first women's game. She was pleased to see a decent crowd streaming into the venue, but quickly realized that there were problems at the gate that made the crowd seem bigger than it was.

Even though the court had been ready for some time, and the offices an even longer time, the staff had not been properly trained or equipped to deal with a crowd, and it took almost fifteen minutes to finally enter the building.

Most of the O'Flahertys had attended the volleyball game the night before, so many of them decided to skip today since Ryan had warned them she wouldn't play much, if at all.

Catherine, however, was right on time as usual. She found Martin, Maeve, Caitlin, Conor, Brendan, Rory and Jamie without too much trouble, and she looked around excitedly while the band played. "This is very lively, isn't it?"

"Yeah, there's more excitement about basketball than there usually is for volleyball. It's kinda cool to have the whole band here."

"Don't forget the full complement of cheerleaders," Conor added with a waggling eyebrow.

Jamie was shocked but terribly pleased when she turned around in response to a tap on her shoulder to find Jordan, Mia and the entire volleyball squad grinning down at her. "You guys are so sweet!" she cried as she hopped up and hugged each woman. They all knew Martin, Maeve, Brendan and Catherine by now, and most of the girls had been chatted up by Conor, but Rory was a new face to many of them. Jamie made the introductions as the team grabbed the empty row right behind them.

Turning around, Jamie patted as many legs as she could reach and said, "I'm really sorry you guys didn't get the NCAA bid. You deserved it."

The women mumbled their thanks, obviously not in the mood to talk about the disappointing news.

The teams came out to warm up just as the spectators got settled. They were wearing a different type of navy blue warm-up outfit, and Jamie turned to Conor to ask what they were. He explained that they were practice warm-ups with snaps all the way down both legs so they could be ripped off without trying to get them over shoes.

Mia was sitting right behind Jamie, and she leaned over and said, "She looks pretty cute in that outfit."

"Yeah, she does," Jamie agreed. The solid color and roomy cut made Ryan look even bigger than normal, and Jamie was always in favor of more of her lover—even if it was an optical illusion.

As game time drew near, the cheerleaders took the floor and stood at attention as the band played the Star Spangled Banner. Introductions began for the visiting University of Nevada. In contrast to volleyball they were distinctly perfunctory. The announcer reported each starting player's name, class, height and her hometown in a near monotone.

As soon as the visiting teams introductions were finished, the cheerleaders formed a long phalanx that the Cal players would obviously run through to reach the middle of the court. Now the announcer came to life as he intoned dramatically, "And now...your University of California Goooolden Bears!" The crowd cheered heartily as he began to introduce each of the players. He called out each of the players by number with the reserves introduced first. Since Ryan wasn't a starter and she had the lowest number she was called first. "A six foot three inch senior forward from San Francisco, California...Number five...Ryan O'Flaaaa-her-ty."

Martin shot Jamie a smile as he asked, "Is that the same announcer?"

"Yep," she replied spotting the red haired man at the scorer's table. Ryan's personal rooting section got to their feet and cheered loudly. The volleyball team chanted "Boomer…Boomer…Boomer," until Ryan looked up and gave them a tiny wave.

Jamie hadn't met any of the players yet, and Ryan didn't have much to say about them since she'd been working almost exclusively with Lynette to get ready to play. She noticed that there were only two people taller than Ryan, a very large black woman named Janae Harris from Inglewood, California, and a woman with a tongue-twisting, unpronounceable name from Croatia.

The starting players ripped off their warm-ups, and Jamie laughed at the gasp from her mother when she spied the uniforms for the first time. "Oh my!" she muttered. "That is the most unfortunate outfit that I've ever seen."

Jamie had to admit that the uniforms were dreadful. They were the very bright gold that normally accented the navy blue of most of the Cal gear. Gold was a fine color as an accent, but a little bright gold goes a very long way, and these uniforms were past any reasonable limit. Jamie mused that very few people looked good in gold, and it was clear that only the darkest black women on the team could pull it off. Unfortunately, only three members of the team were very dark skinned, so the rest of them were doomed to look jaundiced for the rest of the season.

Ignoring the color, which was very hard to do, the cut of the uniforms was absolutely horrid. It looked like the uniforms of the Golden State Warriors had been delivered by mistake but the women had decided to wear them anyway. Most of the players had their shirts hanging out over their shorts, and they looked like men's jerseys, since the tails were quite tight around the women's hips. But as bad as the shirts were, it was the shorts that were the true tragedy. If a woman had a thirty-inch waist it looked as though she wore a forty-inch pair of shorts. They were so outrageously baggy, that they would have been comical if they weren't so unattractive.

As tip-off drew near, the starters tucked their jerseys into their pants as far as they could go, then pulled the waistband of their pants down low on their hips. Next they pulled the jerseys out until they bloused down over the wide waistband of the shorts. After another bout of tugging the shorts down, they were set, until they had to run or jump—which necessitated another round of adjustments.

Mia leaned over and whispered to Jamie, "You have to make her quit this team! She could ruin her whole reputation if she's seen in that monstrosity!"

"Maybe she doesn't look as bad in hers," she said weakly, almost afraid to have Ryan take off her warm-up.

Once she was over the shock of the uniforms, Jamie paid attention and really began to get into the game. She had spent a lot of time in football stadiums when she was growing up, but since her father wasn't a big basketball fan, so she hadn't been either. It was enjoyable and educational to have the volleyball team behind them since many of the girls had played basketball in high school, and they knew a lot about the game. They also provided contagious enthusiasm as they cheered wildly for each play.

The band was located in the section right next to theirs, and Jamie noticed that the drummers rapped their sticks on the rim of their instruments every time Cal scored a point. They began to anticipate the noise, and after a few minutes the volleyball team began to chant with the drummers when a point was scored. After the first three-pointer they all cried, "Bang! Bang! Bang!" as the drums rapped out the crisp staccato.

Cal was clearly the superior team, and by halftime they were leading by fifteen. Ryan did not play, as predicted, but Jamie noticed that she was very intent on watching the game. She sat next to Lynette, and Jamie noticed that she talked to the coach almost constantly.

The second half began in the same lop-sided fashion that the first half had presaged, and with five minutes left Cal was leading by twenty-five. Jamie saw the coach point to Ryan, and the O'Flaherty rooting section went wild as she stood up and shucked her warm ups. The girls shouted "Boomer, Boomer" until time was called and she ran onto the court.

Much to Jamie's disappointment, Ryan looked a little worse than her teammates did. Her golden tanned skin was singularly unsuited to the garish gold color—being exactly the wrong shade to complement each other. Her weight loss made her look absolutely lost in the huge uniform, hiding every attractive element of her lovely body. As Jamie stared at her partner in puzzlement Mia leaned over and pointed out the missing ingredient. "Where are her breasts?"

"I don't know," Jamie murmured. "I'm certain that they were there this morning..."

She wasn't sure how her lover had accomplished it, but her breasts were practically non-existent in the colossal jersey. And given that the shorts hid every hint of her hips and rounded butt, she had to admit that every ounce of her sex appeal was very well hidden. Once her shock at seeing the uniform had passed, Jamie allowed her eyes to roam down and notice that Ryan wore black high-top basketball shoes—with short black socks that barely showed above the ankle. The tall woman reached into her sports bra and extracted a mouth guard, and as she slipped it into her mouth, Jamie noticed that it was a bright blue color. "Oh, that's fantastic," Jamie murmured. "Blue teeth are just the right touch."

Even though Ryan didn't look hot, she played hot. Cal played an aggressive style of man-to-man defense, and Ryan played her opponent so tight that they could have both gotten into the same mammoth uniform together. She was obviously annoying the poor woman, as the overmatched player tried in vain to get away from the pressure. Her opponent wasn't a very good ball-handler, and she was obviously surprised when she tried to hold the ball above her head to make a pass and Ryan jumped in the air and smashed the ball from her hands. The volleyball team started yelling, "Spike, spike, spike!" as the ball skittered across the floor and landed in the hands of Cal's point guard. Ryan took off for their basket as soon as she slapped the ball away, and two passes later her teammate fed her the ball for her first two points—an uncontested lay-up. As Ryan ran back up the court she couldn't keep the smile off her face, while she pointed dramatically at the teammate who had passed the ball to her as the announcer called out. "Ryan O'Flaaa-her-ty. Thank you, Amy Sumitomo."

Coach Hayes left Ryan in for the rest of the game, and even Catherine could tell that she caused the intensity of the game to increase measurably. "She's quite the little fireball," she mused as she smiled at Jamie. "Would it be terribly rude to see if you could have that outfit tailored for her?"

"I don't think that would be a good idea," she replied, wrinkling up her nose.

"Well, ask her to make sure that any photos they take of her will be from the neck up."

Ryan was not given many more scoring opportunities, but she was a potent force on defense. Her lightning-quick body was a blur as she flew around the court, and she managed to block two shots and snag two rebounds in her limited play. Just before the buzzer, she had the ball and Jamie could see her dart a glance down for the three-point line. She dribbled back a foot and launched a beautiful shot that flew through the hoop as she was fouled. "Four point play!" her rooting section cried as Ryan went to the free throw line. She went through the same routine that Jamie had seen the day Ryan had tried out, but Ryan added one little twist. Using her index finger, she made a quick X over her heart, then concentrated and lofted the ball cleanly through the net.

The final score was 99-69, and Jamie noticed that Lynette put her arm around Ryan's shoulders and talked to her animatedly the whole way to the locker room.

As the announcer summarized the game totals, he once again went through Nevada's numbers perfunctorily. When he announced the totals for Cal, the band got involved once again by rapping out the point totals for each player. Even though she had only played a few minutes, after Ryan's name was called the drums banged out six thumps. "Well done, eh, Jamie?" Martin said happily.

"Mighty!" she agreed with a big grin.

Since Jamie had the team all together she said, "We're having a big party on Tuesday after your last game, guys. Bring dates or friends, if you want. Thanksgiving break starts the next day, so you've got no excuses."

Jamie was waiting right outside the locker room, holding a squirming Caitlin when Ryan emerged. "My two favorite girls!" Ryan smiled as she accepted the lunging baby and bent to kiss her partner.

"You did so good," Jamie enthused. "You're gonna be starting in no time."

"Thanks," she said with a shy grin that charmed Jamie to the core.

"Hey, did you see the sign I gave you?"

"When you were shooting that free-throw? I saw it, but I'm not sure I understood it."

"I made an X over my heart. You know, like the sign for a kiss."

"Ohh, you're such a sweetheart. Were you born so cute, or did you just keep getting cuter all the time?"

"Mmm." Ryan paused to consider the question. "I think it's an ongoing process. I don't think I'm done yet, either. There's plenty of unexplored cuteness for you to tap into."

"Now that's something to look forward to."

"You know, you didn't comment yet, Jamers. Did you like our unis?"

"Um, they were very, very…bright," she replied, believing in the maxim 'if you can't say something nice…'

Ryan tossed her head back and laughed at Jamie's faltering tries to compliment her. "I know they're dreadful, but that's how the rest of the team likes to wear them, so I don't really have a choice."

"Well, the uniforms are bad enough, but where did your breasts go?"

"I can't stand to have them bouncing around, so I wear a sports bra that's one size too small and then a compression top over that."

"Well it was very effective. I couldn't see one inch of movement from any of your body parts."

"I'm sorry you don't get to see jiggling," she said as she wrapped her arm around her partner to go find the rest of the family.

"Me too. Now I'm gonna have to actually watch the games."

On the way back home Jamie asked, "Did you have a meeting after the game?" She sniffed delicately and teased, "You sure as heck didn't take a shower."

"Yeah," Ryan smiled. "Coach likes to review the game as soon as it's over. Then at the next practice she goes over it in detail… minute detail from what I've heard. We did get a little good news, though."

"What's that?"

"We can all go to the airport on our own on Thanksgiving.

Apparently, she likes the team to travel together on the bus, but since so many of us will be with our families on Thursday, she's not going to make us come to Berkeley first."

"Wow! What a humanitarian." She looked at Ryan with concern and asked, "Are you sure you're going to enjoy this? She doesn't seem like your kinda coach."

Ryan shrugged. "I hate to jump to conclusions, but so far you're absolutely right."

"Can we discuss this?"

"Discuss…?"

"Honey, I've got some concerns. Can we stop for a cup of coffee or some ice cream? I don't want to discuss this in a moving car. I want your full attention."

Ryan gave her a wink and said, "And you think you can get that when I've got a dish of ice cream in front of me? It'd better be coffee."

They parked in the big public lot next to their favorite coffee shop and snared the front table, watching the Sunday night parade of homeless people looking for a spot to bed down.

"I'm worried about you," Jamie said quietly. "I know you have boundless enthusiasm for things that you love, but I have a feeling that this isn't going to be one of them. You're still very run down, your weight is still way too low, and you've got a load of schoolwork this term. I just don't see how you can do it."

Ryan reached across the table and grasped Jamie's hand, blue eyes searching her face with concern. "Why haven't you said anything before?"

"I have, honey. You know I wouldn't have chosen this for you."

"Yeah, I know, but that's different from being worried about me. Before you were just telling me that you wouldn't do it. Now you're saying that I shouldn't do it. Big difference, babe."

Jamie sighed and shook her head. "I don't want to tell you what to do. That's not the kind of spouse I want to be."

Ryan reached across the table to cup her cheek. She exerted just a bit of pressure and Jamie lifted her head and met her eyes. "You're a wonderful spouse. You're just showing me that you love me."

"I do love you." Her eyelids fluttered closed and she rubbed her cheek against Ryan's hand. "I love you enough not to nag you about this. I just want to make sure you've thought it through thoroughly."

"I think I have. I mean, I can't be sure this'll work out, but I get along well with one of the women and I like the assistant coach a lot."

"That's a small amount of support, love."

"Yeah, but Janae is cool. She's the center and she's also a senior. I know she wants to make a difference this year, and I think that if we work hard we can win over some of the fence sitters. If we can get the control of the team away from the other two seniors I think we could be good."

All of this was a complete news flash to Jamie. "You not only have to play well, you have to orchestrate a coup?"

"I wouldn't go that far," Ryan chuckled. "But the other two seniors are pretty negative and their negativity has infected the team." Jamie was giving her a very wary look and Ryan looked at her seriously and said, "I know you don't understand this, but I love team dynamics. I get a huge boost from trying to toy with the chemistry of a team and turn it into a positive force. Janae feels just like I do—and I think it would be awesome if we could kick some butt and drag Cal out of the cellar for a change."

"This really means a lot to you?"

"Yeah. In a weird way it does. I like it that we play in the big gym. I like it that some of our games are televised. I really enjoy the boost that women's basketball has had in the last few years and I want to be a part of it." Her eyes were shining with excitement and Jamie felt all of her reservations dim when she looked into those baby blues.

Reaching across the table, she grasped her partner's hand and said, "I'm in your corner, baby. If this is what you want, you've got my full support."

"That's worth everything to me."

Chapter Seventeen

On Monday evening Ryan came home from her last double practice, feeling a little down in the dumps afterwards. When she walked in the door, Jordan was already there, setting the table. "You know, this extra hour is about to kill me," she said, grinning. "I'm used to eating by six-fifteen. Can you have your coach move practice up an hour?"

"Come here," Ryan said, smiling sweetly.

Jordan walked over, then immediately let out an outraged squawk when Ryan grabbed the back of her neck and shoved her head into her open gym bag. "That's a toxic dump!" Jordan hollered, bringing Mia and Jamie out of the kitchen to see what was going on. "She's trying to kill me!" she cried.

"Leave Jordan alone," Jamie warned. "She's not used to being around ruffians like you." She approached her partner and gave her a gentle hug. Casting a glance at the gym bag she said, "That's cruel, Ryan. Very cruel."

"I thought you liked the way I smell," she said, feigning hurt.

"I do. I just prefer your scent fresh. When it ferments on your wet clothes, it's a bit much even for me."

"No respect in my own home," she grumbled, heading for the shower for her body and the laundry chute for her clothing.

"Oh, honey, your aunt called. She asked you to call her when you have time."

"Maeve or Moira?" Ryan asked as she ascended the stairs.

"Maeve. She said it's not a rush."

"Let me call her now, okay?" Ryan asked. "She never calls without a reason."

When she reached her room she dialed her aunt's number, smiling when her father answered. "May I speak to the lady of the house, please?"

"Ahh, it's my sweet one. I'll get Maeve for you, love. Are you feeling well?"

"I'm fine, Da. Had my last double practice tonight. I'm back to one-a-days now."

"Good. Here she is. See you tomorrow, sweetheart. Shall I wear a suit?"

"Well, you can if you want, but your normal attire is just fine. Are the boys all going to make it?"

"Of course they are. We'll have a good showing of the cousins as well. Don't you worry."

"I'm not worried, Da. The family has never let me down."

"Hello, Ryan," Maeve said when she picked up.

"Hi, Aunt Maeve. What's up?"

"I heard something distressing yesterday, and I didn't have a chance to talk to you about it after your game."

"What is it?" Ryan felt her heart rate pick up at the tone of her aunt's voice.

"I spoke with Mary Elizabeth Andrews, and she said things aren't going well at their house. It seems that Sara told her parents that she's a lesbian."

"Oh," Ryan said, sitting down hard on her desk chair.

"Yes, apparently Mary Elizabeth wasn't terribly surprised, but Sara's father took the news very badly. He told Sara she wasn't welcome to come home if she was going to choose that path."

"What would he rather?" Ryan snapped. "Would he rather she never know love in her life, or should she marry some poor man who doesn't ever understand why she's so distant?"

"Ryan," Maeve said gently. "I'm on Sara's side in this."

"I'm sorry, I know you're supportive. It just makes me so damned mad. Why must people be so afraid of difference."

"I don't know, but they are. So many parents seem to love their children until they disappoint them. I don't know Sara's father well, but he's always seemed very proud of her and her accomplishments. I guess he can't stand to have his image of her destroyed."

"So what's the bottom line? What's Mrs. Andrews going to do?"

"That's the most distressing part. She acted so helpless. She said that she didn't know what to do other than to hope her husband changed his mind soon. I got the impression that she wasn't going to push the issue—even if it means Sara is forced out of the family."

Ryan took a deep breath, biting back the colorful curse she was on the verge of spitting out. "I thought Mrs. Andrews had learned something from what happened to me," she said softly.

"I think it's expecting a lot for Mary Elizabeth to suddenly have a spine. She's a very, very passive woman."

"With a daughter that's probably absolutely devastated," Ryan said, her stomach clenching in sympathy for her old friend.

⁂

Jordan seemed distracted at dinner and after Ryan watched her pick at her food for a while she finally asked, "What's up?"

"Huh?" Jordan asked absently.

"Is something bothering you? You've been quiet ever since I came back down."

Mia shot Ryan a look, but the question was already out on the table and she couldn't pull it back in.

"Oh. I was just thinking about tomorrow night. I called home to get my messages and my dad called earlier to say he can't make it."

Ryan mentally rolled her eyes. "He can't make it to senior night? Does he know this is a big deal?"

"Yeah, he does. He wouldn't cancel if he didn't have to," she said, her defenses rising. "He has a very demanding job."

"I didn't mean to imply that he doesn't care," Ryan said contritely. "I just thought that maybe he didn't understand that this meant a lot to you."

She shrugged and said, "It really doesn't. I'm sure that lots of people don't have family available. It's just gonna be weird when your whole clan shows up," she admitted sheepishly. "I'm really gonna look like an orphan then."

Knowing she was treading on thin ice, Ryan asked, "Did you even ask your mom to come?"

"No way," she said with wide eyes. "Then she'd know the season was over."

Ryan nodded, not understanding this logic in the least, but knowing that Jordan had her reasons for everything she did—even though they were sometimes elusive.

※

After dinner, Ryan called Sara, but no one was home, and the answering machine didn't pick up.

Jamie came upstairs and lay down on the bed, motioning for Ryan to join her. Ryan cuddled up against her chest, allowing Jamie to soothe her by rubbing her back. "It brings back all of the old memories, doesn't it."

"Yeah, it does. I guess, in a way, Sara knew how poorly this would go. Maybe that's why she was so afraid of being honest."

"Maybe," Jamie sighed. "It's just sad. How can you let something so incidental to your child's total self affect how you feel about them?"

"I'll never understand it," Ryan murmured. "Not if I live to be a thousand." She nuzzled her head against Jamie's chest, soaking up the comfort. "I feel like I need to get in touch with her. Will that bother you?"

"No, of course not. I'd be disappointed in you if you didn't feel that way. The important thing is to be supportive of Sara right now. She must really be hurting."

"Are you sure?"

"Yeah." She smiled warmly. "We'll handle anything that comes up. It'll be all right."

"Thanks, baby. She was always closer to her mom, but she always strived to make her dad proud of her. His approval was paramount to her...and probably still is."

※

Ryan hunted Mia down at lunch the next day, managing to find her sunning herself in front of the science library. "Got any ideas about how to support Jordan tonight?" she asked without preamble.

"Uhh…" Mia squinted up into the sun, then motioned for Ryan to move to the side. "Look, I offered to be there for her—as her friend—even though I'd freak out if everyone knew about us. Don't give me that look. I tried."

Ryan sat down and patted Mia on the shoulder. "I'm sorry. I should have known you'd try." She cocked her head and asked, "Did she just turn you down, or did she give you a reason?"

"Oh, she said that she didn't want anyone to think we were together. But I don't know. I got the impression she just doesn't think she deserves it."

"You're gonna be there tonight, right?"

Mia blinked up at her and gave her a scowl. "How big of an asshole do you think I am?"

"Forget I was even here," Ryan grumbled before heading off to her next class.

⁂

"How are you feeling about tonight?" Jamie asked as she helped Ryan secure her hair in a very neat style for the final volleyball game of the season.

"I'm sad," Ryan said, looking just a little sheepish. "It's hard to describe, since I know that I'll be friends with the women from the team that I really bonded with, ya know? But a team has a very ephemeral chemistry, and when you play your last game of the season—it's forever lost—even if you have the exact same players the next year."

"I think I understand that."

"It's harder than usual for me," Ryan said reflectively. "Probably because I know this is the highest level I'll ever play at. I've peaked, since the basketball team sucks, and that's never happened to me before. It's a little humbling."

"Honey, I know you don't agree with me, but I still think there's a good chance you'll get an invitation to try out for the Olympic team."

"It's not gonna happen," Ryan insisted. "I'm gonna try and just play my heart out tonight, and get on with it. From now on, I'm just a former-college player who will still kick an occasional butt in beach volleyball."

❧

The team was a little jittery during warm-ups, even though they were playing for nothing more than pride. It was important to all of them that they make a statement with their last game and things got even tenser when someone mentioned that a scout from USA Volleyball might be in the stands.

Ryan scanned the crowd in the sold-out gymnasium, and easily found her rooting section. She gave them a signal when it was getting close to game time, and they made their way down to the court. The student manager came to get Jordan and Ryan, handing them their warm-up jackets. They stood over by the huge blue curtain that separated the stands from the basketball court and waited patiently while the lights went down and the announcer began his spiel.

"Ladies and gentlemen—may I have your attention. Tonight we honor two graduating seniors who have combined to lead the Bears to their best finish in the decade.

Jordan Ericsson, a four year starter, is the all-time Bears leader in kills and hitting percentage. A national player of the year candidate, she's also a two-time First-team All PAC-10, and a two time member of the U.S. World University Games team. Jordan was a first team Volleyball Magazine All-America, and was a Junior Olympic All-Tournament team selection. She's from Santa Monica California, and lettered for four years at Le Lycée Français de Los Angeles in both volleyball and basketball. Jordan also played for the Palisades Storm club team for four years, and was the CIF state champion in the fifteen-hundred meters."

Jordan slapped Ryan's hand and started to head out to the court, but Ryan grabbed her jacket and said, "Not so fast. Wait for your cue."

Jordan gazed at her in the dim light, but Ryan just smiled enigmatically and said, "Listen to my bio. It won't take long."

The announcer began again. "Ryan O'Flaherty has made a big impact in only one year with the Bears. A two-year letter winner from the University of San Francisco, Ryan was the PAC-10 player of the month for October, the first time a Bears volleyball player has won that honor. She's from San Francisco and lettered at Sacred Heart Academy in volleyball, soccer, basketball, and softball for three years. Ryan was a member of the CIF championship soccer team in her junior year. She was also the state champion in the two hundred meters."

"Let's give a hearty round of applause to these two fine athletes as they're joined by their family and friends."

The blue curtain parted as the lights went up and no less than twenty O'Flahertys streamed through the opening. A pair of significantly shorter women made their way to the front of the crowd, each bearing a lavish bouquet of roses. Jordan was positively dumbstruck, and Ryan had to tug on her to get her to walk to the middle of the court. The crowd was on its feet, clapping wildly as Jordan and Ryan waved and took a bow.

Even though the applause was thunderous, Jordan was aware of little but the small, warm hand that held her large, clammy one, and the misty brown eyes that gazed up at her with a look that bordered on adulation.

Ryan slung an arm around her friend's shoulders and said, "Isn't it nice to be part of a large family?"

Ryan's prediction was accurate, and the final game proved to be an intensely emotional experience for the entire team. They had little problem with their opponent, the University of Nevada, and were moving along nicely towards a three game sweep. They were leading game three 13-9 when timeout was called. Coach Placer gave them a few instructions during the brief interlude but just before he sent them back on the court he reminded them, "Two more points for the season!"

Jordan shot a near panicked look at Ryan, and as their gazes met it suddenly hit her full force. Despite the short talk she'd had with Jamie, she hadn't given a lot of thought to the end of volleyball, since she was already gearing up for basketball. She realized with a start that she had done this her whole life. She had never had to face the sadness that affected a lot of the women when the season ended, since she always had another one to go to. It was very similar to the way she'd regarded women in the past. When a woman had outlived her usefulness, she was replaced almost immediately with very little emotion. But that wasn't how she wanted to live her life any longer. So she tried to stay with the emotion of the game and really feel what the end of the season meant to her. It was obvious that Jordan was deep in the moment and as their eyes met Ryan wrapped an arm around her. "Let's go out big!" she urged giving her a fierce squeeze.

Jordan looked like she was fighting to maintain her composure, but returned Ryan's hug and nodded her head forcefully. "Let's kick some butt!" she growled her face taking on a look of fierce determination.

The next point was won before Ryan could blink. Erika served a beauty, but the ball was dug brilliantly and returned right to Jordan. The tall woman elevated and slammed the ball down with as much force as Ryan had seen her exert all year. As soon as the ball landed, she jumped in the air and gave a joyous 'whoop' that seemed to energize the entire team. On the next serve, the ball was returned to Ryan's side. Amy and Jordan slid over, and the three of them rose as one, their long arms extended over the net. Ryan had no idea which of them actually got the block, but the ball zoomed off their hands and skidded onto their opponent's court for the final point of the season.

Before Ryan knew what hit her, Jordan had jumped into her arms, and it was only her quick reflexes that allowed her to catch her teammate. Long, lean legs wrapped around Ryan's waist, as Jordan repeatedly thrust her arm into the air in triumph. Ryan gave her an enthusiastic squeeze, but patted her back after just a few seconds. "We have to be good sports. Hop down so we can shake hands."

"I like it up here," she said with a joyful grin on her face. "Now I know how Shaquille O'Neal feels."

A rather firm slap on the butt got her to release her hold, and they politely shook hands with their vanquished opponents. Ryan stood near the center of the court and let the bright lights warm her for a moment as her teammates streamed into the locker room. She lifted her head and gazed all around the gym, just trying to soak up the moment. As her eyes traveled around, they landed on a thin, dark haired woman who was watching her intently. As soon as Ryan looked at her the woman rose from her seat and walked quickly towards the exit. Ryan's stomach did a flip, as it seemed to do every time she saw Sara Andrews.

The celebration continued into the locker room. For a change, everyone took a shower since they were all going to the party. Jamie had told Ryan that she would leave as soon as the game was over, but that Ryan needn't be in a rush to leave. They played around in the open shower area, teasing and congratulating each other with much more enthusiasm than usual. It soon became clear that no one wanted to leave the protective environment of the team, so Ryan finally reminded them that there was a house full of food and drink just waiting for them. That did the trick, and they all dashed out of the room and began fighting over hair dryers.

Most of the women had brought street clothes to wear to the party. With their hair out of the restrictive ponytails or braids that they normally wore they looked like an entirely different group of women when they showed up at the already hopping celebration.

Ryan immediately noticed that some of the cousins were paying rapt attention as they came in, and she had no intention of discouraging them. The boyos could do a lot worse than her teammates, her fondness for her teammates having grown with each game.

As soon as she spied her, Jamie rushed over to congratulate Ryan. Jordan was also the recipient of a kiss from Jamie, but Ryan could see her looking around for a friendlier version as soon as Jamie pulled away. Moments later, Mia came scampering up. She took Jordan by the hand and started to lead her into the library, informing her friends, "I have to give her a private congratulations for her stellar play." Her sexy grin left no doubt that the private talk would go on for a while, so Ryan went into the kitchen to help Jamie with the food.

They had decided to order in rather than cook themselves, so Jamie had ordered trays of cold cuts and platters of antipasto from Ryan's favorite Italian deli in Oakland. She was pleased beyond words when they went into the kitchen to find that her Aunt Deirdre had baked a massive sheet cake and decorated it with a large rendition of a volleyball and the dark blue 'Cal' script outlined in gold. "This is gorgeous!" she cried as she gave her grinning aunt a hug. Her Aunt Deirdre had been the family baker all of Ryan's life, and her skills had increased in proportion to the massive numbers of cakes required in a family that commemorated every occasion with one.

Her aunt blushed a little as she gazed at her creation. "It's not bad at all," she agreed. "And with a slight modification, I can use the design for basketball in a few months."

Ryan made her way around the room, welcoming every relative. When she reached the chairs in front of the library, she was nonplussed to see Jennie talking seriously with Catherine. As soon as Jennie spied her she rushed over to give her a hug.

"I had no idea you were coming tonight! How did you get here?"

"Jamie called me yesterday and asked if I wanted to come. She stopped by and got me on the way over. It was so much fun," she said animatedly. "It was really cool to see you guys play!"

"I'm really glad you got to come." Checking her watch, she asked, "Do you have permission to be out after curfew?"

"Yes, Ryan," she said dutifully. "Mrs. Evans was just going to give me a ride home."

She bent down to kiss her young friend and asked, "Do you have plans for Thanksgiving?"

"Kind of." Her smile faded as she finished her thought. "My mom won't let me come home, but we're having turkey for dinner at the house. The other girls can't go home either."

"That won't cut it, Small Fry. You're coming to my house. I'll call your housemother in the morning and tell her I'll be up to get you at around ten-thirty. I've got to leave for Colorado by three, but one of my brothers will take you home, okay?"

"Like I'd say no to that?" she asked, her sweet face beaming up at her friend. She tossed her small arms around Ryan's waist and said, "It'll be so nice not to get yelled at on Thanksgiving."

Ryan and Jamie made their way around the room, chatting with each relative and teammate for a few minutes. There were so many in attendance that Catherine had returned from taking Jennie home by the time they were finished. "Good party, eh, Catherine?" Ryan asked as she joined her on the love seat.

"Excellent as usual. I've been to some pretty impressive parties, but I never have more fun than I do when I'm with your family."

"Well, I'll let you in on a little secret," she whispered as she leaned over to speak into her ear. "Our parties weren't much fun at all until you started attending. You're the key."

Catherine gave her a kiss on the cheek. "You are such a sweetheart. I don't think I'll ever be sure if Jamie's really a lesbian, or if your charms were just too much to resist."

"I guess it doesn't really matter, Catherine, because I'm going to keep her too occupied to even consider that question for the rest of her life."

"You're pretty confident of that, aren't you?" she asked, her eyes focusing sharply on Ryan.

"There's not a doubt in my mind. Some things you just know, Catherine." She looked at the still thoughtful expression on her mother-in-law's face and asked, "Did you feel that way about Jim?"

Catherine's head shook slowly. "I wasn't nearly as mature as you and Jamie are now. Jim was my first serious boyfriend, and I don't think I had any idea how I should have felt."

"What about now?" Ryan asked, sensing that Catherine wanted to talk.

She laughed with a touch of derision in her voice. "I suppose I should be as mature as you are now, but I'm not sure that I am. I know I have a deep bond with Jim, but I'm quite sure I don't feel like you feel about Jamie." She sighed heavily and leaned her head back against the sofa. "I don't know if it's possible to be optimistic when you have as many betrayals and disappointments as we have had. I think I have to be willing to accept less."

"I don't like the sound of that, Catherine. How can you open your heart to someone that you don't trust?" She scooted to the edge of the cushion so that she could turn and face her mother-in-law. "Being vulnerable with Jamie is what lets us really love one another. I hate to think of you setting yourself up in a situation where you think you have to settle for less than that. You really don't." Her eyes were burning with intensity as she said, "You're a fantastic woman. Any man with an iota of sense would realize that and do whatever he had to do to convince you that he loved you. You deserve to love and be loved with your whole heart. Please don't settle for less."

Catherine nodded slowly, looking touched. "I think I know that. Sometimes I lose track of what my needs are, but I think I'm doing better in this area. I won't go back to Jim unless I can trust him. It's just not worth it." She looked at Ryan for a long minute, her hand lifting to gently stroke her flushed cheek, "I swear you are the best thing to ever happen to our family."

"I know I'm partial, but I think Jamie's the best thing to happen to your family," she teased. "But speaking of family, when can I pick you up on Thursday?"

"Ryan, I give in to nearly every one of your demands, but I'm putting my foot down this time. I'll drive myself, and I promise to behave and not drink too much."

"That's not why..."

"I know you care about me, but I'd feel better if I drove. I know you and Jamie have to leave early for your road trip, and I don't want any of your brothers to have to chauffeur me."

"Okay," Ryan said, seeing that Catherine was adamant about this. "We'll see you on Thursday then."

"What time should I arrive?"

"You know, I think it's about time I let you in on another secret. We don't have starting times for our parties—I just make them up for you. When people feel like being around each other, they head on over. That's the best I can tell you." She shrugged her broad shoulders, and gave Catherine a helpless look.

"All right," she chuckled, "but I should warn you that I might be there while you're still in your pajamas."

"Not a problem," Ryan laughed. "I'll give you a key."

Everyone with a job wandered off a little after eleven, but most of the volleyball team was still dancing at midnight. There were enough hands remaining to make the work move quickly, and by twelve-thirty the place was presentable again. Ryan's teammates finally got the hint and started to walk to their respective homes. Conor offered to give a ride to two of the women who lived a bit farther out and after enthusiastic thank you's and goodbyes, the last of the guests sauntered out at twelve-forty-five. Jamie switched the kitchen light off then grasped Ryan's hand and headed for the stairs. They turned off the lights in the parlor as they turned the corner and were about half way up the stairs when they heard a small crash and a loud string of profanity from the kitchen.

Ryan flicked the lights back on and ran downstairs to find her cousin Dermot jumping on one foot and holding the other in both of his hands. "What's the idea of turning off the lights?" he demanded irately.

"Everybody's gone, Dermot. Everyone except you and Amy," she said as her teammate blushed furiously. "Did you come with your parents?"

"No, I rode over with Dec. Liam and Padraig came in Liam's car. Either Declan assumed I was with the others, or he ditched me!"

"No problem. You can borrow my car. I'll be home tomorrow afternoon, so I can pick it up then."

"Aw jeez, Ryan, I hate to take your car."

"It's fine, Dermot. Amy could use a lift anyway, right?"

"Yeah. It's about three miles. That's a little far at this time of night."

"You haven't had much to drink have you?" Ryan asked.

"Well, I hadn't planned on driving, so I had quite a few..." he admitted.

"I didn't drink at all," Amy said brightly. "I could take you home."

"You two work out your own plans," Ryan said as she tossed her keys to Amy. "Just don't drive my car if you've been drinking, and call your mother if you're not going home," she commanded her cousin.

Now it was Dermot's turn to blush, but Amy wasn't far behind.

"Thanks," he said gratefully. "You're a life saver."

"My pleasure. Have fun you two," she said, giving them both farewell hugs.

She saw them out the front door and locked up again. By the time she got up to her room, Jamie was already in bed. "Dermot and Amy?" she asked, looking surprised.

"Yep. Surprised the hell out of me too."

"Well if you can't get the prize of the O'Flaherty clan, Dermot's not a bad choice."

"Aw, am I really the prize?" she asked as she climbed onto the bed fully clothed.

"No, but Maeve won't let your father go…" she started to say when the full-scale tickle assault caused her to lose her ability to speak.

"Ouch!" Ryan cried as she flopped back down onto her pillow. "What in the heck?" She stuck her hand under the pillow to pull a hard object out from beneath it. "What is this?" she asked with a quizzical look at her partner, pulling the leather covered book onto her lap.

"Open it and see," Jamie said as her face turned up into a grin.

Ryan did so, enormously pleased to find that Jamie had made her a scrapbook of the entire volleyball season. She had included the small articles about each game that had appeared in the campus newspaper, as well as the tiny snippets from the Chronicle. She'd also included the roster from each game that she'd attended, along with her ticket stub. Ryan was delighted to note that her partner had even gone to the trouble of obtaining the press release from the NCAA which announced Ryan's selection as the student athlete for the month of October. The facing page showed the attractive certificate they'd sent her commemorating the event.

A nice 8 x 10 of the entire team took up one page, but the rest of the pages were filled with candid shots that Jamie had taken in the locker room and at the post-game parties at their house.

"I'll add the pictures from this party when I have them printed," she said from over Ryan's shoulder.

Ryan was slowly shaking her head as she surveyed the neat book. "You are the most thoughtful woman in the world," she murmured as she placed the book down and pulled Jamie into her arms. "I've never kept things from my teams, and I find they just all meshed together in my mind. It'll really be nice to look back on this in future years and remember how special this group of women was."

"I'm glad you like it," Jamie said as she gave her a few sweet kisses.

"I love it. And I love you," she said as she pushed her down for a proper thank you.

Chapter Eighteen

O n Wednesday morning, Catherine was watching C-SPAN, in what was becoming a new ritual for her. She had never had much interest in Jim's legal career, but her family had always been very involved in politics, and she had grown up being very aware of the importance that government played in her life. Since Jim was now serving at the highest level of government, she found her interest sparked once again, and she'd taken to reading more and staying much more cognizant of the affairs of the Senate.

She was particularly interested today since Jim had called her the night before to say that one major piece of business was scheduled to be conducted before the Senate went on their extended break. He was planning on speaking against a bill that would solve part of the budget crisis by slashing funding for the National Endowment for the Arts, one of Catherine's favorite programs. She could tell how excited he was to be able to address an issue that was important to her, and she had promised that she would be watching when he got the opportunity to speak.

Having risen extra early to be sure she didn't miss anything, she smiled into her coffee as the junior senator from the state of California rose to speak. He looked particularly handsome this morning, wearing a dark blue, chalk-striped suit with a white shirt and a blue and green rep tie she had purchased for him. He spoke quite eloquently, and she smiled as she considered that some of his points were actually her own—things she had mentioned when they spoke on the phone.

She was so taken aback by the fact that he'd respected her words enough to make them his own that it took her a minute to place the young red-headed woman that came up to his desk and handed him a paper—obviously feeding him some statistics that his staff wanted him to be sure to mention. Catherine blinked slowly, finally closing her eyes as the unbearably sharp pain of betrayal once again lanced her heart.

Pushing the coffee cup away, she crossed her arms and laid her head down upon them, too drained to even force herself to go upstairs. Marta passed by, but didn't say anything, honoring their long-standing, but unspoken agreement. She was always interested, and always available to discuss any matter that Catherine chose, but Marta did her best not to interfere or intrude on her employer's privacy. Even today, when every empathetic part of Marta wanted to find out what was wrong and help if she could, she maintained her respectful distance.

After a long while, Catherine rose from the kitchen table and went upstairs to her office. It took her a few minutes, but she found the papers she was looking for. She sat down at her desk and composed herself as much as she could, and then with a shaking hand, she uncapped her fountain pen and signed her name to the petition for divorce.

At the close of Senate business, Jim strolled into his office, whistling a tune as he passed his secretary. "Has the messenger delivered my tickets yet?"

"Yes, sir. They came just a few minutes ago. Will you need me to order a limo from the airport?"

"No, thanks. My wife will pick me up." He smiled at the sound of that—very much liking how easy it was to be able to rely on Catherine again. "Will you get her on the phone for me?"

"Certainly,"

He walked into his office and loosened his tie, then sank down into his large leather chair and pulled out the bottom drawer. Hooking his heels onto the wood, he leaned back in his chair and hit the speakerphone when his secretary buzzed him. "Cat?" he asked, his voice brimming with excitement.

"Yes." That was all she said…just one word…but he knew something was terribly wrong. He picked up the phone and asked, "What's wrong, honey?"

"I signed the divorce papers today. A messenger picked them up a few minutes ago. I assume you'll be served sometime next week." Her voice was eerily flat, completely devoid of the warmth and affection she'd expressed just the night before.

"*What*! Cat! How can you… Why would you…?"

"I must compliment you for making things easy for me this time. At least this time I had the evidence right in front of me. It never dawned on me that I'd see your mistress on C-SPAN, but I suppose I should be happy that it happened now, rather than after this weekend. Having you want to come and surprise Jamie seemed like such a nice thing. I had the illusion that we were becoming a family again," she said softly, as her voice became ragged with emotion.

"Cat! No! *No*! I swear, nothing is going on between Kayla and me! I broke up with her the day after the Stanford game. I swear I've not touched her since!"

"Jim," she said softly, "why on earth should I believe you?"

"Because I don't lie to you, Cat. I've always told you the truth whenever you asked me about anything!"

"How do I know that?" she asked. "How do I know that anything you say is true? How do I know that the compliments you've been giving me are genuine? How do I know that, Jim?" she repeated, obviously not expecting an answer.

"You have to trust me," he said, finally seeing the truth of the situation. "If you can't trust me, we don't have much to go on."

His statement hung out there in the air, both of them knowing that it was an elemental truth. He was holding his breath as the seconds ticked slowly by.

She sighed heavily and said, "I can't trust you. I wish with all my heart that I could, but I can't."

She started crying softly and even though her words had devastated him, he wished he could be there to hold her and comfort her. "Please, Cat," he said, his hoarse voice just a whisper. "Please try to believe me. I'm telling the truth."

"I can't let you hurt me again, Jim," she murmured. "I can't." Now she was sobbing harshly, crying in a way he hadn't heard from her in years.

"Please, Cat," he said, again and again. "Please let me come home. I can't bear to hear you cry like this. Let me see you."

"No," she sobbed. "I've made up my mind. Don't come home. I can't stand to see you. It's over. It sickens me to say it—but it's over."

"Cat! Please!" he tried again, but the only sound was the flat, uncaring dial tone.

Chapter Nineteen

As soon as she could manage, Jamie was off to the library on Wednesday morning. Ryan had basketball practice at noon, and they were heading to Noe as soon as she was finished. Jamie was pretty sure that she wouldn't get much done if she hung around the house, so she forced herself to maintain her discipline.

Ryan had finished her breakfast and was just about to start cleaning up when Jordan came down in just a T-shirt and panties. "Morning," she said as she came up behind Ryan and gave her a hug and a kiss on the cheek.

"Hi. Want some breakfast?"

"Yeah. Love some. Could I also borrow some clothes? I threw my wet stuff in my gym bag and got everything drenched. I wouldn't even try to fit into anything of Mia's," she needlessly added.

"Sure. You can go up and scrounge around. You know where everything is."

"'Kay. Be right back."

A few minutes later she was back in a hooded sweatshirt and a pair of sweatpants. Ryan's thick cotton ragg socks were on her feet, and she looked much warmer. "So, what would you like for breakfast?" Ryan asked.

"You're gonna cook for me?" Jordan asked with a delighted grin.

"Sure. You name it."

"Hmm, I don't remember the last time anyone cooked for me. I need to exploit this opportunity."

"What part of eating with us every night isn't cooking for you?" Ryan asked with a crooked grin, ruffling Jordan's fine hair.

"You're cooking for each other. We're sponging off you. Big difference."

"You don't sponge," Ryan chided. "We like having you both with us. Believe me, I don't let people abuse me. If I felt taken advantage of, I'd talk to either you or Mia about it."

"Still, this is the first time I can remember anyone cooking just for me." She looked over at Ryan with her eyes slightly hooded and added, "It's nice." Jordan obviously didn't want to waste her chance, and she paused to think for several minutes until Ryan began to make suggestions.

"French toast? Pancakes? Oatmeal? Eggs with hats?"

"Eggs with hats? What in the heck is that?"

"Do you like eggs?"

"Love 'em."

"Then eggs with hats it is." Ryan assembled the items she needed, taking two pieces of sourdough bread and buttering both of them. Then she cut a large round hole in each and put her favorite cast iron skillet on the range. A little more butter in the pan and then she added the bread. When the skillet was hot, she broke an egg into the holes and watched carefully as they started to sizzle. When they were halfway done she flipped each one over delicately and added the cut out pieces of bread so they could toast too. She pulled over a plate, slid the perfectly cooked eggs onto it and added the little cut outs on top of the eggs. "Two eggs with hats," she said as she placed the plate in front of her friend with a flourish.

"They're so cute. How do I eat them?"

"I like to make a hole and eat the yolk with the little circles of bread. But you can be creative."

Jordan dug in and closed her eyes in pleasure. "These are divine!"

"Thank you," she nodded. "My grandmother in Ireland makes eggs this way."

"My grandmother in La Jolla makes eggs by harassing servers in restaurants until they're ready to throw them at her."

"Is that your mom's mother?"

"Yeah. Apple doesn't fall far from the tree, does it?" she asked wryly.

"I don't know," Ryan admitted. "As much time as we've spent together, I'd have to say that I don't really know much about your family. You're kinda reserved about the whole bunch."

"Mmm," she said, shrugging her shoulders. "I don't have much to say. They're not my favorite people."

"You haven't said what your plans are for the holiday. Are you going home?"

Jordan's head shook decisively as she said, "No, I told my mother we're still playing. She now believes that the volleyball season lasts until just after Christmas." She laughed derisively, stopping short when Ryan placed a gentle hand on her arm.

"What are you doing for Thanksgiving? Are you going to Mia's?"

"No," she said, again shaking her head. "She didn't offer. It's no big deal," Jordan added, with a forced brightness. "I can catch up on my classes. That's what I've done for the last three years."

"What about your father?"

"Oh, he and Candy are going to Vail for a couple of weeks. He's a big skier," she said wistfully. "When I was a senior in high school, he and I went there for Thanksgiving. That's the last trip we had together."

"Has he been with Candy that long?"

"No. He had another one before her. I forget her name," she said. "Joni or Jody or something like that. He's not single for long."

"Will your brother be home for the holiday?" Ryan continued, knowing she was prying, but trying to figure out just what the dynamic in the family was.

"Of course," she said, her expression turning into a scowl. "The little prince would never miss out on an opportunity to wallow in self-pity with my mother."

Once again Ryan was shocked by the acrimony that Jordan held for her brother, and she couldn't help but ask, "What's the deal with your brother? Why so hostile?"

Jordan got up to take her plate to the sink. She started running water to do the dishes, and as she waited for the sink to fill she said, "I shouldn't go off on him. It's not really his fault, and I certainly don't want to trade places with him." She turned to Ryan and said, "It's always been the two of them against me and my dad. It wasn't so bad when my dad lived with us, but when he left..." she trailed off, her implication clear.

"So you felt that the two of them were against you?" Ryan asked, not really getting the point.

"No, not so much against us. That's not the right way to put it. It was more like they were the same person. My mom hates my dad, so my brother has to hate him, too. When I was real little, I was more of an outsider, but when my dad left, they both just kinda ignored me. I got more and more involved in sports as a way to be out of the house," she admitted. "Volleyball was great because there's a lot of tournaments and clinics that I could go to that covered almost every school holiday. During most summers I'd go from one camp to the next, barely coming home at all. So, I don't really know my brother that well, in a way. I've never called him on the phone, and I've never written to him. I'm not even sure I have his address."

Ryan tried hard to hide her frank amazement at this situation. She had no idea of what it would be like to have so little connection with family. The compassion was evident in her eyes when Jordan said, "I guess I don't talk about them much because they seem dead to me. I've tried to kill any longing I have to get mothering from her. It's just not going to happen."

Blinking in shock, Ryan considered for the first time the fact that it was actually preferable for her mother to be dead than to have the distant, rancor-filled relationship that Jordan was left with. She approached her friend and wordlessly wrapped her in a warm hug, feeling Jordan's body relax into hers. "I'm sorry that's how it is for you, buddy."

Jordan didn't reply with words, but she greedily soaked up the affection Ryan offered.

"Will you come to my house tomorrow?" Ryan asked.

"Aw, I don't want to intrude. I'm used to being alone on the holidays. Don't worry about it."

"Thanksgiving has a lot of meaning for me," Ryan said as she lifted her head to look directly into Jordan's blue eyes. "It lets me give thanks for all of the people who mean something to me. You're one of those people, so please come to my house tomorrow and share the day with us."

The sad eyes grew a little brighter as Jordan looked at her friend for a long minute. "Did any woman ever refuse you?" she asked fondly as she patted Ryan's cheek.

Ryan smirked at her as she said, "Not a whole hell of a lot of them. You're not going to spoil my record are you?"

"Not a chance. Add me to your list of conquests."

Mia stumbled into the kitchen as they were still holding each other in a loose embrace. "Get your hands off my woman," she growled playfully, pointedly removing Ryan's arms from her lover's waist.

"We were just making our Thanksgiving plans," Ryan said, obliquely chiding Mia for not bothering to make sure Jordan had a place to go.

Mia looked up at her and twitched her head towards the door, giving Ryan a none-too-subtle hint to take her leave. She did so, patting Jordan on the back as she left.

Mia led Jordan over to a chair and sat upon her knee when she was seated. "I've been working on my mom all week, honey, but she's adamant that Thanksgiving is just for the four of us. I don't know why she's so hardheaded about this, but she won't let any of my other relatives come either. It's just a thing for her, I guess."

"That's okay," Jordan said softly. "I don't really mind being alone. It seems important to Ryan that I go to her house, so I will, but it really doesn't matter to me. It's just a day to eat too much."

Mia knew it was more than that, and she suspected that Jordan wanted more than that, but didn't think she'd ever get it from her family of origin. "I wish we would have thought this through," she said, leaning her head against Jordan's. "I would love to go up to Tahoe with you. Maybe rent a little cabin. We could have a big feast in front of a roaring fire." She started to run her fingers through Jordan's hair, knowing that her touch always calmed her. "Then we'd make love all night in front of the fire, sharing a few glasses of wine, and just being together." She sighed heavily and said, "Doesn't that sound nice?"

"Yeah, it does." Jordan's voice was wistful and bore an element of hope. "Maybe someday?"

"Count on it," Mia said, kissing her soft cheek. "We just need to figure out who's gonna prepare that nice dinner for us, 'cause it sure isn't going to be me."

"Hey, don't look at me," Jordan smiled. "I can just manage to make cocoa on a cold night."

"I'd have plenty to be thankful for if I had you all to myself, a big fire and a mug of cocoa."

"Can you build a fire?" Jordan asked, her blue eyes dancing.

"You and a mug of cocoa is plenty, too. And just for the record, the cocoa's optional."

Jordan graced her with a full, relaxed smile, and Mia found herself drowning in those pale blue eyes. "I have to leave soon, honey. Will you come upstairs with me and let me show you how much I'm going to miss you?"

"Yes," she whispered, placing a gentle kiss on the corner of Mia's mouth. "If I can show you the same."

⚜

Ryan sat in her room as she contemplated the phone call she knew she should make. Gathering her courage she checked her organizer and dialed the phone.

"Morris and Foster," the receptionist announced.

"Hi. I'm looking for an associate named Sara Andrews."

"Her direct number is 312-3344. Please hold and I'll connect you."

"Sara Andrews," she answered almost immediately.

"Hi, Sara, it's Ryan."

"Hi," she said sounding winsome. "I guess you did recognize me."

"Of course I recognized you! Why didn't you say hello?"

"I don't know. I saw your whole family there, and Jamie, and I just thought it was best if I didn't. But I couldn't let you play a whole season without seeing at least one of your games. You don't mind too much, do you?"

"Why would I mind? I think it's sweet that you cared enough to come."

"I care an awful lot," she said softly. "I'll always care for you."

Feeling the stab of longing she always felt when Sara expressed her emotions, Ryan tried to fend off the mood with a little humor. "So, what did you think? Do I still have it?"

"You've still got the magic," she said with a chuckle. "I thought you were good in high school but…"

"Okay, okay, I've fished for enough compliments. Now tell me how things are going for you."

"Things are okay. I was spending most of my time on the freeway, so I got an apartment in the city."

"Really? Where?"

"Marina. Where else should a young corporate attorney live?"

"So is the job okay?"

"It's about what I thought it would be. There are some nice people that I work with, but it's not too exciting."

"Hey, don't you get bar results this week?"

"Did you have to remind me? My stomach is in full spasm."

"I thought you weren't that concerned. You told me this summer that it didn't worry you a bit."

"Wishful thinking, I'm afraid. If I don't pass, I have to take three months off work and study like a maniac again. Add to that the humiliation of everyone at the firm knowing that you failed, and it doesn't help me sleep at night."

"I uh…I spoke to my Aunt Maeve," Ryan said. "She saw your mom at church on Sunday."

"Did she tell her about my little coming out party?" Sara asked wryly.

"Yeah, she did. Was it really bad?"

She sighed and said, "In a way it was as bad as I'd ever imagined." There was a short pause and Sara added, "But in another way, it was much easier than I'd dreamed. I did it, and we're all still alive." She chuckled softly and said, "I used to dream that my dad fell over with a heart attack when I told him."

"Your mom said that your dad is being pretty rigid about this. What are you going to do?"

"Not much I can do," she admitted. "He said this is the last chance I have to turn around. He thinks that if he gives me his 'permission,' there will be no reason for me to try to change."

"Does he really think that you can switch your sexual orientation on and off?"

"Apparently so," Sara replied quietly.

"I'm really sorry to hear that. I can't imagine how it must feel."

"I'll survive. I just had to draw a line in the sand. It's not like he just disagrees with me, he feels like he can force his opinions on me; and I can't tolerate that any more."

"So what will you do tomorrow?"

"I don't know. I got a couple of invitations, but it just feels weird to be with someone else's family."

"Would it feel weird to be with mine?"

"What?" she shouted so loudly that her secretary got up and closed her door.

"You heard me. We're having a huge crowd, so it won't be anything formal. Some other friends of mine will be there, so you won't be the only one who's not related..."

"Ryan, I appreciate that you asked, but your father would rather have the Ulster Unionists there before me."

"That's not true in the least. We had a party after the Stanford game and my father was pleasant to Jim Evans, and he practically tried to have me killed."

"So you're saying they'd welcome me with open arms, huh?"

"Well no, I didn't say that," she admitted. "But they'd rather have you than Jim Evans."

That caused Sara to let out a long, low laugh, and Ryan knew she had her. "Oh, Ryan, I miss your sense of humor. Nobody here can make me laugh like you do."

"Then come over tomorrow and get your fill. There's only one way to get comfortable being with each other again, and that's the total O'Flaherty immersion program."

"You know you could always talk me into anything. But I'll only come on one condition: Jamie has to invite me."

"Huh?" she replied weakly.

"You heard me. I'll only come if Jamie wants me there."

"Boy, you picked the right profession," she mused. "You drive a very hard bargain." She paused for a minute then asked, "Why's that important to you?"

"Because of where we left things. You made it clear that you didn't want the temptation of being around me. It's one thing for you and me to assume the risk, but this affects Jamie, too. If this is going to cause one problem in your relationship I won't come."

"Okay. I'll talk to her."

"That's my final offer. I'll be here until five or so, but I'll give you my home number too. If Jamie isn't as enthusiastic as you are it's perfectly all right, okay? No hard feelings."

"All right. I'll talk to you later." She hung up quietly. *Well this should be fun,* she thought with a shudder.

***

Jamie got back from the library nearly an hour after Ryan's practice finished. When she walked into the bedroom, the computer was on but Ryan was lying on the bed, her eyes wide open staring blankly at the ceiling. She was a little afraid of announcing her presence since Ryan's trances were often precursors to some breakthrough or another. But they had to leave soon to avoid Thanksgiving traffic, so she slid onto the bed next to her partner and wrapped an arm around her waist.

"Hi," Ryan said, as though she had fully expected her to join her.

"You weren't in the middle of anything important, were you?"

"As a matter of fact I was thinking of one of the most important scientific discoveries of our time."

"What was it?" Jamie asked when it became clear that Ryan was being playful.

"I was thinking about you," she said softly as she trailed her fingers down Jamie's grinning face.

"Oh, I thought you were doing some math thingies."

"I was. I was thinking of your name and assigning numbers to it. You know like 'j' is the tenth letter of the alphabet and so on?"

"Uhh, yeah, I guess I see what you mean."

"Then I took all of the values, and I added them all together, but that didn't do much for me. So then I multiplied the numbers in your first name together and then did the same for your last name. When I subtracted one from the other I thought I might be onto something. So I did the same for my name. And do you know what I found?"

"No, I'm quite sure I don't have any idea."

"I found absolutely nothing," she admitted with a quirky grin. "But it was fun to think about your name for..." she paused as she looked at her watch quickly, "forty-five minutes."

Jamie reached over and placed her hand over Ryan's chin. Tugging lightly, she turned her face until it was in exactly the same position as her own. She scooted just a little bit closer and laced her fingers through her dark hair as she started to kiss her. Her hand moved softly through the inky strands until it rested on Ryan's smooth cheek. As she lifted her head she whispered, "Having you spend your time like that is more meaningful to me than if you had written me a sonnet."

"Touch me like that again," Ryan asked in a voice that was just a hair above a whisper.

"With my fingers in your hair?"

"Uh-huh, and on my cheek." She closed her eyes and waited for the gentle touch.

Even more softly this time, Jamie ran her fingers all through the ebony tresses and trailed them lightly over Ryan's cheek. She dipped her head and kissed her soft lips again and again until her partner was moaning with desire. "I love it when you touch my face with your hands while you kiss me," Ryan whispered. "It feels so intimate."

"I love it too," Jamie whispered as she closed her eyes and started to nibble on Ryan's soft lips. Her touch was fleeting and incredibly gentle, but after a few seconds Ryan's mouth opened slowly and she drew Jamie's tongue in. Now the intensity began to build as Ryan wrapped her arms around her partner and pulled her on top of her body. Her mouth was fully open now as she hungrily sucked and nipped on Jamie's darting tongue. Grasping Ryan's flushed face with both of her hands, Jamie pulled up just a bit and gasped out, "Do you mind if we get stuck in traffic?"

"There could not be anything further from my mind right now," she replied softly. "I need to feel your touch. Love me," she urged and Jamie immediately decided that a little traffic paled in comparison to the chance to love the luscious woman who gazed up at her.

An hour later they struggled out of the tangle of sheets and got into the shower together. "Have I told you in the last five minutes what a devastatingly wonderful lover you are?" Jamie asked as she rested her head on Ryan's chest to protect her face from the needle sharp spray.

"Five minutes?" she said reflectively. "I don't think so. But if Mia's home, she could probably repeat some of your enthusiastic praise."

"You know she's with her family, Silly. If there was a chance she would have come home I would have closed the door. I had a feeling I was going to ravage you this afternoon."

"Did you now?"

"Yep. I was thinking about your sexy body and the way you smell the whole time I was studying. It was a struggle to stay in the library as long as I did."

"Well, I'm very proud of you," Ryan said as she kissed her nose. "Just for that I'll give you another tumble before we go to bed."

"If you use that tongue like you just did you can tumble me anywhere, anytime."

"My tongue might have gotten me into trouble today," Ryan ventured, having decided to get the issue out of the way.

"Meaning?"

"I invited someone over for dinner tomorrow without checking with you first."

"Ooh, I forgot. So did I."

"Who did you invite?"

"I asked Ally. She called yesterday when we were at the game, and I jotted her number down on my way out of the house today." She looked at Ryan carefully and asked, "You don't mind that I called her, do you? She asked to speak with either of us."

"No," Ryan said, shaking her head. "I don't mind." She realized that she did, in fact, mind that Jamie spoke with Ally, but thought that was childish and didn't want to admit it. "Why'd you invite her?"

"She sounded sad. She called to wish us a happy Thanksgiving, and when I asked her what she was doing, she said 'nothing'. I knew you wouldn't want her to be alone, so I asked her." She looked up at Ryan with her guileless green eyes and asked, "Did I do okay?"

"Of course you did," Ryan said, giving her a gentle hug. "It's always a good thing to offer to share our family with people who don't have one. You did great."

Jamie giggled a little and revealed, "It felt kinda cool. I've never done that before, you know. I never took anyone except Jack to my house for a holiday. It wouldn't have occurred to me."

"I'm glad it occurred to you now."

"Who did you ask?"

"Well, I partially asked Sara," she said. "But she won't come unless you ask her. She took what I said about keeping my distance very seriously, and she wants to make sure that she won't harm our relationship if she comes over."

Jamie's brow furrowed and she asked, "Do you think it will hurt us?"

"No, I don't anymore. I know I'll have feelings for her for a very long time, but I know I'll never act on them. I'm feeling totally secure these days, babe."

"The same goes for me. I don't have a problem with it."

"And you don't mind calling her?"

"No. I think that's probably a good idea, anyway. The last time we spoke I wasn't very friendly."

"You are one in a trillion."

"You're a very generous grader," Jamie teased.

"No I'm not. You deserve a straight A average in the girlfriend department. No one else could come close."

Chapter Twenty

Since so many people were expected, Martin decided that they needed five turkeys. While the churchgoers were at Mass, Conor and Rory got all of the barbecues going—two with mesquite and two with regular charcoal. Martin had put the biggest of the birds in the oven before Mass so when they returned, the whole house was permeated by the intense aroma of the roasting fowl. "My mouth is watering, and it's only ten-fifteen!" Ryan moaned. "How will I be able to wait?"

"I can make you a little something," Martin offered, but she wouldn't hear of it.

"I want to be famished by the time we eat. I'm going to put on a display the likes of which you've never witnessed," she predicted.

"Maybe I should have gotten six turkeys," Martin mused.

"I can load up on the dressing and sweet potatoes," Ryan assured him. "You know how I love Thanksgiving, Da. For the last week I put myself to sleep by thinking of Thanksgiving dinner. I swear I've been looking forward to this meal for a month."

*

Catherine arrived just a few minutes after they returned from Mass. As Ryan went to the door to welcome her she gazed at her fondly, slightly in awe of her impeccable style. Today's outfit consisted of an incredibly soft-looking cashmere turtleneck sweater that was the color of French vanilla ice cream. A delicate gold chain belt hung rather low on her hips, accentuating her small waist.

Chocolate brown suede slacks covered her thin legs and darker brown suede boots finished off the look. As usual she wore just the right amount of perfume for Ryan's tastes, the distinctive scent only noticeable when one actually hugged her. "You look absolutely wonderful, Catherine," she said sincerely as she took in her delicate scent.

"Thank you. I normally wouldn't wear slacks on Thanksgiving, but I wanted to be able to chase my little Pumpkin around the house without worrying about my stockings."

"You really do look lovely, Mom," Jamie agreed. "I like it when you look more casual."

"I like it too," she said decisively. "It makes me feel younger, and I need all the help I can get around you two."

They had to drive to Berkeley to pick up Jordan and Jennie, and Ryan noticed that her teammate was a little reserved when they picked her up. It might be hard for Jordan to get into the spirit of the party, but hopefully the informal nature of the day would loosen her up and let her enjoy herself.

When they arrived at the big craftsman style house that Jennie was staying at, Ryan was amazed at the sight of her coming down the stairs. Jennie was smiling so brightly that she looked giddy. She had on a baby blue cardigan sweater over a white turtleneck and a pair of navy blue wool slacks. The slacks were at least one size too large and about two inches too long, but Ryan had never seen her young friend dressed so normally. "You look really nice, Jen," she said appreciatively. Jennie hadn't shaved her head in several weeks, and the blonde fuzz that she was sporting made her look a bit like a Chia pet, but Ryan thought it best not to comment too much on her appearance or style choices. She knew that one of Jennie's favorite methods of rebellion was through her "look", and she neither wanted to encourage or discourage her in that regard. So she made it a point to comment only if Jennie did something different, just to show that she was paying attention.

"Thanks," she said as Ryan gave her a hug. "I borrowed the pants, but the sweater is really mine."

"Well, you look great," Ryan insisted as they walked through the living room.

Jennie stuck her head into the small den where four high school aged girls were watching TV. "Bye, guys," she called out. "Have fun today."

"You too, Jen," one of the young women replied. The others sat up attentively when they spied Ryan in the doorway. "Who's your friend?" one of them asked.

Jennie grasped Ryan's hand and pulled her into the room. "This is my friend Ryan I told you guys about," she said as she looked up at the tall woman.

"Hi," the oldest looking girl said in a tone that Ryan recognized, but no longer sought out.

"This is J.C.," Jennie said as she introduced them. "And that's Maggie and Skylar."

"Why don't you two hang out for a while," J.C. suggested in a near sultry voice.

"Gotta go," Ryan said quickly. "My lover's waiting in the car."

"Jamie's here too?" Jennie asked.

"Yep. We're just waiting for you." Ryan put her hand on Jennie's back to guide her out. "Nice to meet you all," she said politely.

"You too," J.C. said, but she managed to make it sound like a proposition.

On the way down the sidewalk Jennie laughed as she said, "Well at least they won't think I'm a total nerd."

"What do you mean?"

"I told them that you were coming to take me to dinner, and I said you were really gorgeous. They didn't believe me, but I think you changed their minds," she giggled, sounding just like the fourteen-year-old that she was.

The house was bursting at the seams when they arrived, and they were all amazed at the massive display of appetizers that the other aunts had prepared. But even though Ryan was starving, she steadfastly refused all of the proffered dishes. "I want turkey, gravy, dressing, sweet potatoes, mashed potatoes and cranberry sauce,"

she maintained. "I refuse to surrender my appetite to any other foodstuffs."

Catherine was carrying the baby around, and as they passed, Ryan gave her a pointed look and said, "Time for a change, Catherine. Want me to do it?"

"Oh no, I can handle it," she said easily. She found the diaper bag next to Maeve, and the older woman insisted on helping her. They took the baby down to Ryan's room and got her settled as Catherine worked on her diaper changing skills. "So, how are things going, Maeve? I trust married life is treating you well."

"Oh yes. It's better than I could have dreamed. Now Moira can assure Mam that Martin is the dream both Fionnuala and I have always said he was."

"Whas that in doubt? I can't imagine a mother wanting a better husband for her daughter."

Maeve was pensive for a moment, trying to decide how to frame her reply. "She's never forgiven Martin for taking my sister away from home. Fionnuala was just over here on a tourist visa, you know. I had met the O'Flaherty brothers at church while they were still brushing the Irish soil from their shoes," she said fondly. "We had some shirt-tail relations in common, and one of their cousins was living in the town my husband was from. We all hit it off immediately," she recalled. "My husband actually helped Francis get into the carpenter's union. We made as many calls as we could, and within a few weeks, Martin and Patrick had jobs too, and they could afford to send Malachy to school to learn his plumbing trade. I took Fi to Mass with me at the end of her little visit, and she suggested we have the boys over for tea that day. Well, by the end of the afternoon, my little sister was over the moon for Martin. She stayed past the expiration of her visa and didn't go home until Martin asked her to marry him. She had to go home then just so she could come in legally again, and my mother worked that poor girl over so badly she didn't know up from down! But her mind was made up, and as soon as she got another visa—back she came."

"And your mother never warmed up to Martin?"

"No, she didn't. They didn't spend any time together since they couldn't afford to travel to Ireland together, and my mother doesn't travel at all. So Martin and Fi would save up to send her and one of the children over every year. Martin thought it was important for the kids to know their grandparents, so it made sense to do it that way, but the result was that they've really spent very little time together. Before we traveled there together, the last time they saw each other was when we took Fi back to Ireland to bury her," she said with a catch in her voice.

"Well, I'm sure Moira will give a glowing recommendation," Catherine assured her. "Anyone could see how happy you both are."

Maeve placed a hand on Catherine's shoulder and said, "And I can see how sad you are. Do you want to talk about it?"

Before she knew what came over her, Catherine dropped her head onto Maeve's shoulder and cried her heart out, feeling like the underpinnings of her world had been ripped away.

She cried for the longest time, unable to control herself when she felt the surprisingly firm embrace enfold her. Maeve comforted her, rocking her gently until she could speak. "I've decided to divorce Jim."

"Oh, no," Maeve said. "That's so sad."

"I don't trust him. It's that simple."

"I understand. It's very hard to trust once you've been hurt."

With a sad, wry laugh, Catherine said, "I wish it had only been once. I might have been able to trust him if he'd just made one mistake."

Maeve nodded emphatically. "I know just what you mean. You don't have to explain."

"I feel like I'm going to explode. It's been very hard to hold this inside."

"Haven't you told Jamie?"

"No. I didn't want to upset her today. It's their first Thanksgiving together and I want them to have happy memories of the day."

"But Catherine..."

"No, my mind is made up," she said firmly. "She's leaving for the airport in just a few hours. I'll tell her when she gets back from Colorado. It's not right to have her struggle with this while she's away."

"You know what's best, Catherine, but are you sure she won't find out?"

"No. Jim promised not to call her until I've spoken to her. He owes me at least that much."

Jennie had taken a shine to Rory, their shy personalities merging quite well. He was gamely showing her his accordion when Ryan checked on them. Rory looked up when Ryan poked her head in the room and said, "Your buddy here has some musical talent that you didn't know about."

"Really?" Ryan sat on the bed and watched Rory illustrate the proper way to play his instrument. "What do you play, Jen?"

"Well, I don't know much," the young woman admitted. "I started taking clarinet lessons when I was in fifth grade, but my high school doesn't have music class."

"But you still play?"

"No. We just rented the instrument. My mom sent it back one time when she was mad at me. I was really getting into it too…" she said softly with a faraway look on her face.

"Don't move a muscle," Ryan ordered as she dashed from the room. Two minutes later she was back with two clarinets, one of which she handed to Jennie with a flourish. "I got this one when I was just a kid. When I got better I saved up for three years until I could afford a really nice one." She held the better quality instrument out for Jennie to examine. "I'll make you a deal," she said as Jennie looked up at her with barely disguised longing. "I'll lend you my starter. If you work hard at it and make a lot of progress, I'll give you this one for your fifteenth birthday."

The gaping look that th younger woman gave her nearly made Ryan weep. "Do you really mean that?" she asked, looking like she was afraid the instrument would be ripped from her hands.

"Of course I do. I haven't played in over a year, and my original will be plenty good for the rare occasion I want to pick it up. I'd like this good quality instrument to be played. If you'll promise to play it—it can be yours."

"I will, Ryan," she said. Her smile was bright enough to light up the room. "I don't know a lot, but I'll do my best."

"You don't have to do this alone," Ryan said with a smile. "I'll teach you."

"You…you will?" Years of disappointment and broken promises clouded Jennie's eyes. "But you're so busy…"

"I am, but you're worth it."

"Hey, don't forget about me," Rory piped up. "I'm not a bad teacher either."

"Would you be willing to help?" Ryan asked.

"I'd love to. I've got a lot of time on my hands when we're not touring. Ryan's more skilled with the clarinet, but I taught my little sister to read music, so I think I could manage that part of the lesson plan."

"Really? Will you really?" Jennie asked hopefully, her eyes wide.

"Absolutely," Rory replied. "What's your schedule like?"

"I don't have anything after school. I'm home by three."

"How about Wednesdays?" Ryan suggested. "I rarely have a game on Wednesday, and it's not usually a travel day.

Rory considered the logistics and suggested, "How about if I work with Jennie from five to seven at your house. Then when you get home we can eat dinner together and you can give her a short lesson and some practice exercises for the week."

"That's a great idea," Ryan agreed. "How about it, Jen?"

"I'm in!" she gushed as she slapped Ryan's outstretched palm.

When Ryan came out of Rory's room, she spotted Jordan leaning over the railing of the second floor. She had a wistful look on her face as she gazed down at the boisterous party that raged just below, and was so deep in her reverie that she didn't notice Ryan coming up next to her. "Hey, buddy," Ryan said softly so as to not jar her friend.

"Hi, Boom," she replied as she slipped her arm around Ryan's waist and rested her head on her shoulder.

"What's got you down?"

"Oh, I don't know. Sometimes I just feel like I'll always be outside looking in," she said softly. "I look down on all of your relatives and see how happy and connected to each other they seem, and it feels like I'll never have that."

"I know you'll never have it from your mom, but you can create your own family."

"How am I supposed to do that?"

"Well, one way is to let someone in enough to really love you. When you let yourself really be loved it's not that hard to extend your love to bring in others. Like Jamie," she said as she nodded her head at her partner down below. "It's hard to believe now, but she was very distant from her family when I first met her. She was so starved for connection that she just jumped in with us like she'd been an O'Flaherty all her life. She's chosen to be in my family, and she's added so much to the group in a very short time. Now her mom is one of us, too. It can just grow and build, if you're willing to take the leap."

"So I have to start flying my lesbian flag to get the ball rolling, huh?" she asked with a smirk.

"Nope. That's not required. I choose you as my sister," she said as she wrapped her in a warm embrace.

"I couldn't pick a better one," came Jordan's mumbled reply as she nuzzled her head against Ryan's neck.

It was almost noon, and both barbecued turkeys were just about done. Ryan checked her watch for the tenth time wondering where Sara and Ally were. Both of them were chronically punctual, making her think that each was going to be a no-show. She'd been up and down the stairs to the backyard so many times that she was a little overheated, so she decided to sit out on the front deck for a few minutes to cool off before she began her feeding frenzy. To her surprise, Sara and Ally were out there, sitting on facing chairs, both looking very comfortable.

Ryan stood in the doorway, her hands on her hips, giving her friends a scowl. "Were you two going to come in, or what?"

Sara got up and made a vague gesture between Ally and herself. "We got here at the same time, and for some reason we both confessed to being nervous about going in. We sat down to chat, and we must have gotten carried away." She glanced at her watch and said, "My God! We've been out here an hour and a half."

Ryan smiled at the pair and said, "You're actually here at the perfect time. We're going to eat soon."

Ally got up and wrapped Ryan in her powerful embrace, giving her a gentle, but full kiss on the lips. Sara came up next to Ryan and, as Ally released her, gave her an awkward looking hug. Their mouths nearly collided as Ryan went to kiss Sara's lips, but was offered a cheek. She pulled back quickly, and Sara tried for a mid-flight correction, but now Ryan was aiming for her cheek, managing only to hit her nose. They finally gave up, both looking sheepish.

"Now how do we get you two comfortable? Sara, you know nearly everyone, so you don't need introductions, but Ally only knows Jamie. Do you want to meet everyone, or would you like to fly under the radar for a while?"

"If you don't mind, I'd be grateful if I could just stay in the background," Ally said in her soft, Southern drawl. "I hate to meet large groups of people."

"Stick with me," Sara offered. "I can point out all of the relatives for you, and introduce you to anyone you'd like to meet."

"Now that's the best idea I've heard all day," Ally said, her eyes flashing with interest.

They went in and Jamie spotted them right away. She walked over to them and said, "Hi, guys. Good timing. Would you like me to introduce you to everyone?"

"Already taken care of," Ryan said. Looking around the room she pointed and said, "The lovely woman in that corner is Jamie's mom, Catherine, and I think you know everyone else on the first floor, Sara."

"I do, but some of them are a lot bigger than the last time I saw them."

Ryan smiled and said, "Testosterone does a body good. Those critical early twenties gave some of the boys new bodies."

"That's rather obvious. Boy, you should have asked some of your straight friends over."

"Are you…non-straight, Sara?" Ally asked, showing a level of interest that a bystander would have seen.

Sara froze a little, then she took in a breath and said, "I'm uhm… I'm a lesbian."

"New development?"

Sara looked mortally embarrassed. "No, not really. But talking about it is new."

"Well, welcome to the club. Let me know if you need a tour guide."

She'll never fall for that line! Ryan screamed internally. But to her displeasure, Sara smiled broadly at the larger woman and nodded her head slowly. "I could use a good tour. I just told my parents I've joined up."

"Well, I've been a member for years and years. I'll clue you in on all the attractions."

Ryan stood there squeezing her hands into fists. *If you even think of taking her to try out vibrators, I'll kill you with my bare hands!*

Martin saw Sara come in, and after fighting through the crowd he gave her a warm hug and said, "My goodness, you've become a beautiful young woman."

"Thanks, Mr. O'Flaherty," she said, ducking her head shyly. "I really appreciate the invitation today."

"You're required to call me Martin now." Maeve came up beside him and captured Sara in a hug also.

"We're so glad you came, Sara. I hope we'll see you again often."

"I'd like that Mrs. Drisc…O'Flaherty," she finished weakly.

"It's Maeve, dear."

"Okay, Maeve it is." She smiled. "Do both of you know Ryan's friend Ally?"

"No, we've not had the pleasure," Martin said, his eyes lighting up in surprise. "I've heard Siobhán speak of you for years, but somehow we've never met."

Ally looked a little puzzled, but graciously greeted her hosts. Ryan, was standing across the room, pleased to notice that Sara was introducing Ally to a few important people. Conor came up beside her and asked, "Who's with Sara? She looks like a…I don't know." He stared at her, eyes slightly squinted. "Is she on your basketball team?"

"No. That's an old friend of mine you haven't met."

"Old friend," Conor said slowly. "You don't have any old friends that you didn't..." He looked from Ally to his sister and finally said, "You hit that?"

"Pardon me?" she said with exaggerated slowness.

"Did you hook up with her?" he asked, trying another expression.

"Did you have an operation to remove all of your tact, or did it just seep out through the hole in your head?"

"I asked a simple question. She doesn't look anything like your type so I wanted to know if you bumped boots with her. No biggie."

"Yes, Conor," she said through clenched teeth. "I bumped her boots and everything else. That's my friend Ally."

"That's Ally!?" He said this loud enough to be heard across the room, but luckily the crowd noise was far too loud for his voice to carry.

"Yes, that's Ally. And I'd prefer that you didn't stare at her!"

"You...you...you had sex with her for years," he gasped. "She's... she's so butch! That can't work," he insisted. "You're butch!"

"Well, at least somebody thinks so," she muttered as she wandered off.

Ryan decided that her friends needed to meet Jennie, and she fetched them and took them upstairs. Rory was playing a lively tune on his accordion for his appreciative audience. Jordan was sitting on the floor watching in rapt fascination, and Jennie was sitting right next to her. Jordan had her arm casually draped around the young woman's shoulders, and Ryan briefly thought, that Jordan's reaching out to someone less fortunate was just the thing for her own sadness.

Rory quickly concluded his tune and placed his instrument on the bed as he rose to shake hands with first Sara, and then Ally. His sunny demeanor gave no indication of past ill feelings, and as Jordan and Jennie struggled to get up Ryan urged them to remain seated. "These are my good friends Sara Andrews and Ally Webster," she said. "This is Jordan Ericsson and Jennie Willis."

"Good to meet you both," Sara said as she squatted a bit to

shake their extended hands. "I saw your last game, Jordan. Quite a performance."

"Thanks," she said as she shot her a dazzling smile. "Having Ryan on the team made this season a lot easier."

"You don't have to tell me," she laughed. "She turned our soccer team around in one year."

"We'll feed you guys even without the bull," Ryan smirked. "Hey, you two have something in common."

"What's that?" Jordan asked.

"You're both waiting for some life-changing news."

"I'm waiting for bar results," Sara volunteered. "What about you?"

"I should find out by Monday if I'm invited to try out for the national volleyball team," she said, swallowing nervously.

"That's so cool!" Jennie piped up, but after a second she added, "What's that mean?"

Jordan gave her a squeeze and said, "That's the kind of reaction I like. You think it's cool even when you don't know the significance." She rubbed Jennie's head affectionately. "They have a team that spends about a year getting ready to participate in the summer Olympics. You have to get invited to try out, and they might ask me."

"Wow!" she said with open-mouthed amazement. "That's awesome!"

"Well I'm not sure I'll get invited…"

"You'll make it," Ryan assured her. "You had a fantastic year."

"What about you Ryan?" Sara asked.

"No, I don't think so. They like to see a real commitment to the game. My checkered career doesn't show the focus that they want."

"I don't know, Boomer," Jordan opined. "You might be surprised."

"Boomer?" Sara said with a delighted grin. "Did you say Boomer?"

Jordan got to her feet and lightly touched both Sara and Ally on their shoulders. "Let's go snag some snacks, and I'll tell you all of her many nicknames."

Great, now the whole world will have ammunition, Ryan grumbled to herself.

🐎

Ryan left Jennie in Rory's capable hands and went to search for her partner, who'd been missing for long periods throughout the day.

She finally found Catherine carrying Caitlin around. "Ryan, have you been photographed yet?"

"I don't know what you mean," she said slowly.

"Didn't Jamie tell you what she was going to do?"

"Nooo, not that I'm surprised at that," she smirked.

"Well, let's go outside," Catherine urged, handing the baby off when she started to reach for Ryan. The three of them threaded through the throng and stood on the small open porch off the second floor, overlooking the impromptu photo studio in front of the stately crape myrtle in the far corner of the small yard.

"Where did she…?" Ryan started to ask.

"I have no idea where she got the idea, but she's been snapping away for over an hour."

They walked down the stairs and observed Malachy, Peggy, Padraig, Liam, Declan and Dermot posing for their family portrait. Two large bounce umbrellas were arranged along with studio quality lights and a very large square format camera on a sturdy tripod. They waited patiently while Jamie finished with the family, but as soon as they broke the pose Ryan came up right behind Jamie and leaned over severely. Her face was nearly touching Jamie's and she was rewarded with a gentle kiss. "Like my set up?"

"How…?"

"I wanted to have some family portraits taken. I called around, but it was ridiculous how much portrait photographers wanted to spend a couple of hours here. So I decided to rent a whole set up. I took a few photography classes when I was in high school, and it all came back to me when I went to the camera store to rent this stuff. Cool huh?"

"You are very, very cool," Ryan said with appreciation. "You're positively frosty."

"Well, it's about your turn gorgeous."

"Cool. Can I keep Caitlin?"

"Of course. I want some with the baby, some with you and my mom, and some with your immediate family. Oh, and you and Jennie, and you and Jordan, and you and Sara, and you and Ally."

"How about you and me?" Ryan asked, her brow furrowed.

"Hmm, I guess that would be okay," Jamie mused thoughtfully, hiding her grin.

"Catherine, would you do the honors?" Ryan asked as Jamie showed her how to snap the shutter.

They posed for a few pictures with the baby, but when Jordan, Sara and Ally came down, Caitlin spotted them and immediately changed her allegiance. "Do you mind babysitting for a few minutes?" Ryan asked Sara.

"Only at your own risk," Sara said as she swooped the baby into her arms. "No guarantees on when you'll get her back."

They posed for a few more pictures, and Catherine was very pleased with the result when she suggested that they lean their heads against each other. "You do that so often, it looks very natural."

"Kiss shot, kiss shot!" Jordan urged.

Ryan rolled her eyes, but Jordan reminded her, "It's the only way I see you two most of the time."

One of her props was a small step stool so Jamie climbed onto the lowest step to equalize their heights. Ryan stood very close and gazed at her with such love in her eyes that Catherine had to capture the moment. "We're not ready," Jamie complained.

"Ryan was," Catherine said as she shrugged her shoulders. They leaned in towards each other for a gentle kiss but just before the shutter closed Jamie placed her hand lightly on Ryan's cheek to recreate the sensation that Ryan loved. That caused Ryan's mouth to curl into a sweet smile that was captured perfectly as Catherine snapped the shot just millimeters before their lips actually touched. "Perfect!" she declared as they broke apart.

"Okay, Jordan, hop in with Boomer," Jamie instructed.

The two friends smiled up at the camera with their arms casually draped around each other's shoulders, looking very much like the athletes they were. Next Jamie turned to Sara and said, "You're up."

Sara blinked a few times, but wordlessly handed the baby to Jordan and stood a little tentatively next to Ryan. Ryan obviously felt very comfortable, because she snaked an arm around Sara's waist and pulled her close. She grinned up at Jamie and just for an instant Jamie saw a flash of the innocent, guileless face that graced the high school pictures she so loved of her partner. In that moment, she was very glad that Sara was back in Ryan's life. Anything that made Ryan happy was good for them as a couple.

A cute shot of Ryan with Ally was next, and Jamie smirked to herself as she saw Ryan's whole demeanor change when the large woman put her arm around her. She was certain that Ryan would be surprised by the photo, since she knew Ryan didn't realize how she blushed like a schoolgirl when Ally was around.

Next came a few adorable shots with Ryan and Catherine. They held the baby between them, and Jamie had to laugh when Caitlin looked directly into the camera, just like Ryan did.

Jordan then took a few with Jamie added to the portrait and while Catherine went to grab the boys and Martin and Maeve, Ryan insisted on several shots with her and Duffy. Martin came down the stairs grumbling loudly, "Dinner's twenty minutes from being ready, girls. Do we have to do this now?"

"Yes, Da," she reassured him. "We'll all have our pants unbuttoned after dinner."

Even though he complained, Ryan knew he was pleased to have this opportunity. He was clearly a photo nut, as evidenced by the plethora of shots that filled every room in the house, but very few of the shots were professionally done. He had wanted another formal shot for years now, but it was impossible to schedule the whole group.

It took a few minutes to get all of the boys organized, and they were ready to go when Maeve slid into the group and smiled so brightly that Catherine got a tear in her eye just looking at the scene. Martin gazed down at her with a look of pure devotion, and she snapped the shutter immediately without them even noticing. Several posed shots later, Martin and Maeve agreed to a few alone, and when they were finished they nearly ran back into the house to finish dinner.

Finally, Jamie got a few shots of Ryan and Jennie together, then she called a halt to her duties until dinner was finished.

As everyone filed back into the house, Ally tugged on Ryan's sleeve and said, "Stay outside with me for a minute, will you?"

"Sure." Ryan let Jamie pass her to go in, and she sat down and waited for Ally to do the same. "What's up?"

"First off, I want to thank you for having me to your home. If I'd known your family before, I never would have let you get away. I haven't been at a big family celebration since I left North Carolina, and I've got to tell you—it's given me something to think about. I tend to think of families as mostly evil, and it's really great to see that's an overgeneralization."

Ryan reached over and gave her hand a squeeze. "I'm really glad you came. It's about time my family met the mystery woman."

"You know," she said reflectively, "I know that you've said you've never allowed yourself to fall in love, but unless I'm reading you very wrong, there is, or was something special between you and Sara. Am I off the mark?"

Ryan could feel her color rising, and she decided to be completely honest with her friend. "She was my first love. Things didn't work out from the very start, and she's been out of my life since I was a senior in high school. We just re-established contact this fall."

"But that was a long time ago," Ally said, scratching her head a bit. "She said she was just now coming out."

"I don't want to give away Sara's confidences, but it's taken her a long time to get comfortable being gay. She's just now taking some big steps."

"Hmm…" She looked at Ryan carefully and asked, "How would you feel about me calling her? Be honest with me, Ryan. I'd never do something that'd upset you."

Ryan sighed and looked to the sky for a moment, trying to organize her thoughts. "I love you both, Ally, and there's nothing I'd like better than for the two of you to hit it off. You're both very special people, and I honestly think she'd really like you."

"But…" Ally led.

"But…it would take me a long time to get comfortable with it if you…went out."

Ally smiled gently and said, "I think you mean if we stayed in."

The dark head nodded quickly as Ryan said, "Yeah. It's the staying in part that I'd have to come to terms with."

"Then I won't do it. There are lots of other women out there."

Ryan placed her hand on her knee and said, "No. Really. Don't let me stop you. Every mature bone in my body wants the two of you to find someone to love. There's just a small part of me that doesn't ever want anyone else to play with my toys—and that's something I should get over."

Ally brought her hand up and ruffled Ryan's hair fondly. "I'd never play with your favorite toys with anyone else," she teased. "I'm retiring them to a shrine of honor."

"Oh, that's helpful," Ryan laughed. "Now I feel better."

"I'm just pulling your cute little leg. I know you're referring to Sara. Hey," she said, remembering something from earlier in the day. "What's with this name your father uses for you?"

"He and my grandparents are the only ones who use it. Ryan's actually my middle name."

"Well, it's darned adorable. I really like being around your family, and I hope you invite me again."

"I will," she said decisively. "Hey, if it's not too personal, what happened with Ellen?"

"She wasn't really ready to settle down. I'm going to try to stay away from younger women. I want to find someone who's where I am in terms of commitment."

"I hope you find it, and if it's with Sara, you have my full support. I might have to run in the other direction if I ever see you together, but you'll have my support from a distance." She burst into a laugh and Ally put her arm around her again and held her tightly.

"You're a good woman. I like that you can be honest with me."

"I try. I don't always get it right, but I really do try."

⁂

Maeve pulled Catherine aside to check on her just before dinner was served. "You look like you're feeling a little better. Is that true?"

"Yes, I honestly do feel better. Thanks for letting me cry on your shoulder. Letting out some of the sadness really helped."

"I'll be home all weekend. If you're feeling blue or just want to talk, you call me, all right?"

"I will It's such a comfort to have you for a friend."

"Me too, Catherine. Me too," she said fondly giving her a generous hug.

The feast was spread lavishly on the large dining room table. Everyone stood and admired the perfectly browned birds, but Ryan broke through the crowd and said, "I can't wait another minute. Let's eat."

"You know the rule," Martin warned her. "But since you're in such a hurry, you can just do the honors."

"I'm up for it." She held out both of her hands. Martin grasped one and she urged Jamie to grip the other. Everyone else joined hands quickly as they jammed into every inch of the small room. "We all have a tremendous amount to be thankful for this year," she said conversationally as she glanced around the room. "But the thing I'm most grateful for is friendship. Even though I'm related to most of you, and deeply in love with one of you," she shot a glance at her beaming partner, "I would choose each of you as a friend. So I'd like to offer a blessing for friendship." She closed her eyes for a moment and let her head drop back as she began to speak,

"May you be blessed with good friends and learn to be a good friend to yourself.
May you find the place in your heart where there is both love and forgiveness.
May you feel the beauty of belonging.
And may your friends help you create all of the tools you need to find your home."

She picked her head up and smiled at each of her guests as she loudly proclaimed, "Amen!"

Before the word was out of her mouth, Jamie had thrown her arms around her in a very enthusiastic hug. "That was beautiful, honey. Just beautiful."

"Thanks, " she said, squirming out of her embrace, eyes fixed on the feast, "but I gotta eat."

Half an hour later, five sets of eyes were fixed on the back of Ryan's head. She continued to lean over her plate slightly, as if worried that her food would be taken from her if she didn't protect it. She was sitting on the second step of the staircase and Jamie, Sara, Jordan, Ally and Jennie were all perched on higher stairs. The other women had finished eating fifteen minutes earlier; but Ryan had not only not stopped, she had not even slowed down. When it became obvious that she was deep in her trance, Jamie had taken her own plate and gone to fill it again. When Ryan finished her first helping, Jamie slid the refill onto her lap. Ryan acknowledged the gesture with some sort of grunt but couldn't spare the effort to actually form words. As she neared the end of the second plate, Jamie hopped up again and used Ryan's original for her second refill. Now all eyes were on her to see if she would be up to a fourth. As Jamie started to rise, Ryan placed a hand on her knee and smiled over at her as she said, "Gotta save room for dessert, babe." She popped the last forkful of turkey into her mouth and leaned back, letting out a big breath. "I would give up my birthday and Christmas before I'd give up Thanksgiving."

"You know I could make you this dinner any time you wanted it," Jamie said.

"Nope. It's not the same. It's the entire experience I enjoy."

Martin raised his voice above the din and begged, "Bit of a hush, please." The crowd quieted almost immediately as he announced, "Before we serve dessert, it's our tradition to have each person express one thing they're thankful for this year. I volunteer to begin." He waited for quiet and said, "I have more gifts in my life than any man deserves, but I'm particularly thankful this year for being blessed by the gift of this lovely woman's love." He grasped Maeve's hand and gave it a squeeze as she smiled up at him.

"It's no surprise that my thoughts are exactly the same," Maeve said, giving him a fond smile.

They went around the crowded room as each cousin, aunt, and uncle took their turn.

Catherine was standing on the edge of the crowd, jiggling the baby on her hip. As her turn came she said, "I understand the rules, but I'm afraid I can't name one thing that I'm thankful for. It was hard enough to narrow it down to two," she said with a laugh. "I'm more thankful than I can say for being given the opportunity to really get the chance to know my lovely daughter." She walked over to where Jamie was perched and gently patted her cheek as Jamie turned her head and kissed her palm. "But I doubt that I would have ever done so if it hadn't been for Ryan. Her influence helped us all break the status quo and start to see each other as we really are. For that I'm eternally grateful." Ryan peeked her head up above the banister as Catherine leaned over and gave her an appreciative kiss.

When the spotlight landed on the guests, Jennie went first. "I'm thankful for lots of things, too," she began in her soft voice. "And I can't stop at one either." She shot a shy look at Ryan and said, "I'm thankful that Ryan and Jamie helped me to get to stay at the group home. It's really been great."

Ryan was gazing at the young woman with deep affection in her eyes.

Sara was next up and she looked like she wanted to skip her turn. But she took a breath as she gazed at a point in the center of the room and said softly, "I'm thankful for second chances." Her head lifted slowly and she pasted on a small smile and nodded to Jordan to indicate it was her turn.

Jordan looked directly at Ryan as she smiled and said, "I'm thankful for my friends. One in particular." She stretched her arm out and caught Ryan's hand as she gave it a firm squeeze.

Ally took her turn and said in her softly accented voice, "I'm thankful for being included in a real family celebration."

Ryan was up next. "I'm thankful for a gift I received this year," she said as she squeezed Jamie's thigh. "It's a gift I didn't expect, but I've come to rely on it completely. I look forward to the time we're together, and I can honestly say that it's given me more pleasure than I could imagine. So, I thank God for my Lexus." She giggled as Jamie grabbed her and began to tickle her furiously. "Oh, all of that is true for Jamie too," she gasped out as the assault continued.

"I'm going to be a bit more mature than my little friend," Jamie said when she released her captive. "I'm thankful for so much this year that it's almost impossible for me to fathom. But I'd have to say that I'm most thankful for my very large, very loving family. Some of us are related by blood," she said as she cast a fond glance at her mother, "but all of us are bound by love." She smiled down at her grinning partner and leaned over a bit to lightly brush their lips together. "Especially you, Tiger," she said softly.

"Well done, Everyone," Martin proclaimed. "It's time for dessert." Jennie, Sara, Ally and Jordan hopped up immediately, but Ryan grasped Jamie's hand to urge her to stay for a moment. Everyone was near the dining room so they had a little bit of privacy for a few moments. She couldn't stand to have a whole stair tread between them so she tugged at her partner until she climbed down and came to sit between Ryan's legs. Ryan draped her arms around Jamie's neck and leaned over until their cheeks touched.

"You're the first person I thank God for every morning and the last at night." Ryan was speaking so softly that the sensation of her breath on her cheek was more noticeable than the sound of her voice. "Being with you has exceeded every expectation I ever had about being in love. I'm so very thankful for the gift of your love."

Jamie got to her feet and extended her hand to help Ryan up. "Come with me," she said as she led her from the room. It took quite a while to get through the crowd, but they were finally alone in the backyard. Without a word, she went over to the camera and attached a long cable release, double-checked the focus and positioned Ryan on her mark and stood right next to her. "I want to forever capture the look on your face when you tell me how you feel about me. Tell me again," she urged as she clasped her hands around Ryan's neck and leaned back in her embrace.

Ryan smiled serenely and settled her hips against Jamie's, looking down at her with all of the tender emotions she felt for her partner ill-concealed by her expressive eyes. "I love your very essence," she said softly, smiling a little brighter when she heard the shutter release. "The things that make you most you are the things that appeal to me the most." Another muted snap as the shutter clicked again. "Your generosity, your determination, your perseverance, and your constant quest to make me happy all combine to make you the most desirable woman I could ever hope to know." She was fairly sure that the shutter clicked again, but the warm pressure of Jamie's lips created a faint buzz in her ears as she lost herself to the sensation.

The cable release fell to the ground as Jamie's arms rose to surround Ryan's neck. Their bodies joined, merging into the remarkably secure fit that they had perfected over the previous months with their continuous practice. "You are the meaning of love," Jamie whispered as her lips were claimed by Ryan's.

"Every time I question my beliefs, I just think of you," Ryan whispered. "Only a loving God could create someone as pure and good as you are. You are the most visible sign of God's presence that I've ever known. You give me faith."

"Happy Thanksgiving, Ryan. The first of many, many more to come."

The End

By Susan X Meagher

Novels

Arbor Vitae
All That Matters
Cherry Grove
Girl Meets Girl
The Lies That Bind
The Legacy
Doublecrossed

Serial Novels

I Found My Heart In San Francisco

Awakenings
Beginnings
Coalescence
Disclosures
Entwined
Fidelity
Getaway
Honesty
Intentions
Journeys

Anthologies

Undercover Tales
Outsiders

To purchase these books: *www.briskpress.com*

To find out more visit Susan's website at
www.susanxmeagher.com

You'll find information about all of her books, events
she'll be attending and links to groups she participates
in.

All of Susan's books are available in paperback and various e-book formats at www.briskpress.com

Follow Susan on Facebook.
http://www.facebook.com/susanxmeagher